"LANCREW'

They were from a small city and were small time hustlers on different city blocks. Only to eventually band together for something bigger than themselves. With a lot more money at stake. They weren't just a bank heist crew, because what they did was epic.

They were smart and organized in the way they executed their heists. And more important than all. They gave back to the community they were apart of. What first started local, expanded statewide. They were getting money in a major way. And they were also a very disciplined group. Who wasn't sloppy about any of their work in the streets. A crew that focused could only be stopped from the inside. They all took a vow to be there for one another. And if they had to kill for one another, then so be it. Enjoy the journey of a crew of individuals who worked hard and played hard. Look into the lives of the men and women that were known as "LANCREW".

Chapter One "Those Early Days"

"Give me my muthafuckin money you owe me nigga!! I'm not going to tell your ass again. I'm not playing nigga. I'll let this thing go"!! Travis said. As he pointed his gun at a man.

The dude didn't care what Travis was talking about. And he didn't think at all that Travis would even pull the trigger. So naturally he tested him. To see if he was really about what he said he was about.

"You're not doing nothing with that piece of shit gun you got youngin. And I'm not giving you shit either. Clown ass nigga" the dude said looking directly at Travis and laughing.

Travis just stared at the man and fired. As a loud bang went off and the man dropped to the ground. Travis hit the man with a single shot to the head. Travis then went through his pockets looking for the money that was owed to him. He got fifty dollars out of the man's jeans and ran away on foot into the night.

The two men had met at a city park that night. Travis felt he had to shoot the man because he owed him money and wasn't going to pay him. And honestly took him for a joke. The man figured Travis had no heart and had no business being in the streets. But Travis grew tired of being taken advantage of. And underestimated. He knew if he was going to be in the streets and about that life. He had to send a clear message when anyone crossed him. Mission accomplished. And he felt no remorse or regret for anything that happened that night. That night everything changed. And even though that murder was never solved. The streets knew. Putting in work and laying down that murder game for the first time. Travis grew to have a healthy respect and fear in the streets after that night.

At that time. Travis was only 22 years old. At that age he was robbing cats and selling weed. As he seen it, he was doing what he had to do. And he added murder to his resume. Travis was born and raised in the 7th Ward in Lanc City. Grew up in the Hill Rise Housing Projects. But he was all over the city growing up. He knew people that were in the streets all over the city also. Like Kwame Richards from Ann Street. Who was a hustler and made plenty of money. They knew each other and respected one another. Kwame was older and from another generation. He was what young niggas now would call an OG. At this point in his life, Kwame wasn't the type of cat to get his hands dirty. Or get caught up in some dumb shit. He was a seasoned vet in the game and in the streets.

Kwame had people grinding for him. He had built himself a nice little empire. He was well respected in the city. But like any city. There was always someone that would test you. No matter who it was. Being from a small city made life even more dangerous for enemies. A lot of people knew each other. And there was less space to roam in a small city. At some point you were bound to run into your enemy anywhere. You always had to be on point, if that was the life you were living.   Page 1

Meanwhile Desmond was doing a little B&E in different parts of the county. A dangerous way to make a living. But he always kept that hammer on him. Desmond grew up on Green Street. And growing up on that block is pretty self-explanatory when it comes to the city. It was definitely one of the roughest blocks in the city. He was a young black male with a gift of art. But at the moment. His art wasn't making him any money. And he wasn't the type to hold a job long. So he did what he felt he had to do to survive. Desmond was also 22 years old like Travis. And they knew each other from school. Desmond knew of Kwame from just being from the city. Desmond also knew Kwame was about that paper.

One day Desmond ran into Kwame at a legendary spot in the city Downtown at HOP. Desmond was sitting down and eating. When Kwame came in. Dressed in a white tee, some jeans. And a crisp pair of White Air Force Ones. He had on a thick Cuban Link chain with a large cross medallion. And some dark shades. As he approached Desmond and took off his shades. Desmond reached down in his waistband at what appeared to be a gun. Kwame quickly noticed.

"Hold on youngin. Don't trip. I'm not here to rob you. Nigga. We're in a public place. Fuck you think I'm trying to get bagged quick? We're next to the fucking Police Station!! I don't have no heat on me. I'm here to talk to you. Put that shit away" Kwame said as he sat down across from Desmond.

After hearing that. Desmond raised his hand above his waist and proceeded to finish his food. He didn't say anything, just sat there and stared at Kwame.

"I'm here to offer you a job with me. I know you're getting tired of that B&E shit. That shit isn't going to last forever. Ask yourself if you really want to continue risking getting your head blown off for some goods nigga"? Kwame said.

"What do you want with me Kwame? And what kind of job are you talking"? Desmond replied.

"Well one thing I do know is. You're quick with that piece. So whatever I have in mind will certainly involve that Glock of yours. My plan is basically a dream team of cats taking over and expanding out. Nigga I'm talking bank heists. And I have another surprise when I get all of you together. Let's exchange numbers. And I'll hit you and explain more later. I'll keep in touch. Keep your phone close youngin. Stay out this street shit. I got big plans for all of us" Kwame said.

Page 2

Desmond and Kwame exchanged numbers and Desmond continued eating. Kwame left and went about his way. Over on Chester Street. Angel Styles was growing up and looking better with age. She was now 20 years old and still somewhat undecided about her future. She was working part-time and still thinking about going to college. One thing she was good at was talking to people. And persuading them. She was beautiful and loved guns. And loved going to the gun range. She was damn near a marksman. She knew Kwame too. And with the plan he was coming up with. He could use her. Kwame wanted the best and most fierce in the city. A crew of fearless individuals who wanted that bag. Angel was a young woman with ambition. But she also loved money and desired the finer things in life.

Besides working part-time. Angel was dating a guy who had moved to the Lanc City area from out of town. A guy that went by the name "Bags" who was a few years older than Angel. Bags never told anyone where he was from. He just wasn't from Lancaster. That was clear. At the time Angel was happy with Bags. They had been dating for a little while now. He spoiled her with expensive bags and shopping sprees from time to time. Bags made his fair share of money in the streets. But he mostly kept a low-profile and wasn't seen just anywhere amongst anybody. He ran with only one other person. Bags had a partner he ran with that went by the name of Stacks. Most times Bags would be seen riding through the city in a Ford Expedition. Or his old-school. A Blue drop top 69' Cutlass. That he spent money customizing.

Those two vehicles didn't attract a lot of attention, so he stayed under the radar. He had an apartment outside the city where he resided. Bags was a 21 year old hustling nigga that got money a lot of different ways. Bags and Desmond used to hustle in the same streets. But had a falling out of sorts. And really wasn't on good terms anymore. They would see each other here and there passing in the streets. But that was about it. The strange thing was. Desmond was cool with Angel who was dating Bags. It was always an uncomfortable feeling for Angel when they seen each other out. But Angel kept it together and kept her composure. It was always peace between them when Angel was around. And it was a mutual respect between the men, although neither man feared the other. As long as each man stayed out of the other's way, everything would be cool.

Bags decided to pick Angel up from her job one day. It was something he did from time to time. And as usual. As soon as she got in his truck. There was a Nike bag waiting for her. Inside was some Jordan brand products. Some Jordan's and a matching track suit. As Bags was driving through Lanc City streets. Angel was admiring her gifts and Bags was loving her reaction.

"I got the same pair. So I said fuck it. I might as well get my lady a matching track suit too, so we can stunt on these clowns together" Bags said as he drove.

"Yesss…and I love them. Thank you. Baby. You know just how to spoil your woman. And I'm not going to complain" Angel replied.

Page 3

"So what's good? Are you hungry? We should go to Lucky's" Bags said.

"I can definitely eat something. And that sounds like a plan. You can't ever go wrong with Lucky's" Angel replied.

The two were talking about a classic spot in the city on the corner of Rockland and Green Streets. A Chinese take-out spot that played a major part in the community for many years. If you were from Lancaster City or frequented the area. You knew about Lucky's Chinese Take-Out. The 7th Ward section of the city was home to so many strong and talented people. That went on to be successful in their own right. It was also the most dangerous section of the city. Some made it out and some didn't.

Downtown had went through a rebirth of sorts. What was once a vibrant Downtown back in the 70's and 80's. And part of 90's. Was a ghost town and then made a huge resurgence. To now becoming a trendy and popular Downtown. Bars and restaurants everywhere. And people from the County had started returning to the city's Downtown. The Art Galleries were thriving and alive in the city.

On Lime Street. Dondrake "Wheels" Wells was doing his thing with cars. Stealing them and taking them to chop shops for cash. His nickname was Wheels because he knew how to get cars. And he was good at getting out of sticky situations in vehicles. Wheels knew Travis Clark pretty well. And was like a big brother figure to him. Yeah. The same Travis that had just committed murder. And was known now as a shooter. Travis was young, brash, and wild. Wheels had gotten cool with young Travis over the years. Wheels was five years older than Travis. Wheels was 27 years old. One day on Lime Street the two were standing outside leaning on one of Wheels car's. A 1999 Toyota Camry.

"What's been going on youngin? I hope you've been laying low and staying out of the mix. I heard about what went down the other night. You know some niggas knew that dude owed you money. I just hope you know what you're doing. Because the streets stay talking. Maybe I should get you a one way ticket out of this bitch" Wheels said.

"I'm not going anywhere. And I'm not worried about the streets talking. He owed me money and wasn't going to pay me. Muthafucka took me for a joke. So I let his ass have it. I'm not letting no nigga strong arm me. Fuck that"!! Travis replied.

"You got a point. And that's why you need to get on my team. And leave that bullshit alone. Help me with these cars. You don't have to bust your gun to do this shit. We get the cars on the list, take them down the way. And get that paper" Wheels said as he burned an L. Passing it to Travis.

"You know I'm not into that shit fam. I'm good at what I do. And I haven't seen no jail cell yet old head" Travis replied.

Page 4

"You talk that shit. You think what you're doing will last forever? Nigga there's other shooters out there besides you. No nigga is invincible or immune to getting got. I've been doing this shit for a while. It's legit youngin. Believe me. When you get your head out of this street bullshit. You come see me and I'll put you on" Wheels said.

"Don't hold your breath on that. Thanks for the L. I'll holla" Travis replied leaving.

Meanwhile on Pershing Avenue and Locust Streets. Nakeem "Nitro" Harris was controlling the area. Him and his crew had ran the area for quite some time now. Nitro knew Desmond, and he also knew Angel from Chester Street. Nitro had tried numerous times to date Angel. She was always flattered but never entertained it. Even though she was with Bags, it never stopped Nitro from trying. Nitro was 25 years old. And fresh off doing a five year bid for possession of narcotics. In which he only ended up doing three and half years. Getting out on good behavior. Since being out, he had been trying his best to keep a low-profile. But still stay on his grind. As he drove his Yukon Denali through Pershing Avenue. Checking out his workers. Then driving across Chester and Green. He happened to see Angel at the corner store on Pershing and Green.

"What's good babygirl? You getting me something"? Nitro asked speaking out of his truck.

"Hey. No. You got plenty of money to buy your own. How have you been"? Angel replied.

"You know maintaining as always. You should come take a ride with me. Just take a ride. No funny shit. I know you're with this nigga Bags. We're still friends right"? Nitro said.

Angel just looked at Nitro and smiled. Shook her head and got in the truck.

"And I know it's not going to be no funny shit. Nigga I keep my gun in my purse. And my aim is deadly. You know I'm a marksman" Angel replied laughing.

"I see you still love going to the range. And you should be a marksman as much as you go" Nitro said laughing.

"You know it. I got to. These streets aren't kind and these bullets don't have no names on them. Even a female like myself has to stay strapped" Angel replied.

"You're a different type of female for sure. They don't make too many like you anymore beautiful. That's why I dig you and can still be friends with you. Trust me. I can't hang around too many females unless I'm trying to smash. You feel me"? Nitro said.

"Yeah I get it. And that's good to know we can still be cool. We've always been cool. So where are we going"? Angel replied asking.

"I figured I'd take you to get some ice cream and we can feed the ducks at Longs Park. Chop it up. You always liked to do that back in the day" Nitro said.

Page 5

And that's what they did. When they were younger, they used to see each other out at Longs Park at times with their families. And Nitro always remembered the little girl wanting to feed the ducks. That little girl was Angel. Nitro was five years older than Angel. Over the years they knew each other. They both grew up around the corner from each other. Nitro growing up on Pershing and Angel growing up on Chester. Angel always looked at Nitro as a friend. And he felt the same until she got older and grew into the woman she was currently. So to her, she wasn't disrespecting Bags by hanging out with Nitro. Bags knew they were cool.

"How long are you going to keep running these streets Nitro? You know that quick money is short money too. You have to have a plan my friend. And I know I haven't officially left for college yet myself. But I do have a plan" Angel said.

"Baby girl. I'm not in no streets. I'm past that part on my hustling resume. You just so happen to see me ride through the block. The only time you'll see me out around here is to do what I have to do.

And be gone. I got a nice spot outside the city to lay my head. I lay low for the most part. Every once in a while. I go Down Bottom to get me a drink or two. I hit a few Downtown bars the other week. With a few dudes I'm doing business with. Trying to broaden my horizon a little bit. Feel me? But I have a plan" Nitro replied.

"Well at least you do. That's what's important. I've really been thinking about going to school. But part of me wants to wait a little and chill at home. I don't know why I want to stay here. Especially when I know I can further my education and get a degree. I guess it's how I feel at the moment. Just being out of high school and experiencing life as an adult" Angel said.

"Fuck what anyone thinks. Ultimately. It's your decision because it's your life. Do what makes Angel happy. If it's going to school to further your education. Then so be it" Nitro replied.

"Word" Angel said.

On Beaver Street a cat that went by the name of Rage was living a pretty regular life. Working a full-time job and selling a little weed around his neighborhood. Him and his wife lived on Beaver Street with their three kids. Rage had done a few prison stints when he was younger. But after getting out of prison after numerous times. He married his kid's mother and they lived in the same house he grew up in. Like the others. Kwame knew Rage also. Rage was older than Kwame. Rage was 30 years old. Kwame and Rage had done some time upstate together. They decided to meet for a drink Down Bottom. Kwame wanted Rage to be apart of the dream team of a bank heist team he was building.

"I know you've been trying to law low since you've been out and got married. I can definitely dig that. I'm trying to stay out the way myself. But I have an opportunity of a lifetime for all of us. You won't have to do much the way it's mapped out. I'm talking about taking down banks. All jobs have two teams in two different cars.

Whatever car we take to the bank. We ditch with no prints. We can do this shit Rage, I'm telling you. Put all this neighborhood beef shit a side and band together. And literally get this bag my nigga.
Page 6

Give that money right back to the community. Make a difference however we can" Kwame said.

"Brilliant idea IF we don't get caught. Like anything else. I'm pretty comfortable in my situation right now Kwame. But let me think it over. Extra money can never hurt right"? Rage replied.

"That's all I could ask for. Two more shots of Henny for me and my homie over here"!! Kwame said to the Bartender.

"I have to admit. It's a brilliant idea, but also some dangerous shit too. Risky. Getting niggas from different hoods. Who probably have issues with each other. Trying to get them together? Could be a recipe for disaster. And I hate to be negative. But I'm just saying" Rage replied.

"Trust me. I'm aware of that. But in this case. I'm hoping the fact that I'm cool with all yall niggas. That earns enough respect to try and make it work. We're talking about money fam. It's going to work for all of us if we work together" Kwame said.

"We're cool like we've always been. So for YOU. I'm going to strongly consider it. Some of these niggas I know of and we've crossed paths in the streets. But don't think for a second that I trust any of them" Rage replied as he took his shot.

"That's fair man. Like I said. It's all I could ask for. I'm trying to build this dream team. Could we get some more shots please? Shit. We just getting started" Kwame said motioning the Bartender over again.

Kwame was slowly getting everyone together. Adding the pieces to fit the puzzle. That was to be one of the most fearless and brazen bank heists crews ever.

There were two more people that Kwame had to get with to add to the finishing pieces of the puzzle. That would ultimately be the crew that was known as "LANCREW". Erica "Erotic" Fisher. Who was also born and raised in the city on Rockland Street. She saw a lot growing up on that block over the years. Rockland Street played a major role in the city's 7th Ward. Back in the 80's it was the place to be. The main strip and hangout back in those days. Everyone hung out on the playground. From people rolling through playing their boom boxes back in the day. To basketball tournaments. Festivals in the summer time. Rockland was lit. Erica remembers those days even though she was younger then. Erica was 35 years old. With Lucky's Chinese Take-Out right down the block. And The Boys & Girls Club down the other side of the block. There was always something to do when Erica was growing up.

The Boys & Girls Club had the most impact on the kids in the city than anywhere else. It meant the World to Erica and kids like her who grew up in the city. A second home and major part of the community for a lot of people. It not only provided jobs for people who lived in those neighborhoods. But gave them a chance to mentor kids that they knew and lived around. It was a very positive place. And most of the older members that made up "LANCREW". Were able to experience just what The Boys & Girls Club meant to the kids in the city.

The other cat Kwame wanted apart of the crew was Ron "Chill" Moore. Who hailed from the biggest housing project in the city. Almanac. Which was later name Franklin Terrace. Chill pretty much controlled most of the projects if not all of it. He had a little team that held shit down for him in each part of the projects. Chill was also good at planning heists. He ran with some cats from Pittsburgh years ago and did a few jobs. After being out that way with some relatives. Like others in the crew Kwame was trying to assemble. Chill had also spent some time upstate. And now 32. He was just trying to live his life and stay out of the prison system. Kwame wanted to present him with an opportunity, so he went to Almanac aka Franklin Terrace to holla at him.

"Man. You got shit moving as smooth as I got my shit. I love it. I'm impressed Chill. But this opportunity I got for you. Could make shit a lot easier for all of us when it's all said and done" Kwame said. As they sat outside and watched the kids play down the street.

"Taking down banks huh? I promised myself I was done with that shit years ago fam. A nigga got like two strikes now. If I do decide to be apart of this, I want a small role. I'm not trying to go back upstate bro. Not at all. I have big plans for my future" Chill replied.

"Homie I'm not trying to go back either. But I need you to help me put this shit together. I know you know what you're doing when it comes to bank heists. I need you bro" Kwame said.

"Give me two days to think it over. And like I said. I want to play the background this time around" Chill replied.

"I got you Chill. I have some young niggas in mind to play them frontlines. I'll hit you in two days. I have to get back to the block. Stay up bro" Kwame said. As he got up from his chair outside Chill's house and left.

Erotic was a little easier to convince. She had been boosting along with working a part-time job. She was good at making things disappear, when she wanted them. She was also skilled at doing hair. And dreamt of having her own Hair Salon one day. Which was also one of her side hustles. The pieces to the puzzle were coming together. And after he would finally get an answer from them all.

His plan could be put into action. And they could map out their first bank heist.

Travis was a shooter, and fresh off a murder. That local authorities had no leads on. He was still in the hood doing what he normally did. Like nothing happened. And Travis was another person that Kwame wanted apart of the team. And wanted on the frontlines because he was a shooter. Travis was a young ticking time bomb. Had a compulsive violent temper. And couldn't be told anything. And whoever was planning the heist had to keep in mind that Travis was a loose cannon. Around his home turf in Hill Rise Housing Projects. He was known as "Let Off". For being the type that would open fire anywhere and at any time.

Hill Rise Housing Projects spanned numerous blocks. Locust, Rockland, Howard Avenue, Chester, Green, Lime, Dauphin, and Duke Streets. One of the biggest housing projects in the city. Travis grew up on the Howard Avenue side of Hill Rise. But was all over the projects. Being cool with people on the Chester and Green Street sides. And they all grew to know Travis was someone not to cross. Most times he was alone. Walking the streets or just somewhere in a bar having a drink. Kwame now wanted Travis to deal with some people he wouldn't normally be around. But for the right price. He would co-exist with some cats to get that bag. And that's exactly how Travis looked at it. It was business to him.

Kwame was at home when he got a call on his cell from Wheels.

"What's good fam. You can count me in, I'm down" Wheels said.

"Cool. You know where you fit in Wheels. No need to even speak on it. I'm just glad you're apart of the team. Everybody has a role in

this thing. And as long as we all play our roles. This shit will all work. And we won't be stopped. I'm just waiting to hear back from the rest. After that I can get all of us together" Kwame replied.

Not long after Wheels agreed to be apart of the team. Others followed. No matter what issues any of them had with each other. They put it a side for a greater prize. This wasn't just going to be a bank heist crew. It would be a group of individuals who also invested and gave back to the community. It was a major plan, an operation of sorts. Angel was the latest to agree to join the crew. Chill was in after being hesitant at first because of his criminal record. Kwame was always a man of his word. So Chill trusted what Kwame said they could do. After everyone agreed and was in on the plan. Kwame was looking to get everyone together. And that wouldn't be hard because everyone was local.

A few days later. Kwame had everyone meet Down Bottom to discuss some plans. It was during the day when less people were in the bar. He didn't want a lot of people around anyway. For this meeting. He had a space cleared out for them toward the back. Kwame got there earlier. Followed by Wheels, Desmond, Chill, Travis, Angel, Nitro, and Erotic. Rage would catch up with the team later. He was working at the time at his day job. And would be put in the loop by Kwame at a later date.

"I got you all here so we can go over the initial plans. First off. We're getting Jason type masks. For part of the team that goes in the banks. Secondly. We'll be using two cars for each job. One that will take us to the bank, and another waiting in the wings after we ditch the other. Three man teams. And two cars with one other crew member driving the other getaway car. And we NEVER use the same teams on heists. We switch up on they ass so they can't get no descriptions. We start small ladies and gents. And work our way up that food chain. Less attention the better" Kwame said.

"So you're saying it's not going to be that much money in the beginning? And that means we're still going to be doing our thing in these streets" Desmond replied.   Page 9

"You're a grown man dawg. You can do as you please. But what I would advise all of you to do is. Stay out the mix locally. So you won't draw no attention to yourselves over no dumb shit and lose focus on the bigger picture. The money we could make will let you leave that street shit alone" Kwame said.

"What kind of money you talking about us making"? Nitro asked.

"I'm talking potentially millions. That's if we keep our execution tight. And don't fuck this up" Kwame said.

"Let the man finish. I'm interested in hearing this shit" Wheels chimed in.

"Wheels will be our primary driver. But we of course will switch up on that too at times. Wheels will be in charge of getting us the cars. He knows the ins and outs of all that shit. The main thing is getting in and out of them banks quick. Get in and do what we have to do. Flawless execution. And get the fuck out of there. First team up is Desmond, he's good at handling shit. Along with Angel. She will lure the security guard over to her. Travis will be right by her side because he's also good at handling shit quickly. Wheels will have Rage with him. Wheels in the one car, and Rage in the other. Desmond, Angel, and Travis. You all hit those tellers hard. And get to that bank vault. Let me get some drinks over here for my friends. Get them whatever they want on me" Kwame said to the Bartender.

The plan was coming together. And the crew that was known as LANCREW was forming and coming together nicely. Kwame was amazed himself that he could get a bunch of wild individuals together. That didn't necessarily hang out together on the same page. Him being cool with all of them was the piece that held shit together. Especially in the beginning. But Kwame had to be a man of his word and make this work. And more importantly. Put the crew in position to make money than they would in the streets.

"I have to say. I admired the way you got all these wild ass niggas together. And agreeing to this plan. Thought for sure somebody was going to get into it. Maybe even guns being drawn. But niggas actually listened and remained cool" Wheels said to Kwame.

"I told you fam. When money is involved, niggas will listen. You could get the craziest cats together to do some shit for money. That's the power of the almighty dollar. We can make a lot of money Wheels. And make a difference in a lot of people's lives" Kwame replied.

Meanwhile Rage was getting off work. And as he rode home hitting a few blocks to collect some money he was owed on the way home. Rage had his hood Beaver Street on lock. And the surrounding blocks. And was well-respected in the area. In particular for his hand game. He could fight really well. As he got close to his house. His cell phone rang, it was Kwame.

"What's good bro? Everybody met Down Bottom. I wanted to put you onto the plans. First run out, I have you and Wheels driving the cars. Wheels takes them to the banks, and you bring it home. You'll be waiting in the wings for Wheels to tell you that the job is done, and they're coming to you. Give yourself a little distance between the rest of the crew and the bank. If we execute this shit right, it'll work every time. We'll all get together again before we go into the first heist and finalize it all. Going to need you there. Keep in touch bro" Kwame said.

"Ok. Sounds good to me. I'll be waiting for you to hit me back. Be safe Kwame" Rage replied.

Now that everyone knew their role on the first heist. All that was left was the last minute details and preparation for the actual heist. Which bank they were hitting first and which two cars they planned to use. And last but not least. The very day the heist would go down.

Erica "Erotic" Fisher was still doing her thing boosting to make ends meet. Anything you wanted, you could put a request in. And she would get it most times. But she was growing tired of getting her money that way. That's why she was so eager to join the crew and do something else. And make way more money than she could ever make boosting. Erotic was at the time seeing a guy that went by the name Stacks. He had been living in Lanc City for a while now. And his partner Bags was dating Angel. Who ironically enough was also in the crew. Angel and Erotic both knew each other. He was coming down Rockland Street in his cherry red Jeep Cherokee as Erotic sat on her porch.

"What's good baby"? Stacks asked as he stopped in front of her house.

"Hey. I was just about to text you. What you up to? Erotic replied asking. As she stood outside the truck on the driver's side.

"I was coming through to see your sexy ass. Let's take a ride, get in" Stacks said.

Erica got in the jeep like Stacks said. And they proceeded to drive off. Erica lived with her Grandmother on Rockland. From time to time, her Uncle would stay there also. As her and Stacks were driving, they had a conversation.

"You still boosting? You know you don't have to do that shit. You're MY girl now. You don't have to risk getting jammed up for that bullshit. Just keep that little part-time gig you got. And everything else. I got you" Stacks said.

"I told you before Stacks. That's MY thing. I make my own money. I never been the type of woman to depend on a nigga. The gifts are nice and I appreciate them. But I have to make my own way" Erotic replied.

"Cool. I could understand that. But in case you ever change your mind, you know I got you. And I have a surprise for you" Stacks said.

"I was just about to ask you. Where in the hell are you going? I see you're pulling into County Park" Erotic replied looking on. Page 11

"Just chill woman. I got this. Close your eyes please" Stacks said as Erotic put her hands over her eyes.

They drove a little further and then pulled into a spot where Stacks parked. He then got out of the Jeep and opened Erotic's door. Guided her out of the Jeep, with her hands still over her eyes. Walked a few feet and told her to open them. There was a nice blanket laid out on the grass with food and a bottle of wine. Along with some roses for Erotic. There was a chef there that had prepared the food. After they arrived. Stacks motioned him to beat it for a while, so he and his lady could enjoy their food.

"Wow. This is really nice Stacks. I love it. And I appreciate it too. It's been a while since you've done something like this for me" Erotic replied.

"I told you. I got you. You know your man is a man of his word. And I wanted to show you how much you mean to me. Now let's get this grub on and enjoy some of this wine" Stacks said.

Stacks treated Erotic well. They were an item for a little over six months now and they cared a lot for one another. They sat, ate, talked, laughed, and enjoyed each other's company. It was a calm and peaceful early Spring day and the wind was blowing. They had a great time. And they were only down the hill at County Park. It was a little break from Erotic doing her day to day grind. An hour and a half later. Stacks dropped Erotic back off at her house on Rockland Street.

Chill was in his Franklin Terrace neighborhood watching the neighborhood kids play football in the parking lot. He had actually bought the kids a few footballs so they could play with. And from time to time in the summers. Chill would have cookouts for the kids and people of Franklin Terrace aka Almanac. Which most of the older generation knew it by. Chill was loved throughout his projects. Just as he was watching the youngins. His cell phone rang, it was Kwame.

"What's good homie? I need you to run somewhere with me. Over in the 6th Ward" Kwame said.

"Yeah. Come through, I'm outside now" Chill replied.

Kwame went to pick Chill up and they were off to a warehouse tucked in the city's 6th Ward on the North Side. Chill and Kwame walked in the warehouse on North Plum and Liberty. There was a man inside waiting on them both when they got there. The man greeted them both with a handshake. A Spanish man with a full beard.

"This is my homie Chill. He knows what's good. Chill this is Chino" Kwame said introducing the two men.

They then went to the back of the warehouse where there was a box that Chino showed them. They opened it and there was Jason type hockey masks in it. There were also guns in the warehouse. They were brand new guns with scratched off serial numbers. Of course the guns they would use in the bank heists. Page 12

"This is our ticket bro. Clean guns, the masks and all. We pretty much got the plans ready. We just have to execute. But I need your *expertise to tie the loose ends. Make sure shit is extra tight. Everybody plays their part, and we're in business" Kwame said.*

"I mean I been in some wild shit in my life. This is real creative fam. Once I get that steel in my hand, shit will get real for me" Chill replied.

"Indeed. We all have to be on point, it's a matter of life and death. Shit is creative. But could be real dangerous. If one of them guards get brave and want to play hero" Kwame said.

"Man. You know I'm always on point nigga" Chill replied. As him and Kwame laughed a little.

Kwame and Chill walked out of the warehouse that day after seeing all the resources they had to them. Confident and with a swagger like they knew it all was going to work. While driving back to their hoods. Kwame and Chill had a conversation. About when they were young cats and County Park had Splash Parties.

"I was thinking about Splash Parties in County Park. We were young niggas but that shit was live. Music blasting from the speakers. Food, and everybody in the city there. The pool was jam packed. The baddest chicks in the city there looking beautiful as ever in their bathing suits. If you was somebody in this city. You remember and know about Splash Parties in County Park nigga. And the most important thing was. Everybody was good and there was no drama and no beef. Just the city having a good time. When we start making some of that real money. We're going to bring that shit. Word. We're going to bring that shit back better than ever playboy" Chill said.

"That would be dope. Real dope. And I know the city would love it too. Get this doe and that's one way we could give back to the community. Throwing the Splash Party. Right in County Park where it began. Free of charge to the public" Kwame replied.

The two continued chopping it up until Kwame dropped Chill off. On Lime Street. Wheels decided to walk up the block to Lime and Dauphin to the corner store. Wheels grew up going to Mr. Cee's store. Him and Mr. Cee had a unique relationship Mr. Cee was a well-respected man in the community. His store was an important part of the community for many years. He knew Wheels since he was a young kid growing up on Lime Street. And he knew Wheels parents. Wheels had the upmost respect for Mr. Cee. And looked at him as a father figure. He made sure he went to the store at least every other day. To see Mr. Cee and purchase something from the store.

"I remember watching you and your friends run around this neighborhood as kids many years ago. Coming in the store everyday after school. Getting that penny candy you kids always loved. And I also remember giving you your first job. Sweeping up out front. Remember"? Mr. Cee replied asking.

"Yeah. Of course I remember. You made sure you had my favorite candy in stock. Because I always reminded you to get more when I worked here. Jaw Breakers and Swedish Fish. And the first job was major Mr. Cee. I appreciate that" Wheels said.   Page 13

"Those were the good old days. When community meant something. People took more pride in it, than they do now. People cleaned up trash from out in front of their doors. There was more respect amongst the young and old. People had more morals. I'm glad you stayed out of some of the mess that's gone on around here" Mr. Cee replied.

"I hear you Mr. Cee. And you're right. How's things been going around here"? Wheels asked.

"I'm good. And things are as good as they can be. I've been here a long time in this store and on this block. I've seen a lot of things over the years. And I'm still here and blessed" Mr. Cee replied.

"Yes. You're very blessed to have been here in this store on this block this long. And that's why I come by and check up on you every once in a while. And this whole city appreciates you. I have to get going Mr. Cee. Take care. And I'll come through in a few days and check up on you again" Wheels said. Shaking Mr. Cee's hand before leaving.

"Be safe out there son" Mr. Cee replied as Wheels left.

Travis was sitting in his housing project hallway puffing on a blunt. Something he did from time to time in his section of the houses. Not too many people said too much to Travis. He was somewhat of a loner and kept to himself. A quiet young man with a quick violent temper. Which already resulted in him committing murder. And he didn't have a problem killing again if he had to. Travis wasn't a troublemaker by any means. As said before. He kept to himself and minded his business. As young boy he was bullied and took advantage of. But as he got older, he got bolder. And a lot more dangerous. And he vowed that anyone who crossed him, would pay dire consequences. Always strapped with a gun on him as an adult. People knew he was a loose cannon.

As Travis sat there, a lot of thoughts ran through his mind. He thought about his life and where it was headed. At the moment he knew he was content on the life he was currently living. But for how long? He was curious about the opportunity to work with Kwame and others. Being apart of the bank heist crew. And getting some real money. Travis was a grimy dude. That most times only looked out for his best interest. He never trusted anyone, so it was hard imagining him working with others for a common goal. He naturally walked around with a chip on his shoulder. Much like his young counterpart Desmond from Green Street. Him and Desmond were cool, but not close at the time. They went to school together, and just knew each other from growing up in the city. They were both two young and wild dudes. And two important pieces of the crew.

The two that would be on the frontline. Kwame knew Travis and Desmond had no problem emptying a clip in anybody that resisted during the heists.

Even though the two were somewhat alike and knew each other. They hardly spoke. But now they would come together and form a unit with a few other individuals from different areas of the city. With one common goal. Get money and get away with it. At the end of the day, that's what it was about. Everyone would be present for the next meeting of the minds.   Page 14

To finalize the plans for the heist. One thing the crew that would be known as LANCREW all agreed upon was. Leaving any personal shit between them in the past and get this money. They were all working together in the name of business. They realized they could all be stronger together, rather than being apart. They stayed out of the local scene as much as they could, to not draw attention to themselves from the local authorities. They had bigger fish to fry and a lot more at stake. Even though doing what they planned to do was illegal also. There was a lot more money in it. And that made it worth the risk to them.

Nitro was sitting in his truck on Pershing Avenue. Waiting for this chick he was seeing to come out of a house around the corner on Howard Avenue. Nitro was growing a little impatient. So much so, that he was about to get his cell out and call her. But just as he was about to, he saw her coming in his rearview mirror.

"What the fuck? I was about to leave your ass. I hope you got what you wanted. Glad I didn't have no work on me" Nitro said as she got in.

"Chill. Damn nigga I didn't take that long. Impatient ass. But anyway. Where we going baby"? The woman replied asking.

"We're going back to the crib. I got some Henny and some burn. We could order out and make a night of it" Nitro said as he continued to drive.

Rage was at his Beaver Street home and decided to make a run to Prince Street to another legendary spot in the city. POS. POS was known for having some of the best fried chicken in the city. And that was exactly what Rage was getting on this late Spring early Summer night. He loved their fried chicken. So it wasn't unusual for him to make a run to the spot from his nearby Beaver Street neighborhood. A lot of people who hung down at POS knew Rage. So it was always love when he came through. But this particular night there were a few dudes that walked in POS that didn't look familiar.

Rage peeped it right away, as soon as they came in. He was sitting at a table with a few other dudes having a beer when they came in. As they walked in. They stared at Rage a little longer than a usual stare down. It just seemed funny to Rage as he sat there. Rage wasn't concerned. But he noticed as he sat there. He then went back to what he was doing while waiting for his food to be ready.

Five minutes later his order was ready, and he was about to leave. As he walked out of POS. He noticed the same dudes that were inside POS standing outside as he came out. He locked eyes with the both of them again. And kept walking. But he was definitely ready for whatever, and on point for whatever was going to go down. Rage was a strong dude, stocky. And one of the reasons he got his name was his brute strength and his fight game. He could've easily been a boxer, and even took up the sport for a short time. But eventually got disinterested with it. And gave it up. Many of days after work, he would workout down in his basement. He had a punching bag down in his basement, and a speed bag. That night it was nothing.   Page 15

And Rage walked back to his Beaver Street neighborhood with no problems. The next day everyone met up on a Saturday. So guys like Rage who worked full-time. Could attend the meeting. It was an important meeting because it was the last meeting before the heist. All the detailed instructions and planning would be laid out. It would be up to the crew to execute the plan to perfection. The crew all met at the same warehouse Kwame and Chill was at before. In the 6th Ward. Kwame, Wheels, and Chill basically planned the first heist. Chill knew the ins and outs of banks. And of course Wheels was an elite get away driver. Kwame was good at organizing shit. The three men had already staked out the bank three days straight. Checking out the routine of the overall business of the bank.

The bank was in Dauphin County. And the three men did their homework on the bank. After getting to the warehouse. Kwame got everyone's attention. And began going over the plans. Wheels and Rage were the drivers. Travis, Desmond, and Angel would be the first and only three in the bank. They knew their roles. Angel would enter the bank first and distract the guard with her beauty alone. To make way for the gunmen Travis and Desmond. The two young guns, whose blood stayed hot. And they loved the action of gunplay. But the plan was for them not to have to use their guns. ONLY if they were drawn on by the security guards. They were to execute the plan. And try to do so without shooting anyone. Which was asking a lot. But was the plan.

Get in quick and get out quick, plain and simple. The plan was to be in the bank no more than twenty minutes flat. They wanted to hit the tellers and hit the vault. And get out of there. Angel would wear a wig and some sunglasses. While Travis and Desmond would wear the hockey masks the team had to put over their faces. The crew would have interchanging parts. The purpose being, that the authorities would never get their identities. Or a real read on them. Chill was one who was experienced in bank heists. And studied bank heist crews in American history. He noticed flaws in each of them. Not huge flaws, but some small flaws. And details that led to their capture. On this heist. Chill, Nitro, and Erotic would sit this one out.

Despite Chill planning it. He was clear when he said he wanted a small role. So he as well as the others would wait back in the warehouse in the 6th Ward. For the rest of the crew to get back with the money so they could count it. Kwame included.

"We're set ladies and gentlemen. Two days away from our first job of many together. Let's get rich. We have to be sharp on our execution and very precise with our time. No bullshit while we're in them banks. Angel do what you do. And once Angel give you two that text. You two do what you do best. Storm that muthafuckin bank and get that cash. Hit those tellers and hit that vault. And get the fuck out of there!! Wheels will be waiting in the car" Kwame said.

"You know with them guards in there. We may have to pop somebody trying to be a hero. I can't see no resistance with that. I know you want us to keep this shit violence free and all. But that may be impossible. The shit is what it is fam. We may be young, but we're ready for this shit. Believe me" Desmond replied.

"I know you two are ready. I wouldn't put you two on the frontlines if you weren't. I know you young niggas are trigger happy. That's exactly why we put you two in the action. Trust me. There's a lot of niggas in the city that would love to be apart of this shit. And THINK they could be successful doing it. But we're the chosen few. We're those niggas. And in the end, we'll be the ones eating. There's a lot of money to be made, let's get it"!!! Kwame said.

"Nigga you could talk a nigga into a plan, even if he may not even be interested. Kwame a slick talker yall. Yall got to watch this nigga. But I fucks with you all day Kwame. I have to get out of here, got some shit to handle" Nitro replied before he left.

The rest of the crew then started filing out after him. Leaving the warehouse and going their separate ways. The masterminds. Chill,

Wheels, and Kwame were the only ones still back in the warehouse. They were all confident that their plan would work. They just wanted to execute the plan and get as much cash as they could. Kwame knew one thing. Which Desmond had mentioned. If anyone in that bank showed any resistance. They were dead. So Kwame was hoping for the best. Armed robbery was one thing. But armed robbery and murder was another. The crew was less than forty eight hours away from their first heist.

"Everything looks good and we got the right people in the right roles for this. Especially for the first heist. The youngins will be on point. And won't let shit past them. You already know the nigga Travis is a shooter. You know I got the whip game on lock so we're good on that. Rage been in the game a long time, he knows what he's doing. Trust it, we're good Kwame. We don't have shit to worry about it. I'm hungry as shit. Let's hit HOP or Lucky's" Wheels said.

"I think we did a good job getting shit started. In less than forty eight hours, we'll see if it all works. Get your game face on Kwame. We're about to see our plan put into action" Chill said.

"I'm just a little worried about the youngins popping somebody before they need to. You know both them niggas are trigger happy. I just hope they're patient like I told them. Popping somebody will bring even more heat on us before we even get started" Kwame replied.

"Yeah. But who would you rather have on your team? Some young hungry niggas that don't have no problem letting that thing off if they have to? Or some timid niggas that are scared and might end up going in there getting shot AND bagged"? Chill asked Kwame.

"You're right. I have to trust the plan. Let's see how it works out. Let's hope these young niggas don't fuck this up. We can hit HOP for *something to eat. And go Down Bottom for a drink or two" Kwame replied.*

On Green Street. Desmond had just came back in from the block. After being outside for the last forty five minutes. Watching things go down on his porch. When he decided to go in his house. He went inside and went in his kitchen to finish a drawing he was working on. An amazing drawing he did of a city block. The city block was of course his hood Green Street. And it wasn't just a painting. The painting was vibrant and alive with people all through it. From Hustlers on the block to little girls sitting on porches listening to music.   Page 17

To little boys playing basketball on a make shift basket made out of a milk crate. Hung from a pole. The painting captured the block in so many lights. Even though throughout the city it was notoriously known as a violent block. Desmond showed the block in a different way. A more positive way. The block wasn't all bad, it had produced some very meaningful people. That went on to become successful in their own right. And Desmond was trying to capture that in his drawing. Like any other Urban area in America. The entire 7th Ward produced some smart, creative, talented and successful people. Despite the negative perceptions of the city's Southeast and it's residents. Success stories were alive and well. And being felt all over the World. Not just in Lanc City. Authors, basketball players, football players, artists, doctors, nurses, military servicemen and women. Teachers, baseball players, singers, rappers, etc. Were all born and raised in the 7th Ward.

Even though Desmond was in the streets, he was very talented at drawing. It was his passion. He had his drawings all over his house. He didn't let too many people in his home. So a lot of people didn't know just how good he was at drawing. But those that were lucky enough to see his drawings, knew how talented he was. They witnessed the greatness of his drawings. As he was sitting there working on another masterpiece. He suddenly heard a knock at his door. Desmond grabbed his 9mm handgun off his table. And went to answer the door. No one would just come to his house without calling first. Anyone that knew him, knew that. It was why Desmond grabbed his gun.

He approached the door and looked out the peep hole. To his surprise, it was Travis. Desmond didn't know what to think. But he knew he and Travis were going to be on the frontlines together in this heist. Off the strength of that, he opened it.

"What's good nigga? What you doing here"? Desmond asked as he opened the door.

Travis just smiled and replied.

"Nigga you going to let me in or what"? Travis replied standing there.

Desmond with his gun still in his hand, let Travis in. They eventually went into Desmond's kitchen to chop it up.

"This is some nice shit. I heard you could draw. Interesting street shit too. I like that" Travis said as he was checking out Desmond's drawings.

"I didn't even know who the fuck you were, knocking on my door like that. Most times I don't even answer my door if niggas don't call me first. You were about to get shot" Desmond said. Sitting across from Travis at the kitchen table.

"I knew you wasn't going to shoot me. We got a lot of money to make together. And as young niggas, we've got something to prove to these old niggas who put us on. They don't think we can handle this shit. But they put us on the frontlines because they don't want that work. But we do. And we're more than ready aren't we"? Travis replied.   Page 18

"If they didn't think we were capable of doing it, they wouldn't have recruited us. And fuck what they think. I'm about this paper. That's the only reason I'm in it. And I'm sure that's why you're in it too. At the end of the day, that's all that matters" Desmond said.

"No doubt" Travis replied agreeing.

It was really the first time the two young, brash, and wild little niggas. Got a chance to talk to one another for an extended time. They knew each other from going to school together. Because they were the same age. But just wasn't close enough to have a full conversation with one another. But they were now two young dudes surrounded by mostly older men. Angel was the youngest out of everyone in the crew at 20 years old. She was the only one younger than Travis and Desmond. Travis felt they had something to prove to the older cats in the crew. Desmond didn't care. He was all about getting money. Travis surprise visit to Desmond's Green Street home was essentially to get some sort of chemistry amongst each other. Since they would be guarding each other's lives during the heists. He wanted to make sure they were on the same page. Stakes were at an all-time high, and lives would be on the line.

On Ann Street. Kwame was in his home enjoying his dinner with his lady and young son. Afterwards sitting on his recliner and watching some TV. And thinking about the crew's first heist the next day. A lot was going through Kwame's mind. He had more at stake than anybody in the crew. Being the man that put it all together. People that was handpicked by himself. From his perspective. This had to work. He was confident that the plan would work, he just didn't want any blood on his hands. Tomorrow couldn't come any quicker for Kwame. To say he was anxious was an understatement. Each individual spent the night before the heist doing what they normally did in their lives. To the best of their ability. Without drawing any unnecessary attention towards themselves that seemed suspicious.

On Chester Street. Angel was doing her hair and getting herself ready for tomorrow. Preparing the wig she would wear. And holding a pretty chrome 9mm handgun. That she would use the next day. Angel was a marksman and knew how to handle guns. She wasn't doing it so she could shoot people. She went to the range to practice her shooting, in case God forbid she had to shoot someone. It was for protection and just being prepared in case. Angel would go to the range with her older cousin Tisha. Who lived nearby in the Garden Court Housing Projects. Angel was still considered underage. So Tisha would go with her when she went. One thing she didn't do, was tell her cousin Tisha any crew business. The heist the next day was just between crew members, and crew members only. Tisha had no idea what Angel was going to be doing the next day. Angel knew what she signed up for, and she was ready.

Chill was at his home the night before just enjoying a normal night at the house. And Chill wasn't going to be actively participating in tomorrow's heist. He would be part of the team that would count the money. After being in his house, he went out front to see what was going on out there. Franklin Terrace was always live. So there was always something going on. This night was no different. Cars drove past bumping their music loud. Kids were outside still playing.   Page 19

Some members were anxious, some members were nervous. Collectively they had a job to do, and the next day would be the first chance to do so. Five in the morning and Kwame was wide awake. He couldn't sleep much the night before. And he was up now for good. He went downstairs and ate some cereal and watched a little TV.

By the sun slowly rising. You could tell it was going to be a nice day. So the crew wouldn't have to worry about a heist in bad weather. Which obviously could've potentially caused problems with the execution of the heist. No problems on that front, it was a go.

The Day Of The Heist Act 1

Wheels awoke early that morning also. Looked out of his window. And let the sunshine in as he looked out onto South Lime Street. He had one of the cars that they would use for the day. His car of choice? An older Buick sedan. Wheels figured a sedan would be better than a coupe, so each member of the crew could get out of their own separate doors. Better for when they were getting away quickly. After getting dressed. Wheels made his way downstairs, out the door. And into his car then off to Chester Street to pick up Angel. When Wheels came up East End Avenue and then onto Chester. Angel was waiting on her porch. She got in and then they were on their way to get Desmond on the corner of Pershing and Green. And lastly to Hillrise Housing Projects to pick up Travis.

"What's good girl? I know you ready right"? Wheels said to Angel as he drove.

"Hell yeah. I'm ready. It's an opportunity to make some real money. I'm always trying to make some real money" Angel replied.

Then Desmond got in the car. Followed by Travis. And they met Rage down the street from Travis on South Duke. Rage was in the other car that would bring the team home after they ditched the first car. The crew made the forty five minute drive up to the Dauphin County bank. Wheels and the team that would do the heist. And Rage following right behind them. Once they got closer to their destination, Rage would fall back to a location only the team knew. And wait.

The drive up, everyone was quiet and focused in the car. Angel had her wig on. Desmond had his mask in his lap. Gloves on and gun in hand. Travis was sitting in the backseat relaxed, like what they were about to do was nothing. Gloves on as he was holding his gun and looking up and down every few seconds out the window. The drive seemed like forever to the crew. They were getting antsy.

"Damn Kwame picked a far location for this first heist. Shit. Feels like we're never going to get here" Desmond said sitting behind Wheels.

"Patience youngin. Patience. All this shit has to be done carefully and precisely. You can't rush shit like this. The further away, the harder it is to catch us. Especially with Rage behind us. Focus ladies and gents. Focus" Wheels said as he continued to drive.

Angel looked out of her sideview mirror from the passenger side and saw Rage pull over near an overpass. She knew then they were getting closer to the bank. The car became completely silent as they got closer to the bank. Everyone had their game faces on as Wheels pulled into the Dauphin County bank. Wheels parked and Angel put on her blonde wig and shades. Then proceeded to get out of the car and enter the bank.   Page 21

Angel entered the bank with a blonde wig on and some shades. As she approached the teller, she handed her a note. She then proceeded to text Desmond and Travis. Who were waiting in the car outside for her text. The teller looked at Angel and Angel nodded as if to say. "Yes I'm serious, this IS a bank robbery". As soon as Desmond and Travis got the text, they stormed out of the car. Masks on as they walked across the parking lot to the bank. Weapons already in hand as they entered the bank.

"Everybody get the fuck down!!! Now!! And don't do no stupid shit to get your ass blasted. Get down!!! Face down on the ground!! Fill this muthafuckin bag up bitch and shut up!!!Desmond yelled as he tossed a bag to the teller.

Travis quickly hopped over the teller counter and instructed that teller to head to the back to the vault. Angel and Desmond held down the front, as Angel herself was now armed also. Angel walked over to one of the armed guards that was now on the ground. And kicked his gun away from him.

"Hurry up and open this fucking vault!! Move it!! If you don't get to this safe, it's over for you" Travis said pointing his gun at the woman as she nervously was opening the vault.

Another text was sent out to the team saying they had ten minutes. The vault was finally open. And Travis sprinted inside. He filled his bag with as much cash as he could. Then telling the teller to go back out front as he came running back out. Once Travis came running through, that was the cue for Angel and Desmond to be out right behind him. With their weapons drawn, they got back out of the bank. And sprinted to the car where Wheels was waiting. Wheels did what he did best. Wheel the shit out of that Buick and off into the day. They all got back to where Wheels was. And ditched the Buick Sedan and got in a Mini-Van. Heading East back to Lanc City.

With the five of them in the van, they had plenty of room. And there was no sign of any cops pursuing them. They immediately went back to the warehouse in the city's 6th Ward. Where the rest of the crew would be waiting to count the money. Up until this point, the first heist was successful.

Rage had got them all back to the warehouse. The crew had three bags of money. Kwame, Chill, Nitro, and Erotic would count the money. The heist team emptied all the money on the table. Stared at each other for a minute. Until Wheels shouted. "Yo. WE did that shit. We really did that shit"!!

The rest of the crew laughed and gave each other daps. Realizing they had really done what they set out to do. But this was just the beginning.

"Yall all know what it is. The heist team. Good work. Yall did yall thing. We'll count the money of course. After we get this counted. Everybody will get their cut. We should celebrate. Go Down Bottom get lit up. And then hit some Downtown bars. We should be finished counting this, and the night will still be young. Whatever yall want to do" Kwame said.   Page 22

"If I'm hitting Downtown. I'm hitting HOP up. Those steamed shrimp in the red sauce!! A Lanc City Classic" Chill said as he sat next to Kwame.

"Kwame we out. Just make sure we get our cut. Hit me on the hip when it's ready for us to pick up. I'll be expecting that call" Desmond said. As he and Travis got up and left.

That's just how the youngins were. They were straight and to the point. And serious about putting work in and getting their money. They may have been wild on their own time. But when it came to getting money, and doing whatever they had to do to get it. They were focused. They would go all out. Kwame knew that, that's why he put them on the frontlines. He also did it to test their composure. He knew both of them would open fire in a heartbeat. Like most young niggas do nowadays. Putting them in a high pressure situation where they may not have needed to fire a single shot. And see how they react. From the looks of the first heist. They both passed that test. No one was harmed, and not a single shot fired.

Most the crew had left the warehouse. All but the men and woman counting the money.

"Seems like them young niggas handled shit well. Hopefully that's a good thing moving forward. And hopefully it will continue. I'm just ready to get in this shit now. It's my turn. The next team is up, and we'll be ready" Nitro said looking anxious to get in the action.

"I'm glad you all will be ready. Because in a few days, we're going to map out the next one" Kwame replied. As he and the rest of team continued counting. The counting didn't take that long because they were using machines. They stayed until they were done counting. By the time the crew got done counting. The first heist netted the crew over $250,000. Nice take for the crew's first time out. After leaving the warehouse. Some of the crew wanted to celebrate. Wheels and Chill went Down Bottom to have some drinks. Nitro decided to get a penthouse suite high above the city at the Convention Center Downtown.

The youngins? Well they went back to Desmond's house on Green Street. He was showing Travis some more of his drawings. Travis had bought two bottles of Hennessy for the both of them. And some Lucky's take-out.

"The rest of the crew was probably shocked at how we handled shit today. I told them niggas we were ready" Desmond said.

"Like you told me before nigga. If they didn't think we were capable, they wouldn't have had us out there. They knew damn well we were ready for whatever. I'm just ready to get my cut" Travis replied.

"I did say that, didn't I? Fuck it. Let's just celebrate tonight and enjoy the fact we have some serious cash coming our way soon" Desmond said.

Two shrimps on a stick and a few cheeseburger combinations. Two favorites of Desmond and Travis at the popular city take-out spot. Page 23

In Dauphin County. The authorities were looking for clues to solve the bank heist a day earlier. They were interviewing potential witnesses. All the authorities had was an African American woman in a blonde wig. Accompanied by two masked gunmen. Beyond that, that's all witnesses in the bank saw. Police were hoping that someone saw the getaway car or the license plate number or something. As of this point, no one seen anything outside the bank. The crew got away quietly without busting their guns at all. Which was what they wanted. The people in the bank did what they said, in fear of their lives. Travis and Desmond immediately made their presence felt. And let everyone in that bank know, they weren't fucking around. And they would shoot you if they had to. It was a brazen daytime robbery executed flawlessly like the crew had hoped.

They were already back in Lanc City. And the money had already been counted. And was about to be split up. The plan worked to the tee. And there were no leads in the heist. This was just the beginning, and the crew was about to choose another bank to hit. With a whole different team playing different roles. They would be hard to stop.

The next day came and Erica Erotic Fisher was laying in her bed. When she heard a knock at the door. She quickly got up to answer the door, so it wouldn't wake her grandmother. Got her robe on and went downstairs to answer the door. Before opening the door, she looked out the peep hole. It was Stacks. She was wondering why he was knocking on her door so early in the morning for.

"Where the fuck you been? I've been hitting your phone for over a day or so. And no answer"!! Stacks said.

"Nigga if you don't chill the fuck out and keep it down. My grandmother is sleep. What is wrong with you coming to my house this damn early in the morning? I had some shit I had to do. And something is wrong with my phone" Erotic replied. Pushing Stacks back onto the porch and closing the door.

"Regardless of how busy you were. You couldn't call your man? You've been real distant lately. You fucking with somebody else or what? Let a nigga know if that's what it is" Stacks said.

Erotic just looked at Stacks and shook her head. And then replied. "Are you done? Because I'm about to go back to sleep. And I don't appreciate you waking me up. Assuming shit. I've been getting money like you've been. I told you I like getting my own money. And you better hope you didn't wake my grandmother up. You know she will cuss you out if she has to. Especially waking her up".

"If it's just you two in there. Let me come in. I'll put that ass back to sleep" Stacks said smiling.

Erotic just shook her head and yawned. And then closed the door. Stacks shook his head in disgust and got in his car. And left. That's just how their relationship was, on and off. Because Erotic was always doing her thing. Making money one way or the other. Since being apart of the crew. She stopped boosting. Like anyone else, she was not allowed to tell Stacks anything about the crew. He had no knowledge of what she was apart of.   Page 24

There was no way Stacks would've wanted her involved in any bank heist crew. Not that it would've stopped her. Because Erotic was the type to do what she wanted to do, if she really wanted to do it. Little did he know, Erotic was about to be the lead lady in the next heist. She was excited about getting the same opportunity her counterpart Angel did. To lead the team into the bank. The ladies were free to wear whatever colored wigs they wanted, as long as they switched them up. Kwame was hoping the money from the first heist would keep the crew out of the streets locally. And out of any petty shit that would draw any attention towards them. That was asking a lot from a crew of individuals that made their way in the streets. But so far so good.

The question was. How long could all of them fallback from the streets? Only time would tell. After a few days. Kwame wanted everyone to meet at the warehouse to get their cut from the heist. It didn't take long for each of them to make their way to the 6th Ward warehouse. The take was $250,000. The crew split the money between them, and paid Chino some money for using his warehouse. Everyone was happy to finally get their money. But before they left, Kwame had some news for them.

"Check this out. We got another bank in our sights. A bank up in Franklin County. Hoping this time we get even more money than the first time. Different team like we discussed. Nitro, Erotic, and Travis. You all will hit the bank. Wheels and Chill will bring it home" Kwame said.

"The quicker we hit this next bank, the quicker we can blow through this money we got now. Or do whatever the fuck yall plan to do. Best believe I'm ready to cash in. We're getting more than the first heist" Nitro said sounding confident.

"What you trying to say? What's that supposed to mean? We didn't do it right the first time nigga?!! There was a quarter of a million dollars on that table my nigga"!! Travis replied. Clearly agitated at what Nitro said.

"Just chill!! Nobody is saying shit. No need to argue about no shit like that. We in this shit together. The first heist was successful. No matter how much money it was. This is all extra money to us. Wasn't nothing Travis, just chill youngin" Kwame said.

"You all enjoy your cut. I'm stacking my doe. I'm not spending shit" Wheels said.

"Well that's all I have for you ladies and gents. I will keep you all posted on the details of the next heist as it gets closer. Keep your phones on you and stay out of the mix. Don't spend all that doe in one place" Kwame said. As the crew was leaving.

Rage was very much a family man and could use the extra cash. He was looking to get work done on his Beaver Street home. His long term goal was to eventually sell his home and move outside the city. He wanted to give his kid's a better life than he had. And the streets had changed over the years. Rage was well-respected. But he just didn't want his kids in that environment anymore. So the plan was to get the repairs done on his Beaver Street home and eventually sell it and move. This money would definitely help with that.   Page 25

Rage had been in the streets since he was a youngin. But was in a different space in his life now. Being married and having kids now. Definitely changed his mindset about things. Kwame was on his porch on Ann Street just standing outside looking up and down the block. Watching everything from the cars going up and down the street. To the many people that were on the block. Something he liked to do from time to time. To reflect on everything he had been through. A few prison stints. And being stabbed in the stomach prior to that. The master plan he, Wheels, and Chill had put together was just getting started. Kwame stashed a lot of the money he made. Except splurging a little on his girl and his son.

The crew wasted no time getting back at it. While the bank heist investigation was ongoing in Dauphin County. The Police had no leads. But had surveillance camera footage from the bank. The footage showed three people involved in the heist. What authorities already knew. Detectives watched as one of the mask gunmen led a teller back to what seemed like the vault. The whole thing happened in like a little over twenty minutes.

For now that's all the authorities had to go on. They had Detectives comb the outside of the bank and all around it. Looking for clues to solve the case. Over $250,000 was stolen from the Dauphin County bank. The crew had already got their money and some were splurging on themselves. While Wheels and Kwame were stashing their money. Wheels already kept a fleet of cars. He knew a lot of people that could work on cars. And he restored a lot of them. He enjoyed it. Investing his money into rebuilding cars. Wheels himself currently had three cars. He loved his old-schools.

Wheels was a student of the old-school crews of the city. The posse's of the late 80's and 90's. The crews from the 80's like HBO and CC. He learned some things from each crew and era that came before him. Meanwhile Angel had done a little shopping. Picking up some new wigs for the upcoming heists. And getting a few things for herself. Part of what made the crew unstoppable was their ability to hide their true identities. Their different disguises and interchanging parts. Made it hard for authorities to pinpoint a specific description about the crew. Only Angel's blonde wig. Even with surveillance footage, there wasn't much the authorities could make out. As far as any identity. The next heist would feature a totally different female with a totally different style wig.

But before that. Angel was enjoying a full day at the spa. A manicure and pedicure with her cousin Tisha. And to cap the day off. They had lunch after doing some shopping. It was an enjoyable day for the two women. As Angel was enjoying the money she made, and treating her cousin to a good time in the process. It was a nice day with her cousin and best friend.

"Thanks. Angel. For everything today. I really appreciate it. It's been a while since I've been able to get something for myself. With the kids and all" Tisha said.

"Don't worry about it cousin. I'm just glad we were able to hang out. It's been a while with us both working. Glad we made it happen" Angel replied.   Page 26

"Have you decided yet if and when you're going to school? That WAS your dream to further your education" Tisha said to Angel.

"I plan on going back to school cousin. I'm just taking my time. I'll know when it's time. And before you even say it cousin, I'm not going to take too much time" Angel replied.

"Right. Because you know how Lanc City is. If you're not doing something productive with your life. You can easily get caught up in some shit in the mix. And you know I don't want that for you cousin. You're better than that, and you're smart. Go get that degree and chase your dream" Tisha said.

"Don't worry Tisha. I'm good and I'm not giving up on my dream. Just taking my time and moving at my own pace. I have a plan" Angel replied.

The two ladies continued with their day together. Shopping. To the Spa and lunch. It was a great day and they both had a great time. Angel and Tisha were very close. Neither of them had a sister, so in essence they were sisters. And had a sisterly bond. Even though in reality they were cousins. Angel growing up in the first block of Chester Street. And her cousin Tisha growing up in Garden Court on the Marshall Street side. Which was only a few blocks from each other. So they were always at each other's house. Tisha was older than Angel, and they always looked out for each other. That's why it was nothing for Angel to treat her cousin for a day.

Angel didn't want to tell Tisha how much money she had. She couldn't. Tisha would ask where the money came from? She told her she had worked some extra hours to get the money to pay for the day. For now. That's what Angel wanted Tisha to believe.

Chill and Rage decided to go down to HOP for some wings and drinks. As they were sitting at the bar. Rage glanced out the big glass window at the entrance of the spot. When he seen some cats he thought looked familiar. After thinking for a moment. He remembered. It was the same dudes he seen at POS. After taking a sip of his drink. He and Chill had a conversation about it.

"You see them niggas over there Chill"? Rage said. Looking over toward the two dudes.

"Yeah. What about them"? Chill replied asking.

"Seen them down POS one night. They were looking at me all crazy and shit. But then again maybe I was tripping. Because nothing popped off. And I was by myself too. I was onto them niggas quick though, because I had never seen them down at POS before" Rage said.

"If they didn't do shit that night. And it was two of them, and you were dolo? They don't want no smoke. But it's good to know who they are though" Chill replied.

"True. We have bigger fish to fry anyway. This first heist was cool, and it only took twenty minutes. We couldn't have asked for an easier payday. I've been really thinking about moving out of the hood with my money. As much as I love Beaver Street, shit is just different now. But it'll always be my hood for life. Page 27

My kids are getting older now. And I want them to see more than I seen growing up. I've lived on Beaver all my life fam. My kids too. That's why all the money I'm making with the crew, I'm stashing for that dream house" Rage said.

"Sounds like a great plan. That's why we do this right? I have some ideas myself. But that will come when it comes. Until then. Let's enjoy the ride homie. Embrace the reality of us having a little money now" Chill replied.

"I heard Kwame say this next bank is in Franklin County. I see we're branching a littler further out" Rage said.

"We have to. So these people stay off our trail. And the next team is up. And even though niggas know how I get down. I'm ready to show and prove that I can still do this shit for real. That's why I feel *so confident about this shit. I wouldn't have never left from in front of my house in Franklin Terrace. If I wasn't confident that I could still put in work. I was making good money in the projects, still am" Chill replied.*

"I feel the same way bro" Rage said. Taking a sip from his drink.

The two continued having drinks and chopping it up. Authorities in Dauphin County had found the older model Buick. At the time they didn't know if the Buick was tied to the bank heist or not. But they did find the car on the side of the road by an underpass. After towing the car, they would dust it looking for prints. Problem with that was, everyone wore gloves, including Wheels who was one of the getaway drivers. There were still no leads in the Dauphin County bank heist. And the crew was already planning their next heist. The authorities had no clue who anyone from the crew was. No description at all of any of them. But Angel. Who wore a blonde wig. And was someone that people in the bank said they remembered during the heist. The authorities had no clue if the bank heist crew would strike again, or where they would strike. But they were about to find out.

Kwame was driving through Lanc City streets when he decided to drive down South Lime Street. Where just like he thought, Wheels was outside cleaning off one of his cars. By this time it was getting closer to Summer. But not quite. It was mid Spring. It wouldn't have mattered If It was In the dead of Winter. Wheels always made sure his cars were clean. Kwame pulled up and had a conversation with him.

"I knew your ass would be out here wiping one of your cars down. If it's nice out. I always know what you're doing bro. You can clean mines next. If you want nigga" Kwame said smiling.

"You got some money? That's the only way I'm cleaning anybody's car but mines. Pay me and I got you" Wheels replied. As they both laughed.

"But on some real shit. You ready for this next go round? A longer distance to drive. But hopefully a much bigger take also. We're all feeding a lot of people, so we need to raise the stakes a little higher this time" Kwame said.

"You know I'm ready. Small thing to a giant dawg. Besides. I may even surprise your ass and get on the frontlines for a heist" Wheels replied smiling.

"Homie you don't have to prove shit to me either way fam. I know how you get down. I put the youngins on the frontlines because you know they love that action. But anytime you want to step out front, just say the word" Kwame said.

Wheels just smiled. He was happy with being the get away driver. He just wanted to let Kwame know if he wanted and was needed on the frontlines. He could do it. The youngins being out front worked for the crew. If it wasn't broke, the crew weren't trying to fix it. They would keep the same formula that has worked for them.

Wheels was an OG and had nothing to prove. He had put in work in the streets and was well respected. Ever since he was a young boy growing up on Lime Street. These days Wheels was just trying to get a little money here and a little money there. He grew himself a decent size fleet of cars. His homie Miles who grew up with him on Lime Street was a Mechanic. And was his partner in getting cars and restoring them. And in some instances, selling them. Wheels was a hustler. And his homie Miles had his own garage on Manor Street. Any cars Wheels had, he would take them to Miles. They worked together and got money together. They had a good system going. And as much as Wheels wanted to let his homie Miles know what he was doing. He knew he couldn't say a word.

The next day the crew met at the warehouse to discuss the next plan of action. Which was a Franklin County bank. Each heist was strategically planned out as far as location. They didn't want anyone onto them. Or for anyone to have a clue when and where they would strike next. Authorities were still investigating the Dauphin County bank heist, with no more leads than they had before. Everything was going according to plan, but it was early in the game to tell if it would continue. Kwame arrived at the warehouse first. Along with Nitro and Wheels. Ten minutes later, the rest of the crew arrived. They met on a Saturday again so Rage could be there.

"This is our second time around. And we're looking to make a lot more than we did before. I'm changing it up a little. Nitro and Desmond will be on the frontlines. Along with Erotic. Wheels and Chill, you two will bring it home. The rest of us will be back here waiting to count that money" Kwame said.

"I guess you want me out of this one huh Kwame"? Travis replied with a smirk on his face.

"Not at all. We do what we have to do. You know that. This time I wanted to make a switch, nothing personal playboy. Everybody will get action and everybody will have to sit it out. We all eat and we all ride for each other. That's how it works" Kwame said.

"Yeah. I hear you. We're still getting paid right? I'm not tripping, ya'll get that money" Travis replied smiling.

In his sick twisted mind, Travis was being sarcastic. He was just thrown off like that. A loner with nothing to lose, and he lived every minute of his life like it. Most people in this situation would've loved to have survived one heist. And sit on the sidelines for another. While getting paid to do so. A person would be happy. Not Travis. He loved being in the thick of the action. Whatever that may have consisted of. It was a rush to him. But in this situation. He had to be a team player and be patient. After answering Travis comment, Kwame continued talking to the crew.

"This time out it's going to be more difficult. It's a longer stretch being that it's an hour and a half away. It's very important that we get this shit right. In and out quick. We enter here. Erotic goes in and does her thing. When she gets in the bank and sends you that text. Nitro and Desmond, you two come through guns drawn ready for whatever. Hit those tellers, and Desmond you take the other teller to the vault. Wheels and Chill will be waiting for the team to bring this shit back home. Any questions"? Kwame said.

"An hour and a half Kwam? That's pretty steep. Long drive for a heist, but I guess you know your shit. And I trust you'll put us in the best position to get that bag" Erotic replied.

"Trust me. The further we expand out the better. But if it makes you feel better, we'll choose a closer location next time" Kwame said.

Despite the skepticism about the distance to and from the bank. The crew were all confident in the plan either way. It was the last meeting before the next heist in two days. But before that. Travis decided to throw himself an old-fashioned house party. It was something Hill Rise Housing Project was known for back in the day. Some of the best house parties in the city took place in those projects. This would be no different. Travis spared no expense as he had three apartments reserved for the party. Despite mostly being a loner. Travis got some people he talked to within the projects. And threw a party. The people were happy to party with Travis, rather than be at the other end of his gun.

There was a DJ in one of the houses. And he had some huge speakers that were placed outside so everyone could hear the music. The party was lit and there was food and drinks for anyone that wanted to come through. Travis invited some of the crew to the party. Desmond, Erotic, and Chill all came through. And they were all having a good time.

"You got this shit popping tonight Travis. Damn near the whole projects is here. Good shit homie. I never knew you was the type of nigga to be throwing parties. I do the same shit down in my hood in Franklin Terrace. Well I know it as Almanac. You young cats might call it Franklin Terrace. Later in the summer I plan on throwing my annual cookout down Almanac. You all have to come through" Chill said. Passing an L between himself, Desmond, and Travis.

"Shit is nice bro. And they're some bad ass broads here too......damn!! I know you have to be bagging one of them. Which one is it nigga? So I don't end up trying to holla at her" Desmond said laughing a little.

"Nigga. You couldn't handle the chicks I deal with. They aren't checking for you. I got a few bottles in the crib for us to pop. We're getting lit tonight" Travis replied.

The DJ was playing all the latest bangers, and everyone was enjoying themselves. People from the Locust Street side of the projects also came down to party. As well as the Rockland, Chester, and Green Street sides also. Like Chill said. Damn near the whole projects was at the party on the Howard Avenue side where Travis resided. The whole front yard was jam packed with people, as well as up and down Howard Avenue. Over a hundred people attended the party that night. Even though not everyone knew Travis personally. But they heard the music banging from blocks away. And the party was the talk of the city that night. Of course the cops came through the party and told Travis he had to keep it down. After the Police left, the party continued.

Stacks and Bags were also in attendance. Two people who didn't really care too much for Travis. But still made their way to the party.

After driving down Howard Avenue and seeing what was going on. Somewhat surprising to see them both there, but they showed up anyway. They both walked up to where Desmond and Travis were standing. Erotic and Chill were amongst the crowd of people. And watching from not that far away. As they both saw when Stacks and Bags walked up. Being that Erotic was dating him.

"What's good Travis.....Desmond? Shit is live. I'm surprised you Lancaster niggas did it so big. Reminds me of how we did shit back home up North" Stacks said looking around. As he pulled Erotic close to him.

"Yeah. And I'm surprised you niggas came through to a party like this. Figured it was a little too small time for your taste. I'll let you and Erotic do your thing. I got a party to host" Travis replied walking away.

"You do that homie. Another time for that Stacks. We don't want to ruin the vibe with your lady here and all" Bags said. Interrupting Stacks and Travis. As Travis left to mingle with his guests.

Desmond and Chill stood side by side watching from a far. But it was clear there was bad blood between the men. Travis brushed it off as nothing. He was enjoying his party. And would get back to the street shit tomorrow. Basically unbothered. Because he knew nothing was going to go down with all the people that were there.

"Hey. I didn't even know that you were coming. Not that I got shit to hide, just having a good time with my peoples. Anyway. Welcome to the party" Erotic said. As she stood talking to Stacks.

"Let me holla at you for a minute. We need to talk" Stacks said. Grabbing Erotic's arm and pulling her over towards the street and away from everybody.

"I didn't know your ass was going to be here. What the fuck is up with that? I went to your grandmother's crib and you pushed a nigga away. And now you're here"? Stacks added on.

"Why are you even tripping? These are my people's. You knew damn well I was going to be here. I don't see the issue in it. I'm surprised you and Bags pulled up. And Angel isn't even here. You two don't get along with Desmond and Travis. That's why it's crazy to see you two here. I'm here because my boy invited me to his party" Erotic replied.

"Who fucking Travis? He's a fucking bum and you know it. We were just riding by and seen all these people out here and stopped. We didn't know it was this nut ass nigga's party. Where did he even get the money to do some shit like this? We're about to head out, this shit is getting tired. You coming with me, or staying at this bullshit ass party"? Stacks asked.

"I'm staying at this bullshit ass party. As you like to say it. With my people's like I attended to do" Erotic replied.

"Suit yourself. We out. Let's bounce bro" Stacks said walking back over towards Bags.

"Where you two going? The night is young fellas. You two aren't going to stay and party with us? Plenty of food and drink" Desmond said in a sarcastic manner to Stacks and Bags.

"No thanks. We're good. Another time and place though nigga. That's my word" Stacks replied. As he and Bags walked back to his truck.

The tension between the four men obviously wasn't going anywhere anytime soon. It was only a matter of time before it boiled over. Kwame told the crew to lay low and stay out of the street shit. Especially locally. They didn't need any heat on themselves, especially in their line of business.

Nitro was having some drinks Down Bottom with a female friend of his. Listening to one of Lanc City's finest DJ's rock out on the ones and twos. A good amount of people was in the bar this night. Nitro had his usual seat when he was Down Bottom towards the back of the bar. That's when he seen Stacks and Bags come in the bar from his seat towards the back. He knew them both from being in the streets. Although they never dealt with each other. It was a small city. And if you were somebody, people knew you. Or knew of you. Stacks and Bags weren't originally from the Lanc City area. But people knew them from them spending a lot of time in the city. And getting familiar with the people and the way of life of the city.

Nitro watched as they ordered some drinks and sat at a table near the DJ set. He had a viewpoint where he could see them, but they couldn't see him. It wasn't like he was going to go over and speak to them. They knew each other, but that was about it. Nitro knew he was apart of something a lot larger than local beef. He was apart of a crew who had major plans. The last thing he wanted to do was stir up any unnecessary bullshit. That really had nothing to do with him. But did have everything to do with his fellow crew members Desmond and Travis. Nitro continued having his drink and enjoying his night. And remained focused on the task at hand. Which was the next heist the crew had planned.

On Chester Street. Angel was doing her nails and watching TV. She had been at the mall shopping earlier that day. Got herself a few pair of shoes and a few outfits. Ended up dropping almost a stack in the mall alone. She also put some of her money away for school. Like she had promised her older cousin Tisha, and the rest of the family. About her eventually going back to school. She was going back to school. But was undecided on the exact time she would go. Her plan at this point. Was to stay home for a year. And then go to school. What school? She had a few she was considering. All within driving distance of Lanc City. After joining the crew and making money from the first heist. She was eager for more. The hunger to get that bag amongst the whole crew was real. It was the night before the next heist.

Erotic was up next. It was her turn to lead the crew into the bank. Despite having an important role in the heist the next day. Erotic partied well into that morning with Travis, Desmond, and Chill. The party brought back memories from house parties in Hill Rise back in the 80's and 90's. The projects really showed out and enjoyed Travis party. By the end of the night. Travis had passed out. Chill helped him into his crib and got him straight before he went home himself. And Desmond made the short walk to Green Street to his house.

The Second Heist Act 2

Early morning around six. Erica Erotic Fisher awakes to the bright lights of a Police car parked out in front of her Rockland Street home. She was almost scared to look as she peeked out her bedroom window. She looked down from her second floor bedroom window to see it was Stacks. He was up against his truck. And Police were searching his truck. Erotic was shocked and didn't know what to do. This couldn't be happening right now. Especially on the day of the heist. She just sat back on her bed and didn't know what to think. She had no clue of what was going on. And why Stacks was in front of her house at six in the morning. More importantly she was scared for Stacks and what may be in his truck. She hoped he didn't have any work on him.

After about ten minutes. The Police car drove away. And surprisingly. Stacks got back in his truck and drove away. But before he did that, he looked up at Erotic's bedroom window. She ducked her head back away from the window out of sight. She definitely didn't want Stacks to think she had anything to do with the cops stopping him. In a few hours Erotic had an important job to do, she had to get her mind right.

It was three hours later. And Wheels had just picked up Erotic. Desmond was already in the car, and they were on their way to pick Nitro up on Pershing Avenue. He had stayed in the city last night on a house on Howard Avenue. Something he did before each heist so far. After that they were off. Chill would meet them on Route 283. And then they would follow each other to the bank in Franklin County.

An hour and forty minute drive. As they drove the car was silent like the previous heist. Everyone was focused on the job at hand. Erotic put on the bright red wig she would wear. Which damn near covered her face. You could hardly see her pretty brown eyes. Desmond sat directly behind Wheels as he clutched his gun in his hand. Wearing black gloves as he stared out the window as they drove. Nitro sitting behind Erotic just stared out the window, with his gun in his lap. Ten minutes later, Wheels broke the silence in the car.

"Don't get restless and shit. I know it's drive. We needed to branch further out, throw these muthafuckas off you know. We don't need anybody onto us. Especially this being only our second time around" Wheels said.

"Yeah. I can dig it. I just hope the next one is a little closer. Niggas are anxious to get this shit popping. We get a bigger take this time, it'll definitely be worth it" Nitro replied.

"Of course" Wheels said as he drove.

Desmond just sat in the back not saying a word. He was focused the whole trip to the bank. Erotic didn't say much either. She was a little nervous. This being her first heist and all. But she knew she had a job to do. Boosting was something she had done for years. And was good at it. This was a whole other ballgame. Completely different, but she was up for the challenge.

After finally arriving in Franklin County. The crew slowly approached the bank. Desmond and Nitro slumped down in their seats as the crew rode by the front of the bank. Putting their masks on as Wheels parked. After they parked. Wheels looked at Erotic and she proceeded to look out her sideview mirror. Straightened her wig out and got out of the car and walked a few feet to the bank. Wheels watched from his rearview mirror. Desmond and Nitro still slumped down in their seats, waiting for Erotic's text message. After about ten minutes, the text came through. Desmond and Nitro quickly got out of the car and headed to the bank. Guns in hand and walking fast towards the bank. Entering the bank Desmond and Nitro quickly went to work.

"Everybody get the fuck down!!! Down I said!! Hurry up"!!! Nitro shouted. As he and Desmond stormed the bank.

Desmond then tossed the gun to Erotic. She quickly hopped over the teller counter and demanded the teller to fill a bag with money. Nitro continued holding down the front of the bank, as Desmond led the other teller to the back. Towards the vault. Just then. The armed guard towards the front that dropped his weapon upon order from Nitro as he entered the bank. Attempted to recover his gun again. Only for Nitro to see him and quickly go over towards him, gun in hand. Pointing the gun towards the guard's head.

"You raise up off this ground one more time, and I'm going to blow your brains all over this floor. You hear me? Don't be stupid" Nitro said. Kicking the guard's gun away from him.

Another five minutes went past and Erotic hopped back over the counter with two bags full of money. And not long after that, Desmond came from the back.   Page 34

With a bag of money as he sprinted towards the front, realizing they were on a timer. And had to be out of the bank and in the getaway car. Not a minute after twenty minutes. Their heists had to be done in twenty minutes. No more no less.

"Let's go"!!! Desmond shouted as he ran out of the bank. Followed by Nitro and Erotic.

After they left. One of the armed guards ran to retrieve his weapon across the bank. And then sprinted out the door after the crew. He got outside just as the crew were pulling off. He fired two shots and radio for backup and gave the description of the getaway car. One shot had hit the passenger sideview mirror. And scared the shit out of Erotic as they sped away. Wheels was headed to the Interstate. Where Chill was waiting in the other car. The crew quickly got out of getaway car and into the car with Chill. Back down 283 East headed to Lanc City.

"We did that shit!!! Muthafuckin guard almost shot us. Once they find that car and see that bullet hole in that mirror. They're going to know that's us" Nitro said.

"I just hope we got more than we did the first time. That was the goal. And even if they do find the car. No prints in there, we all wore gloves. We're good. Just get us back to the city Chill" Wheels replied.

"I tried to get as much cash as I could out that fucking vault. You clean up E"? Desmond said to Erotic.

"Hell yeah. As much as I could fit in this bag" Erotic replied.

"Chill out. We get back to the city and head straight to the warehouse" Chill said as he continued to drive.

For the second straight time. The crew successfully executed a bank heist. And were on their way back to the Sixth Ward warehouse. The rest of the crew were waiting to count the money. The authorities in Franklin County were onto the car that left the bank. After firing two shots at the car, the armed guard was able to get the plates. But little did he know, the crew had ditched that car. And got in another car. And was damn near all the way back in Lanc City. It was early in the investigation. And the Franklin County authorities only had the description of the getaway car. But other than that, they had no leads. The people in the bank saw a woman with bright red hair come in the bank. Followed by two masked gunmen.

This was all on surveillance camera from the cameras in the bank. And even though it was on tape. The two gunmen had masks on, so their identities were hidden. And you couldn't make out the female's face clearly. Authorities in Franklin County didn't know if this heist was connected to the heist that happened in Dauphin County. Or if it was a separate heist. With Dauphin County authorities having little to no leads. It would be difficult to tie both heists together. But local authorities in both counties continued to work diligently on solving both cases.

To the authorities their thought was they were dealing with a three person robbery team. But in reality they had no idea what they were up against. Over an hour and a half later and the crew was back at the warehouse. As soon as the team got back from the heist. They walked in the warehouse and dumped all the money on the table like always. Total silence. Until they all looked at each other and laughed. Celebrating yet another successful heist. And they were all anxious to see how much they made on this heist.

"Ok. Good shit. Looks like the team did well. As our rule states. The team that did the heist can go. The team that was waiting here, let's get started counting this money. I mean what the fuck else would we want to be doing then counting money right"? Kwame said smiling.

"Nigga I could name a whole bunch of shit I'd rather be doing. Like being up in some ass right now. But I will say. This would be on my list, because I'm about that paper. I'm about to be out. Holla at me when you know how much we came up on" Nitro replied.

"Do you my nigga. Appreciate your work team. Let's get to counting this money" Kwame said. Sitting down at the table with the money.

Desmond left with Chill, and they definitely weren't ready to go home. Even though they were in a tense situation being in a bank heist. They weren't tired. So they both went Down Bottom for some drinks. As they walked in, they seen some people they knew. Shook some hands and greeted a few people. Before they sat at the bar. They were sitting near the back of the bar. As they sat there having drinks. They noticed Stacks and Bags sitting at the bar across from them.

"I see this nigga Stacks is in here. Bags too. You remember them niggas right? They came to Travis party in Hill Rise" Desmond said. Sipping on his drink.

"Yeah I remember them. Who the fuck are they anyway? I mean I heard of them from a few people. But I don't know shit about them dudes. So to me they not making no noise, so they aren't a threat to us" Chill replied.

"Not at all. But I don't trust them niggas at all. Bags and I have a little history together. We used to hustle together in the streets. Had a falling out because the nigga thought I cheated him out of some money. But I didn't. I don't have to. We haven't been on good terms since. It's crazy that both them niggas fuck with the two chicks in the crew. Neither of them niggas like or get along with Travis either. He's ready to bomb on them niggas right now. But I have to remind him, that we have bigger and better things going on. Focus on our thing. And leave this street shit alone" Desmond said.

"You sound like Kwame nigga" Chill replied laughing.

"Whatever nigga. But he's right. Why waste our time on that petty shit. When we can be getting this real money. I'm not trying to be doing this shit forever. But do it enough to be financially straight. And I've been thinking about going to art school. Maybe pursue a career in Graphic Design" Desmond said.   Page 36

"Sounds like a plan. And a good one too. That's the first time I heard you talk about going to school youngin. It's inspiring. I heard you could draw your ass off. Follow your dreams bro. You know I wish you the best. We're all in this to make some money and invest to make more. Take care of our families. Put this money away, because that short money won't last long. Get what we can while we can. And be smart with it. Except your boy Travis. We already seen how that nigga loves to spend money" Chill said. Laughing a little.

In Franklin County. The authorities were still doing their investigation into the recent bank heist. They finally found the getaway car that the crew had ditched. On the side of the road off the Interstate. The bullet holes from the armed guard's gun that had been fired at the crew were still visible. It was all the local authorities had. Along with the surveillance camera footage from the bank. Which wasn't much to go on. It didn't even cross the minds of the authorities in Franklin County. That maybe, just maybe. Both heists could be connected. The crew were always two steps ahead of the law.

The money was finally counted at the warehouse. The crew came away with $550,000 in cash. Later that night. Stacks had called Erotic and asked to pick her up so they could talk. She agreed to do so. And she was a little nervous about talking to him after the last time she had seen him. He was in front of her Rockland Street home being stopped by Police. She decided to bring her 9mm with her. She usually kept the gun in the home for protection with her and her grandmother living there. Erotic stepped outside and waited for Stacks to come through. After about five minutes, his truck pulled up and Erotic got in.

"What's good? So what are we doing here? You going to keep being distant with me or what"? Stacks asked as he drove.

"I've been busy Stacks, not distant. You know I'm not the type female to just sit on my ass and watch my man get money. I grind too" Erotic replied.

"Yeah. I hear you. You always say that shit. Anyway. I know you seen me outside of your crib the other day. Fucking cops pulled me over on some bullshit as usual. Talking about some parking tickets when they ran my shit. I was just passing through the neighborhood. And no. I didn't have shit on me either" Stacks said.

"Good. That was going to be my next question" Erotic replied.

"Come on now. You know damn well I stay on point out here in these streets either way baby" Stacks said. Smiling while he continued to drive.

"That's what you say. And until otherwise I have to take your word for it" Erotic replied shrugging her shoulders.

"I do have some shit I need to talk to you about though. It's been irking me, so I'm going to tell you now. I don't really dig you being around Travis and them niggas he runs with. I don't rock with dude at all, don't even like the nigga. Just rubs me the wrong way. I wanted to see you, and then I see you at this nut ass nigga's party. Shit just seems like it's changing between us. Especially since you've been around them dudes" Stacks said.

"I understand we haven't been spending that much time together lately. But I promise when I do get the time. I'm yours. And as far as my people. My people are my people Stacks. You know I went to school with Desmond and Travis. We've always been cool. Before you even came to Lanc City" Erotic replied.

"Can't believe you on that bullshit. Your choice" Stacks said. Clearly not happy about what Erotic just said about the crew.

Rage was doing a lot of thinking. He sat down and talked to his wife about the possibility of moving out of the city. Beaver Street was home for so long to him his wife and three children. He was still in the process of doing renovations to their current home. With thoughts of selling it eventually. And moving to the county. Rage had stashed the money he made from the first heist. And planned to do the same with the money from this one. He was saving for the family's dream home. He was making money from his full-time job. His little side hustle on the block. And his work with the crew. He had plenty of money coming in.

Over in Hill Rise. Travis was sitting on his front step drinking a bottle of Hennessy. He had a few females with him. But they were about to leave. He met up with them at a Downtown bar. And after being persuaded by Travis. The ladies decided to come back to the projects with him. Travis was a young fly flashy nigga. And a shooter. A handsome dude who the ladies loved. With a violent compulsive temper. Travis became fearless and heartless on the streets. After many years being the weak that the strong preyed on. Now HE was the hunter. But he didn't prey on the weak. Just those that crossed him and forced his hand. After throwing that party in his projects. He became a project legend. Still very young. And Travis relished in the moment doing it that big in his projects.

The ladies all gave Travis a kiss and left. He was sitting there watching TV. After coming back inside his apartment. Travis was enjoying the money he was getting from his work with the crew. And couldn't wait to get his hands on the next lump sum of cash that the crew would be getting from this current heist. But he was also eager to get back in the thick of things. On the frontlines in the action. The shit that Travis loved. He felt a little slighted that Kwame took him off the heist team at the last minute. Even though he knew he would have to sit out sometime.

Wheels hadn't been over to visit Mr. Cee in a little while. So he stepped out of his Lime Street home. And walked up the block to Mr. Cee's store.

"Hey Mr. Cee. What's going on? Haven't been by in a while, thought I'd stop by" Wheels said. Entering the store. Page 38

"Dondrake. Hey buddy. I'm doing good. Glad to see you. What's new with you son"? Mr. Cee replied.

"Everything is cool Mr. Cee. Just maintaining you know. Wanted to make my usual visit. How's business been around here"? Wheels asked.

"Business is the same as always. The usual neighborhood kids daily after school. The adults around the neighborhood that come and get various things from cigarettes to household products. The families from around the neighborhood who shop here. And every once in a while I see a new face. Lately I've been seriously thinking *about retiring and giving it up. And selling the store. I've been doing this for a long time" Mr. Cee replied.*

"Wow. Really? Just promise me before you sell it, that you give me first dibs on buying it from you. There's so much history with this store in this neighborhood. In the city period. This store was everything to us as kids growing up. Just like The Boys & Girls Club was to us. Many of nights coming from there. I would stop here before I went home. I wouldn't want someone who wasn't from the neighborhood to get the store" Wheels said.

"And where would you get the money from to buy this store son? You know I'm never one to pry on someone's business. But I'm just curious. And since you seem to be genuinely interested, I will let you know when I plan to sell it. Would be nice for you to take over, if you could. Since you know the neighborhood so well" Mr. Cee replied.

"I've been saving for a while now Mr. Cee. Plus me working and getting the money I'm getting now. I have a nice amount of money put away. I have to get going. I'll take these two bottles of water. And I'll be through again in a few days like I always do Mr. Cee" Wheels said.

"Ok. And you be safe out there Dondrake. Take care" Mr. Cee replied.

Wheels was a little shocked that Mr. Cee was thinking about selling the store. And he also knew Mr. Cee had been around a very long time. Serving the community like he did was one of the main reasons Wheels respected him so much. And admired the man he was and continued to be. Wheels just wanted the store to be left in good hands. Because it was and continues to be. A very important part of the community. And what better person to have the store than Wheels himself. He was born and raised on the block. And continued living there till this day. Eventually becoming a store owner was something Wheels had to think about now.

Angel's cousin Tisha was walking down East End Avenue from her Garden Court apartment, to Chester Street. To visit Angel. She finally made her way to Angel's house and they went to her room.

"Damn girl. Look at all these clothes and shoes. I know you're going to let me wear some of these clothes girl. You can't possibly wear all these clothes" Tisha said. Admiring the clothes in Angel's closet'

"Of course cousin, I got you. You can borrow whatever you want. As long as I'm not wearing it AND you return it. Did you even wear the clothes we bought when we were shopping before"? Angel replied asking.

"I wore the one outfit. Went Down Bottom for Thirsty Thursdays. And girl my ass looked so nice in that outfit. Niggas jaws dropped when I came in" Tisha said as they both started laughing.

"Cousin you're so crazy. I'm glad it looked good on you" Angel replied.

"Angel. Did Bags buy you all this shit? That nigga took you shopping"? Tisha asked.

"No. Bags didn't buy any of this. I made my own money and bought my own shit. Like I normally do. He's bought me gifts before. But cousin you know I'm an independent woman. Who makes her own money. I'm not like a lot of these bitches out here looking for a come up" Angel replied.

"Oh no doubt cousin. I know you're independent. We're family and it runs in the family. It was just a question. Because I know how a lot of these niggas get down" Tisha said.

"Let's go to HOP. I'm starving" Angel replied. As her and Tisha went to the Downtown spot to get something to eat.

It was Friday night. And like most Friday nights. Downtown was lit. Especially first Fridays of every month. People from the county as well as the city converge Downtown to party. All the bars and restaurants are open late. It was a unique way to breathe life back into the Downtown area. That for many years felt the loss of a lot of businesses and excitement. But over the last ten years has risen again. And in a major way. From the First Fridays, the thriving Art District in the city's Downtown. The opening of new bars and restaurants Downtown. The resurgence of classic city businesses that remained relevant. It was a good time to live in Lanc City.

While Angel and Tisha were out, they ran into Nitro. Who was sitting at the bar when they walked in.

"What's good Angel? Tisha? How are you two beautiful ladies doing"?

"We're good. Just came down to get something to eat. And enjoy the festivities which is First Fridays. I see you're enjoying it too" Angel replied. As her and Tisha were standing next to Nitro at the bar.

"Shit. You know me. I be where ever the wind takes me. You feel me? I might go Down Bottom a little later. We should link up and meet down there" Nitro said.

"We don't have any plans after this. We might do that, if my cousin Tisha wants to swing through there. If we do. I'll hit you. I still have your number. Be safe Nitro" Angel replied. As her and her cousin Tisha went to the restaurant side of the spot.

After eating at HOP. Angel and Tisha walked Downtown amongst the many people who were Downtown for First Fridays. A lot of county people loved to come in the city to party for First Fridays. Prince Street, King Street, Lime Street, Orange Street, and Queen

Street were jam packed with people. The main Downtown blocks. After walking around Downtown a little. The ladies made it back to Angel's car and drove home. It was a nice night that the cousins hung out and enjoyed themselves. They then called it a night.

The next day. The crew was to meet at the warehouse to get their cuts from the last heist. And Kwame had some news for the crew. He would be involved in the next heist. In the action instead of being one of the masterminds behind it this time. He felt somewhat useless after just being apart of the planning. It was almost like Kwame had something to prove. Not only to prove to his crew members, but also himself. That he still could do what he had to do. Given the opportunity. And Kwame had an idea to put himself and Travis on the frontlines together. He wanted to test the youngin. See how he could handle himself side by side with Kwame.

The next target would be a Berks County bank. Kwame, Wheels, and Chill staked it out a few days before the next heist. They had a good plan in place. And were eager for the next heist to make even more money. For now. They all reaped the rewards from yet another successful heist. The crew decided to let little time in between their next target. The crew was making money but was far from comfortable in their minds.

Travis took his money and turned his apartment into a palace of sorts. A big screen TV, brand new furniture. A beautiful twenty gallon aquarium. And any other thing he wanted. Travis was in the company of women most of the time. Beautiful women of all races would come to hang out with him in Hill Rise. He was a loose cannon that had the charm to pull any woman. That mix of a personality was a turn-on to some women. He knew how to treat women. And at the age of twenty two. He had already committed murder and got away with it. And made a lot of money. He felt almost invincible, and in total control of his life. Even though he was living reckless. Travis felt so good. That he wanted to take a trip to Atlantic City.

Wheels, Nitro, Travis, and Desmond decided to make the two hour drive to Atlantic City for some fun and gambling. Nitro drove one of his trucks. As the four men rode down, they were banging that 90's Hip Hop and R&B. And chopping it up as usual. They finally got to AC and went straight to the Casino. As they were gambling. Travis went over to Wheels and they had a conversation.

"What you think about Kwame being on the frontlines in the action"? Travis asked Wheels.

"You really asking me this shit now? While I'm gambling my nigga? It won't be the first time Kwame has been on the frontlines. I know it's been a minute since he's been in some action, as far as gun play. But once a street nigga, always a street nigga. Well. For cats like me and Kwame that is. Trust me. You don't have shit to worry about youngin" Wheels replied.

"You know him better than I do. And since I have the respect I have for you. I'll take your word for it" Travis said.

The fellas got back to gambling and enjoying themselves. Desmond betting big and Wheels playing Blackjack. Like most people they won some and they lost some. Travis gambled a little. But mostly walked around the Casino watching others play. Nitro was on the slot machines. Finally cashing out after winning over $500 cash money. Wheels won the biggest take of them all. Winning two grand on the Blackjack table. After winning. Wheels promised to take the four of them out to eat. After a night in the Casino, the four men enjoyed a nice dinner courtesy of Wheels.

"You all thought shit was going to be like this? You know reaping the benefits of this heist shit, and enjoying ourselves like we are? Shit being this easy? I didn't. I can't even front" Nitro said.

"I mean I knew it was possible for shit to be this easy. And yeah. I can say I was a little skeptical about it at first. When Kwame walked in HOP that day. Looking like he was hunting me down. At that point. I thought maybe this nigga may be onto something. Now enjoying this and getting away from Lanc City for a little. We need that break. Makes it all worth it" Desmond replied.

"It does feel good to get away. And the nigga that we would least expect to give us advice on relaxation. Travis loose cannon ass. Good idea youngin, you know I love you like a little brother. We all need to go on some more getaways, you only live once" Wheels said.

"Dawg I got vacations planned already this year for myself. I'm going a few places. Vegas, Jamaica, etc. Sitting on the beach somewhere surrounded by beautiful women. And a drink in my hand. That's my vision" Nitro replied.

Travis just sat there after eating dinner looking around the restaurant. He wasn't used to much. And this was his first time in Atlantic City. He always wanted to come to AC. Saw images of AC on TV. And now he was finally here in awe. Travis was usually a quiet cat at times. Real observant. Nitro, Wheels, and Desmond all knew this. They also knew when he was quiet he was usually plotting something. Nobody questioned him about it or said anything to him about it. They let him be in his own World. If and when he wanted them to know, he would tell them. After a late night meal. The four men went back to their luxury hotel suites. Accompanied by women, each of them called it a night.

They had each met some beautiful women who went back to their luxury suites with them. These women knew they had money. And *was there only for a good time. The one night the four men stayed in AC. They barely got any sleep. And were up damn near all night. In Travis room. After a few rounds of some wild sex with the beautiful female he had in his room. Travis walked out on the balcony. High above Atlantic City as he looked out over the beach and city skyline. Just zoning out and enjoying the moment. As he looked out from the balcony. He thought about how far he had come in his life. How he was such an outcast amongst his peers. And now having money and a lot of respect on the streets. His life had changed drastically.*

Travis didn't have to be in the streets like he once was. Well in the short time he was. The bank heist crew money was plenty of money for him to live comfortably. He had a great time in AC. After being the one who had the idea of going. And invited some of his crew members. He was ready to get back home to Lanc City. And back to the thick of the action of being apart of a bank heist crew. That next morning the four men were headed back to Lanc City. And back to their daily lives. Although the night they all had before. Was more of the life they envisioned for themselves in the future.

Desmond returned home to his Green Street home. When he walked in the door and saw his drawings. He knew he was home and back in his element. His dream was to have his art displayed in one of the Downtown Art Galleries. He was unsure if the city's vast Art District community would be able to understand and appreciate his Urban Art. Desmond was really considering entering his art into a contest locally. The Lancaster art scene was thriving and growing more and more each day. Desmond wanted to be apart of the city's vibrant art scene. He would be sitting out this next heist. As Kwame and Travis would take center stage on the next one. He would now have more time to dedicate to his work.

Desmond had bet over three grand down in A.C. And lost most of it. Won back about $800. Before coming back home to Lanc City. He had a great time down there with the fellas. He was thinking about getting a new car also. Because the car he currently had was always giving him trouble. In reality. Desmond could move off the block and into a better neighborhood if he wanted. But he was too much into staying on Green Street. He felt more comfortable on Green Street. Where he was loved, and somewhat of a star in his own right.

Things were going great for the crew. And everyone was eating. So there was no jealousy at all amongst the crew. But on the outside. One crew member had a problem. Stacks and Bags didn't care too much for Travis. And weren't necessarily too fond of Desmond either. But Travis and Desmond weren't the type to shy away from confrontation. Neither Stacks and Bags or Travis and Desmond were going to back down from each other. And of course there was the conflict of interest being that. Angel and Erotic were good friends of Travis and Desmond. But were dating Stacks and Bags. All young people that were living different lifestyles. And were on a collision course to crash at any moment.

Chapter Three "The Turning Point"

The next morning. Rage was awakened by a knock at the door. He got up wondering who was at the door this time of morning. He naturally grabbed his Glock 40 handgun from under the bed. And went downstairs to open the door. It was a dude he knew from down the block. After answering the door the man told Rage there was a man down the street harassing his workers. He came to get Rage because the man had gotten out of control. And since Rage ran shit, he was the man to go get in a situation like this. Rage quickly ran upstairs to put his shoes on and proceeded to walk down the block.

Rage got halfway down the block and encountered a man that was towering over people. And was very angry and yelling. He noticed Rage walking up to him. The man shoved another man a side that was trying to get in between them. And shouted at Rage.

"What the fuck are you going to do bitch"?!! The man said.

Without saying a word. Rage gave his gun to his boy. And took his shirt off, as both men squared up in the middle of the street. The man immediately rushed Rage driving him back. But Rage had his hands free and began throwing uppercuts. Connecting on a few. Driving the man back a little off of Rage. Rage then hit the man with consecutive right and left hooks. Connecting on both. Which initially made the man even angrier. And he rushed Rage again. This time Rage stepped to the side. As the man's momentum made him fall on the ground. This would be his demise. As Rage quickly ran over and stood over top of the man delivering blow after blow. Until the man was knocked unconscious. By the time Rage stopped punching the man, his knuckles were bloody. Some of it his blood, but mostly the man's blood.

Rage got back up after several people attempted to pull him off the man. And got his gun back from his boy. And walked back down Beaver Street to his house like nothing had happened. The man was still lying in the middle of Beaver Street. Completely out of it and bleeding heavily from his face. The very reason Rage got that nickname was because of his fight game and how good he was with his hands. And he earned every bit of that nickname from his past. Over the last several years he was a dedicated family man. Being married to his wife and raising his kid's. Working a full-time job and having his side hustle on the block. And his role with the crew. For the most part. Rage kept to himself and his family, and definitely wasn't a troublemaker. But when he needed to bring the street side out of him. He would, without any hesitation. He protected those who were close to him.

The guy that came and got him was like a little brother to him. And he had known the man for years. They were close. And Rage felt like he had to defend his boy. Who wasn't a very big guy at all. Especially against a man that was the size of the dude Rage had knocked out. Rage was a big stocky guy. He could definitely handle a man that size. And he did just that.

At the end of the day, it didn't matter what your size was. It was all about your skills. And Rage came from an era where that's how it was. Even at an older age, Rage still had his skills. And was glad to display them, rather than being in a gun fight on the block. And possibly killing someone. He was happy when he was able to square up with the man in the middle of the street. They fought and lived to fight another day. Although I doubt that the man wanted any more parts of Rage. The bottom line was they fought like men, and no one died from gunfire.

There were people on the block that seen the whole thing. They heard the commotion outside and came on their porches to watch Rage. Do what he's done many of times on the block. The people on Beaver Street was used to seeing Rage handle cats. After Rage was back down the street and already in his house. The man had gotten up from being knocked out. Some people helped him sit up, as he was still clearly dazed. After about another ten minutes the man rose to his feet. Someone handed him a towel to wipe his face, which was bloody. Rage had a feeling that it wouldn't be the last time he'd see that man. he was sure they would run into each other again. After getting home. Rage walked in the house, as his wife just looked at him and shook her head.

He didn't even try to explain anything to her. Because he wasn't going to explain having his people's back. It was just how he was. That's why he was respected and got so much love on the block. It was also why his wife was hoping they eventually would move off the block. Regardless it was over now. And they were onto bigger and better things. It was dismissed as a minor bump in the road and they moved on.

Kwame was sitting on his porch on Ann Street just chilling like he normally did. Sipping on a drink. Watching the people and cars down the block. When he seen a beautiful black BMW come down the block slow. And parked a little down from Kwame's house. Kwame just looked, eager to know who it was inside the car. To his surprise. It was Wheels. Kwame knew that Wheels could get just about any car he wanted to get. He had connections in Philly, Newark, New Jersey. And New York City. After getting out of the car. Wheels calmly walked up to Kwame's porch and greeted him.

"Do you see me? I said do you see me nigga"?!! Wheels said smiling.

"Indeed. I do. Shit is nice bro. Real nice. I see you spending that doe. You trade your other whip"? Kwame replied asking.

"Hell no. I kept that shit. I love my Maximum. And I still got my old-school too" Wheels said.

"You just burning blocks huh? You get the car for the next heist yet"? Kwame asked.

"Yeah. I got to ride that bitch. See how she rides. About to burn out on Route 30. Push that bitch. And test out them cylinders. Had to roll through Ann and see if my nigga was out. And you were. And yeah that car thing is handled for the next heist. We good" Wheels replied.

"I know niggas are tired of me just sitting back planning shit, and not in the action. Before you ask. That's why I feel like I want and need to be on the frontlines. Everybody has been in the action but me" Kwame said.

"Dawg you don't have to prove shit to no one bro. I'm just doing my driving shit, that's my role. I told you that from day one. Let the youngins get out there and do what they do. That was the plan. And I know we have to switch up. The respect for you is always there. You're one of the OG's. And these young niggas that's running with us. Respect OG's. Because we expect it. And we give that respect right back to them" Wheels replied.

"Nigga you trying to talk me out of it? I'm in bro....I'm in" Kwame said.

"I'm not trying to talk you out of nothing. I'm just making sure you're good with this. And you have nothing to prove. But anyway. You want to hit a few blocks? Burn on something"? Wheels replied asking.

"Cool. Let's dip" Kwame said. As he got up and got in the BMW. And left with Wheels.

As they were riding through Lanc City streets, they had another conversation.

"Travis seemed a little worried when he found out you were going to be on the frontlines with him. I told him. He didn't have shit to worry about" Wheels said. As he drove.

"The fuck is he worried about me for? I can always handle my own. Young nigga better ask around. I knew his young ass was a loose cannon. Unpredictable and grimy as hell. I respect him as a man. But he better learn to respect the rank" Kwame replied.

"I know fam. That's what I told the nigga. They act like we weren't in these streets before their young asses. We're a team, and we'll get it done as a team like we've been doing. And get this money. The main thing is us continuing to co-exist as one unit. And we can keep getting this money as long as we want to" Wheels said.

"And that's why I'm going to let that bullshit go. Because like you, I see the bigger picture. Besides. His young ass should be glad he's getting some real money. Fuck all that nonsense anyway. About this next heist. Berks County it is. We need to get together with Chill to finish the plan of action. Sometime this week" Kwame replied.

"Sounds good to me. I was talking to Mr. Cee and he was telling me he was thinking about retiring and selling the store. Which is crazy. The store has been around since we were young boys. And I hate to see anybody get that store that doesn't know the history and what that store has meant to the community. I told him. If he plans to sell it, I might buy it" Wheels said.

"That would be dope bro. Own a store in your own hood. That's that movie shit. A proud black business changing owners but remaining a black owned business. That's what it's all about. And that's what we used to talk about and heard older cats preach. Ownership in our own communities" Kwame replied. Page 46

"No doubt. That's why I'm seriously thinking about doing it. Of course being the good honest man Mr. Cee is. He wanted to know how I would get the money to buy the store. I told him I was saving, and I am saving. One thing I don't want him to find out is what we do. He would never sell me the store. And I don't plan on using any of this heist money to buy it. I have too much respect for Mr. Cee to be dishonest to him. If I'm going to do it, I'm going to do it right. The man is like a father figure to me. He watched me grow up on the block. And knows my parents" Wheels said.

"I can dig it man. He always looked out for a lot of kids in the city. I remember plenty of times coming from The Boys Club. And stopping by the store to stock up on candy and snacks. Good people in the city that's made that kind of impact on the community. Are hard to come by the longer time goes on. You have to appreciate them while they're here. Nowadays there's no respect, no code, and no morals" Kwame replied.

"Word. And that's why it means so much to me to get the store and keep the legacy going in my neighborhood. For Lime Street. For the city" Wheels said.

"Now you know what to do. Continue to stack up and buy the store" Kwame replied.

"You know it"!! Wheels said agreeing with Kwame.

They drove a little more through city streets finishing the L that Wheels had rolled before dropping Kwame back off on Ann Street. It was a good conversation between the two like always. They both understood each other's journey in life. Both having been locked up before. And knowing each other from back in the day. That's why they got along so well. And it was important that they did, because they were key pieces in the puzzle.

A few days later. Wheels, Chill, and Kwame made one more trip to the Berks County bank. Sitting in the car. They all had a conversation.

"I've really been thinking about us hitting one of them armored trucks. That shit is risky, but we're going to get to that eventually. For now. We need to hit this bank we're looking at for huge cash. Clean this muthafucka out. You heard me? Should be our largest take, and it's a shorter distance than the other ones" Kwame said.

"We only hope to. The main thing is getting out of that bitch without killing anybody. You know them young niggas are itching to pop off. I hope none of those guards get brave. You know the one did. And shot at the car. I'm just saying we don't need that kind of heat. We have to avoid that shit at all costs. I'm not going back to jail" Chill said.

"Always fellas. Always. We got this. Make this money. And get out of this game with doe stacked" Wheels replied.

"We need to meet up at the warehouse in a few days. Let the rest of the crew in on new business as well as what else is ahead. Time to head back to Lanc City" Kwame said. As he drove off heading back home.   Page 47

Authorities in Dauphin County were starting to think maybe the heist in Dauphin County may be connected to the bank heist in Franklin county. They weren't positively sure, but the thought was starting to run through their minds. The State assigned a Detective to the case. Detective Herman Boyd was a veteran on the force of over twenty years. And had worked all over the State of Pennsylvania. His main focus right now was seeing if both heists were connected. And if they were. He could then piece together the evidence and leads in each case. One thing was for sure. In both heists they were two women who led the bank heists teams into the banks. A Blonde hair African American woman in the first heist. And a bright Red hair African American woman in the second heist. At the moment the authorities had no clue if the two women were the same women or two different women.

Detective Boyd had to figure out a lot of things in order to even begin to solve the case. And he took it as a personal challenge to solve the case. Detective Boyd was clearly at square one as far as the case was concerned. Because the only description he had of the two bank heists. Were the descriptions of the two women. The bank heist crew was two steps ahead of law enforcement. And had plans of moving even further ahead. Detective Boyd was in a race against time before the bank heist crew would strike again.

In the beginning, it was all Detective Boyd. And he relished in the moment at being the man that was running the investigation. He started in Dauphin County questioning employees of the bank there that got robbed. At first it looked like a longshot at solving this case with little evidence. But Detective Boyd vowed that he would get the case solved. All the case needed was a new lead to break the case wide open.

Nitro was riding through his hood on Pershing Avenue. And stopped for a little and chopped it up with the youngins. He would do that from time to time. To let them know that he was visible and men just like them. The youngins he had working for him felt connected to him because of it. This particular day he decided to pick them up in his truck. And took them out to eat. Three of his workers who worked on Locust Street and Howard Avenue went with him to get something to eat. The youngins that worked for him used to see Nitro on the block when they were kids. Hustling and grinding. Spring, Summer, Fall, and the Winter. Out on them blocks. And they wanted to be apart of it. He appreciated them and saw the same drive in them that he had in himself at their ages. So he put them on. He really wanted them to make enough money that they could eventually get themselves off the streets. And take the money they made and save it or invest it. It was something he talked to them about a lot.

Nitro definitely didn't want them in the streets for too long. Because he knew what that life would eventually lead to. And he didn't want that for them. Even though they worked for him. He wanted the same for them as he wanted for himself. After they went out to a Chinese restaurant and ate. He dropped them back on Pershing Avenue. And before they got out of his truck. He reminded them of what he said about their long-term goals to get off the block.

Page 48

Nitro enjoyed the time with his workers. And after dropping them off back on Pershing Avenue. He headed home. The next day the crew was to meet at the warehouse. And for the first time, everyone beat Kwame there. He came late. And you know some of the crew let him know about it.

"I see the chief master planner is late today. We have to mark this date down fellas. Mr. Always On Time was late on this date" Travis said. As a few of the crew started to laugh.

"Whatever nigga. I had to drop my kid's off to their grandmother. Glad everyone is here, and I'm sorry I was late. As we discussed. The next target is this Berks County bank. Like always. Me, Wheels, and Chill staked the bank out and now know their routine. The heist date will be in three days. And yes. I'm still on the frontlines with Travis. As much as we love how Wheels gets us out of the situations. Once we're out of them banks. He's going to sit this one out. Rage and Nitro will be behind the wheel this go round. Remember we have to keep switching shit up, so no one is onto us. Keep that in mind. Shit. They're still investigating that Dauphin County heist" Kwame replied. As everyone laughed.

"I saw that shit too. I couldn't help but laugh when I seen it on the news the other day. I'm thinking. These muthafuckas are two steps behind us" Desmond said. As a lot of the crew kept laughing.

"And that's how we want it to be. The plan isn't to be in this shit for long. We all agree on that" Kwame replied.

"At least this trip is closer. Those long rides have a nigga anxious. I couldn't wait to get to that Franklin County jawn. I was ready" Nitro said.

"Damn Rage. What the fuck happened to your hand fam"? Kwame asked.

"Some bullshit happened on the block. I had to handle somebody, that was trying to rough up one of my people's. Light work. I let my people's pick his big ass up. After I knocked his ass out and sent him on his way. I did take the heat down there with me. Because I didn't know what I was running into. But the nigga actually wanted to fight. So I'm like. Cool this is right up my alley. Handed the 40 to my little homie, and gave the boy work. Big muthafucka too. And he fell hard" Rage replied. As everybody fell out laughing.

That was the crew. A bunch of wild crazy cats. Who were getting more brazen by the day. But they were smart enough to keep it to a minimum. And not draw too much attention to themselves. They loved the fact that law enforcement had no idea who they were.

"And oh yeah. Angel you're back up baby. You know one of these times we're going to have you and Erotic on the same heist. Shit would be dope right you two"? Kwame said.

"Kwame you always coming up with some shit. But it would be dope though, I can't front. If it makes dollars it makes sense" Chill replied.   Page 49

"Word" Wheels said. Sitting back in the chair.

After that the crew that was on the next heist. Listened intently to the specific instructions. It would be the first heist without Wheels driving one of the getaway cars. Sitting out his first heist, and his boy Kwame on the frontlines for the first time. This heist would not *only be a test of the crew's strength and depth. But just interesting because it was closer to Lanc City. This time around. Angel would be wearing a Gray wig. She had prepped it since she knew she would be up next. As she was in her Chester Street home, there was a knock at the door. It was Bags.*

"What's good? I thought maybe I would finally catch you at home" Bags said. Giving Angel a hug and kiss as he came in.

Angel was a little surprised seeing Bags. Being that he came to her house unannounced without calling. Something he never did. Because he knew how much Angel didn't like it.

"You got some balls coming here unannounced. I mean we rock together and all. But you know I don't even like my family coming here unannounced" Angel replied.

"Whatever. I had to do this shit to see you. I wanted to see your fine ass. My homie's cousin seen you and your cousin Tisha shopping out at the mall. I know you work part-time. But what else are you doing to have money like that? You told me you were saving for school" Bags said.

"Why all these questions? I was doing me. Like I do sometimes. You know that I like to shop, I don't know why this surprises you" Angel replied.

"What you out here hustling? You cool with Erotic and you both cool with that bitch ass nigga Travis. I know you're not working for that nigga. Please tell me you're not" Bags said. Sounding curious and concerned at the same time.

"Are you serious right now? Why would I be working for him? I don't work for nobody but my part-time job and myself. And why all this jealousy towards Travis? We're just cool. Nothing more than that" Angel replied.

After all the back and forth between Angel and Bags. They ended up sitting down together on the couch and watching a movie. Angel knew that there was tension between her two homie's Travis and Desmond. And Stacks and Bags. The two pair didn't like each other at all. And the tension was building. One thing Angel didn't want to do, was get herself involved or between the men. She was seeing Bags and their situation was going well for the most part. Angel was more concerned about her future and her plans to go to school. The stigma of the city kept her home, plus the fact her and her crew were making a lot of money together. So for the moment. It was hard to think about going to school now. So Angel continued to do her.

She needed to get focused. And in less than forty eight hours. She was once again going to be apart of another heist. Her second time around, after being involved in the first heist in Dauphin County. Page 50

The Day Of The Heist Act Three

Chill woke up early and looked out of his second floor Franklin Terrace window. Out onto the street. The projects were quiet. Many of mornings Chill would look out that window each day. Almost looking out over the projects before he stepped out the house each day. Chill would sit this one out. And would be at the warehouse waiting for the rest of the crew to get back. To count the money. He was hoping this heist would go as well as the first two. Chill played a huge part in planning out the all the crew's heists. And staking out the locations. He had all the confidence in the World in all his crew members. Because he knew they were all hungry and determined.

Chill finally got up and went downstairs to eat breakfast. That's when he turned on the TV and saw Detective Boyd. Who was the lead Detective on the bank heist case. He was thinking to himself.

"Oh shit"!! Detective Boyd was the same Detective that investigated his cousin's murder in Harrisburg. And someone Chill really didn't care too much for. He just looked at the TV in shock. And shaking his head in disgust.

Nitro had come out of his house and got in the car that Wheels had got for the heist. He would be bringing the crew back home. He had an important role in the heist. He had to be on point. Rage would get the crew to and from the bank. He picked Kwame up on Ann then hit Chester to get Angel. And lastly. Over to Hill Rise to scoop up Travis. Then they headed up 222 North to Berks County. With Nitro following right behind. As usual the ride up was quiet. Everyone was focused on the job at hand. For the first time in a while. Kwame would be in the thick of things. Something he was used to from being in the streets when he was hustling. When Kwame built the crew of individuals that made LANCREW. He had a vision of older G's like himself, Wheels, and Chill. Playing the background while letting younger cats like Travis and Desmond get into the thick of the action because they loved it and invited it. There was a reason that Kwame had switched shit up and decided he wanted to be on the frontlines.

He had something to prove to not only himself. But also his fellow crew members. He wanted to let them know that he was willing to get in the thick of the action if he had to. And he was more than able to handle his own. Although he had the respect of his crew members. Kwame wanted to be on the frontlines for himself. And he was more focused than ever.

He would be alongside the wildcard of the crew. The young wild and brash Travis. Someone he has had a somewhat rocky relationship with. Travis hardly listened to anyone. But Kwame knew when it came down to it. He could trust Travis in the heat of battle. And he really had no reason in hell to trust Travis. Being that Travis *was unpredictable. There was too much money to be made for Travis to try and play Kwame.*

Travis was disciplined when it came to crew business. He might've had his own mind when it came to his personal life. But times like this, he stayed within the crew and was a team player. They were getting closer to the bank. Angel put her wig on, along with her shades. Rage pulled down the street from the bank. Wheeling the car there and parking. His hand still healing from him knocking that guy out on Beaver Street. A week prior. Once they parked. Angel looked out her sideview passenger mirror before getting out of the car. And walking towards the bank. She made her way inside the bank, as Rage watched from his rearview mirror.

Kwame and Travis in the backseat with masks on, sitting low with guns in hand. Waiting for the message to storm the bank. At that moment. A cop car came riding by. Rage was a little shook seeing the cop car coming down the street unexpected. But he kept his composure and didn't look suspicious. As the cop car passed him and continued riding down the street. The crew was hoping to get in and out of the bank without any issues. After about ten minutes. The message was sent and Kwame and Travis stormed the bank. As soon as they entered the bank, they were in complete control. Angel was already hitting the teller drawers in the front along with Kwame. Travis took the manager to the back towards the bank vault.

All of a sudden. One of the armed guards who was ordered to get on the floor. Attempted to reach for his gun. Kwame saw him just as the guard fired a shot at him. Kwame dove behind one of the teller counters. He then returned fire. Letting off three shots as the guard tried to run behind something but got hit in the back. As he fell to the ground.

"You all see what the fuck just happened?!! Don't be stupid like him. Stay the fuck down on the ground with your faces. Face down. Anybody else get up like he did, you're getting shot too"!! Kwame shouted.

Travis came from the back with a bag full of money. Angel a little after came from behind the teller counter with another bag. As they all then sprinted out of the bank and ran to the car. As soon as they all got in the car. Rage sped off. Heading towards the Interstate where Nitro would be waiting in the other car.

"I shot one of them guards. Shit!! Muthafucka pulled his gun on me and fired a shot at me. Damn near hit me too. We don't need the heat that comes with shooting an armed guard in a fucking bank"!!! Kwame said. Sounding concerned.

"Yeah. I heard that shit from the back and seen you standing there. Said to myself. Ok. Kwame out that bitch holding shit down in the front. He got that. So I went back to the money. Man fuck that guard. He had it coming to him, he should've stayed the fuck down. And I thought I was going to be the first nigga out of the crew. To pop someone. Well that's what you all thought" Travis said laughing a little.

Page 52

The crew ditched the getaway car off Route 222 South heading back to Lanc City. Nitro of course was waiting for the crew after they left the bank. After ditching the car on the Interstate. All four crew members. Angel, Kwame, Travis, and Rage. Hopped in the car with Nitro and they sped off. Heading back home to Lanc City.

They finally got back to Lanc City. Getting off at the New Holland Avenue exit and headed straight to the Sixth Ward warehouse. Where Wheels, Chill, Desmond, and Erotic were waiting to count the money.

"It looks like the team racked up. How did it go"? Wheels asked. As the rest of the crew came in the warehouse with bags full of money.

"Kwame shot an armed guard and he's bugging out because of it" Travis said laughing a little.

"Look youngin. I'm about tired of you running your muthafuckin mouth"!! Kwame said. As he was walking towards Travis. But a few crew members got between them.

"Man. You cats are bugging. You niggas can sit here and argue. I did my part. The money needs to be counted. And whenever it is. Let me know about my cut. I'm out. I got shit to do tonight. I'll holla at yall later. Be safe crew. One" Nitro said as he walked out.

"Just chill fellas. We got this money to count. It's business. We're all here with a purpose. To get this money. And what happened Kwame"? Wheels replied asking.

"I was out front holding shit down. When this guard reaches for his shit and fires a shot at me. I ducked behind this desk and almost dropped my gun in process. Then I gathered myself and returned fire. Fired three shots and hit his ass once. I believe in the back. But this is what I didn't want. Now these muthafuckin cops are going to be on our ass"!! Kwame said. Sounding worried and angry at the same time.

"You did what you had to do at the end of the day. It was either him or you. He's the one who initiated the gun fight. You had to know at some point. One of these guards was going to try and play the hero. The important thing is everybody got out of there. I say we lay low for a little while. While this shit dies down about this guard

getting shot. Let's hope he doesn't die. We all got plenty of money. We can afford to chill for a minute" Wheels replied.

"I agree. Wheels got a point Kwame. Let's chill and enjoy this money dawg" Chill added on.

"It sounds like a plan. You all know what to do. I'm going to the crib. Need to be with my family" Kwame said. As he walked out.

"Well let's get started ladies and gents. We got paper to count" Chill said. Clapping his hands and smiling.

Angel also left. And on the way home, as she drove back to Chester Street. She had a lot of things running through her mind. Did she really want to continue dealing with Bags? Being that she didn't want to be in anything serious. She didn't know when she was going to decide to go away to college. Angel was torn about what she wanted to do. Seeing Kwame almost getting shot that day, was also on her mind. Before she could even return fire to protect Kwame. He had already returned fire hitting the guard in the back. On a positive note. She was thinking of taking advantage of the time off the crew planned to take. And going on a vacation. Angel wanted to take her cousin Tisha with her on vacation.

Her and Tisha always wanted to go to Miami. They used to talk about it since they were little girls. The timing was perfect. Angel got them plane tickets to Miami. She felt it would be a great way to clear her mind and have some fun. A week later. Tisha and Angel flew out of Philadelphia International Airport to Miami, Florida. The city they both dreamed of vacationing to when they were growing up.

"Can't believe we're finally here cousin. Thanks so much for the trip. Girl let's hit South Beach" Tisha said. Sounding excited.

Angel had just as much fun on the trip, watching her cousin's excitement throughout the trip. The two women had the time of their lives in Miami. Hitting South Beach. Going shopping in all the finest stores. Sitting on the beach and enjoying the water. As their hotel suite was just off South Beach. Eating at some of the finest restaurants in the city. And by night, they enjoyed the nightlife of Miami. Hitting some of Miami's hottest clubs.

Meanwhile back in Lanc City. Erotic was in her room counting some of her money. She didn't want her grandmother to know about the money she had. Because she knew there would be plenty of questions. She stashed her money under her mattress. And she wasn't selfish with her money either. She did do a lot of things to the house her and her grandmother were living in. she bought new furniture. And she made several repairs to the home that needed to be repaired. She would meet Stacks later for dinner that night. Erotic was glad that the crew was planning to lay low for a little while. She definitely didn't need any heat on her. She didn't want her grandmother to worry.

Detective Boyd by now had heard about the current bank heist in Berks County. He had made his way up there to check out the scene. A guard was shot in the back. So not only was this a bank heist, but someone had been shot also. The guard was in serious condition. The word was he could be paralyzed for the rest of his life. After getting home after the heist. Kwame couldn't do anything but watch the news, hoping the guard wouldn't die. The last thing he wanted anyone in the crew to do was shoot someone. He knew it would only bring heat on them from law enforcement. But he also knew. In this line of business, it was always a chance it could happen. In each heist they were in, it could happen. Kwame just never thought it would be him to pull the trigger at this point in his life. But like Wheels said. It was either him or the guard. And Kwame had   to   make   a   quick   decision.

The next day Kwame found himself at the Mercedes Benz dealership. He was always fond of the cars. And he had stashed enough money that he could splurge on himself on something nice. Of course it would be a later model Benz, but a Benz nonetheless. After talking to the salesmen for a few minutes. Kwame brought in a duffle bag full of cash money. And put it on the counter. Much to the man's surprise. And about ten minutes later. Kwame was driving a Benz off the lot. A Black Benz at that. With as dark a tint allowed by the state of Pennsylvania. After getting in his Benz for the first time. Kwame just sat in it, admiring the ride. Then it was off to the city. He had to burn some blocks before he went back home to the block on Ann.

First all through the Eighth Ward. Manor, Filbert, High Street, St. Joseph, Lafayette, Vine Street, Strawberry. And so on. Hollering at people he knew as he rode by. As much as he didn't want to draw too much attention towards himself. He was living in the moment as he rode in his Benz. After going through the Eighth Ward. Kwame drove through the trendy Downtown section of the city. Before driving through parts of the Sixth Ward and heading home to Ann Street.

Later that day. Kwame made his way down Lime Street driving his Benz. He was hoping to see Wheels out on the block. And just like clockwork, Wheels was sitting on his front step. Some young kids that were on the block, were wiping down one of Wheels cars. Wheels handed them twenty dollars a piece and they were happy. The kids then ran back up the block to play two hand touch football.

"Hey man. Get your ass up and wash your own car nigga"!! Kwame shouted out his black Benz.

As Kwame was sitting in the middle of South Lime Street. Wheels got up to see who it was, looking down into the car from a distance.

"Man. Go ahead with that bullshit. This you"? Wheels asked looking surprised.

"Of course it's me my nigga. I wouldn't be driving anyone else's shit. I just got it about an hour ago. What you up to? Fam get in so we can chop it up" Kwame replied. Pulling over a little further up the street.

"Shit is nice bro, real nice. And you got black too. Smart choice. But you have to keep them black cars clean. This is a mix between sporty and luxury. Like my BMW. That's the way to go. I just think the shit makes a statement when you're driving it. And riding through. It speaks of class. How long you think we should lay low"? Wheels asked.

"I'm thinking maybe a month or so. Make them think the shit is over. We're far from done. But we're going to damn sure make them think we are. I told you before. I've been thinking about us hitting one of them armored trucks. There's a shitload of money in there fam" Kwame replied.

"Yeah. But that shit is risky as hell. And it will bring even more heat to our front door. Think about it. We need to really think about our moves going forward K. You know I'm all about that bag. And I dig your ideas. But we have to keep shit in perspective" Wheels said.

"I hear you. But I'm not giving up on that idea though bro. I believe we could really do it. But for now, we'll continue to lay low" Kwame replied.

The two sat in Kwame's Benz and talked a little more until Kwame went home.

Meanwhile over in Hill Rise. Travis was standing outside of his door just enjoying fresh air. And natural noise of the projects. It was starting to get warmer outside, after yet another brutal Northeast

Winter. The kids from in and around the projects were outside playing. Cars were driving by the Howard Avenue side where Travis resided. Banging music from their systems. Travis just stood outside his door smoking a cigarette. When he saw a truck roll down Howard Avenue. In the truck was Stacks. Him and Travis both glared at each other as he drove past. Travis being who he was, just laughed a little and continued smoking his cigarette. Five minutes later, Travis put the cigarette out and went back inside his apartment.

After Stacks rode by Howard Avenue. He made a left onto South Duke Street and preceded to go by one of Bag's cribs. Over in The Clairemont Homes on the Chesapeake Street side. Once Stacks got to Bag's house. He was amped.

"It took everything I had not to hop out my truck and handle this nigga Travis dawg. I'm telling you, it's only a matter of time" Stacks said pacing back and forth.

"Don't worry about that shit. Fuck him. I got a plan. Let's get right and worry about them clowns later" Bags replied.

Angel and her cousin Tisha were back from Miami. And back in Lanc City after landing at Philly International Airport. They both had a great time. And not one time did Tisha ask Angel where she got the money from to pay for the trip. They were just glad to get away for a few days in sunny Miami. The women loved and enjoyed the entire trip. One of the best times they've had together in their lives. Definitely a trip to remember. But now it was back to their city and back to reality. Chester Street and Garden Court Apartments.

Angel spent well over three stacks in Miami. And that was including the whole trip. To her it was well deserved and well worth it. She didn't splurge that much on herself. She had been stashing money for school.

Nitro and Chill decided to go Down Bottom for some drinks and to hang out for a little. Listening to the many talented DJ's in the Lanc City area. The bartenders knew them both and knew what they liked. They both sat in their usual seats towards the back of the bar. They were taking shots and having a good time. Sipping on some mixed drinks. About fifteen minutes later. Stacks and Bags walked in the bar. Nitro knew of them. But didn't know either of them personally.

"Chill you know them two cats right there? That's Stacks and Bags isn't it"? Nitro asked. Taking a sip of his drink.

"Yeah. That's them niggas. They were at Travis party in Hill Rise. They got some kind of issue with Travis and Desmond" Chill replied.
Page 56

"I know Travis could be an asshole at times. The young nigga is reckless. But what I seen that night at his party. Right at his front door in Hill Rise. Was them niggas Stacks and Bags fucking with him. Talking shit. I watched Travis walk away. And you know like I know. That nigga doesn't walk away from nobody fam. The kid is a shooter. But you never know what Travis did to them dudes. Regardless. His young ass is with us now. And we can't let him get caught up in this local beef shit" Chill said.

"Yeah I did hear that they had some beef with Travis. That young boy shit. We got bigger fish to fry. And if I need to remind Travis of the bigger picture I will. You can believe that shit. He's not fucking our shit up for some petty local shit. Enough about that. You here anything more about the investigation in Dauphin County"? Nitro replied asking.

"No more than before. They don't have shit on us fam. Nothing" Chill said.

The next day Desmond got up in the morning. Got some of his artwork and put it in his backpack. He was heading Downtown to talk to some of the Art Gallery owners. He was looking to get some of his drawings displayed. Desmond was confident, that once they seen his work. They would love it. So as he walked up Prince Street, one of the main blocks Downtown. And also home to the city's Art Galleries. He walked into the first Art Gallery and a man approached him as soon as he walked in.

"Hello. Can I help you sir"? the man asked.

"Yeah. You can. I'm Desmond by the way. I have some art I would like you to look at. And you can tell me what you think honestly" Desmond said. Taking the drawings out of his backpack.

After Desmond took the drawings out of his backpack. The man looked at them amazed.

"Desmond these are really good. Amazing talent you have. And you did all these yourself"? The man asked. Happy

"Yep. All me. I've been drawing since I was ten years old. I want to get my work seen and appreciated" Desmond replied.

"Understandable. And you should want to get your work seen, as talented as you are. Have you been to any other of the Art Galleries here Downtown yet"? The man asked.

"No. I haven't been to any other galleries. This is the first place I came to" Desmond replied.

"Ok. I wont even have you go to any other galleries. I will speak to the owner about your artwork. And hopefully we can display some of your work. They are very unique drawings. The way you display street life in your work is unique. You don't see that much anymore. What street is this"? The man asked.

"Green Street. The block I grew up on here in the city" Desmond replied.

The man just nodded and replied. "Oh ok".

Desmond was halfway towards accomplishing his goal. And walked out of a Downtown Art Gallery. Happy to know that one day one of the Galleries may be displaying his artwork. A kid from Green Street in Lanc City would have his work displayed within a bustling art scene in the city. The thought was to get Desmond's artwork more exposure to people not only in the city. But the county and surrounding areas. Along with tourist who would frequent Downtown after touring the city and county. Pretty much a broader audience.

Desmond felt great that day. And it let him know that he had another avenue for success besides doing what he was doing. IF everything went the way he hoped. That was yet to be seen, so for the time being. Desmond would continue to get money the way he was currently. Desmond was still sitting on a lot of money from the bank heists the crew had done. Each crew member had well over a quarter of a million dollars each. That's why it was the right decision to lay low for a while after their last heist. And an armed guard getting shot, made matters worse. It was stressed for the entire crew to be smart with their money. Each individual was grown and could ultimately do what they wanted. But it was only smart for them to make their money work for them. They all knew they couldn't do this forever.

Detective Boyd was now in Berks County investigating the latest heist. After leaving the scene. He made his way to a local hospital to visit and interview the armed guard who was at the bank the day of the heist. After talking to some law enforcement that were guarding the man's room. Detective Boyd was allowed to enter the room. After entering, he started his interview.

"Sir. Tell me what you seen the day of the bank heist from start to finish"? Detective Boyd asked.

"Well there was a female that came in first. She went to the bank teller, and I think she gave her a note. I was watching her, because she didn't look familiar. And something just didn't seem right. Then about ten minutes later, that's when two masked gunmen stormed the bank. Before I could react, because I was watching her. They told everyone to get on the floor face down. So I did. One of the gunmen along with the girl stayed up front with us. The other one had a manager take them to the bank vault. I don't know what I was thinking grabbing my gun and firing. I guess I thought I could do something to help the situation. Ended up getting shot in my back. I'm hoping I can walk again. But I felt like I had to do something, or they were going to kill us" The man replied.

"Sir you did what you thought was right. You were doing your job defending the bank. No need to be so hard on yourself. We're hoping and praying that you come out of this fine. And I believe you will. I'm sure the people that were in that bank appreciate your efforts. You did a great job, it's unfortunate that this happened to you in the line of duty. Is there anything else that you can remember about their appearances"? Detective Boyd asked.

"Well the female that came in the bank had gray hair. That's the one thing I remembered that stood out" The man replied.

"She was about what age? Younger woman? Older woman"? Detective Boyd asked.

"I really couldn't tell. I don't believe she was old" The guard replied.

"Anything else you noticed"? Detective Boyd asked.

"No. That's pretty much all I remember besides the masked gunmen" The guard replied.

After being in serious condition when he arrived at the hospital. The guard was doing better and recovering. After surviving a gunshot wound in his lower back. He could talk well enough to tell his story. But he wasn't out of the woods yet. So to speak. Because it was still a chance he could be paralyzed.

Detective Boyd had to wait for almost a week before the guard was out of surgery and recovering. Before he could actually interview him. It was clear that the man had come a long way in a week. He was still shook up from the heist. From the information that the guard gave Detective Boyd. He began thinking the crew that did the bank heists in Dauphin and Franklin Counties. May have done the Berks County bank heist also. He knew he had to focus in on who those individuals were. Getting their identities was key, and Detective Boyd was trying his best to do just that. Just the information he got from witnesses and the security guard. He knew he was looking for a bank heist crew. And in this latest heist in Berks County. The crew netted over five hundred grand.

As soon as Detective Boyd left the hospital, he hit the ground running. Trying to track down who these people were who were apart of this bank heist crew. Back in Lanc City. Travis had just purchased a brand new forty five caliber handgun. And he couldn't wait to use it. That very day he decided to go to the range. And Angel. Who stayed at the range herself, decided to join him. As they fired at their targets side by side, it was obvious that they both had a love for guns. Especially Travis. Who owned three guns, but loved his new forty five. After taking a break from target practice. The two chopped it up.

"What's good Travis? You been laying low? Haven't seen you in a while" Angel asked.

"The best way to be right? Especially with what we do. I just mind my own business. But we both know some people who aren't necessarily doing the same. I know you have a thing going on with

Bags. And his girlfriend Stacks got this thing going on with Erotic. This city is small and word travels quicker than you think. I really didn't know them niggas like that. Desmond knows them better than I do. I know they're not from here. For some reason they think they know me. I just wanted to let you know in case you wanted to know where I stood with it. Because I'm sure you know they don't like me" Travis replied.

"I'm aware of that. I just stay out of it. You all are grown men. And you all can handle your situation. That's where I stand with it" Angel said.

"Cool" Travis replied.

Travis had done his best to stay out of the local scene. But knowing Travis like he knew himself. There was no way he could stay low for long. He loved the spotlight and attention too much. Travis really had no reason to be on the streets. He had a lot of money and still was living in the projects. But his growing issues with Stacks and Bags could possibly force his hand into doing what he's done before. He was obviously a known shooter. And had no problem shooting again. Either way Travis was ready for whatever. He never thought about living and dying, he was too occupied with enjoying life. Good times and getting money. He never cared how he got it. After hitting the Berks County bank for over a half a million dollars. The crew would split yet another take.

One day Travis took the short walk from the Howard Avenue side of Hill Rise to Green Street to hang out with Desmond. And as always Desmond had all the drinks you would want at his house. Where he had a make shift bar that he always had fully stocked. From Hennessy, Ciroc, to Patron. They sat in Desmond's living room and drank.

"I went Downtown the other day. Took my artwork down there and one of the employees liked it. He told me that he would show the owner and get back with me. They might give me a spot down there to display my artwork. Maybe have my shit out there on First Fridays, where the city and county people can see my shit. He was bugged out when I told him the background of the drawing was Green Street. He couldn't deny the talent once it was in front of him. No matter where I was from. He knew my talent belonged with the rest of that artwork down at the Art Gallery. And it felt good for someone I didn't know to like and appreciate my work. You feel me? Anyway. Enough about me. What's good with you soldier"? Desmond said.

"Just chilling fam. Trying to stay out the way. And congrats on that possible opportunity you have. I know your work belongs down there too. You got that art shit on lock, crazy talented with that bro. I was at the range with Angel the other day. We were talking and I told her that we're cool and always will be cool. But what happens in the streets is in the streets" Travis replied.

"As it should be. Bro them niggas don't want nothing man. They're just trying to bait you into some bullshit. They might both be crazy to think that they can strong arm you. Which is funny as shit when you think about it" Desmond said. As him and Travis started laughing.

"Does a nigga look like he's worried"? Travis replied. As they continued laughing.

It was one of those moments where you knew at that moment. Both Desmond and Travis knew how to handle the situation. And they had no concerns at all about it. They then went outside and sat on Desmond's porch and drank. Talked shit and had a good time like they always do. You could call it a celebration of sorts. Being that a local Art Gallery was interested in Desmond's artwork. That night they celebrated till like four in the morning.

The next morning. Kwame was downstairs in his Ann Street home watching TV. There was news about the crew. The newscaster was explaining to the TV audience that the heists all had one thing in common. They all had women involved. They also had surveillance camera footage from each of the heists showing Angel and Erotic. It made Kwame think about if he needed the ladies to fallback for a minute. Now that the focus was on them. And he needed to holla at one of the crew members. That crew member was Nitro. Who was gifted at computers, and hacking them. Along with getting past alarms. Kwame had in mind what he had been thinking about recently. Having Nitro get into the security systems of the banks, including the surveillance cameras.

From that point on. Kwame switched up Angel and Erotic's roles moving forward. They would both fallback and have the roles of counting money in the warehouse. It was what was best for them at this point. Even though the authorities didn't have their identities, they knew that women were involved in all the heists. Kwame called Nitro and told him to meet him Down Bottom to discuss some things over some drinks. Fifteen minutes later, they were sitting at the bar chopping it up.

"I was watching the news earlier. They know they were chicks involved in each of the heists. So from now on. Angel and Erotic will be counting money. We have to switch shit up. We have to let this shit die down before we strike again. Niggas got plenty of money, we just have to be smart with it. In the meantime I'm going to watch this investigation closely. May give me an idea about how we move going forward. Maybe even out of state" Kwame said.

"Whatever works and keeps us paid. We had to know at some point these muthafuckas would be on our ass. Right? About two more heists and I'm good anyway" Nitro replied.

"I met you down here to discuss your technology skills. Maybe work on the security systems before we enter. Like the surveillance cameras and shit. Disable all that shit once we enter the bank. I know you know your shit, that's why I knew I had to holla at you" Kwame said.

"Say no more. I'll see what I can do. Shit definitely won't be easy bro. If I can't do shit with the security systems, we'll stay with the plan of letting the ladies fallback" Nitro replied. As the two men continued sitting at the bar drinking.

Kwame's boy Chino owned the warehouse in the Sixth Ward. Where the crew counted the money. And had most of their meetings and planning at. Kwame and Chino grew up together and kept in touch with each other throughout the years. After founding out Chino had a nice size warehouse in the Sixth Ward. Kwame wasted no time in discussing the use of the warehouse for the crew. Chino was well compensated for renting out the warehouse. And even though it was his warehouse. He stayed out of crew business. And he never asked any questions. He was just happy to be getting paid well. He knew Kwame for years and trusted him. Trusted that he wouldn't put Chino in a bad situation. Everybody was eating and the crew was still on its hiatus from the action. Everyone was enjoying the money they made, and shit was all good.

Both Kwame and Wheels had keys to the warehouse. In case either of them would be late to a meeting, and the other one had to be there. As the investigation continued statewide. The crew continued to lay low. Three counties had been hit. Dauphin, Franklin, and Berks county. They were all hit for over a million dollars. They had got away with all of them to date. And the only description they had of any of them. Was the fact it was a female that went in the bank first in each heist. Beyond that. The local authorities didn't have a clue.

A few days later. Stacks and Bags were sitting outside the warehouse in the Sixth Ward. Just watching from their car. They had followed a few crew members there a while back. And had been watching the place ever since. You ask why they were there? To rob the next person that went inside the warehouse solo. Ten minutes went by. And here comes Chino by the warehouse. Doing his usual check to make sure shit was cool. Chino was a Hispanic man with a muscular build. Bald head and tatted up with a reputation for putting in work. And most times he kept a gun on him, today would be no different. But as Chino opened the door of the warehouse. Stacks and Bags with ski masks on. Both rushed him before he could get his gun out. And took the gun from him. And both had their guns pointed at his head. They then ordered him inside the warehouse.

"Where's the money nigga?!! And don't say there isn't no money in this muthafucka. Because we know there is. We've been watching this muthafucka for days. Where's the money"?!!! Stacks said to Chino.

"I don't know where no fucking money is. I own this warehouse and just came to check on my shit. There's no money in here. I don't know who told you that shit"!! Chino replied.

"Muthafucka shut your ass up!!! You talk too much. Now you got ten seconds to tell us where the fucking money is. Or I blow your head off right here right now. That's all I want to hear from you nigga. You hear me?!!! Ten....nine....eight.....seven...." Bags said.

"Ok. Ok man!!! There's five grand in the drawer over there. And that's all that's in here. I swear on everything" Chino replied.

Stacks and Bags both looked at each other through their ski masks. And went over to the drawer and got the money. After getting the money. They both could be overheard trying to decide whether they were going to kill Chino or not. Chino just sat there in the chair fuming. He wasn't the type to get robbed. This was the first time he had ever been robbed. Stacks and Bags had caught him slipping. And it paid off to the tune of five grand. And just like that. Stacks and Bags had boldly hit the crew's warehouse. And didn't even know it.

Chino was left in the chair tied up. Stacks and Bags left. And Chino was getting enraged by the minute. Only thing on his mind was getting loose and getting revenge. After twisting and turning for over an hour. Chino was finally able to get loose. He immediately called Kwame. Kwame was Down Bottom having drinks with Chill. When Chino called. Kwame couldn't hear too good because of the music. He stepped out of the bar so he could hear better.

"Say what?!! They got what"? Kwame asked sounding concerned.

"Some niggas just robbed me I said!! Two dudes came behind me when I went by the warehouse. And was opening the door to check on shit. Muthafuckas were talking about where's the money and all this shit. How do these niggas know we had money in the warehouse anyway?!!! I told them there wasn't any money in here. Then they put both guns to my head and asked me one more time. What the fuck you think I was going to do? They got five grand from the warehouse. And I know part of this shit was my own fault for not being more on point. My bad, I fucked up. But we have to get those muthafuckas bro......we got to. I don't know who they are, but we've got to find them niggas man" Chino said. Still angry as hell about the whole situation.

"I'm wondering the same shit. Worst thing I could think of right now is a leak in the crew. We all knew the rules to this shit when we started this. Everybody understood what this was. Just let me get a chance to figure this shit out. I'll hit you back. That five grand aint shit, we'll make that back in no time" Kwame replied.

"If I see any trace of them cats, I'm handling the shit myself. That's my word"!!! Chino said.

"You're a grown man and can do as you please. But think about it Chino. Is it really worth it now with what we got going on? That warehouse is in your name. You catch a case, that shit is gone bro. That's nickel and dime shit, you know we're REALLY chasing that bag homie. The choice is yours. If I have to move the crew's operations somewhere else I will. Just let me know" Kwame replied.

"Some of that money was mines Kwame. And I need my fucking money" Chino said.

"Listen!! Fam let that shit go. I'll give you the five grand. I'll holla nigga. I'm in the bar" Kwame replied as he hung up his phone and went back in the bar.

The crew at the time had no idea that the two men that robbed them of five thousand dollars. Was someone a few members already knew. And were enemies of Travis and Desmond. Stacks and Bags were fearless street hustlers. They had no problem killing you if they felt they needed to. And they had a personal vendetta against Travis. And pretty much anyone he ran with. That now meant the crew. Even though at one time Desmond was cool with both of them, they had a falling out. And Desmond had since bonded with Travis since they were both apart of the crew. And both being the same age. It all made things interesting moving forward. And the beef was only going to get hotter after this latest incident of Chino getting robbed at the warehouse.

It was something the crew was trying to avoid. Local beef. It was not the time to go to war, when the crew was currently laying low. Stacks and Bags knew they were targeting some heavy hitters in the city. And they didn't care. All that mattered to them was they were five thousand dollars richer. Which was a come up in their eyes.

Wheels needed to ride down to Philly to handle some business. So he asked Travis to ride with him. He and Travis had a good relationship. Travis always looked at Wheels like a big brother. Getting out of Lanc City for a little would do Travis some good. He had so much heat surrounding him with the Stacks and Bags shit, amongst others in the city he had issues with. Riding on the Pennsylvania Turnpike. The two chopped it up.

"What you been up to youngin"? Wheels asked as he drove.

"Shit. Spending some of this money and having fun like I'm supposed to. Enjoying my life and staying sucka free. You feel me"? Travis replied.

"I heard that. Kwame called me earlier and told me someone robbed the warehouse of five grand. Some niggas had Chino at gunpoint. Which is crazy because Chino is the type of nigga that always stays strapped. I told Kwame somebody had to be watching the spot" Wheels said.

"I know if I see some funny shit around me or a nigga even looks suspect, it's over for him. Whoever did it, better hope I don't get to them first" Travis replied. As he pulled his brand new forty five caliber handgun out of his waistband.

"Youngin you're tripping. Put that shit away. Still can't believe they caught Chino slipping. The important thing is, the homie didn't get shot. Lanc City is small. So I'm sure whoever they were, if they haven't already left the city. And they're still in the city, we can track them down. The truth always comes out, we'll find out who robbed the warehouse" Wheels said. As he continued to drive.

"I know we're supposed to be taking a break and all. But I'm ready to get back into the action. This staying stagnant shit has got me antsy" Travis replied.

"I figured your wild ass would say some shit like that. Take a trip like we're doing now. Get away from the city for a change. I mean far away. May do your ass some good. You remember how much fun we had in A.C." Wheels said. As they were now entering the city of Philadelphia.

"Yeah. But I'm not trying to go nowhere man. I'm good. I just want to make some more money" Travis replied.

Wheels had to meet up with some cats in Southwest Philly over some business. Taking Travis along with him could've been a good thing or a bad thing. Either way he was along for the ride. Wheels trusted that when he was around him, Travis wouldn't do no shit to put them in danger. Travis was a loose cannon to most and very unpredictable. So he could do anything at any given time. You just never knew with Travis. This day he was reserved and was just keeping Wheels company. And had his back in case anything went left.

As Wheels met with the cats he had come to Philly to meet with. Travis stood back off to the side. Every once in a while. Travis would look over at Wheels and the other men to make sure everything was cool. Travis stayed looking around his surroundings. And he had his forty five caliber handgun on him. The meeting took about twenty five minutes. And Wheels and Travis was headed back to Lanc City. But before they left. They headed to East Passyunk Avenue and Pats Steaks for a World famous Philly Cheesesteak.

Later that day. Erotic was out to dinner with Stacks. And she noticed lately how Stacks had been spending money. Bought an expensive bottle of wine while they were eating dinner. Erotic didn't drink much, and was a little surprised Stacks was spending money like he was.

"Did you hit the lottery or something? Something you didn't tell me about"? Erotic asked. Sounding curious.

"No. Why? I'm just out here in these streets getting money. Me and the homie came up on something. And I felt I would show you a good time. Well I always do. But just wanted to do something nice for you" Stacks replied.

"It is nice. No complaints. I was just curious is all" Erotic said.

"Enjoy this. Where the money comes from don't matter. Money is money baby. That shit is all going to spend the same" Stacks replied.

Erotic quickly dropped it and continued eating. At the time. She had no knowledge of the warehouse being robbed. Only a few of the crew knew. Part of the crew that knew didn't want to make it more of an issue than it really was. It was only five thousand dollars. Which was nothing compared to the money the crew was making. Angel and Erotic were kept in the dark so to speak, when it came to the warehouse being robbed.

Detective Boyd continued his investigation. He went to each location that had been robbed by the bank heist crew. He was basically working with the state and local authorities. Trying to solve the bank heists. At the present time, he had little of nothing. Oddly enough. Detective Boyd was waiting for the crew to strike again. Hoping to get a leg up on them in the next investigation. But Detective Boyd also knew that the more the crew continued to strike. The more likely someone might be in danger of losing their lives. He as well as local authorities had gathered what little evidence they had. And was hoping to obtain more in their pursuit of solving the cases.

The crew was still in Lanc City trying their best to lay low and stay out of the bullshit. They knew that they had the attention of local and state officials. Even though local and state officials didn't actually know who they were pursuing at the moment. In the midst *of that, and the warehouse recently getting robbed. What did Kwame do? He decided to have a meeting with the crew at that same warehouse a few days later to discuss their plans moving forward. He felt it was important for the crew to return there. And as expected. Everyone came strapped to the meeting. And ready for whatever.* Page 65

After everyone got there. Kwame had something he had to announce to the crew. Something positive amidst all the other shit that was going on.

"I'm sure we all remember saying when we came up on some real money. We were going to give back to the community that raised us. Now is the time to do just that. I'm talking about a Splash Party in County Park. Like they used to do it back in the day. Food, drinks, music, games for the kids. A big cookout by the day. And an adult pool party by night. The fucking city will be there. And we'll be hosting it, doing our part in giving back. Shouldn't be no more than a few stacks a piece from each of you to fit the bill. Come out your pockets and give back ladies and gents" Kwame said.

"I'm sure nobody has a problem with giving back. We been doing it in our own hoods anyway. I'm having my annual cookout later this summer down Almanac" Chill replied.

"So it sounds like everybody is down. And as far as the music is concerned. We're going to have all the local Lanc City DJ's on the ones and twos. We're booking them all. I'll get some people to get fliers and pass them out all over the city announcing it. It's on" Kwame said. As he smiled.

Everyone in the crew agreed to give their part of the money to fund the Splash Party that the crew were planning to have. There hadn't been one in years. Not since some of the older members were youngins themselves. But they do remember. And they remember what it meant to the people of the city. The crew was excited about bringing the party back to the city. The Splash Party was planned in a month from the present day. And it was free to anyone in the city that wanted to attend. After the announcement for The Splash Party. Kwame, Wheels, and Chill were thinking. It was only a matter of time before they find out who robbed the warehouse. The streets talk, and they always had their ears to the streets.

Rage was at home chilling watching some TV with his kids, when he got a knock at his door. It was his boy from down the street. This time he had some news he thought Rage would like to hear. The guy told Rage he overheard a group of dudes talking about this guys Stacks and Bags who robbed this warehouse on the city's North side. Rage had told his boy to keep his ears open for any word on some cats robbing a warehouse. Rage didn't know Stacks and Bags personally. He remembered hearing their names in certain circles. But didn't know them. Now Rage could run that information back to the crew and they could handle it how they saw fit to. He wasted no time in calling Kwame. He told Kwame and Wheels to meet him Down Bottom. So they could discuss it.

"Cat on my block came to the crib and said he needed to holla at me about something. I'm thinking at first. Does this nigga need me to knock somebody else the fuck out or what? Anyway. It wasn't that. He said he overheard some niggas talking about some dudes name Stacks and Bags robbing a warehouse. That's why I called you down here. Because I knew they were talking about our warehouse in the Sixth Ward. You two know these dudes man"? Rage said.

Kwame and Wheels just looked at each other.   Page 66

"We know of them. They have an issue with Travis and Desmond. More so Travis than anybody. Funny thing is. I don't believe they know who they robbed. Either way, if they did rob the spot. Its now a crew problem. And I can't be sure if Chino finds out, that he won't be on their ass moving forward. I told Chino to let it go. He has too

much to lose. But at the end of the day. A man is going to do what he feels like he has to do" Kwame replied.

"The only niggas I know brave enough to rob any spot is stick-up kids. But if you say these cats got issues with Travis. Then this shit is more personal than anything. Anyway. I came to you two with that info because I knew the warehouse got robbed. And I had my people from my hood with their ears open in case they heard anything. So now you guys know" Rage said.

"No doubt fam. I appreciate the info. Tell your people I got a thousand dollars for them for the information. The conflict of interest here is. Those two niggas fuck with Angel and Erotic. It's a sticky situation and I don't want either of them all worried or emotional about the shit. So it's best we don't let them know about this. These niggas have to get dealt with" Kwame said.

"Oh indeed. They do need to get dealt with" Wheels agreed.

"For now. We get back to planning this Splash Party in the park. This is huge for us and this is huge for the city. This will be the first official time that we give back. This shit has to be epic. The type of party that people will talk about for years to come" Kwame said. Sounding excited.

"The big dreamer. My nigga Kwame. I can dig it bro. It does sound exciting and it will be nice to give back to the community" Rage replied.

"Well fellas. I have to get out of here, I have a date a little later. Met this bad ass chick earlier, and we're going to link up. You cats be safe. Hit me if anything pops off" Wheels said. Finishing his drink and leaving.

Kwame and Rage just continued sitting near the back of the bar, having more drinks.

"How much longer you trying to do this shit man"? Rage asked Kwame.

"Shit. As long as we can continue getting this money without getting caught. We're just chilling now until shit cools down. Then we strike again for even more doe. And we're switching up. Angel and Erotic are no longer leading us into the banks. They know females have led us in all our heists. So from now on, we'll let them count money. I know you're loving that money. You buy that new house yet dawg"? Kwame replied asking.

"I'm stacking and planning to. I never thought I would want to leave Beaver Street. But after having the money now and being able to afford it. It's opened my eyes and changed my mind. I've been on Beaver Street all my life. But I know I want better for my kids. And now that I have the chance, I have to seize the moment" Rage said.

"I mean why not move bro. That's why we're in this to make better lives for ourselves and our families. Especially for us older niggas who have families. Young niggas like Travis and Desmond have a lot longer than us out here on these streets. That's the difference between us and them. We stack and them young niggas spend. I feel everything you're saying dawg, trust me. You have an opportunity to get out of the hood and make a better life for your family. Do that shit nigga, and don't hesitate. You never know if you'll ever get that chance again" Kwame replied.

The two finished their drinks and Rage convinced Kwame to leave his Benz Down Bottom. And he would take him home. Kwame had been drinking all day almost. The next morning. Kwame would walk the short distance from Ann Street to Down Bottom on South Duke. To get his car that next day.

Chapter Four "The Streets Are Hot"

Fliers were placed all over the city announcing the Splash Party at County Park. And the buzz was growing stronger by the minute. All the local DJ's were recruited to DJ the party. And they were all excited to be apart of the crew bringing Splash Parties back to the city. It was indeed a no drama event. Any drama from anyone, that person or persons would be put out of the party ASAP. The party was about the community, and the people who were apart of it. During the day the party would be for men, women, and children. Around nine the party would shift to an adult pool party. Of course the weather would be hot, it being held in the Summer. The nice weather always brought everybody out in the city.

Erotic, Angel, and her cousin Tisha were sitting on Erotic's porch on Rockland Street. Hanging out and enjoying the weather.

"Girl I see that Gucci bag you got over there. You done splurged and didn't let your girl know. We could've went shopping together. Where did you get it? In Philly"? Angel asked admiring Erotic's purse.

"Stacks got it for me. He's been spending a lot of money lately. We went out to dinner. He bought me some shoes and this bag. It was a little strange because he doesn't usually spend like that. I mean he does nice things for me. But these last two gifts were a little expensive" Erotic replied.

"Bags took me to dinner the other day too. But he hasn't been necessarily spending crazy. Regardless girl, I wouldn't trip. You know how many women would love for a man to buy them shit like that? Enjoy that girl. I know I would" Angel said.

"Oh I am. Don't get it twisted, I'm not complaining. I appreciate everything he does for me. Trust me" Erotic replied.

"Shit. If you ask me. Both yall bitches are lucky to have niggas spending money on yall. Shit. They got any brothers or cousins? Well on second thought. Any Uncles? I'm older than yall young asses anyway. I don't need his ass to take care of me, I get my own. A bitch just needs some help sometimes. A few gifts, and some vacations" Tisha added on. As they all started laughing loud.

The women all continued sitting on Erotic's porch talking and laughing. Having a good time while enjoying the Summer weather. A little while later. The ladies walked a few feet away to Lucky's. To get some shrimp on a stick and some fries. Tisha got the cheeseburger combination. They then walked back down to Erotic's house and continued sitting out front and eating their food. Angel and Erotic had no clue that the money being spent on them. Was actually their crew's money. After Stacks and Bags had robbed Chino at the warehouse of five grand. The two had money to burn. But Angel and Erotic had no knowledge of what was going on around them.

The Splash Party at County Park was a week away. And the buzz around the city was at an all-time high. Everyone was talking about it. The party was going to be nothing short of amazing. The crew had invested a lot of money into the party. Providing top notch food and entertainment. By paying all local DJ's their fee to DJ the party from early afternoon until midnight. The park itself was massive and spanned a large amount of area. And clearly was the biggest park in the city. But the Splash Party itself would only be in the pool and surrounding areas. The entrance being on Chesapeake Street. The crew wanted to keep the Splash Party the same way they remembered it back in the day. That same feel.

Desmond and Nitro were at Reservoir Park playing some basketball. Something they both loved to do from time to time. When they had time. After playing for another half hour of one on one. They both took a break from the hot sun. And sat down on the side of the court. Both drinking big bottles of water. They chopped it up. Just the two of them.

"Any word on who robbed the spot"? Desmond asked Nitro.

"Not that I know of. Nobody called me and told me anything about that. Whoever it was, got some balls to rob the spot like that. I don't believe these niggas know who they're dealing with fam. I'm sure it won't be long before we find out. Lanc City isn't that big" Nitro replied.

"True indeed. I was thinking the same shit. Can't be too much of a mystery, the streets talk" Desmond said.

"Always. But this Splash Party is going to be bananas!! We're bringing the whole city out playboy. And the crew invested a lot of paper on this shit. It's going to be epic. I'm just proud I could help bring back Splash Parties to the city and County Park. I remember my older brothers used to talk about those parties. Now I'm going to be able to experience the shit for myself. And you youngin. You weren't even born when Splash Parties were at County Park. You're really going to get an experience dawg. Shit is going to be lit" Nitro replied.

"It does sound like it's going to be crazy. I'm ready to unwind and party. Holla at some bad ass broads. Because I know they're going to be there. In them skimpy ass two pieces....I can't wait. Definitely looking forward to that. And just being around the whole crew. It's been a while since we've all been together. Since we've been on this hiatus and all" Desmond said.

"I've been meaning to ask you something anyway. How's things going between you and them cats Stacks and Bags? I mean I don't know the niggas like that myself. But I seen them Down Bottom a few times and around the city. I heard that they do stick-ups here and there besides hustling. And I have a strange feeling that they may be behind the warehouse robbery. Now I'm not sure. Because nobody told me shit. But it's just a thought. Since they're in that line of business. Chino said the niggas that robbed him had on ski masks.

We don't have no concrete proof right now. If it's them, they most certainly have to get dealt with. I'm sure everybody feels that way. Including Kwame" Nitro replied.

"There was a time that I hustled with Stacks and Bags. We had a falling out about money. I got cool and close to Travis since running with the crew. And them niggas never got along with Travis. They never liked him. Me being cool with Travis made me their enemy also. Fuck it, I'll take that. It is what it is. We have to do what we have to do. And if that means them clowns have to go, then so be it. Robbing the warehouse is a violation. But I can't front, I've never known them to be stick-up kids. But who knows. Maybe they're on some different shit now" Desmond said.

"Like we both said. We know the streets talk, so we'll wait on it" Nitro replied.

The two men walked to Nitro's truck and were off to their houses after playing some basketball. Basketball was a sport that a lot of the crew members enjoyed. Something else they were planning to bring back. Was the basketball tournaments in the Eighth Ward at Brandon Park on the hill. Something that was also popular in the city in the 90's. The crew was planning on sponsoring their own team in the Summer Basketball League. They would also fund the league for kids across the city. But for now. All the focus was on the Splash Party in County Park. There was still some work to do before the party that next week.

One thing was for sure. The crew getting the money they had, made their lives and the people's lives around them a lot better. Rage was getting the necessary repairs done on his Beaver Street home. So he could eventually sell it and move his family to their dream home. Kwame had stashed some of his money. And bought himself a Benz. Wheels added to his already large car selection, by buying a BMW. The others had plans with their money also. On top of the fact the crew had outlined a plan to help the community for years to come. A five year plan. To not only bring back Splash Parties and Summer Basketball Leagues. But other community initiatives. All positive programs to uplift a community that needed it.

The whole crew felt emotionally connected to the city because they all were born and raised in the city. And they felt they needed to all give back to the community that raised them. And the Splash Party in County Park would be the biggest party the city has ever seen.

Chino was at Kwame's Ann Street home, in his kitchen. Talking about everything that was going on lately.

"Any word on who the fuck robbed me? And when are we as a collective going to hunt these niggas down? I'm tired of waiting Kwame" Chino said sounding frustrated.

"Chino you need to chill bro. We're going to find them. This city isn't that big fam. Just let the process play out. We'll find them, and you'll get your money back. Take this other shot" Kwame replied. Giving Chino another shot. As the two were drinking.

"Yeah. If you say so. Just make sure when you find them muthafuckas, I get a piece too. I want to look in those niggas eyes and let them know who the fuck they robbed. And to NEVER cross me again" Chino said. Still sounding angry.

"Plus we'll be back in action after the Splash Party. Make that money back in no time. You have too much to lose playboy. With the warehouse and all. You go to jail catching a case out here, and your warehouse is gone. Which means the crew has to relocate, and you won't get paid your rental fee. So think about that when you want to act on this right now" Kwame replied.

"I hear you Kwame. And I saw that Benz outside when I pulled up. Shit is nice bro, real nice. The crew is getting it. I have to give it to you niggas. You all know your shit and what your doing. Well oiled machine huh? I'm going to need to raise the rent. Since you don't want me to act. And shit is getting expensive" Chino said.

"I get it and understand. We'll give you an extra stack. Sound good enough for you"? Kwame asked.

"Hell yeah. That'll work" Chino said.

"It's just that simple Chino. You help us and we help you. That's why that little petty ass five grand don't mean shit. We're talking about making millions. Maybe you can take that extra money and get you some better security around the warehouse" Kwame replied.

"Maybe more cameras on the outside. But other than that, I've been holding shit down at the warehouse forever. They caught me slipping that day, but that shit won't happen again. I promise you that my nigga" Chino said.

"Whatever you feel like you want to do to prevent it from happening again, is up to you. Everybody will be strapped regardless from now on. We'll be back in business soon. Hold it down" Kwame said.

Chino just nodded his head in agreement. He knew realistically. Dealing with the crew was a win all the way around. They paid Chino well for using his warehouse. And Chino didn't have to do much of anything, it was easy money. There's no way that Chino was going to fuck his relationship up with the crew and risk easy money. Chino was just frustrated about being robbed and wanted revenge in the worst way. There was no way Kwame was going to tell Chino who a few crew members thought and were told robbed the warehouse. Because he knew what Chino would do. He would immediately turn the city upside down, looking for Stacks and Bags. Thus drawing unwanted attention to himself and possibly the crew. Kwame wasn't going to risk that.

It was a Friday night and Down Bottom was jam packed. Stacks and Bags were seated at their normal seats when they were there. By the DJ booth. That same night Nitro and Desmond were Down Bottom also. They arrived after Stacks and Bags. When Nitro and Desmond first came in the bar, they saw each other. Glanced at each other, and then Nitro and Desmond went towards the back of the bar.

"You seen your friends when we came in"? Nitro said. Laughing as they sat down at the bar.

"Fuck them niggas. I see them around a lot. They don't bother me. I haven't really even said shit to them dudes since Travis party in Hill Rise" Desmond replied.   Page 72

"The wildcard is Travis. You're with him more than any of us. And their issue seems to be more with him. I'm sure you feel if you're with him, you got his back. He's crew. We all feel that way about it. But I hope it doesn't come to that. we have to stay focused on these heists. And out of this local beef shit, we don't need it" Nitro said.

"I'm as focused as ever man. Hopefully getting my drawings Downtown in one of those Art Galleries. Besides the crew business. Like Travis. I'm ready to get back to bank heist business. And as far as their beef with Travis. Of course now that's crew business. They have a problem with him, they have a problem with us" Desmond replied.

"I can't wait for this Splash Party. I know some of Lanc City's finest will be in attendance. Beautiful bad ass women in bathing suits. I wouldn't miss it for the World. The crew is going to show up and show out. This party is going to be epic" Nitro said.

On the other side of the bar. Stacks and Bags were sitting at their table listening to the DJ and having some drinks. After about ten minutes and finishing their drinks, they decided to go outside. They stood over by Stacks truck.

"Desmond's punk ass in there. Got Nitro with him tonight. I guess he left his girlfriend Travis at home. We got the warehouse. And we're going to get Travis next. And if Desmond or any of them other niggas get in our way. We're getting them too. Run through that whole fucking crew if we got to. I'm sure they'll step up security at the warehouse. But we want Travis. Get him and he'll lead us to the rest of them" Stacks said. As he stood against his truck talking to Bags.

"Say no more. You know I'm down for whatever" Bags replied.

Meanwhile back in the bar. Nitro and Desmond were finishing their drinks. After that. They walked outside to go to their car. Because they were leaving. They both walked past Stacks and Bags. And exchanged stares but kept walking to their cars, as neither party said anything to each other. You could feel the tension. Although there was no drama that night.

The next week had come. And the Splash Party was in a few days. And it was still the talk of the city. The crew was expecting a huge turn-out. Lancaster County Park officials were bracing themselves for a large crowd of people at the party. Probably the largest crowd to ever be at the park at one time. A drama free event that was going to be a party for all by day, and an adult pool party by night. Large grills were moved near the pool area to make all the food for the event. Local caterers that would handle the side dishes for the event, as well as the beverages. There was excitement in the air all over the city. And you could feel it.

It was a few days later and the day of the Splash Party in County Park. Which was to start around one in the afternoon. That's when the families and younger kids would arrive at the party. Get in the pool, enjoy some games that were brought out to the event. Food and drinks. Along with other activities that brought the community together. From just before one and the start of the party. Cars were lined up bumper to bumper on Chesapeake Street at the entrance to the park. Page 73

Cars were parked all along the grass and parking lots leading up to the pool area. It was a nice and hot sunny day. The pool had been thoroughly cleaned and treated. The pool area looked great. The surrounding areas also. As they were activities and games for kids all around the pool area. The grills were going. And the music was banging through the large speakers placed throughout the party area. All local DJ's were scheduled to get on the wheels of steel all throughout the day into the night. The party would continue to keep going.

It was an honor and pleasure for each of the local DJ to rock out for the community. It was a very inspiring and positive day. Just like the crew had hoped it would be. It was an event that brought the whole city together. People of different races, religions, gender, ages, etc. It was definitely an event for everyone who wanted to come out and just celebrate being apart of this community. Great food from hot dogs, burgers, cheesesteaks, fish sandwiches, barbecue chicken, etc. And it was all free to the community. It seemed like the whole city was there. Even before any of the crew members had arrived. The park was jam packed. People were lined up to get their food not too far from the water tube. Set up for the kids in one area over where the food was. There were also older residents of the city that came out to support the event.

Not a whole lot of political people from the city. Although some was sure to have been in attendance along with the others. Local government were definitely aware of the event. An hour later some more of the crew started to show up. Angel and Erotic had both arrived at the party with their bathing suits on. With little dresses around their waists covering their lower bodies until they got in the pool. Erotic arrived with a few of her friends, and Angel arrived with her cousin Tisha. All beautiful women, as they all entered the pool area together. Travis and Desmond arrived together. As they were accompanied by a few of their homies from their neighborhoods. Green Street and Hill Rise.

Travis had to enter the party with a bang. Despite it being still daylight. Travis had two bottles of Belair Rose he entered the pool area with. Handed both bottles to one of his homie's and went immediately to the diving board. And just like Travis being the life of the party. He posed for the many people in the pool area. And then proceeded to jump in the pool from the highest diving board. The people went wild as Travis hit the water. Travis was full of life and loved to have fun. And he relished in the moment that day, being one of the hosts of the party. He was young, wild, and crazy with a lot of money.

Desmond was walking around the pool chatting with different people that was in the pool. As he was walking. He walked past Erotic and Angel sitting in the pool.

"Hey Desmond. What's good? Where's the rest of the crew"? Erotic asked.

"Just chilling and mingling. What's good E? Angel? They should be here soon. Kwame and Wheels said they were leaving to come down here. The last time I talked to them. I'll holla at you two later" Desmond said. As he continued walking around the pool.

Nitro had arrived with his people from Pershing Avenue. And a beautiful female friend he had on his arm. As expected. Each member of the crew came through the party with people. From their respective blocks. People that knew them more than anybody. Rage arrived with his wife and kids, and a few homies from Beaver Street.

"Girl everybody in the city is here. I haven't seen this many people all together in a long time. I don't even remember ever seeing it honestly. This is really nice. Whoever threw this party. It's well appreciated by me. As well as everyone else here. And it's a good thing. Bringing the city together on a positive note. We need more of this. I'm sure it cost a lot of money too. There's a lot of stuff out here. Fun stuff for the kids, very nice. Somebody got some money" Tisha said. As she sat in her tube in the pool. Next to Angel and Erotic.

"I'm just glad everybody is getting along and there's no drama. Today it's all about showing love. This is what it's all about, a good time" Angel replied. As she was dancing to the music blasting through the speakers. As she sat in the pool.

Not long after that. Kwame, Wheels, and Chill made their entrance to the party. The whole crew and the people from their neighborhoods found a spot up on the hill under a shade tree to chill. That was where most of the crew stayed throughout the day. Except Travis of course. He stayed being the life of the party. Mingling with everyone in the pool. Most of them with wifebeaters and shorts. Some with short sleeve collared shirts over top. With all the latest flyest sneakers you could think of. Where the crew stood was like the V.I.P. area of the party. Overlooking the pool area. It was a blazing hot Summer day. Tisha, Angel, and Erotic all got out of the pool and walked up the hill where the crew was at.

"This shit is lovely right? Nothing but love today. Love for the city and this community. I'm so glad we could do this. Truly amazing. I thank each and everyone of you for helping to contribute to this" Kwame said. As he was admiring the crowd from up on top of the hill.

Travis was still in the pool and still being Travis. At the moment he was real close in the pool with a Puerto Rican beauty. That he was whispering something in her ear at the moment. She was smiling and clearly loving what Travis was saying.

"This nigga Travis still in the pool trying to be a playboy. You know the youngin is a rare breed man" Chill said sipping on his drink.

"That's my nigga Travis being Travis. And I bet you all he got shorty's number. And will probably leave with her" Desmond said. Sounding confident that Travis would pull the beautiful Puerto Rican woman he was talking to.

It was a blazing hot Summer day. So much so. People were pouring ice cold water over their heads. Trying to stay cool. Of course there were a few huge fans that were set up around the pool area. Most of the crew had on visors and shades. The food was smelling good as it came off the grills. There were four large grills going. Making all kinds of food for the community. And the community loved it. Everyone was having a good time.   Page 75

Man, woman, and child enjoyed the festivities of the city's first Splash Party in years. Great music, great food, and great entertainment. And a lot of positive energy. County Park was the place to be. The streets were damn near empty. Everybody in the city, and some from the county. Were at the Splash Party. Two people who weren't there was Stacks and Bags. As they both drove through city streets amazed how dead and empty they were. That is until they drove down Chesapeake Street and saw all the people and cars. They continued riding past the party, and on about their business. They had no desire to go to the Splash Party.

"That shit looks packed. But then again. It's free food so everybody is going to be in that bitch. I'm not surprised at all" Stacks said as he drove.

"Fuck that party. I just hope all the niggas we've robbed are in there getting money. So we can keep robbing them" Bags replied.

"Oh indeed we are" Stacks said smiling.

Back at the party. The day time part of the party was winding down. The crew was on the hill overlooking the pool. As they popped bottles of Champagne and other bottles that they had brought to the party. The crew had mingled with everyone, because most people in the city knew them. Even though they had taken a lot of money, and was sitting on a lot of money. They all remained in Lanc City on the same blocks they grew up on. Rage of course was planning on moving eventually. But was currently still on Beaver Street. They were all having a great time with the people. And that's when none other than Wheels stepped to the DJ set and grabbed the mic.

"What's good everybody? I hope everyone is enjoying the Splash Party. We brought this back to the city because we as a community needed this. WE needed something positive for US. For all of us. Put all this local beef shit aside and have a good time. Come together. Yall see this? All these people out here having a great time. This is what it's about. Now I have to shoutout all the blocks that's represented up here. That made all this possible. My hood Lime Street....where my Lime Street peoples at? Rockland, Chester, Green, Beaver, Ann, Hill Rise, Franklin Terrace is in here!! Pershing Ave, Marshall, Juniata, Dauphin, and the rest of the 7th Ward. 8th Ward, 6th Ward. The whole city!! And one more thing. This party is dedicated to all the soldiers and queens and good people we've lost over the years in this city. Rest easy we love and miss you all. Now let's get back to the party. Let's get it"!! Wheels said as he gave the mic back to the DJ. And walked away.

The music started banging again, and the party turned back up. Some people were dancing in and around the pool area. The early evening was approaching. As a lot of the families and younger kids *were leaving. The night was young. As the exclusive adult pool party was a few hours from officially starting. It would be the night cap to a great day and evening. Travis had finally gotten out of the pool. And came up to where the rest of the crew were.*

"Travis. The crew over here talking shit fam. Because you were still in the pool with shorty. I told them. My homie is going to take shorty home with him watch" Desmond said smiling.

"You know it. It' s a done deal already. We're linking up later. She's going home with the kid. Time to put the kids away, it's time for the adults to play. You feel me"!! Travis replied.

"We need some more bottles Kwame. We're running low. Need to go on a store run"!! Nitro said.

"You cats are crazy as hell if you think I'm running to the store getting anything. We ran through a whole case of Champagne already. Crazy" Kwame replied. Amazed at how fast they ran through a case of Champagne.

It's a party playboy. Niggas are drinking mothing but Champagne. Didn't nobody touch the beer. Which made it easy to run through this Champagne" Wheels said laughing.

Even though a lot of people had left, like families and young kids. There was also other people who were just arriving for the exclusive adult pool party. The grills were still hot, but cooling off a bit. The cooks took a break after cooking all day in the hot sun. And enjoyed some of their own cooking in the process. The crew was still in their same spot, talking shit and enjoying themselves. That's when Chino had arrived and walked up to the crew. He had pulled Kwame aside to talk to him.

"I'm going to ask you this one more time Kwame. What's the word on the niggas that robbed me"? Chino asked.

"We're onto them dawg. I told you that shit. Let us handle it. And leave the shit alone. We may have an idea of who it may be" Kwame replied.

"A good idea of what Kwame"? Travis asked interrupting as he walked by.

"Nobody Travis. This conversation is between Chino and I bro" Kwame replied.

"I was just asking who. I'm apart of this shit too you know. What we got secrets now"? Travis said. As he walked away.

"What's their fucking names Kwame? Stacks and Bags"? Chino said. Insisting on continuing to talk about it.

"Stacks and Bags? They robbed the fucking warehouse Chino"? Travis asked. Looking directly at Chino.

"They robbed me at the warehouse Travis. I had to hear it through the streets. Isn't that right Kwame? Muthafuckas got away with five grand too" Chino replied.

Kwame just looked at Chino and shook his head. After telling Chino numerous times to let it go, the crew would handle it. He just wouldn't let it go. So now the cat was out of the bag so to speak. If Chino and Travis knew, the whole crew would know now. Kwame didn't want that distraction for the crew. Especially not in the midst of what was going on at the moment. The Splash Party for the community was the main and only focus right now. And that's what Kwame wanted to get back to.

"Them cats are becoming a problem Kwame. That shit is clear. It's one thing to have beef with me. The streets are the streets. But now these niggas are taking money from us. It's my beef that started this shit, so I'll handle it. They have to go" Travis said. As serious as he's ever been.

"No!! Both yall niggas chill the fuck out and enjoy this party we got going on here. It's not about us today. Or that other shit we got going on. Not now. This is about the community today. Let's get back to what's really important" Kwame replied. Visibly frustrated with the whole conversation.

"Yeah. Let me get back to this party" Travis said. Just staring at Kwame as he walked away. And smiled. Shaking his head yes.

The party continued going on until midnight. That's when people started leaving. It was an epic event like the crew had hoped. And a great turn-out like they had hoped also. Everyone had a great time. And more importantly, no drama at all. The only people that raised their voices that day. Were Kwame, Travis, and Chino. Despite that moment. The crew were very proud to show out for the city and it's people. Rage and his family had left earlier. Along with Travis and the beautiful woman he had been talking to. And was with most of the day. They both left not too long after Travis and Kwame had that exchange. The other crew members were heading right up the hill to Down Bottom. To have some more drinks and entertainment to close out the night. Kwame, Wheels, Chill, Desmond, Angel, Erotic, and Tisha. All headed to the bar. Right after they left County Park.

Meanwhile. Stacks and Bags were riding up Duke Street heading North. When they stopped at the intersection at Duke and Church Streets at the light. Stacks and Bags were talking and staring at Farnum Street Towers in front of them. A conversation began.

"Regardless of them having that warehouse more secure now. We have to hit them again at that warehouse. Some different shit though. These Lanc City niggas don't really want it with us. Yooo.....what the fuck is"? Stacks said. Before six shots rang out.

Boom!! Boom!! Boom!! Boom!! Boom!! Boom!! Six shots fired consecutively into Stacks truck. Both Stacks and Bags were shot in the head and chest. It was late night into early morning. Police were called immediately as the shots were heard. As you could hear the sirens loud in the summer night air. When Police arrived, Stacks and Bags were dead on the scene. Both still in Stacks truck lifeless. As Police were on the scene. Residents of South Duke Street started to come out of their homes looking at the scene.   Page 78

Police had the area yellow taped off. And Stacks truck was covered with a tarp. To cover his and Bags bodies. Both men had been shot three times. Twice in the chest and once in the head. Most of the crew was still Down Bottom. Not knowing that right up the block. Two guys that were becoming their enemies had just been murdered. But that was about to change. As a dude that some of the crew knew. Came in the bar and gave everyone the news about Stacks and Bags. As soon as everyone found out. They immediately went up the street to the crime scene.

"Kwame I'll drive up. You cats are wasted" Nitro said as everyone got in his truck.

Nitro, Kwame, Wheels, and Chill were in Nitro's truck. Desmond, Angel, Erotic, and Tisha were in Desmond's car. As they reached the intersection there were people everywhere. As well as law enforcement. And as they arrived. The Coroner had already made it there. And they were about to take the bodies out of the car. The Police had blocked the crime scene off. You couldn't see a whole lot from where they were standing. What some in the crew did notice, was Stack's truck. They knew he was in there. And he and Bags were always together. They knew the man in the passenger seat was Bags.

"Desmond. That's Stacks truck. Oh my God!! Oh no!! You have to be fucking kidding me. What happened"?!!! Erotic said. As she was visibly upset.

"It IS his truck. And Bags was with him. Shit"!!! Angel replied. Upset also at what happened.

"You two just chill. Calm down. No need to draw anymore attention to ourselves than we already are" Desmond said. As they all stood there watching.

Everybody there knew that this wasn't a good situation for either Stacks or Bags. Anyone knows when you see yellow tape. It's more than likely a violent crime scene. And in this case it was. As two men had lost their lives. By this time. Angel and Erotic had stepped away from the scene. And they both sat in the grass in front of Hill Rise Housing Projects. Away from the scene. They cried together. And they grieved together. The two men that they both were dating were gone. Just like that. Stacks and Bags deaths were clearly affecting the two women. And at the time. The last thing on their minds were wondering who did it. They were just still in shock and confused. That two men they had grew to know were gone.

Travis was watching the crime scene from the back door of his apartment in Hill Rise. Which was facing South Duke Street. Staring out and puffing on a blunt. As he watched with a smirk on his face. There was clearly no love lost between Travis and the two men. Their dislike for each other was evident. And now the two men were dead. And the crew no longer had to worry about handling them for robbing the warehouse. Knowing Travis. He could've been smirking because of his own reasons. One thing about it. Travis was glad they were gone. After finding out about the robbery. He felt it was time for them to go anyway.

Back on South Duke Street at the scene. A lot of the crew were still standing there after the bodies were removed from the scene. Stacks truck was now being towed. Word spread fast about the murders and local Police were gathering all the information they could. That's right around the time the crew had all left and went their separate ways. The last thing they wanted was to be questioned about a murder they had no information about. Plus being who they were and doing what they do. They didn't need ANY attention.

Police were stuck. And Wheels decided to walk up the Howard Avenue side of the housing project. To check on Travis. He hadn't seen or heard from him since he left the Splash Party earlier. Wheels knocked on his door, and after about five minutes Travis answered the door.

"What's good OG? How you? And what brings you to the crib this late"? Travis asked.

"Why did you leave the party so early for bro? We went Down Bottom until somebody told us that Stacks and Bags got murdered. Right out there at the light. Duke and Church. Shit is crazy out there right now. Police everywhere" Wheels replied.

"Oh that down there? Looks tragic. A lot of people down there too. I heard what sounded like shots. Just didn't look out. Gigi and I have been here since I left the party. Nigga that's why I wasn't worried about that shit down there. You feel me"? Travis said laughing and smiling.

"I hear you youngin. I'm going to let you get back to what you do. But be straight up with me nigga" Wheels replied.

"Don't look at me. I was here bro. I just told you what I was doing. I wasn't tripping on them niggas man. After the party all I wanted to

do was chill. And that's what we've been doing dawg. I have to get back to this, so I'll holla at you tomorrow" Travis said motioning over toward Gigi.

"I'm going to act like I believe your ass. I want to believe you. Either way. We were going to handle them collectively. As a unit like we discussed. Let's hope none of us are suspected of this shit. I'm glad you're good. We'll talk more tomorrow" Wheels replied as he left.

Travis just nodded his head yes. But no matter what Wheels or anyone else said. Travis was always going to be Travis.

Detective Boyd was continuing to piece together the bank heists. And something happened that completely shocked him. The bank heists just all of a sudden stopped. And then one day he came across a Lancaster newspaper. A double murder had recently happened in the city. For some strange reason, the murders interest him. He decided to look deeper into it. And paid a visit to Lanc City himself. He didn't know what he could get coming to the city. But he wanted to give it a shot. He first wanted to work with local law enforcement to get the facts on the double homicide. The report said that there was a lone gunmen. That fired six shots into the passenger and driver. Killing both people pretty much instantly. It was believed that the first shot hit Bags in the head. Followed by two more shots to his chest.

Stacks got shot the exact same way. And it seemed to happen quickly. When Stacks body was removed from his truck. And as the door of his truck was opened by the Coroner. A gun fell out of the truck as soon the door was opened. Stacks was armed like always and seemed to be about to return fire after Bags was shot. But was too late, before he himself was struck in the head with the first shot fired at him. It was basically an ambush and a barrage of bullets *fired at the two. They didn't have a chance because they didn't see it coming sitting at the light on Duke and Church.*

Detective Boyd got what he could from the local authorities about the double homicide. He explained to them that he was investigating bank heists. And he was looking at cases not only Lancaster. But York and Harrisburg. And around the York County and Dauphin County areas. As well as Reading and the Berks County area. They assisted him on his search for information. The bank heist crew had terrorized South Central Pennsylvania banks. And got away with a lot of money in the process. Over a million in total. And the crew was still laying low, but some members were getting antsy. And ready to get back in action.

Still dealing with Bags death. And helping Erotic do the same dealing with Stacks death. It was almost unreal what happened. How just last week she was talking to Bags. Talking about what they were planning to do that weekend. Angel had a range of emotions. From thinking seriously about going to college. And leaving the crew for good. Stacks and Bags deaths really shook Angel and Erotic. Angel had enough money to pay her way through college. And she had a partial scholarship. So she was only going to have to pay for part of her tuition. It was all there for her. And even though she had experienced an unspeakable tragedy, she still wasn't ready to leave her home city. And leave everything behind. There was something else keeping her in Lanc City. Besides the fact she was apart of LANCREW. And she didn't know what it was, but she could feel it.

Nitro and Wheels were Down Bottom in the back. Shooting pool.

"When are we getting back in the real game? Niggas are still hungry for more doe. We need to get back to what we do fam" Nitro said. Shooting a shot.

"We've been checking out some spots over the last few days. We have to be a lot more careful now. They're investigating all that shit.

I'm not trying to go to jail. Been there done that. I'm too old for that shit now man. We can still do what we do. We just have to really be on point to keep them cops off our ass. They don't have a clue, and we want to keep it that way" Wheels replied.

"Don't none of us want to go to jail nigga. They haven't even questioned any of us yet. They're too far behind dawg. We got this. We need to get back to work" Nitro said.

The next day Wheels made his way to Mr. Cee's corner store. A place he loved since he was a kid. And a place he made sure he would visit at least once a week.

"Mr. Cee.....it's Dondrake" Wheels said as he came in the store. Mr. Cee happen to be in the back when Wheels came in.

"Hey there buddy. I was in the back checking on something. How are you doing young man"? Mr. Cee replied.

"I'm good Mr. Cee. You had me a little worried when I first came in. I didn't see you or hear anything. How have you been"? Wheels asked.

"Son you don't ever have to worry about me. This is a nice neighborhood and I've been here a long time. I know we live in a treacherous world. Like what happened to those two men that got killed in the city the other night on Duke and Church. Believe it or not. Most people still respect an upstanding citizen. That minds his or her business and goes about their way. It's sad and unfortunate what happened to those men. I pray for their families" Mr. Cee replied.

"Yeah. I heard about that. It's a shame" Wheels said.

"I thank God every day. For keeping me out of harm's way anywhere I go around this city. I know its far from the most

dangerous city. But it has its moments. So have you thought about what we talked about"? Mr. Cee replied.

"I'm glad you asked that. Because I have thought about it. And I'm going to take you up on your offer. I can't let this opportunity slip away. An opportunity to continue the legacy that you started. A legacy that means so much to this neighborhood, to this city. I have to be the one to do that. it would be an honor Mr. Cee. But I do need some time. Like maybe a year to make it official. Does that sound good to you"? Wheels asked.

"Yes. That sounds great son. I was thinking the same thing. I'm not as ready to give it up just yet. But in a year. I'm sure I'll be" Mr. Cee replied smiling.

"Ok. Great. You know the store will be left in good hands. I promise you that. I just want you to know that. I have a lot of respect for you Mr. Cee. And everything you've built here. You know how much this store meant to me growing up here. And to the whole community. If I wasn't coming here before or after school. I was coming here after being at The Boys & Girls Club" Wheels said reminiscing.

"I'm sure you'll do well here. I have all the confidence in the world in you son. And I'm sure you'll make me proud. Get your business in order. And a year from now, you'll be running this place" Mr. Cee replied.

"Indeed. I will Mr. Cee. I have to get going. I'll take this drink here, and I'll be about my way. I'll see you Mr. Cee. Take care" Wheels said before leaving.

"Ok son. I'll see you later, be safe out there" Mr. Cee replied.

Page 82

Angel was at her home on Chester Street. When her cousin Tisha came over to keep her company. She was still grieving the deaths of

Stacks and Bags. There were still no leads in the investigation. Stacks truck was still at Police Headquarters being searched for evidence by Detectives. Those Detectives determined that the shots came from the passenger side of the vehicle. So the shooter had to be on that side of the vehicle. They would also look at surveillance cameras that were all over the city. To see if they caught any footage of the shooter. The bullets recovered from Stacks and Bags bodies. Determined that the murder weapon was a 45 caliber handgun.

The local authorities suspected it was a planned hit. And the shooter knew where Stacks and Bags were that night. And obviously knew they would be at that intersection at that time. With local law enforcement believing it was a planned hit, wasn't good for the crew. It was known within the city that Stacks and Bags had issues with Desmond, Travis, and Chino for robbing him. Being that the streets talk. Local authorities were hoping that someone would come forward with information as to who had problems with the two men. Stacks and Bags weren't originally from the Lanc City area. But had been around the area for years. So Police wanted to talk to people who were cool with the two men first.

Within a short time. Local Police had got information on who the two men were dating. Angel and Erotic's names were the first to come up. Which is something they definitely didn't want. They both asked to come Downtown to be questioned. And they both did so with Lawyers. But before they did. They both had a conversation about it.

"I know we don't have shit to do with this E. But I hate having to be questioned about it. It's bad enough we've been grieving already. And we have more money to make" Angel said to Erotic

"I know. I wasn't expecting this. But we have to do what we have to do. I'm going to tell them the truth. I don't know shit" Erotic replied.

Both women went in one at a time accompanied by their Lawyers. Angel was questioned first. Detective Boyd started off by asking Angel if she wanted anything. She didn't and so he started the interviewing process.

"I'm Detective Boyd and I have you here to ask you some questions about Antonio "Stacks" Smith. And Charlie "Bags" Harmon. I understand that you were involved with Mr. Harmon. Is that true"? Detective Boyd asked.

"Yeah. You could say we were seeing each other for a few months. I knew them both for a little over a year. Angel replied.

"Did you know of anyone that they had problems with? A street beef or something"? Detective Boyd asked.

"No. Not that I know of" Angel replied.

"Come on now!! You were Bags girl. I'm sure you knew personal shit that was going on in the man's life. Including people he was enemies with. And if you care for him like you say you do. You'll give me this information to help capture his killer. Their killer" Detective Boyd said.

"Even before he was killed. We weren't talking as much as we used to. He was doing whatever it is he does. And I was working my job and saving up for college like I've been. We were both really busy. Lately we'd been more like friends than anything. But I honestly didn't know anything about what he did. And who were his enemies. He kept that part of his life away from me" Angel replied.

"You had to know your friends Stacks and Bags were drug dealers. Did you see any of them do anything criminal"? Detective Boyd asked.

"Not around me. So I wouldn't know" Angel replied. With a straight face. As she kept her composure throughout the whole interview.

"I have one more question for you. There's been a bank heist crew that has been involved in several bank heists. And have gotten away with stealing over a million dollars. All across the state of Pennsylvania. Dauphin County, Franklin County, and Berks County. There looks to be two women that are also in this crew. Well that's what surveillance cameras showed. You know anything about that" Detective Boyd asked.

"Why would I know anything about that? I don't know anything about a bank heist crew. Sorry Detective. I can't help you. Can I go now"? Angel replied asking.

"Yeah. That's it. You can go now. But stay close, because you are someone that knew both victims. And I may need to speak to you again" Detective Boyd said. As Angel left with her Lawyer.

Angel walked past Erotic as she walked out of the office. They glanced at each other. And Erotic walked in the office to get interviewed next.

She sat down across from the Detective. She was chewing gum, and Detective Boyd told her to remove it. She rolled her eyes a little and threw her gum in the trash.

"Word is you and Stacks were pretty close" Detective Boyd said. Looking directly at Erotic.

"It depends on what you mean by being close. I used to date him if that's what you're wondering" Erotic replied.

"Right. That means you knew a lot about what was going on in his life right"? Detective Boyd asked.

"Wrong. I just dated him. We never lived together, and our relationship was never serious. We just hung out a few times. Went to dinner a few times. And the movies. That's it. I knew nothing about the man's personal business" Erotic replied.

"Where were you the night in question"? Detective Boyd asked.

"Me and some friends were at a bar. Having some drinks and having a good time. Angel was one of my friends that was with me that night in the bar. That's where I was" Erotic replied.

"You know anything about a bank heist crew? That's been robbing banks across three different counties. Maybe you know something about that"? Detective Boyd said.

"No. I don't Detective. Sorry" Erotic replied.

"Ok. You're free to go. But don't go too far. I may need to question you again" Detective Boyd said.

"Yeah. I hear you Detective. Good day" Erotic replied. As she got up and left.

The Detective's attempt to get any kind of information from Angel and Erotic failed. He was back to square one within the investigation. Just like he was in the bank heist investigations. Very little leads and minimal evidence. And at this point. Detective Boyd had ran out of people to talk to. He wasn't that familiar with Lanc City. He would let the local authorities continue their own investigation into the double homicide. He would get back to the bank heists where he started. The Detective was stuck on whether he should stay in Lanc City or not. He really wanted to break one of these cases badly. Detective Boyd worked night and day trying to solve both cases.

After Angel and Erotic left the Police Station Downtown. Kwame was parked down the street from the Police Station. He was there to pick them up. And after standing there for less than two minutes. Kwame pulled up and both women got in Kwame's Benz. Then proceeded to leave the Downtown area.

"How did it go? Let me guess. They grilled both of you about the double murder. As if you two knew anything about it" Kwame said. Looking over at Angel. Who was riding in the passenger seat.

"Yeah. That's basically what happened. But get this. That Detective is onto us. And the bank heists we've committed. He questioned both of us about it" Angel replied.

"Yeah. Me too. He questioned me. Asking if I knew about any bank heists. How the fuck does he know about us Kwame"? Erotic added on.

"How the fuck am I supposed to know? I didn't expect any Detectives to be in our fucking backyard hunting us down like dogs. If he knows we're here, this could be a potential problem. This shit isn't good for us. I mean we changed up by taking you two out of leading the teams in the banks. I don't know how much more we can change. And I know everybody is eager to get back into action. We need to do another heist soon" Kwame said.

"Kwame I can't front. This questioning shit has me bugged out. And has me thinking more about going to college sooner. That's where I want to eventually be Kwame. College not jail. This next heist might be my last go round" Angel replied.

"Shit got me bugged out too. I'm down for one last major hit, and then I'm out. I've been stacking doe anyway" Erotic said.

"If we get what we're trying to get. We may all be done with this shit anyway. Remember the plan was for all of us to invest our money. If niggas are doing what we've talked about, they should be good. We're in the process of planning the next heist now. In about a week we'll all meet at the warehouse. And finalize everything" Kwame said. As they continued driving through Lanc City streets.

Detective Boyd knowing of the crew. Had Angel and Erotic shook. And had them contemplating whether they wanted to be apart of this thing anymore. Regardless of it all. The crew had their minds focused on the next heist. They all believed in what they were doing. Because up until this point. They've done it without getting caught. And it's made them all a lot of money. So in that regard. They were fearless and didn't mind taking chances. After riding a little longer. Kwame dropped Erotic and Angel off. And went about his way.

Desmond was sitting on his porch on Green Street just chilling. Enjoying the summer weather. A wifebeater and some shorts on this hot summer day. And some crisp white Air Force Ones on. As Desmond was sitting there. He saw a sleek black motorcycle race up the block flying. The rider then made a u turn at the end of the block and raced back up the block. Until it made a sudden stop in front of Desmond's house. He had no idea who this person was. He didn't know whether it was a hitter. And he needed to pull out his gun or what. After parking the rider pulled off his helmet. It was Travis.

"What's good my G? Do you see me right now my nigga? You see what I'm riding on playboy"? Travis said. Standing next to his bike posing.

Travis had a brand new Ducati Panigale V4 R. Motorcycle had 221-Horsepower. In the bike world it's known as a superbike. Travis paid forty thousand for the bike. A gift to himself out of the money he made with the crew.

"Yeah I see you. Nice bike bro. I didn't even know you was into bikes. I thought you were getting a new car"? Desmond replied asking.

"Just got this shit about an hour ago. Always wanted one of these. I got the money now, so why not? I was going to get a new car. But I think I look better in this shit for the summer. I'm going to be racing through the streets in this bitch. You trying to take this shit for a spin fam? You know I got you. Take it for a spin, I'll watch the crib" Travis said. Trying to get Desmond to ride his bike.

"No. I'm good dawg. I don't fuck with bikes like that. But thanks anyway bro. I heard our friends got dusted off last weekend" Desmond replied.   Page 86

"Yeah. I heard about that too. Crazy thing is it happened right in my backyard. Now people think I did it. And I'm sure you as well as the crew have been wondering if I did it right? Imagine if I did do it. Don't you think I would've hit them niggas with more than three shots each? As much as I didn't like either one of those bitches. I could definitely see myself doing it. If it came down to them and me. Hell yeah. I would in a heartbeat. And what if I told you I did do it? Then what"? Travis said. Looking directly at Desmond.

"You know what it is with you and me. As long as we've been rocking together, you shouldn't even have to ask that question" Desmond replied.

Travis just smiled and laughed a little. He felt the humor in messing with people in sometimes serious situations. Especially with the perception of him being a loose cannon. He loved using that to sometimes intimidate and pressure people into doing things he wanted them to do. Travis could be laughing one moment. And ready to kill you the next. He just had a bizarre unpredictable personality. Like buying that new bike. No one knew Travis ever rode bikes. But then again. We're talking about Travis here. They both sat there on Green Street at Desmond's house chilling and having a good time in the neighborhood.

"They called Angel and Erotic Downtown for questioning in Stacks and Bags murders. I know they were solid, and there's no need for us to worry about them saying anything. Because we were all Down Bottom when the murder occurred anyway" Desmond replied.

"I'm just glad neither of them were in the truck that night. Would've been bad" Travis said.

They talked for a little while longer before Travis put his helmet on and sped off down Green Street. And off into the distance. Chill was home and in the midst of planning his annual cookout in Franklin Terrace aka Almanac. The projects always enjoyed Chill's cookouts. In which he had been having them for the last three years. This particular year, Chill had money. So he wanted this year's cookout to be his biggest yet. Being from the biggest housing project in the city. Chill felt like he had to represent for his project. And show out for the city.

Nitro would be helping Chill organize the big cookout. And this was also taking place after the epic Splash Party at County Park. It was only natural that Nitro came down to Franklin Terrace to talk to Chill. So as Nitro pulled up, Chill was sitting out in front of his house.

"What's good playboy? What you been up to"? Chill said. As Nitro walked up and sat down.

"Laying low and in the wind homie. You know how it is out here. I just try to stay out the way. What are you thinking for this party fam? You got a DJ"? Nitro replied asking.

"Not at the moment. But I'm planning on getting one soon. Of course a no drama event just like the Splash Party. We never had any issues before, so I don't anticipate any problems now. Of course this year I'm going bigger than ever" Chill said.

"Sounds good to me. And there won't ever be any drama at any of our events. People in this city know we aint about that bullshit. Shit is always live down here when you have your cookouts. My birthday is coming up, and I'm planning to throw myself a party. I'm getting shit together now. I have about a month and a half. Hopefully by then we'll be back in action" Nitro replied.

"Kwame, I, and Wheels met up to discuss the next heist. He said we should be having a meeting collectively soon. To finalize everything. We're definitely coming back. There's more money to make" Chill said.

"I remember back in the days in Almanac. They had some house parties and some parties in the community building. I used to run through here as a youngin. Had some friends that lived in these projects. We used to do all kind of shit down here. From playing tackle football, to riding our bikes over these hills. Hide and seek, basketball. Got a lot of memories down here bro. Shit has changed but yet still the same. The Boys & Girls Club was everything to us kids growing up. Those were the days fam" Nitro replied.

"Hell yeah. And how South Duke Street was like the dividing line from the hood and the real bottom. All those blocks below South Duke was fierce fam. Some of the roughest looking blocks in the city. And that area produced some of the precious diamonds that were good people and stars in the city. The city produced stars from all over the city" Chill said.

"Yeah. You're talking the bottom part of Green Street, bottom part of Chester, Christian, Woodward, North, Locust, Strawberry, Atlantic Avenue, and Andrew. All the way down to Rage's hood on Beaver" Nitro replied.

"Just growing up in the city was an experience in itself. There's no place like Lanc City. I tell niggas this shit all the time. I remember I *was locked up with niggas from up North. They thought I was bugging when I was talking about my city. You just have to be here in this city to experience what it is. If you weren't born and raised here. Or been here for an extended time period, you wouldn't understand it" Nitro said.*

"Word. And I'm glad the crew has done what it set out to do. In giving back to this community. We still have things we would like to do, that we haven't done yet. But it's going to get done one way or the other. One being my annual cookout I'm having for the city. Especially for my people in Franklin Terrace. Me, Wheels, and Kwame are planning to give turkeys away this Thanksgiving also. We have a lot of plans for the future, as long as we keep getting this money" Chill replied.

"Sounds like great plans. I'm always down with doing something positive for the community. Always willing to give back to my city. I have to get going fam. I need to go by the block and pick-up. I'll holla at you later to finalize everything for the cookout" Nitro said. Getting up out of his chair in front of Chill's house. And got back in his truck and left.

The two men had a great time reminiscing about the times they had growing up in the city. Even though Lanc City was a small city. For those who were born and raised in the city. All noticed how distinctively different it was to any other place they had ever been to. Some natives have left the city and only return to visit. Others have left the city and came back to live. All depends on the person. One thing was for sure. If you were from this city or had ties to it. You kept those ties in tact. So you could always return. Over the years the city has become more culturally diverse. Housing projects like Hill Rise and Garden Court would be remodeled and fenced in for better security. As time passed. Community staples like The Boys & Girls Club and The Elks in the 7ᵗʰ Ward would eventually close and disappear as if it were never there. Even Lucky's Chinese Take-Out would eventually close. Things were definitely changing in the city. And in the World as a whole.

On a positive note. Places like The Attucks and The Mix continued to thrive in the city. Expanding its continued growing legacy of serving the community. All were not lost in the closing of some monumental and influential places that in part changed lives. Downtown became even more trendy as the years passed. A lot of money was invested in the city's Downtown. And it showed. If you were a lifelong city resident at the age over 35 or older. You saw Downtown go through a serious transition. And resurgence. From being vibrant with department stores when you were growing up. To Downtown being a ghost town. To it now being trendy and live as shit. Especially on the weekends and First Fridays. Along with the ever-growing Art scene in the city. Made Downtown a must visit destination for people from the city as well as the county. Even some people from out of state.

But that was Downtown. Which seemed worlds away from where all of the crew was born and raised in the 7ᵗʰ Ward. Southeast Lanc City. An area where the city didn't spend much money. That's why it was so important for people like the crew to give back to that community. They saw the faces of the parents and kids all day at the Splash Party. How that party brought so much joy to the city. That was just the beginning as far as the crew was concerned. Because they were planning to do a lot more for the community. Chill, Kwame, Nitro, and Wheels all met at the warehouse the next day. They were all sitting at a table discussing their plans.

"Next hit. Lebanon County bank. It's closer and we won't be using Angel or Erotic to lead anymore. They'll be sitting it out again and waiting here to count money. Like the last time. Wheels I'm going to

put you on the frontlines this time. And I know we talked about this. But I need you this time dawg. Desmond and Travis will be right by your sides fam. I'm switching shit up to keep these clowns off our ass. We haven't struck in a while. They aren't going to know what hit them when we come back on the scene. That's why we planned it like that. Everybody on board with this? If so. We can tell the rest of the crew" Kwame said.

"If putting a nigga like me on the frontlines at this stage of my life. To get this money. Then so be it. Let's do it" Wheels replied.

The crew had done several heists and only shot one person. That was Kwame shooting an armed guard in the Berks County heist. Wheels was hoping to avoid shooting anyone in his role on the frontlines. His strength was driving, although he could grip the steel when he needed to. Wheels was no stranger to the streets. The crew only shooting one person over several heists was quite remarkable. Considering the fact, they were so brazen in their heists. And each crew member was capable of being violent at any time. The crew wanted to avoid shooting anyone moving forward. The next day all four men traveled to the Lebanon County bank to stake out their next location to hit. It was crucial for planning, timing, and execution.

After staking out their next target. The crew would have an official meeting with all the crew members at the warehouse to discuss the next heist.

Travis was sitting on his front porch. Smoking a cigarette looking out onto Howard Avenue. As cars rode by. Travis was alone in his thoughts on many of days. He was a loner for the most part. Hanging around Desmond here and there. But that's about it. If Travis trust anyone in the crew, it would be Desmond and Wheels his OG. Those are the only two people you could say he was close with in the crew. As long as everybody in the crew was eating, everything was good. What Kwame promised was working, and they all believed in his vision. The proof was in their pockets.

The crew members were seeing more money than they had ever seen in their lives. And most of them were being smart and investing their money. Like Wheels was hoping to buy Mr. Cee's corner store. Kwame had made some investments himself with a personal Financial Advisor. Chill and Nitro were doing their things in real estate. Angel was planning to go to college. Desmond was an artist and was hoping to have his work displayed in the emerging Lanc City Art scene. And now the crew was embarking on their next heist. Hoping to have their biggest heist to date. They were looking to get over two million dollars in cold cash. They had to work fast and precise. Going for that type of money came with a risk. But the crew was willing to take that risk.

On Beaver Street. Rage was having a conversation with his wife. They were talking about officially going house shopping in the County. They had both lived in the city all their lives. Rage lived on Beaver all his life. They were both looking forward to leaving the city and moving to the suburbs. After talking to his wife about planning to go house shopping. Rage walked out on his front porch on Beaver Street. And just looked up and down the block. The kids playing outside riding their bikes. The cars going up and down the narrow block from both directions. Rage was just taking the block all in. And at the same time thinking about his and his family's future. He was letting his mind wonder in the moment. As he stood on the block that meant so much to him over the years.

On the other side of South Duke Street. Who many felt was the dividing line between the hood and the bottom. On the corner of Green and Rockland to be exact. Desmond told Travis to meet him at the old spot where Lucky's used to be. By this time the spot was vacant. So as Travis stood on the corner waiting for Desmond. He *just stood there staring at the spot where Lucky's used to be. And reminisced about the times he spent in and around the place.   Page 90*

And that's when Desmond walked up. And their conversation started.

"What's good bro? How you been? We got a meeting at the warehouse" Desmond said as he walked up.

"Oh we do? That's news to me. It's funny how this nigga Kwame doesn't relay messages back to me. He better be glad we're getting this money together. Might be the only thing saving his ass" Travis replied.

"Relax bro. it wasn't meant like that. They know we're close so they knew I would see you. And I told your ass. Now let's get to the money. Stay focused on the bigger picture fam" Desmond said.

"I'm focused and I'm good like always. And you know I'm always about that money nigga…..always" Travis replied.

"We can't let no petty shit divide us. we have some good shit going for us right now. And after this next heist. We all maybe able to give this shit up and do something else. I know you and Kwame don't see eye to eye on shit. But don't let that fuck up the money. Because trust and believe. He won't let it get in the way of him getting his money. Kwame is too smart for that bro. Been in the streets too long. And I know bro. Kwame and I didn't necessarily get off to a great start either. I thought I may have had to shoot the nigga in HOP. When he first approached me about this bank heist shit. The man gave us both an opportunity to get real money. Give him that. You know how many niggas from the city would love to be a part of this shit"? Desmond said.

"I hear you. I'm anxious for some action dawg. The sooner this next heist the better. Plus some more paper for these pockets" Travis replied.

"I know you didn't run through all that money did you? There's no way. Me myself. I've been stashing my doe" Desmond said.

"Nigga. Hell no. I didn't spend all my money. You crazy? I'm good fam. You never have to worry about me" Travis replied. With the devilish grin he would have on his face from time to time.

Lucky's had finally closed its doors for good a few weeks back. And that part of the block was never the same. Lucky's was another one of the city's landmarks. That was a major part of serving the community in the 7th Ward. When it left. It was almost like an era had ended. In particular. Cats like Travis and Desmond who were younger. And only got to experience a small part of the historic spot in the city's Southeast. The small amount of years that they had a chance to enjoy it. They loved it. Older cats like Kwame, Wheels, Chill, and Nitro. Could tell you stories for days about Lucky's and the area surrounding it. The generations that had the chance to enjoy the place for what it was. Got a treat, and memories that last a lifetime.

It was summertime in the city. And Lanc City summers were always eventful. Everybody would be out. Beautiful women of every race and religion were very visible throughout the city. Corner stores all over the city with music banging and their doors open.   Page 91

Cars going up and down city streets, with their stereos blasting the latest bangers. The crew was sponsoring a basketball team in the summer basketball league. In which the most talented local basketball players were apart of. That would also be going on. First Fridays in the summer brought the city's Downtown more alive. Bars all through Downtown would be open late for the big street party. Plenty of music and entertainment. The summer also brought a wave of violence throughout the city. Like a lot of inner cities, the increase in violence could be attributed to a lot of things. The weather and increase of people outside on the streets. Either way, that element was always present in Lanc City. Things could get violent at any time.

As witnessed by the violent deaths of Stacks and Bags recently. There still were no leads in that case as it remained unsolved. As Travis and Desmond stood on the corner of Rockland and Green Streets talking. Erotic walked the short distance up the street from her home on Rockland Street to greet Travis and Desmond.

"I knew I heard you two down here. Desmond and Travis, what you two doing on my block? Lucky's closed a few weeks back" Erotic said.

"Shit. Just chilling" Desmond replied.

"What's good E"? Travis added on.

"I know you two heard about Angel and I getting questioned about Stacks and Bags murders. They questioned us as if we knew anything about it. Just because we were involved with them. I honestly hope they both get the justice they deserve. I cared a lot about Stacks. I really did. His death fucked me up, I can't front. We weren't serious in our relationship together. But we did spend some time together. And had a lot of fun with the time we spent. As you know I was Down Bottom with you and the rest of the crew Desmond. And that's what I told those Detectives" Erotic said.

"Yeah I remember. Don't worry about that shit. They don't have shit on us. And as of now they still have no leads in the case. That's why they were reaching for yall. Them niggas had more enemies besides us. Anybody could've done that" Desmond replied.

"It's just sad to find out they died the way they did" Erotic said.

"The streets are the streets and the game is the game. There will be casualties" Travis added.

"Indeed. There will be" Desmond said agreeing with Travis.

"I figured you two would say some shit like that" Erotic said. Shaking her head.

The three of them had managed to walk back down the block and sat on Erotic's front step. And continued talking. Until they all went their separate ways. Meanwhile. Chino was over on Ann Street at Kwame's house. Discussing some things with him.

Page 92

"I see the two niggas that robbed me got handled before I could get to them. Was that us"? Chino asked Kwame.

"Hell no. That wasn't us. And would it have mattered anyway? The last thing we need is more attention drawn to us by some local murder shit. Bottomline is they're gone. And no longer a concern of ours. Shit. I never thought the niggas were a concern of ours. But anyway. That's done. Now we can move on. We got bigger and better shit ahead of us" Kwame replied.

"Maybe you're right. But I still wished I could've got my hands on them first. Would've made shit even sweeter" Chino said.

"I got some shit I have to do. So if we're done here. I'll holla at you later Chino" Kwame said.

"Yeah. Ok cool. I have to get going myself. Meeting my girlfriend for dinner over on the West side. Stay up. I'll holla" Chino replied as he was leaving.

For the first time ever. Chino had asked about crew business. Something he hadn't dared to do up until this point. It had Kwame thinking for a minute while he was talking to him. Not that Kwame couldn't trust him. Because if he couldn't trust him, Chino wouldn't be around. Warehouse or not. Him and Chino went back to their days of growing up on Ann Street. Living a few houses down from each other. Chino lived on Ann until he was like thirteen years old. His family then moved to the East Side. Over on East Orange Street. They remained close even though Chino and his family had moved off the block. He didn't want to think the worst about his good friend.

But he also knew it was a dirty game because the game involved money. And anytime you have any type of relationship with most people. It's all good for the most part, until it involves money. When money gets involved, people can and will get out of character. Family, friends, associates, whoever. But on the other hand. Kwame felt Chino had too much of a sweet deal, to want to fuck that up. He just didn't think it made any type of common sense for Chino to do anything against the crew. The heist was in two days. The crew had already had their meeting at the warehouse. And the plans for the next heist were set. Wheels, Desmond, and Travis would be on the frontlines. And Chill and Nitro would be behind the wheel. After Kwame had changed back to their original format, which has worked for them. Of having two get-away drivers instead of one, like Kwame had thought about because of the shorter distance between Lancaster and Lebanon.

The goal was to get two million dollars in cash, or more. It would be a steep challenge, but the crew was confident and determined to pull it off. This heist was what you may call. A personal heist. Being that the three front men. Wheels, Desmond, and Travis all had a pretty good relationship. And the drivers. Chill and Nitro had become close since being involved in real estate and having some of the same business interest. Nitro would take the team to the bank, and Chill would bring everybody home. The stage was set, and now it was all about execution. And doing it in a very fast and precise manner to reach their goal. It would be a challenge they had not yet faced. But they were all eager to face that challenge head on.

"I got my old head with me on this one. This shit is going to be fun. Let's get this money" Travis said smiling.

"And I got that wheel to the bank. Chill will be bringing it home. And hopefully by the time that happens. We'll be over two million dollars richer" Nitro said.

"So I guess me and E are out of the action again" Angel said chiming in.

"Has to be. They got the drop on you two. We could keep switching the wigs, but they were zeroing in on the fact there were females leading the heist teams in the banks. They got surveillance camera footage on you both. So you know what it is. For yall sake, counting money is better for you both at this point. You want to go to college right"? Kwame replied.

Angel then nodded understanding why her and Erotic were playing the positions they were playing.

"All this shit will make more sense when it's over. When yall sitting on a beach somewhere. Or some Caribbean Island surrounded by palm trees. Rich as shit. Laughing about the ways and what we had to do to get this money. But knowing in the end, it all worked. That's why your asses will be sitting on that beach or relaxing on that island" Kwame said.

The heist was the next day. But before that. Some of the crew met Down Bottom for drinks. Chill, Desmond, Travis, and Wheels. All of the heist team that was set to be in action the next day, was down at the bar. Except Nitro. He was the only one that wasn't there. The bar had a decent amount of people there. Of course they were all in the back of the bar where the pool table was. Their usual spot.

"Are you all comfortable with this being our last go round? Like for good"? Chill asked as he took a sip of his drink.

"If we get what we've set out to get. Hell yeah. I'm comfortable with it. I've been stashing my doe fam" Wheels replied.

"Me too. I'd be good. Plus I'm hoping by then. My Art will be bringing in some paper for me" Desmond added on.

"Even if it is the last. I'll get money other ways. You never have enough money. And one thing is for sure. If I am broke. It won't be for long, because I'm going to get it either way I can" Travis said smiling.

"Nigga you damn right you shouldn't be broke. All the money we've done took. We have to be smart with our money. Travis I know you've heard me and Kwame say this all the time. And no matter that you choose to ignore it. It's true. We got in this shit to make money another way that keeps us off the street shit. We've been doing that. Take advantage youngin. And stack your doe. I'm not trying to be fucking around on these streets forever" Wheels replied.   Page 94

"Wheels is right on. Save and invest your money. I know I'm not going back to that street shit. This is it for me. I got to make this work for me. Besides helping with the Splash Party. And having my annual cookout in Franklin Terrace. I've been stashing my doe too. I definitely have plans" Chill said.

"Every man has got to have a plan. No doubt about that" Desmond added.

"I'd hate to see one of yall out here begging for money and shit. After having a shit load of money. That's embarrassing and just stupid. How can you ask the same poor people you probably looked over for empathy? After you done fucked up enough money they could've lived the rest of their lives off of. Shit don't even make no kind of sense fam. We've got a major job tomorrow. A goal that we must reach. Have your game faces on tomorrow and be focused. We're bringing them 2 M's home my niggas" Wheels replied.

"Day Of The Heist Act Four"

Nitro woke up to the sunlight shining through his window. He stayed on Pershing Avenue the previous night. Like he always did the night before a heist. Got himself ready as he grabbed his 9mm handgun. Put it in his waistband. And then proceeded to walk downstairs and got in the getaway car. In route to pick the team up. He drove down Pershing and picked up Desmond on the corner of Pershing and Green.

"It's showtime. You ready young gun"? Nitro asked. Excited as ever. As he as well as the others were anxious for some action.

"Ready as I've ever been. Of course I'm ready to get this money" Desmond said showing his 9mm handgun.

Nitro continued driving down Pershing, then made a right on Dauphin. And a left onto Lime Street to pick up Wheels. Who was waiting on his porch.

"About time. What took yall so long"? Wheels said as he got in the car.

"Whatever man. Just get in fam" Nitro replied.

The last person the team would pick up was Travis. As they headed to Hill Rise to pick him up. Travis was still in his house. And had armed himself with two guns. That 45 caliber handgun that he loved. And a Glock 40 that he also had. He didn't tell any of the crew he had two guns on him. This would be the first time that he would carry two guns with him to a heist. Why? Only Travis knew, and only Travis could answer that question. Or form some type of logic as to why he did it. In his own sick mind. As Nitro approached the Howard Avenue side of the housing project. The crew waited about five minutes before Travis came out and got in the car.

"You should be telling this nigga about time Wheels. Travis is always running late" Nitro said as he continued driving.

"Late. But ready to get this money. And get back into action. It's been too long yall. Don't worry about me nigga. Just get us to the bank" Travis replied.

"He stays on point. He better" Wheels replied to Nitro's comment.

"My OG knows how I get down. Nigga this whole city does" Travis said. Winking his eye and smiling like always.

That was Travis. Always a jokester, but when it was really down to ride. He was definitely a soldier you would want on your team. Despite him being loyal and down for whatever. He was also a killer that was grimy. And wasn't the type of person you could trust. Unless you had that type of personal relationship with him. Page 96

After that exchange the car grew silent. And as the distance got shorter each individual grew more and more focused. They were all hoping that this would be their biggest heist to date. They had a lot riding on this moment. As the car went up Pa. 72 North towards Lebanon County. There was a sense of urgency as they got even closer. Chill was following behind and about to pull over. And wait for the team to finish the job in the bank. And as usual. The rest of the crew was back in Lanc City at the Sixth Ward warehouse. Waiting for the team to get back from the bank, so they could count the money.

After the forty nine minute drive to the Northern Lebanon County bank. The team had finally arrived at the bank. And were ready to go to work. As soon as Nitro parked the car a little ways from the bank. Wheels looked in his sideview mirror to see what was going on before he got out. He then quickly got out of the car and approached the bank. Wheels had a hat on and some shades. He went up to a teller and produced a note telling the teller what to do. After doing that. Wheels sent the text to Travis and Desmond. They then quickly got out of the car with masks on. And stormed the bank with guns drawn.

"Everybody get on the fucking floor!!! Now!!! I said get on the floor, don't make me say that shit again"!! Desmond said. As he had his gun pointed across the room.

Travis immediately ordered the bank manager back to the bank vault. The team had to stay in the bank and get as much cash as they could. The goal was two million. Travis was still in the bank vault and Wheels was cleaning out the front teller drawers. While Desmond had everyone at gunpoint on the floor in the front of the bank.

"Stay the fuck down!! Anybody else stick their heads up, I'm popping off. Try me"!! Desmond said. As he walked around the front of the bank.

As Desmond was holding down the front of the bank. He turned and encountered another armed guard who had his weapon drawn. Boom!!! A single shot hit Desmond in the shoulder. As he fell to the floor and took cover behind a desk.

"Fuck!! Ah....shit"!! Desmond said in pain holding his shoulder.

That's when Wheels came from behind the teller counters and returned fire at the armed guard. Firing three consecutive shots at the guard. Boom!! Boom!! Boom!! Wheels fired another two shots at a guard on the ground about to reach for his weapon.

"Let's get the fuck out of here!! Let's go"!!! Wheels yelled to the team.

Travis came running from the back where the bank vault was. With two bags filled with cash. On the way out. Wheels helped Desmond up as he was holding his shoulder. And they all ran out of the bank and to the car. Where Nitro had the car already running. They got in the car quickly and sped off.

"Fucking guard hit me in the shoulder. Shit!!! Didn't even see his ass" Desmond said. Holding his shoulder. It was bleeding heavily. As he rode in the backseat.

"Rather it be that, than in your head. Be glad for that shit bro. What the fuck happened out front you too? I could've gotten more doe" Travis said.

"What happened was the guard came out of nowhere and hit Desmond. And I had to pop a few shots at him to get him off Desmond's ass. Don't know if I hit his ass or not. I just know those shots stopped. Push that shit Nitro, we have to get to Chill" Wheels replied.

Nitro was going at a high rate of speed trying to get to Chill, who wasn't too far from the Interstate. Waiting for the team to hop in his car so they could head back to Lanc City. They finally got to Chill and they ditched the getaway car. And was off. Back down Pa. Route 72 South. Towards Lanc City.

"Damn Desmond. You got shot bro? Chill asked as he was driving and looked in his rearview mirror.

"Yeah. This guard came out of nowhere and hit me in the shoulder. Shit hurts like a muthafucka too. Have to get in touch with someone who can stitch. Stitch this shit up, because I know I need it. I can't go to no hospital" Desmond said.

"I'm sure we can get someone to handle that. We know a lot of nurses that live in the hood" Wheels replied.

The getaway car was ditched as planned. The crew knew at some point that Police would find the car. It was apart of the plan. They didn't know at the time if they had reached their goal or not. They would figure that out once they got back to the warehouse. Angel, Erotic, Kwame, and Rage were all waiting back at the warehouse. As *they got back to Lanc City and back to the warehouse in the Sixth Ward. Kwame saw Desmond.*

"What the fuck? Desmond you got hit"? Kwame asked. Looking surprised when Desmond came in.

"A guard got brave just like that guard got brave with you. Muthafucka took a shot at him. And hit him in the shoulder. He'll be fine. Calling one of my homegirls that works at the hospital, to come stitch him up" Wheels replied.

"Fucked up. But we have to count this money" Kwame said.

"I know I grabbed as much cash as I could. A bunch of stacks in those bags. Plus what Wheels got from the tellers. We should be close to our goal" Travis said.

"I just talked to my sister. We can go to her crib, she's a nurse at the hospital. She can stitch you up. She lives on Broad Street. Let's roll Desmond" Chill said. As he led Desmond out of the warehouse and onto his sister's house on Broad Street.

"I'm still wondering if I hit that guard after I returned fire. Shit has been weighing on my mind since we left the bank. I know I hit him at least once" Wheels said. As he sat there deep in thought.

"All I know is. With all this shit going on, and Desmond getting shot. And you might've shot a guard like I did. This may be the end of all this shit fam. We all got enough money if we stopped today" Kwame said. Pacing back and forth.

After finding out everything about what happened in the latest heist. The crew wasn't focused on the job at hand. Which was counting the money. They were all thinking about what was to happen next. Was the guard that Wheels thought he hit dead? Did *he even shoot the guard? He knew he fired at him after the guard had shot Desmond. They knew they had a lot of money, but if an armed guard was killed. It would put immense attention on the crew. And the feds would most likely get involved. Which would increase the heat from the law on the crew. Something they didn't want. It was a tense time for the crew. Not to mention a high profile double homicide that was dominating the local news. Law enforcement was already chasing a shadow that was the crew. They just didn't exactly know it at the time.*

After discussing a few things that transpired with the latest heist. Rage, Kwame, Angel, and Erotic. Started counting the money. Most of the team that did the heist that day, had already left and went their separate ways.

Driving home in his BMW from the warehouse in the Sixth Ward. Wheels was doing a lot of thinking. Hoping and praying he didn't kill that guard. As he replayed the heist in his head time after time again. He finally got home and showered. After showering. He stood in his bathroom looking at himself in the mirror. He sat on his bed in his bedroom wrapped in a towel. Turned on his TV and watched the news hoping for the best. Wheels was relieved to know that the man wasn't dead. He had no intention of shooting anyone that day. But when that guard shot a crew member of his, he had to return fire. Wheels felt like he did what he had to do. And if he didn't, Desmond might've been dead right now.

The guard was in a Lebanon County hospital in serious but stable condition. It was a major weight lifted off of Wheels shoulders. He could now focus and get back to his normal life. After that day, it seemed like everything changed. After that close call, Wheels seriously thought about getting out of it all. And living on the straight and narrow. He had serious plans of buying Mr. Cee's corner store. Something that meant a lot to him. And he didn't want that to be in danger. That future business venture stayed on his mind daily. And he wouldn't put that at risk for no one.

The next day came. And Nitro found himself lying next to a chick he was dealing with at the time. After a night of heavy drinking and partying. He was almost surprised she was there. Either way. He paid for it. Waking up with a terrible hangover that morning. He had to get up because he had a meeting later that day about a real estate opportunity. Something Nitro had always had, was an interest in real estate. And as soon as he got some real money. He invested his money in the real estate game. And had several properties all over the city and county. And he had been recently encouraging Chill to do the same. Nitro was a natural born hustler at heart and smart dude period. He was always a get money nigga.

The crew was planning to give out turkeys to families in the city and surrounding areas for Thanksgiving. Another service the crew had promised for the community. And was honored and glad to do. The crew was doing what they set out to do when they formed as one. Which they were all proud of. They all felt obligated to give back. And at the same time, they naturally wanted to. They enjoyed seeing families smiles on their faces. Man, women, and child. Enjoying themselves at the expense of the crew. Giving the less fortunate families turkeys for Thanksgiving. To have less of a burden on themselves meant everything to the crew. The Splash Party was a great day in the city. And the turkey giveaway would be also.

Nitro got himself together. As the female he was with left. Nitro sat on his bed when he got a call from Kwame. It was a little after noon. And he asked Nitro if he wanted to get some lunch at HOP. Nitro was down so they met Downtown.

"What's going on Kwame? You look stressed my brotha" Nitro said. As he was eating his fries.

"Nothing major. Just wanted to get out of the crib for a little. I haven't been down here in a while. Not since Lucky's closed. Wanted to ask you a question though. On that last heist. Was the youngins running wild? And were they composed after Desmond got hit"? Kwame asked.

"When we were in the car going and coming back. Everybody was focused like always. After Desmond got hit. We were just trying to get back to the city. Get the brotha some help, he was bleeding a lot. The man you might want to ask what happened is Wheels. He was the one in the action. I'm glad he returned fire on that guard's ass too. I'm just glad we all got home in one piece. These guards are brave though. First you pop a guard, and now Wheels. Shit is crazy, but it's apart of the game we're in. and necessary in our line of business right"? Nitro replied.

"Yeah. I guess you could say that. I just hope that guard getting hit doesn't turn out to be bad for us. We didn't need that. Although we both know it was necessary. It may be the end for us and this line of business" Kwame said.

Chapter Five "Things Change"

The summer was in full swing. And like it was said before. Lanc City summers were live. Which made Chill's annual cookout at Franklin Terrace another major event in the city. Much like the

Splash Party. There would be a few grills going, making food for all the guests. Chill himself loved cooking on the grill. But this particular day he would have people cooking for him while he played host. The cookout would be in a few days. The whole crew was all invited and expected to attend. There would also be one of the hottest local DJ's in the city spinning the hottest tunes.

The day before the cookout. Travis was on Green Street at Desmond's house visiting him. Desmond was recovering from a gunshot wound to his shoulder. And had his arm in a sling. Chill's sister was able to help Desmond. And get him stitched up and in a sling. He was sitting in his living room chilling and watching TV. As Travis sat across from him.

"It's hard to believe as long as I've been in these streets, this is the first and only time I've been shot. And the shit didn't even happen in the streets. It happened in a bank. Crazy right? How long have we've known of each other? Since Junior High right"? Desmond said laughing a little.

"Yep. Junior High. And I thought when we first met, that we would be fighting each other everyday. We were both hard-headed little bad ass kids. That wasn't backing down from anyone. And I was still a small ass nigga getting bullied by a few niggas from around the city. But I still had the heart to fight most kids if I had to. Those were the days. And look at us now. Grown men getting money and we run the city now. Nobody in this city is fucking with this crew" Travis replied.

"Obviously we weren't as cool and close to each other as we are now. Up until us becoming apart of the crew together. That's how it was. But I'm glad real recognized real. And we've united and become stronger as one. Nothing but love and respect for you bro, and that's from here on out. For life bro. We're both from the same generation and both were young niggas brought in by older niggas to be apart of this. And we've done it successfully. We've both showed these OG's that we can hang with them. And even though we're wild, we can still keep our composure and focused to get the job done. We can't front. We've learned a lot from these cats. And fattened our pockets in the process. Life is good" Desmond said.

"You have a point bro. You definitely have a point, and I love the money" Travis replied. As they both laughed.

"Word is we didn't reach our goal. We came up short. I think they said we got about $950,000. Nice take, but over a million less than what we were shooting for. But fuck it right. It's all free money. Stack my cut right with the rest of the money I've earned. Either way. Everybody should be straight if they were smart with their money" Desmond said.

"I remember you telling me you had a plan for your money. What you plan on doing with your money"? Travis replied asking. As he sat there.

"I've really been thinking about going to Art School. Maybe try to get a career in Graphic Design for a major company. If or if I don't get my drawings displayed Downtown. I've still been thinking seriously about going to Art School. Maybe travel the World some day. I've never been on a plane before dawg. I'm half tempted to ask you what you're going to do with yours. But you don't seem like the type to have a plan" Desmond said.

"You're right fam. I live in the moment. I definitely want to travel though. West Coast, Miami, New Orleans. And many other places if I can" Travis replied.

"Listen to us. Talking about future plans. Crazy right? Less than a year ago, we were two wild young niggas on different paths. Weren't even as cool as we are now. Shows us just how much we've *learned from the OG's and how much of an influence they've had on us. I know a lot of times we don't listen to the old heads. But at the end of the day, they mean well. They've walked this path before us. I've had a lot of time to think. Being in my house shot with my arm in a sling. Just thinking about how far the crew has come and our futures. I want all of us to make it out of this shit without going to jail or getting killed" Desmond said.*

Meanwhile a few blocks away in Garden Court Housing Projects. Angel was over at her cousin Tisha's house. They were just hanging out. When Angel did something that completely shocked Tisha. She pulled out forty stacks in cash money.

"Oh shit!! Where did you get all that money from"? Tisha asked shocked out of her mind.

"Shhh....chill out. Don't worry about how I got it. It's mines, that's all you need to know. I need you to do me a favor. Stash this here at your house for me. You're the only one I can trust" Angel replied.

"You need to tell me Angel. Because I'm not trying to get my door kicked in for nobody. I need to know cousin" Tisha said.

"You're not going to get your door kicked in Tisha. I promise you that. Just trust me on this, I've never did you dirty. I just need you to keep this here with you. This is some money I'm planning to use for school. I can't tell you everything right now. But at the end of all this, I will. You have my word" Angel replied.

"You're my cousin. You know I got you. Now I see how you had all that money to take us to Miami. I just hope you know what you're doing cousin. Having that kind of money. You couldn't have got it in a positive and legal manner. I would hate to see you go down for some bullshit cousin. Please be careful" Tisha said.

"I plan to. Don't worry Tisha. And I'll break you off some for stashing it for me. Everything is going to be fine cousin" Angel replied. Reassuring her cousin Tisha.   Page 102

And just like that. Angel had stashed some money at her cousin Tisha's house. In case for some strange reason Police would take her in. With her and Erotic being questioned in Stacks and Bags murder investigations. She was being extra safe with her money moving forward. She splurged a little by going on her trip to Miami with her cousin Tisha. And did some nice things for herself. Now was the time to be smart with the money she had. By investing and planning for her future.

After leaving Tisha's apartment, Angel met Erotic at the gun range. They both had been out of action for quite some time. Ever since the authorities had caught onto the two women. Kwame had them on the shelf counting money. But they didn't complain. It was easy money for them. And they loved it. The crew was meant to be interchangeable from day one. That's why it was so hard for authorities to pinpoint who the crew actually were. There were so many members, and their roles changed with each heist. A brilliant idea by Kwame, Wheels, Chill, and Nitro. It took different minds to figure out the different ways the crew could execute each heist. The local Police were still investigating the double homicide that happened a few weeks back. And still had no leads.

Statewide the investigation was heating up into the bank heists. Four bank heists that resulted in over millions of dollars in losses. And two armed guards had been shot. Detective Boyd was still leading the investigation. Him along with other law enforcement officials statewide. Were frustrated that the investigation wasn't running as smoothly as they had hoped. And hadn't got any leads leading to arrests of any suspects. It was frustrating to everyone involved in the investigation. Detective Boyd was far from giving up, it wasn't in his nature when it came to solving cases. He was confident at some point. They could crack the case. Meanwhile the crew were busy living their lives. And being smarter and investing their money. Sensing the end was near.

Rage and his wife had decided on the house that they wanted. For the first time in his life, Rage wouldn't be living on Beaver Street anymore. It would definitely be weird at first and something he'd have to get used to. His family were ready to move onto the next chapter in their lives. Even though they were loved on Beaver Street. They were excited about moving into their new home. They found a beautiful home in Eastern Lancaster County. After finalizing everything. Rage wanted to celebrate with some of his crew members. So he decided to meet a few crew members at one of the many Downtown rooftop bars. Kwame, Wheels, and Chill joined Rage Downtown for a few drinks.

"Toast to my homie Rage's purchase of a new home for his family. Congrats my G. I hope you and your family enjoy your new home. Best of luck to you fam" Kwame said. Holding up his glass to toast with everyone else.

"Thanks to you all for being here on such short notice. My family and I appreciate all the well wishes. Love yall man" Rage replied.

"No doubt bro. We weren't going to miss this for the World. We knew how much this meant to you. It's a big moment in a man's life when a man buys his own home. Right under getting married and having children. It's huge. I plan on buying my own home one day too. And yall remember tomorrow is the cookout. Make sure you all come through" Chill said.

"Thanks Chill. I appreciate it. You know I'll be there bro" Rage replied.

"I can't call you no Lanc City cat anymore dawg. You're going to be out there in the County now. With the rich folk" Wheels said. Laughing as he embraced Rage with a handshake and hug.

"You know better than that. I'm going to be a Lanc City dude for life. Whether I'm living here in the city or not. We may leave the city, but the city never leaves us" Rage replied. As he winked and smiled.

"Of course homie. You know I had to fuck with you bro. We're all happy for you fam. And we all know you'll be right back in the city hanging out like you used to" Wheels said.

"Man. My wife is overjoyed. Already talking about doing interior decorating and all that shit. I'm just going to let her do her thing. As long as I get my Man Cave" Rage replied.

"Hell yeah. You have to have that in the crib fam. Just in case some of the crew wants to come over and watch some football. Or the fight" Kwame said smiling.

"Don't worry fam. I made sure I bought a big enough house to get my Man Cave for sure" Rage replied.

It was a good time amongst the older members of the crew. That had real life goals that they were accomplishing. Of course their plans would defer from the way Travis was thinking. Travis may have been the only member with no clear direction. Or future plans for himself. As he said. "He lived in the moment". Older members like Rage were looking to move away from the city and nicer areas for their families. There was still some heat surrounding the crew. They knew one slip up could be the end for all of them. But somehow they always ended up being two steps ahead of law enforcement. Knowing how to adjust to what they were facing. There were rumors going around locally that the double murder may have been tied to them. But no witnesses with any information ever came forward.

After Stacks and Bags were killed and their pictures were on the front page of the local newspaper. Rage noticed that they looked familiar. Then he thought back. They were the dudes that he seen at POS that night he went to get some chicken. And they were looking at him all crazy. It was all coming back to him now. He had gotten a bad vibe from them both the minute he first saw them. And even though they both looked at him crazy that night. Nothing happened, as all three men went about their business. What could've potentially been bad, ended in nothing at all.

Page 104

With Chill's cookout finally here. He had no idea what to expect as far as the amount of people that would attend. But he anticipated a big turn-out. Being that everything was free like the Splash Party in County Park. It was certainly buzzing around the projects. Franklin Terrace would be the place to be today. Chill planned to have a huge trampoline for the kids.

Meanwhile Desmond was still recovering from a gunshot wound to the shoulder. And laying low out of the public eye. But he does plan on attending today's festivities. He promised Chill he would come through the cookout. His arm was still in a sling. And he really didn't want to answer any questions why. Or draw any attention to himself. He was going to the cookout to be lowkey and lay in the cut. He just wanted to heal from this and move on. He still hadn't heard from any of the Art Galleries Downtown. But he wasn't giving up hope. He wanted to prove society's stereotypes wrong. Him being from one of the most notorious blocks in the city. And him also being the most ambitious of his generation. It was a contrast of sorts. But it was just who he was. Desmond was just trying to make an opportunity for himself. And if he could get through the door. He would hopefully provide an opportunity for others from his neighborhood and surrounding areas. Desmond wanted to inspire others through his gift of Art.

The city was always rich with talent. From great athletes to singers, rappers, cooks, comedians, designers, motivational speakers. Lanc City had it all when it came to talent. That was never a question. The question always was. How ambitious was that person going to be with that talent? And how determined were they to have the passion enough to succeed with that talent. Because having talent is one thing. But having that passion to succeed with it is another thing. Some did it and it worked for them. Others were successful with it for a short time and had nothing but memories when they spoke on it. At the end of the day it was up to each individual. The misconception amongst many in society is that inner city people had no hope and dreams. No ambition. Which was the furthest thing from the truth. Young men like Desmond who had basically been in the streets most of his life. Didn't want that life for himself anymore. All he had was his talent and his dream to inspire. And he would do everything in his power to make it happen.

Something the city was also known for was its destruction of its own. It was a small city of people who were all trying to make a name for themselves. Some in the same areas of life. And not just locally, but nationally and some worldwide. Either way if you did get support from most if not all the city. Be thankful because it didn't happen much. Most people who supported your dreams were people who wanted to see you win and succeed. Genuine people who wanted to see whoever win, because they weren't jealous or envious. And they had their own things going on. There were plenty of people like that in the city, and those people were the ones you wanted to work with. Or wouldn't mind even having a conversation with. Because for the most part you two would be on the same page. Desmond felt like he was meeting people like that here and there each day.

People around the city were pretty much cool with most of the members in the crew. For one. The crew fed and gave back to the community. And that included those that may have been jealous and envious of the crew at one time or another. When it was time to eat and the giveaways. None of that petty shit mattered. People around the city knew the crew was a force to be reckoned with. And they would kill if they had to. They had known shooters apart of their crew. The only people that had a problem with the crew was Stacks and Bags. And we all know what ended up happening to them. And even they didn't really know who they had a problem with at the time. Their main focus was on Travis. The crew had money, enough money to make shit happen if they wanted to. But yet they never imposed their will on the city. Because they didn't have to. Their business was mostly outside of the city, in their line of work. That's why they didn't concern themselves with any shit that didn't involve them locally.

Angel was in her Chester Street home sitting on her bed. After a few minutes. She reached under her mattress and pulled out twenty thousand dollars in cash money. She then put the cash in a handbag and sat it under her bed. She was preparing if she had to get out of town quickly. Angel was still a little paranoid about Detective Boyd questioning her and Erotic. She gave her cousin Tisha forty thousand to stash for her at her house. She suddenly felt like the walls were closing in on her. One thing she didn't want to do was lose her money. And she knew if they found any money on her or at her home. When they decided to come after her. They would keep her money. That's why she stashed some at Tisha's house in Garden Court.

It was the day of the cookout. A beautiful summer day. And Chill was up bright and early as expected. Putting the final touches on the event. Wheels was the first one down to Franklin Terrace helping to set things up. Not long after that, Kwame showed up. Followed by the rest of the crew as other people were filing into the projects. Desmond still with his arm in a sling. And Nitro. The DJ arrived and got set up. As cars pulled up to the main area of the cookout. You could see smoke rising off the grills that were cooking and preparing the food. More residents of the housing projects began coming out of their homes and over towards the cookout. You could hear the DJ on the ones and twos as soon as you entered the projects.

"You got to love this shit Chill. Look at all these people having a good time. And it's still early" Rage said in amazement.

"Yeah man. I love giving back to my community. After all. They do support my business within these project walls. It's only right to give back. Makes me feel good about my hood. Doing this for all these people I've known for so long. It's truly a blessing" Chill replied. Sounding proud.

The cookout was going great as more people were arriving. Kids were playing on the trampoline that Chill had rented for them. There were at least three grills going. And beautiful women were everywhere. Walking around in shorts and short mini-skirts. Looking their best. The men mostly were in wifebeaters and shorts. White tees and shorts. Some with towels over their heads, as it was a hot day. Even still the cookout kept going. And was growing as the day went on.

The DJ kept the crowd moving. They were people dancing in areas surrounding the cookout. And everyone was having a good time. As Chill was getting some ice for a drink. Travis came from behind him, with the same chick he was with at the Splash Party. Spanish woman by the name of Gigi. Who was beautiful from head to toe.

"What's good bro? Nice cookout fam" Travis said. As Chill turned around and greeted him.

"Travis!! Glad you could make it bro. And hello there to your beautiful friend. Everybody is having a good time. That's all that matters to me" Chill replied.

"Yeah. This is Gigi Chill. Gigi this is my homie Chill. You remember him from the Splash Party" Travis said. Introducing the two.

The beautiful woman greeted Chill and then she went over to get herself something to eat. There was a woman she knew that was over by where the food was being served. Travis stayed over and continued talking to Chill.

"I see you're showing up to more functions with shorty. I can't blame you though. She's bad as shit dawg. You two serious now"? Chill asked smiling.

"When we're together, we're together. When we're not, we're not. That's the best way to explain it fam. She loves a nigga's swag, but she also loves money. And niggas who got money. We have a good time together. And right now. That's all I'm looking for" Travis said.

"What's your future plans for you, when all this shit is over? I hope by now you have some kind of plans" Chill replied asking.

"I told all of you to stop worrying about me man. I'm good. I don't know where my life is going to take me. Wherever it does, I'll be good there too" Travis said.

"Travis!! What's good youngin? How you? Chill what's good bro"? Wheels said. Coming over to where Chill and Travis were standing.

"The big homie and Lime Street's finest. Wheels is in the building!! I'm good homie, just trying to enjoy this cookout like everybody else" Travis replied.

Angel and Erotic had arrived. Along with Angel's cousin Tisha. You could tell all three of them had been shopping. And they all looked great as they came into the main area of the cookout. Angel had some Gucci shades on along with a very nice outfit. Erotic had some tight jean shorts on with some very nice shoes. Tisha had on a sundress. Heads definitely turned when they arrived at the cookout. Chino came through. And was standing over near where most of the crew were. Also at the cookout unbeknownst to most of the crew at first. And amongst the crowd was Detective Boyd. He was mingling with the rest of the people there. As if he was apart of the community too. The only people that knew what he looked like was Angel and Erotic. Chill noticed him first. That he seemed out of place within the crowd. He knew him also. From investigating his cousin's murder in Harrisburg years ago.   Page 107

Nitro, Rage, and Kwame were standing over in the same area and talking. Enjoying some cold drinks on a hot summer day.

"I got some shit going on out in Arizona. Invested some money out there on a venture. Hoping for a big return" Nitro said. Taking a sip of his drink.

"You hear this nigga man? Sounding like he on Wall Street or some shit. That's good to know you're being smart with your money. That's what we preach to others. But you know I had to fuck with you" Kwame replied laughing.

"Yeah. I hear Nitro the financial wiz at work" Rage said smiling.

"No bullshit. I might fly out in a few days. If it's about the money I'm there" Nitro replied.

"As you should be. You know they're still investigating those heists right"? Kwame asked.

Just then. Angel came over to where they were standing and whispered something into Kwame's ear and then walked off.

"That Detective is here. This muthafucka actually came to Chill's cookout" Kwame said in somewhat shock.

"To answer your question Kwame. I know they're investigating them. But they don't have shit on us. Why should we be worried about a Detective anyway? This is a community event. He can't do shit" Nitro replied.

Rage just stared over towards where Detective Boyd was standing. As he was eating a burger and talking to a few people enjoying the cookout.

"It's nothing that some misguided direction can't handle. I don't see how he would have proof we did anything" Rage said.

"He doesn't have shit on us. But him showing up here in our environment around our people can't be good. This dude is sniffing around us for a reason dawg. And what do you have in mind Rage"? Kwame asked sounding curious.

"Lead his ass on a wild goose chase. All around the city. Make him think he's onto something. The hood got us all day. He won't get shit from them" Rage replied.

"Oh no doubt. That may just work" Kwame said.

Meanwhile. Desmond and Travis were playing with the kids. They both had water guns having water gun fights with the many kids that were in attendance. The kids had fun chasing them too. As they were people everywhere. At this point. You would be lucky to get in Franklin Terrace. As it was crowded with people from all over the city. Everyone was having a good time, much like they did at the Splash Party in County Park. Yet another positive event for the community organized and funded by a member of LANCREW. Page 108

Angel's cousin Tisha was around the crew at each event they had. So much so that people started to wonder if she was apart of what they were doing. But she wasn't. And she didn't ask any questions about what they were doing. She just enjoyed the moments she was around them all. Tisha was well taken care of by her cousin Angel anyway. Angel always made sure Tisha was good. And vice versa. While the crew were all standing near each other. Some of them started taking pictures. Something that Kwame was somewhat cautious about after being notified that Detective Boyd was at the cookout. He didn't want attention drawn to them to tip the Detective off to who they were.

There was a local professional photographer on hand to capture all the moments from the cookout. Chill had put together a very nice event for the people in Franklin Terrace. And they all appreciated the event. Chill was always loved and respected in those projects. That's because he showed the same. He made his fair share of mistakes like any man has in his life. But he did what he could for his people. And showed love. This wasn't his first cookout at Franklin Terrace aka Almanac to most city residents. But it was his biggest cookout. And the biggest turnout he's had ever. People were really enjoying themselves.

The cookout had whined down. And Chill was in front of his house on his front step. Desmond, Nitro, Travis, and Wheels were all standing in front of Chill's house with him. The rest of the crew had left. Travis was still there with his lady friend Gigi. But they were about to leave themselves.

"Chill I loved the cookout bro. Appreciate everything fam. Me and shorty are out. I'll holla" Travis said. As he and his lady left.

"No doubt bro. Thanks for coming. You two be safe" Chill replied.

Travis and Gigi then got in her car and left. Little did they both know. They were being followed. Followed by Detective Boyd. Who left the cookout early and waited in his car. For the first person he thought looked familiar from that crew. Which was the crew standing all together. Detective Boyd really didn't know exactly who he was following. He was just hoping that Travis and Gigi would lead him to something or someone. Who may be able to help him with the investigation. Travis was a little drunk, after drinking most of the day. He had his passenger seat almost all the way back. As Gigi drove through Lanc City streets. They finally made their way back to the Howard Avenue side of Hill Rise where Travis resides.

Detective Boyd watched them park as he rode by and went about his way. Disappointed that they really didn't lead him to anything. Detective Boyd had already questioned Angel and Erotic about the double murder of the men they were both seeing. They both had no clue who killed them. And now the Detective had spotted Travis at the cookout amongst the crew. And figured he was apart of the group. Travis was now on his radar as a fresh face of interest to the Detective. He didn't know who Travis was at the time. But he had thought he overheard someone at the cookout mention Travis name. And looked over in the direction at the man he had followed from the cookout. So he was pretty sure the man they were talking about and the man he had followed was the same man. Travis. Page 109

Angel and Erotic's story checked out. The bartender Down Bottom confirmed their story of who was with them that night. And Travis wasn't one of them. And that fact alone had Travis on Detective Boyd's radar. But there was no murder weapon found. And no trace of it anywhere.

Kwame was at his Ann Street home looking over some papers about real estate classes. He had talked to Nitro and Chill about investing more of his money into it. He wanted to get his real estate license. One of the masterminds behind what would be known as LANCREW. Was looking towards his future and wearing a new hat so to speak. The balance in the crew is what made it so unique. The older members who were investing money in their futures on different things. And a few of the younger members who were still trying to figure things out. In the end. They all helped each other *grow throughout their experiences together. It was all about respect and discipline.*

Detective Boyd was onto Travis. But he knew he couldn't just go up and question Travis. That wasn't going to work. So he was going to do the next best thing. Question the woman he seen Travis leave with. The one he followed to Travis house in Hill Rise. Detective Boyd watched from a far at Chill's cookout. Watching Travis and Gigi before they left. He was watching how they interacted with each to tell just how close they really were. The traits of a Detective. The Detective did a good job of blending in with the many people who attended the cookout that day. He knew if she knew Travis well. She knew things about him that could possibly help the Detective with his case. He just had to wait until she was alone. And once she was alone. Hoping she would talk to him. Which wasn't going to be easy.

Meanwhile. Moving day was approaching for Rage and his family. And the last three days. Rage has been soaking up everything that was of his block he called home for so many years. Knowing he could always come back. But not living on the block wouldn't be the same. He was onto a new journey now. Him and his family. He finished his cigarette outside and looked up and down the block. One more time before he went back inside and started moving things.

Wheels had saved a lot of money over the years. And was soon hoping to take over Mr. Cee's corner store. He felt good that he would be taking over the corner store he used to frequent a lot with his friends as a young kid. As well as a teen. Young man and now a grown man. He couldn't just let anybody take over the store. Knowing how much it meant to the community. Wheels wanted to take on the responsibility of carrying on the legacy. The legacy of a man who meant a lot to him and watched him grow from a child to a man. Wheels made one of his usual visits to Lime and Dauphin to see Mr. Cee.

"Hey. Mr. Cee. What's going on"? Wheels said. Coming into the store.

"Hey young man. I'm doing ok. How have you've been"? Mr. Cee replied.

"I'm good. Just came to check up on you. I also came to tell you. I can give you some money up front for the sale of the store. Cash money. And before you ask Mr. Cee. It is legit money. Nothing illegal. I've saved for years to do something big in my life. And this is it for me" Wheels said.

"I'm glad I could help you do it. And it's great timing because I'm getting to that point where I'm ready to step down and retire. Enjoy the rest of my life with my family. My wife and kids. It's been a great ride serving this block this community. And the city as a whole" Mr. Cee replied.

"And we appreciate you Mr. Cee. I appreciate you. I'm sure you're going to miss this place. It's been apart of your life for so long. Honestly I'm just honored to carry on the legacy" Wheels said smiling.

"Yeah. I'm sure I'll miss it some days. But things change son. As you get older your mindset changes. About everything in life. I'm really going to enjoy spending time with my wife as senior citizens. We always talked about growing old together. After the children were up and out of the house. We were going to enjoy the rest of our lives together. She's waited on me a few years now, to retire. I've kept putting it off and kept running the store. I was really holding off also. Wanting to sell it to someone that would keep it here. In the same community it's served for decades. And here comes you. Out of nowhere. Someone I've known and seen grow up. And knows what this store stands for. I didn't want them tearing it down. To be apart of the gentrification that is soon to come to this area in the future. I'm glad that you'll be taking over" Mr. Cee replied.

"Thanks Mr. Cee. That means a lot to me. Like I told you before, I promise you it's in good hand" Wheels said.

"I believe that son" Mr. Cee replied. As the two men shook hands before Wheels left.

Wheels would hire someone to work in the store on a daily basis. He wasn't planning on being there everyday all day. But he would be hands on with the daily operations. He had other things going on with him selling cars. Buying them and having his partner fix them up and re-sale them. When he takes over the store. He actually believes life will slow down for him a little. Because he planned to be at the store daily.

The crew had split the money from an earlier heist. Each getting $85,000. By this time they all had plenty of money. And did their best to invest, to in a sense hide it. And still make a profit. That was the original plan. Yeah. Buy yourself and your family some nice shit and give back to your community. And the rest invest. Most of them did just that. Nitro's birthday was coming up. And he planned a huge party Downtown at the Convention Center. Renting out one of their ballrooms. Everyone from Pershing Ave to Locust Street to Howard Ave were in attendance. As well as the crew were planning to attend. A day prior and before the party at the CC. Travis and Desmond made a trip to A.C.

To do a little gambling and partying. The two were still very young guys with a lot of money. Desmond's shoulder had healed. And his arm was out of the sling. From the gunshot wound. He wanted to get out. Out of Lanc City. After being pretty much in the house the last few weeks. Letting his wound heal. He was happy to get away. And come back to the city tomorrow night and celebrate Nitro's birthday. It would be an eventful weekend for sure.

Besides buying a brand new motorcycle. Travis bought himself a new car also. A 2018 Nissan Maxima. Black with tricked out rims. And he wasted no time putting it on the road. He had just got the car hours before him and Desmond made the trip to Atlantic City. Once they got down there. They gambled, they drank, and had about four women in their penthouse suite. High a top the Atlantic City skyline. They were both drinking Louie.

Back in Lanc City. Detective Boyd was still working hard on his cases. Working locally Downtown at Police headquarters. Since early that day. He'd been tailing Gigi. He was following her and she didn't even know it. All over the city. From Orange Street to Reynolds Avenue to Prince Street. All the way back to South Christian Street. Where she parked her car and went in a house. Detective Boyd pulled up a little further and parked. He waited there looking through his sideview and rearview mirrors. Trying to see what he could. After sitting there for about twenty minutes. Gigi reappeared. Coming out of the house and getting in her car. The Detective then started his car and proceeded to follow her.

He wasn't too far behind her when he decided to stop her. He had a feeling she had something on her. But he really had no probable cause to stop her. But then again. He was apart of law enforcement. Not having probable cause has never stopped law enforcement from stopping someone. Needless to say. Detective Boyd decided he was going to stop Gigi anyway. He stopped her on South Duke and Chesapeake Streets. Gigi was driving a Lexus. And from the very start, Detective Boyd tried to scare Gigi into giving him information. At first it didn't work, until he told her that he had been following her. And saw her go and out of a house. And he suspected she had drugs in the car. That's when Gigi agreed to go Downtown for questioning. With one condition. She would come with her lawyer.

While this was going on. Travis and Desmond were still in Atlantic City having the time of their lives.

After arriving Downtown for questioning. Gigi was taken to the back room. Once they all entered. She sat at a table next to her lawyer and across from Detective Boyd. And the questioning began.

"Your name is Gigi"? Detective Boyd asked.

"My name is Gina. My nickname is Gigi" Gigi replied.

"Ok Gigi. I have you down here to ask you a few questions. About a few cases. First off. Did you know two guys that went by the street names Stacks and Bags? Are you familiar with those two gentlemen"? Detective Boyd asked.

"No. I didn't know them, but I did know of them. I saw them around the city from time to time. A lot of people knew them. They were here for a while" Gigi replied.

"Did you know they had problems with your male friend Travis"? Detective Boyd asked.

"No. I had no knowledge of that. Whatever beef Travis had with anyone, was none of my concern. We're only friends. He never discussed any of that with me" Gigi replied.

"Come on Gigi!! You're in the streets, you know what's really going on don't you? Don't try and play me by lying!!! That is if you want to stay on the streets, and not go away. For what's in your car right now. Cut the bullshit and tell me the truth"!! Detective Boyd said. Sounding frustrated.

"I'm telling you the truth" Gigi said. With a straight face looking directly at Detective Boyd.

"Ok. Ok....cool. How about. Do you know anything about a bank heist crew from this area? Or at all"? Detective Boyd asked.

"No. I don't. I've never even heard of a bank heist crew" Gigi replied.

"I guess you want to do this time then. For the product you had in the car that day? Because you aren't giving me anything here. Looks like these charges will keep you behind bars for five to ten years. Are you built to do that much time Gigi"? Detective Boyd asked.

"I told you what I know sir. I don't know what else you want me to tell you. Travis and I are friends. And he never discussed anything with me about his personal life or business. He never did" Gigi replied.

The detective was getting more and more frustrated by the minute with his case. Gigi stuck to her story of not knowing anything about the double murder. Or the bank heists. She made a pick up for her cousin. Not Travis. Gigi hustled for her cousin and Detective Boyd was tailing her when she made the pick up.

"The night of the murders. Where were you"? Detective Boyd asked.

"I was at Travis apartment in Hill Rise. We were together after the Splash Party in County Park. We were together the whole night" Gigi replied.

Once again. The detective was stuck. In both cases. The frustration was apparent and mounting. As Detective Boyd didn't know what his next move was going to be. He got the information he already had from a street informant. Being that the streets talk. There were rumors going around about the double murder. And who may have committed the brutal murder on the corner of South Duke and Church Streets.

The street informant that Detective Boyd had, knew members of the crew. And had caught a charge himself. And was doing everything in his power to find as much information about the crew as possible. Overall within the city. Different members were cool with different people, as expected. They all were from Lanc City. And all knew a lot of people from the city. As a whole the crew was pretty much cool with most people. But like anyone or anything that was successful. There was jealousy and envy. The crew was getting real money.   Page 113

And no one had the money they had. Or the muscle they had. Regardless of all that, they still had haters that wanted to see them fall. Anything that was done to the crew by anyone was done indirectly. Hoping to catch one of them slipping. Or like the informant, trying to take them down by ratting them out. Most of the information that was provided was about the double murder. The streets were talking. And Travis was the name mentioned most times. As much the crew gave back to the city and its people. Some people didn't care and wanted them to fall regardless.

Either way. The informant was getting information in the streets and any other place he could. After another successful event at Franklin Terrace. The crew were getting ready for Nitro's party Downtown at the Convention Center. It was going to be a big party. Nitro was expecting over 200 people at the party. Some family coming as far as Chicago. It was Nitro's party and an invite only affair. Wasn't open to the general public. And the party was a day away.

On Ann Street. Kwame was home talking to a real estate agent about showing a property he was investing in. Kwame was new in the real estate game. It was a different challenge than drawing up plans to pull a bank heist. But that was just it, it was a challenge.

And Kwame was loving every minute of it. Learning the real estate game had his interest more than anything. More importantly. It was another avenue for him to make money. Everything was going according to plan as far as the crew was concerned. And Kwame was growing his portfolio.

Erotic was always a gifted hairdresser. And just as gifted at boosting, something she had been doing for quite some time. Before linking up with the crew. She was making enough money now that she didn't have to boost ever again. She was making way more money now than she ever could boosting. She had money and was looking to invest. And invest in something that she loved, something she could call her own. She had seen a place on West Chestnut Street. Which was right off of Downtown. Prime real estate to most in the business world locally. Erotic wasted no time in going to see the place. She took Angel with her. As they entered the place, they liked it right away.

"This is nice E. Real nice. Still walking distance from the hood too. And you're basically Downtown. So you can appeal to the business crowd as well. Good location" Angel said. As they both looked around the place.

"It is nice. And I like the spacing in here. I can have my sinks right here washing hair. Another one here. Maybe a barber chair here. And the receptionist desk right here" Erotic replied.

After seeing the place is when she started to feel the excitement of wanting to own it. She would really be the owner of her own Hair Salon. Something she had dreamed of, but never thought would come true. Because she didn't have the finances to own her own shop. Erotic was now in a position to do just that. And she had every intention to take advantage of the opportunity, after seeing the place. She would have to hire a staff. Which wouldn't be a problem because she knew plenty of women around the city. That were talented enough at doing hair and nails. She would most certainly give those women an opportunity to work for her at her Salon.

Page 114

"You really think I should take it"? Erotic asked Angel.

"Hell yeah girl. This is your dream. You have to take your shot when you get it" Angel replied.

"Girl you know I'm taking it. I was just playing. Ayyyeee"!!! Erotic said. As they started dancing around the shop.

Erotic then went and delivered the news to the seller. It was another big moment for a crew member. And a clever move to hide and invest her money she had made in the bank heists. Money tied up where no one could trace it. They were all making moves. It was important for their livelihood being that they could be out of the game. They wanted to survive off their grind. And they all individually wanted to do it their own way. This was just another example of it. Erotic and Angel planned to celebrate.

"We have to turn up tonight girl. You got your shop now, and shit is on"!! Angel said.

"Yes!! We're definitely popping bottles tonight. I'm inviting the rest of the crew" Erotic replied.

"Why not. I'm sure they will come out and support. Maybe one of the downtown bars. If that sounds good to you. It's your night" Angel said.

"Sounds good to me. Let's do it. Downtown it is" Erotic replied.

Later that night. Erotic, Angel, and Angel's cousin Tisha. Went out on the town to celebrate Erotic's big news of finally getting her Hair Salon. They all went bar hopping through Downtown Lanc City. Starting on Queen Street then Prince and then King. While they were

Downtown. They got a call from Travis and Desmond. And they would eventually join them Downtown.

"Congrats E. What's good Angel? Tisha"? Desmond said as he and Travis walked in a Downtown bar.

"Congrats E. Happy for you" Travis added as he walked in behind Desmond.

"Thanks. I was hoping some of the crew would come through. I appreciate you two for being here. Can I get another two rounds for these gentlemen over here" Erotic replied talking to the bartender.

That was all of the crew that showed up that night. Most of them were gearing up for Nitro's party the next night. At the Convention Center Downtown. Erotic understood why most of the crew couldn't make it out on short notice. So the five of them sat at a table and had a great time celebrating Erotic's big accomplishment. After that they went to another bar and did the same thing. As they sat there at another bar. Erotic had a conversation with Desmond.

"Are you going to have some barbers in your shop E"? Desmond asked.

"I definitely plan to. I mean in the beginning I want to be hands on and be a presence at the shop early and often. ButUntil I get things rolling.   Page 115

Hire some more people. I know there's a lot of young talented barbers in the city. And I'm willing to give them a shot if they want it. Then I can fallback and watch my business grow. That's the plan" Erotic replied.

"Shit. It's good you have a plan. I'm sure your Hair Salon will be a success. I've seen your skills on some of the chicks I dated. So I know you're nice with it" Desmond said smiling.

"Thanks Desmond. Damn I'm drunk as shit. But enjoying myself with my people" Erotic said struggling to get up. Before sitting back down.

"Just chill E. Let them drinks settle. We got you. We aren't going anywhere" Desmond said. As he laughed a little.

"She good? You good E? Travis asked coming back over towards their table.

"Dawg she is fucked up. But we got her. Don't worry" Desmond replied. Getting Erotic to her feet. As Angel and Tisha helped.

They all got in two cars and took Erotic back to her Rockland Street home. It was a fun night for all five people. And Erotic really got it in. Celebrating the accomplishment of owning her own shop.

Meanwhile Nitro was gearing up for his big birthday bash that was planned for this evening at the Downtown Convention Center. Nitro spared no expense paying for the big party. It was a major event and the guest list was invitation only. That guest list ranged from local Lanc City people. To people from Philly, Harrisburg, York, and even as far as Chicago. That all knew Nitro and were coming to help him celebrate. Nitro had connections with a lot of people, some through the real estate game. And some of his real estate associates would be in attendance also. And of course the whole crew were planning to attend.

Detective Boyd was still hard at work trying to build a case of some sort against people he suspected were involved in the double homicide. And that could be tied to a member of a local bank heist crew. He had little evidence, but he wasn't giving up. That wasn't an option to him. He stayed within the city. After hearing about a local beef that may have been connected to the double murder. Detective Boyd even showed up at Chill's cookout over in Franklin Terrace. Trying to hide himself within the crowd of residents of the city.

He was becoming bold and fearless in his pursuit of solving the case. But he had to be careful. Because Erotic and Angel made him out at Chill's cookout. They remembered him from being questioned by him Downtown at Police Headquarters about Stacks and Bags murder. The crew were definitely aware of the detective sniffing around. They were onto him like he was onto them. The crew was always a few steps ahead of law enforcement. They didn't have to worry about the detective being at Nitro's party. It was an invite only party.

Downtown Lanc City would never be the same after this night. It was the night of the biggest birthday bash the city has ever seen. The night would be ruled by Nitro and the crew. Guests arrived early at the Convention Center. And some were waiting in the Convention Center lobby. Some of them were waiting for Nitro's grand entrance. He would arrive to the party in a rented black Rolls Royce Phantom. Accompanied by a date. Which was a beautiful brown skin woman, who looked flawless as she stepped out the vehicle. Nitro's people from Pershing Avenue were also in attendance at the party.

The dance floor was packed with people. Beautiful women and guys in their best shit. Just enjoying the party. Two local DJ's were on the ones and twos for the night. And the V.I.P. area was occupied by Nitro and his closest friends. Bottles being popped all through V.I.P. The hood made it Downtown. And had the city lit for an epic night to remember.

Kwame stepped up to the mic on the DJ set. And announced a toast to Nitro for his birthday. Above anything and like always it was a drama free event. And everyone was having a great time as usual. Nitro, Kwame, Desmond, and Wheels. Were all in the same area talking.

"This party is live bro. And packed like sardines in this bitch. And you deserve it all bro. Happy Birthday my G" Desmond said. Shaking Nitro's hand.

"Hell yeah. This shit is live in here fam. Happy Birthday bro" Wheels said. As the music was bumping. And the many people on the dancefloor as he watched holding a drink in his hand.

"Thanks fellas. And thanks for coming through to help me celebrate. I wanted to do this shit big. You never know how many of these you have left" Nitro replied.

"Word" Kwame said. As he finished off a bottle.

Travis and Chill were on the other side of the party mingling with the rest of the guests. When they both stepped aside and chopped it up.

"You still rocking with that Spanish chick Gigi Travis"? Chill asked.

"If you want to call it that. We're cool. Why"? Travis replied.

"I just asked. No particular reason" Chill said.

"We have that on again off again thing going on. She's a good woman. Loyal to a nigga till the end. If it was anybody. I think about riding with me on some ride or die shit, she would be the one. But you know this life we live and how we live fast on these streets. I never know when I have to just haul ass out of town. And leave this bitch at a drop of a dime. And I know if I wanted her to go with me, she would. But then I also think. I don't want to destroy shorty's life. I care about her as a person because she's just good peoples. And like I said. She's loyal to me and she knows I can't stay faithful" Travis replied.

"Spoken like a true young man. I can see where your mind state is. Because nigga I been there. All that will change as you get older. But *for your sake I hope it's not too late. And trust me youngin. I'm not here to preach to you. I'm saying what I'm saying because I got love for you. Now they're plenty of fine ass women in here right now. The best in the city is out tonight for sure. But how many of them loyal to you like her? Me. Nigga I'm here with my lady of the last six years. We go through our shit, but nobody got my back like she does. And this I know. Some food for thought" Chill said. As he took a sip of his drink.*

"Yeah. I think about that too. I really do. But at this point I don't know what I'm going to do. Despite her being who she is, and me caring about her. I'm willing to take that chance. Because I'm going to live my life" Travis replied.

Chill knew Travis was the only one in the crew with a lot of money and no real direction in life. He was just living in the moment. That was Travis all of his life. Since he was growing up, he was steady trying to prove himself. He was young with a lot of money and a compulsive violent temper. That had already led to murder. The older members in the crew always kept an eye on Travis. And tried to guide him in the right direction within his life. But Travis being Travis rarely listened to anyone. But it didn't stop them from filling his head with knowledge that could help him in his life.

Meanwhile the next day. Gigi had been laying low after being questioned by Detective Boyd. The always loud and boisterous Latina was now falling back. And hadn't been seen for days in the streets. After she was pulled over and cocaine was found in her car. Cocaine that she was carrying for someone else. Detective Boyd was trying to put the squeeze on her for information about Travis. An associate of hers that was suspected of killing two men in the city. She had pretty much planted herself in her home. Nervous and paranoid, she hadn't spoken to Travis in days. But she knew at some point she had to. And little did she know, it would be sooner than she thought.

As she was watching TV in her living room at her home in the Clairemont Homes. She heard a motorcycle pull up. And she knew it was Travis. And it was him. It was still Summer. And Gigi had her door opened and her screen door locked. As she seen him walk up and knock on her door.

"Gigi. What's good Ma? Where you been"? Travis asked. As he came into her house.

She answered the door in some skin tight shorts that exposed her nice thick ass. And proceeded to give Travis a hug as he walked in.

"I've just been chilling. Laying low. And I have something to tell you" Gigi said. Before being interrupted by Travis.

"And why have you've been laying low? What's good Gigi"? Travis asked.

Gigi just paused for a moment and looked at Travis.

"I got bagged the other day for handling some shit for my cousin. They're trying to put me away for a while Travis" Gigi replied. Sounding upset.   Page 118

"What's the catch? They want you to give somebody up right? Who the fuck do they want Gigi"? Travis asked.

"The detective was asking about that double murder on South Duke and Church. And he asked if I knew anything about a bank heist crew" Gigi replied.

"And what did you tell him? And who the fuck is this detective"? Travis asked.

"A Detective Boyd" Gigi said. As she pulled out his card.

"That's the fucking detective that was at Chill's cookout. This muthafucka is becoming a problem. Being where we be at and shit. I need to get somebody on his ass. Because someone has been telling him where we be at. You sure you didn't say anything"? Travis asked.

"No. Travis I told you what he asked and I didn't say anything. But these muthafuckas are talking about locking me up for a long time!! I have to do something"!! Gigi said sounding concerned.

"I'll take your word for it until you show me different. Come on lets take a ride on the bike" Travis replied.

"No. Travis I'm good" Gigi said. Declining his offer.

"Listen!!! We'll take a ride on the bike. Just a quick ride. Then you can come back and chill. And I'll even buy you dinner. Come on. You know you love riding the bike with me. Let that pretty hair blow in the wind. Let's go let's do it"!! Travis replied.

"Ok Travis. Let's go" Gigi said. As they both got up and went outside and got on Travis bike. Then sped off.

After getting on the bike and speeding off. Travis with Gigi holding on tight behind him. Sped through Lanc City streets. At times at high rates of speeds. Travis always liked to ride his bike fast. In and out of traffic through Downtown. Then through the 8th Ward then going through the 6th and 7th Ward. Before returning to Gigi's place. They rode through the city on a nice hot summer day as the streets were packed. Lanc City summers. Everyone is out. Gigi was glad she had finally told Travis about the detective. It was weighing on her mind heavy. The last thing she wanted was to lose her loyalty to Travis. Or make him think for a second that he couldn't trust her. She knew why he took her for a ride on that bike. At high rates of speeds and reckless at times. To show her how much he had her life in his hands. At that very moment.

On Lime Street. Wheels was out in front of his house hand washing his BMW himself. Instead of getting it detailed or having some of the youngins cleaning it for him. He decided to clean it himself for *once. The neighborhood kids loved to see him wash his cars. It became a legend on the block. Wheels washing his cars. Here comes all the neighborhood kids to watch him. Whenever you came down Lime Street on a hot summer day. You were sure to see Wheels washing one of his cars.*   *Page 119*

As Wheels was outside washing his ride. Coming down Lime Street was a jet black Benz. And of course it was Kwame. He pulled over and parked.

"What's good OG"? Kwame asked as he got out of his Benz.

"Aint shit. just got done getting the whip right. What's good with you playboy? Might step out tonight" Wheels replied.

"Just riding through. I knew it was going to be nice out and figured you'd be out cleaning the cars. I know we said we were out of the game for now. But I've been thinking about getting a few crew members together for one last go round. I want some more money" Kwame said looking directly at Wheels.

"As hot as shit is right now, and you're talking about going at another bank? Nigga you're bugging. We all have enough money. That Detective Boyd has been sniffing around us dawg. He was at Chill's cookout remember? I was talking to Travis the other day. He said that dude was talking to his girl Gigi. Asking about them out of town niggas getting hit. And a bank heist crew" Wheels replied.

"I thought we were past all that bullshit man. People still speculating that murder was us? They have no proof that any of us committed that murder. And as far as bank heists. They don't have shit on us with that either. I'm not giving up on hitting another bank" Kwame said.

"I think I'm sitting this one out. I'm about to get this store. And I got plenty of doe. I'm good" Wheels replied.

"True indeed. And I'm proud of you too fam. It's cool. I just wanted to put that out there in case you were down" Kwame said.

"Thanks fam. Yeah I'm good" Wheels replied.

That was the one thing about them two since they became friends. They were always able to have a conversation and talk about things. Man to man. Even when they disagreed with each other. In this instance. Kwame had an idea of one last heist. While Wheels was content with the work they've already done. And the money they've already made. They were all supposed to be out of the game. And focusing on the next phase of their lives. Which was investing their money into their futures. To become real bosses in some form or fashion. Word on the streets were the crew was tied to Stacks and Bags murders. But it was all speculation at this point. And the crew weren't tripping because they knew local law enforcement didn't have any proof.

Things had changed as time went on. If by some chance law enforcement got any evidence on the crew for the double murder or the bank heists. Like Travis said. Any of them would have to be able to get the hell out of dodge at any given time. And they all would be fighting for their lives. But then again. The chance of that happening was slim.   Page 120

Local authorities were still trying to piece together what happened the night of the double murder. Authorities believed that the shots were fired from the direction of the bushes. Whoever it was, came from out of the bushes and fired the fatal shots into Stacks truck. Killing him and Bags almost instantly. And then fleeing on foot. Cameras that were all over the city didn't catch the murder in progress. But did show the truck rolling towards the concrete that divided the intersection at Duke and Church Streets. After the fatal shots were fired. And of course no one in the surrounding areas seen anything. It was very early in the morning. Around 3 am when the murder occurred. The murder weapon was a 45 caliber handgun.

Desmond decided to pay his homie Travis a visit. It had been a little while since they hung out. Just them two. After arriving at Travis apartment. The two youngins sat down in Travis living room and watched TV on his 65' TV. Travis had a bottle in the fridge he brought out. And the two sat and chopped it up.

"So. What's good Travis"? Desmond asked. As he watched Travis poor them both a glass.

"Chilling bro. Just staying out the way. Gigi got bagged on a coke charge. Doing some shit for her cousin. They took her ass Downtown and questioned her. Asking about that double murder and the bank heists" Travis replied.

"Well your girl didn't say shit. Did she? And why the fuck they think there's a bank heist crew here anyway? Who told them"? Desmond asked.

"No nigga. Gigi is straight, she's a rider. She's not going to say shit. But she is bugging about going away for a while on that coke charge. I wish there was something I could do to get her out of that shit. I can't even go to her crib anymore like I want to. Because I know they're watching her ass. I have to keep my distance from her. But I do have to be real with you my nigga. That double murder was me. I had problems with them niggas for a while. And after they robbed the warehouse, I had to get them. They were becoming more and more of a problem. And that shit was spilling into the crew. And I couldn't have that" Travis said. Looking Desmond right in his eyes.

Desmond was a little shocked at first upon hearing that Travis had murdered Stacks and Bags. But at the same time he wasn't. Because in the back of his mind. He had thought that maybe his boy had did the deed. But he didn't want to believe it, until he actually heard it *out of his own mouth. And now he had confirmation. That Travis had now murdered three people. He knew Travis was capable of doing anything at any given time. He was wild and young. Had money and a crazy violent compulsive temper. And he had history and beef with Stacks and Bags like Desmond did. Once Desmond found out what the murder weapon was. A 45 caliber handgun. He knew Travis owned one. It all came together.*

"That's crazy Travis. If that's what you felt you had to do. You know I'm going to ride with you. And you know that secret is safe with me bro. You know there wasn't any love lost between me and them cats either" Desmond said.

"I just know I'm not trying to go to jail. Gigi told me that the detective mentioned my name. She said he was following us. That's how he knew me and her were close. Gigi don't really know shit anyway. I didn't tell her I got them niggas. I just slipped out of the crib while she was sleep and did that. I watched them niggas drive down South Duke and stop at the light. I had my chance and I took it. You know I always got that thing on me. I hid behind them bushes in front of the towers and got in position. Then popped off. I got good aim too, because I hit both of them and killed them. I made sure nobody was around or out on the street to see anything. Them niggas never seen it coming. Which was crazy because they were in my hood" Travis replied laughing.

Desmond just shook his head and didn't say much at all. He was still in disbelief that Travis was telling him this. Travis hadn't even told him about the first murder he committed. Him providing the details of the double murder was shocking to Desmond. Him and Travis had a close relationship after being apart of the crew together. And Travis trusted Desmond. Which said a lot, because Travis trusted very few people. They related to each other more than anyone in the crew. Because they were both young. Travis saying he wasn't going to jail meant a few things. If law enforcement ever caught up to him, he wasn't going down without a fight. Or it could've meant he was taking his own life. Before he would ever surrender.

Desmond remained over at Travis house for another fifteen minutes. Just chopping it up and finishing the bottle they started. On Chester Street Angel was sitting on her bed. Waiting on her cousin Tisha to come over. So she could help her pick out her future path to college. And into a potential career. Tisha had finally arrived at Angel's house after walking from Garden Court Apartments down the street.

"Hey cousin. Sorry I'm late. I was talking to this dude I've been seeing. And yes, I've still been focused on helping you put this plan together. Don't worry" Tisha said. Coming in the house.

"Girl. I knew you would be late when you told me you were talking to him earlier. It's cool" Angel replied.

"Anyway. I know you said not to bring it up again. But what do you want me to do with those forty stacks you gave me"? Tisha asked.

"Just hold onto it for me a little longer. I'll have plans for it soon" Angel replied.

"Girl. I hate to get into...." Tisha said. Before being interrupted by Angel.

"Don't Tisha. Like I told you, it's my money. How I got it doesn't matter. Its mines and I'm going to make great use of it. Just trust me. And trust that I got this" Angel replied.

"Cousin I do trust you. I just worry about you. I've never seen that much money in my life. And for you to have it. It scares me a little" Tisha said.   Page 122

"Tisha I'm good. And you know if I have any problems. A sista stay at the range. These people aint stupid. Nobody bothers me. And I wouldn't get myself into some shit I couldn't handle. I got this cousin" Angel replied.

"I know you can handle yourself. But I'm going to worry about family regardless. I hear you though. You're good. So I'll heed to your words" Tisha said.

"Ok. Now we can get down to this college situation. I've been really thinking about Temple. Good school and not too far from home" Angel said.

"You don't want to leave Lancaster do you? Girl you better branch out and see the world. There's more out there besides this city" Tisha said.

"I know that Tisha. But so much of my life is here and tied to this city. But who knows where I'll be in the future. We shall see" Angel replied.

The two women were very close. Cousins but more like sisters in a sense. Still Angel never told Tisha how she got the money. She was sworn by oath, not to discuss crew business with anyone. Except crew members. But Tisha wasn't stupid, she knew her cousin was doing something. She was starting to put the pieces to the puzzle together. As to why her cousin was around the people she was around.

The summer was winding down. And what an eventful summer it was for the crew. From the Splash Party in County Park. To Chill's annual cookout in Franklin Terrace to Nitro's birthday bash at the Convention Center. The fall would bring other things the crew were planning to do. Turkey give away on Thanksgiving. Gift giveaway on Christmas. All giving back to the community that raised them. The crew kept their word of giving back to the community.

The two armed guards that were shot by Kwame and Wheels were still recovering in local hospitals. And the investigation was still ongoing. But at the moment the crew was out of the game. Despite them being out of the game. Didn't mean law enforcement wouldn't stay pursuing the case. And pursuing them. Detective Boyd was still very determined to solve the case. And after a while the case became personal to him. It was coming up on his longest case to solve to date. As each day passed. It became more difficult to solve the case.

The crew was living their lives. And doing their best to invest the money they made from the bank heists. In different business ventures. The summer was coming to a close and the basketball tournaments were coming to an end. It was the playoffs and championship games. And a few of the crew members were amongst the crowd watching the games. In which three were going on at the same time. At Brandon Park in the 8th Ward. Some of Lanc City's best basketball players have played in those tournaments. It was the place to be in the summertime. And always had a big crowd of spectators. Men, women, and children all came to the games to watch Lanc City's best.

On this particular day. Desmond, Chill, and Wheels were out at the park watching the basketball tournaments. Amongst the large crowd watching the games too. Crew members were almost like local celebrities. When they arrived they were greeted with handshakes and hugs. And shown a lot of love.

"You have anyone in mind to work in the store when you take over for Mr. Cee"? Chill asked Wheels.

"I have a few people in mind. I can start giving interviews once I officially get in there. Why what's up"? Wheels replied.

"I have a cousin that needs a job. If you need help, let me know. He really needs a job bro" Chill said.

"Oh ok. I will bro. I definitely will. Give your cousin my number. I'll get him an application and then I'll interview him once I get settled in" Wheels replied.

Wheels was getting closer to taking over for Mr. Cee at his corner store. Wheels didn't really know how to run a store. But he watched Mr. Cee run the store flawlessly for decades. So he had a great teacher. He knew the neighborhood because he was born and raised there. And Mr. Cee himself. Had the most confidence in Wheels carrying on the great legacy of the corner store. Lime Street was everything to Wheels coming up. Lanc City is a small city. Which meant whatever neighborhood you came from meant that much to you. There was the city and it's blocks. Each crew member took pride in the block they came up on. But came together collectively to represent the city.

Despite getting major money from doing bank heists. The crew still lived on those same blocks they grew up on. Wheels in particular wanted to remain on Lime Street after he bought the store. He felt it was important to remain in the neighborhood. Around the people he's known most of his life. And some of his would be customers.

Detective Boyd was still putting the squeeze on Gigi for information. And Gigi was starting to realize that she was in a no win situation. She wasn't going to snitch. Because in reality, she had no real information to tell. She was a woman of the streets and that was against the code. She would never snitch and leave her family in danger. Gigi was just in a romantic relationship with Travis. A young cat who was a loner. And who also happen to be a killer. Gigi knew as soon as she got caught with cocaine in her ride. She was going *away for a while. Her loyalty for Travis went beyond their relationship. Detective Boyd elected to leave Gigi on the streets so she can try and gather as much information as she could. From anyone that was on the detective's radar.*

Gigi was preparing herself to do hard time. And she was still on the street which was dangerous. Rage and his family were enjoying being new Lancaster County residents. And getting used to their new neighborhood. Far from the normal city noise and now hearing birds chirping. Rage and his family was excited about this new experience. The kids were excited about being enrolled in new schools.   Page 124

And as soon as the family got settled, Rage had planned to have a cookout before Fall turned to Winter. After another workday, Rage decided he wanted to have a drink. He hadn't been Down Bottom in a while. He called Kwame and told him to meet him down there.

"So how's life in the County for the fam"? Kwame asked.

"It's cool man. Just getting used to shit being so quiet out there. My wife loves it and the kids are excited. It's all good. It's just coming from Beaver Street and moving to the burbs is somewhat of a culture shock" Rage replied. As him and Kwame laughed.

"That's what it's all about fam. Living a good life and giving that life to the people you love. That's why we did the shit we've done. Speaking of that. I know we said we were out the game and all. But I got one more heist in me. Hopefully we get a cool million or more" Kwame said.

"Kwam I really don't think I'm down for anymore heists bro. The family is good. And I did what I had to do to fulfill my commitment to the crew. I'm good financially also. For me there's no need to get back in it" Rage replied.

"Yeah I get it bro. I understand. We made enough money right? I mean we're all good to my knowledge financially. I just wanted to see if we could get that million. Its what we always talked about when we put this shit together. Flawless execution. Niggas did numerous heists without ever getting caught. And we all grow old together telling our stories. And counting money from the investments we made. We got ours, and we gave back to the community. And we will continue to give back. I just want a shot at that million" Kwame said.

"We did that. Now it's time to live off our investments. I can't believe you want to take the chance of getting back out there. Risk going to jail? Can't do it. For the most part, we got away with it bro. Nobody is dead or in jail my nigga. Think about that, before you really make a decision about this. We have a detective right now riding around the city questioning muthafuckas about us" Rage replied.

"I hear you fam....I really do. But I've got this one planned to damn near perfection. We'll be fine. And get in and out of there. Like we always do playboy. Believe it" Kwame said. Smiling and winking his eye.

"Anyway. I heard you and Nitro got your feet wet in the real estate game. How's that coming along"? Rage replied asking.

"It's cool. I'm new to the game. Nitro has dabbled in that shit for a while now. I'm learning more and more each day" Kwame said.

"As long as we're investing and putting our money to good use for ourselves and our families. That's all that matters. Buying that house was the smartest purchase I've ever made. And my family is happy and comfortable. I did part of my duty as a man. and I still got some doe I'm sitting on. So I'm happy" Rage replied.

"The only nigga I worry about in the crew moving forward is Travis. You know he's wild and reckless at times. Even though we talk to him all the time. At the end of the day he's going to do what he wants to do anyway. So fuck it" Kwame said. As he took a sip of his drink.

The two men finished their drinks and went about their way. After yet another productive conversation between the two. Kwame had a better idea of who would be down for another bank heist. One thing he did know. Wheels and Rage were out. He knew Travis was always down for some action. Kwame figured if Travis was down, Desmond would be down too. It was Kwame's last chance at getting some crew members together for one last heist.

Chapter Six "What We Did Was Epic"

Gigi was running out of time. Travis being who he was and him knowing what was going on with her. He kept his distance from her. He figured that law enforcement might end up making Gigi wear a wire to try and get information from him. Information that could potentially incriminate him and put him in prison for a long time. As far as Travis was concerned, that wasn't going to happen. And he wasn't giving law enforcement a chance to get close to him. Gigi didn't have any information on Travis. Not anything serious that could get him put away for a long time.

Later that day. Accompanied by her lawyer. Gigi turned herself in on charges of possession. She went Downtown and turned herself in. Not wanting to cooperate with authorities for lesser time. She wasn't going to snitch no matter what. She would take the time they gave her. She never told Travis she was turning herself in. She didn't have to, it was expected. Gigi would be facing a lot of time behind bars.

Life went on. And Kwame was about to offer Travis an opportunity he couldn't refuse. Kwame and Travis had an up and down relationship. They weren't friends by any means. Didn't even hang out with each other. You could say they were business associates and they made that work. Travis was young, wild, and reckless. Kwame was an OG. And like many of the older members of the crew. He as well as the others, tried to school Travis on different things pertaining to his life. And like a lot of the younger generation. It was a roll of the dice. If and when Travis would actually listen to anything anybody had to say. The bottom line was. Kwame just wanted to get a few crew members together. To see if they wanted to do one final bank heist. To reach the goal of a million dollar take. Which would be the most the crew got at one time for a bank heist.

The two people he thought he could convince were the two young guns. Travis and Desmond. He wanted to talk to Travis first. Because he felt if he got Travis, he could get Desmond to be down with the heist. Kwame went over to Hill Rise Housing Projects to pay Travis a rare visit. After knocking on the door. Travis opened the door and let Kwame in. They went in the kitchen and sat at the kitchen table. Travis took a bottle out of the fridge and opened it. Poured them both a glass. And they began to chop it up.

"You don't visit me much, if ever. This has to be some business shit right"? Travis asked. Sitting across the table from Kwame.

"You're smarter than you look youngin. It's definitely about business. One last heist to try to get that million. With it only being us, and hopefully convince Desmond to join us. It's a nice split" Kwame replied.

"I take it the OG's turned this down. So now you're coming for the young niggas. Me and Desmond huh? Let me think on it K, I'll get back to you" Travis said.

Kwame just sat there for a moment, finished his drink. Looked at Travis and replied.

"You do that youngin. You do that. I have to get going. I'll holla at you later. Thanks for the drink homie" Kwame said. As he got up and left.

The fact that Travis and Kwame had the type of relationship they had. Always made things interesting between them. Ultimately they would once again have to work together to complete a successful heist. Like they'd done in the past. So that wouldn't be a problem. Travis told Kwame he'd think on it. Just to make Kwame sweat it out. Because he hardly got along with him, and in essence. Travis knew that Kwame needed him after he learned some of the other members had turned it down.

Nitro was fresh off of one of the biggest parties of the current year. That he threw for his birthday Downtown at The Convention Center. The party was lit, bottles were being popped all night in the V.I.P. Guests from as far as Chicago and as near as York and Harrisburg attended the party. Of course there was plenty of beautiful women that attended the party. All of Lanc City's finest chicks were there. Most if not all of them knew Nitro. It was back to everyday life as Nitro stood on Pershing Avenue just watching. Watching the youngins put in work on the block. But thinking to himself how much he wanted so much more for them. He would tell them all the time. there was a lot more to life than this. Yeah Nitro knew it didn't help that they were working for him.

He was contributing to them being in the streets. That's why he stressed to them, how much more he wanted for them. But he knew like Travis was. You can tell them what you want to tell them. Ultimately. It was their decision. And that's how he was with them. Nitro had one foot in the streets and another in the real estate game. He would hire cats that were from the streets to work on his houses. Guys that were skilled in carpentry, electrical work, and plumbing. And the ones he didn't hire. He'd say he was coming back for them to get them out of the streets. And hire them to work on his houses. Nitro had seen so much growing up in the 80's and 90's about what the streets would do to people in the city and surrounding areas.

He didn't want anyone he cared about and loved to go through that. They were all appreciative of the opportunities he gave them. And they never let him down. It always felt good to Nitro. To be able to put the people he cared for the most on. That was everything to him.

Erica "Erotic" Fisher was preparing for her new Hair Salon to open. "Erotic Styles". Downtown on Chestnut Street. Angel helped. Along with her cousin Tisha. They had all been together a lot lately. They were helping Erotic get her shop ready for grand opening. The grand opening was a little over a week away. And the three women were working hard to get the shop to Erotic's liking. As the women were working. Someone knocked on the front window. It was Chill. The women were a little surprised to see Chill there. He had come to offer his support.

"What's good ladies? How's everything going? Look I know this isn't the grand opening yet. But I brought you a gift E" Chill said. Handing Erotic a small board where she could write down her upcoming appointments.

"Thanks Chill. I really appreciate that. You might get a free hair cut for this homie. I plan on having a few barbers in the shop" Erotic replied. Giving Chill a hug.

"Not much going on. Just finishing up the little odds and ins homie. You here to help or watch us"? Angel asked. Smiling.

"I just stopped by to check yall ladies out. I was on my way to HOP. Get me something to eat and have a few drinks.

Angel, Erotic, and Tisha just looked at each other. And said at the same time. "We'll join you".

And just like that. Chill had company with him that joined him at HOP. So all four of them walked down the street to the restaurant and bar.

Travis made his way over to Green Street to hang out with his boy Desmond. And to tell him about the business proposition that Kwame had presented him with. Desmond opened the door and Travis came in. As Travis came in the house he noticed more drawings that Desmond had recently done. Desmond stayed working on his craft.

"Damn fam. You've been putting in work. Nice. I'm not even an Art type of nigga, but this shit is so dope. They got to put this art Downtown in them galleries. They just got to. Can't deny your talent homie. So what's good"? Travis said. As he came in and sat down.

"Thanks homie. I sure hope so. I'm just being patient and waiting on my shot. I know my work should be on display. They can't stop the sun from shining you feel me? My time will come" Desmond replied.

"No doubt. That time is coming homie, just keep believing. Anyway. I talked to Kwame about wanting to get back into action again. He wants to do one final heist to get a million cash" Travis said.

"I thought we were out of the game. Thought niggas were putting their guns away for good" Desmond replied.

"This is Kwame's shit dawg. I guess some of the OG's told the nigga no. So now he's coming for us. I figured since the split would be bigger, we would be interested. I know I am. And Kwame knows this shit. It's tempting fam. I'm down to be honest with you. You know I love the money. I figured you'd be down. Being the split between us would be bigger" Travis said.

"I mean Kwame has always been straight with us from day one. He feels good about it, why not? Easy money. And if you're down to ride one last time. We going to ride together homie. Tell him I'm in" Desmond replied.   Page 129

It was now official. Travis and Desmond were in to do the next and final heist. The two young guns. Kwame had himself and the two young guns. Desmond had agreed pretty quickly. And although Travis knew he was down also. He still wanted Kwame to wait to hear back from him. Unbeknownst to Travis and Desmond, Kwame also recruited his boy Chino to be apart of the heist team. Chino. The owner of the warehouse in the 6th Ward where the crew's headquarters were. And where they counted the money they took in the bank heists. Chino always wanted to get in the action himself. Now was his chance, and he couldn't have been more happy. In Kwame's mind the crew was set. A four man crew of him, Travis, Desmond, and Chino.

Once he heard back from Travis and Desmond. He could finalize the location. He had one in mind once everything was finalized. That's how Kwame and the rest of the OG's worked, and it was always successful. So they stuck with it. No different this time around. As Kwame once again took the lead. He thought it would be better to choose a bank that wasn't in their plans to throw law enforcement off. So he had his eyes set on a bank in Perry County. Which was an hour and twenty two minute drive from Lanc City. And this time it would only be them in the getaway car, no back-up car. For the first time ever. This heist more than any of them, had to have flawless execution. if not it could cost the four men their lives or freedom.

The heist would be the most brazen and riskiest they've ever done. Regardless of it all. The four men were still down and focused on making the heist successful. Wheels was driving through city streets as he did often. Wheeling his black BMW down block after block. He happened to look through his rearview mirror. And seen a car following him. He continued driving down Dauphin then made a quick right onto Palm Street. And then a right on Green Street pulling up to Desmond's house. Desmond just so happen to be standing on his porch when Wheels drove up.

"What's good bro? Where you come from all of a sudden"? Desmond asked.

"I think that fucking detective was following me man. Like from Downtown to here. First this muthafucka was at Chill's cookout. Now he's following me. What the fuck"?!! Wheels replied. Sounding concerned.

"And I just agreed to do another heist with Kwame, as hot as shit is. This shit has me really thinking man. We called ourselves laying low, and this detective is still on our ass" Desmond said. Shaking his head.

"I told Kwame I was done with that shit man. I seriously thought about it. I'm not going to lie to you. The money was tempting. But then I said to myself. I still got money, and I'm about to have this store. This store means everything to me. Carrying on Mr. Cee's legacy means everything to me. If you're down and agreed. Just have confidence that yall can get the job done successfully. But I could also understand why you wouldn't want to do it either. I don't even believe this detective is even apart of local law enforcement. I never seen him before. Until Angel and Erotic told us he questioned about that double murder. Chill said he knew him from investigating his cousin's murder in Harrisburg" Wheels replied.   Page 130

"He probably followed you because you're a black man driving a BMW. Assuming you're a drug dealer. Probably wanted to arrest *you on the charge of DWB. Driving while black. You know these fucking cops nowadays" Desmond said laughing.*

Desmond and Travis personalities were vastly different from their older counterparts. They both lived life a little more carefree. And didn't worry about much until the situation came to them. Wheels still little shook about the detective following him. Wheels was flawless behind the wheel, it's how he got his nickname. Wheels used to go on high speed chase all over the city. He knew the city so well. All the backblocks and alley way streets. He could lose anyway in a matter of seconds. But he couldn't lose Detective Boyd. That concerned him at first. After later calming down. Wheels realized he wasn't cut out for this life any longer. He was about to buy a store that was important not only to his neighborhood. But the whole city as a community.

On this last heist. The crew members who were left to do the job. Wouldn't have the services of Wheels. Kwame recruited Chino to drive for the last heist. Kwame trust that Chino could handle his role. For the most part. Chino held the warehouse down the whole time the crew were doing their thing. And local authorities had no clue where the crew headquarters were. Only thing on his record as far as dealing with the crew. Was getting robbed by Stacks and Bags. Which still fucked with Chino till this day. Kwame had a way of getting people together. He was able to put a crew of street niggas together to form an unstoppable unit. Along with two sexy seductive females that were street smart and was ready for whatever. Kwame amazes himself till this day that they all were able to function flawlessly as they've done. For the time they did as a unit.

"You got jokes. You laugh nigga. Don't be surprised if he starts following your ass" Wheels replied.

"He probably will now. Nigga you brought him to where I live" Desmond said. Shaking his head and laughing.

On this last heist, the motivation was clear. Their goal was to get a million dollars cash money. That was it. Get into the bank, execute flawlessly and get out. Kwame would stakeout the bank in Perry County that next day.

Chill got up early that next morning. Stepped out on his front steps with his robe on. Some pajama pants and house shoes. Sat in his chair outside his house and just stared around the projects. Something he would do from time to time. He was deep in thought about a lot of things. Chill was thinking about his next move. He was still sitting on a lot of the money he made from the heists. He was doing the real estate thing with Nitro and Kwame. But he wanted more, something he could call his own.

Chill always dreamed of owning a nightclub. But he didn't have the money to own one out right. He would need some partners. In other words. Some investors to sink their money into building the club. He was seriously considering asking Nitro to be one of his partners. Nitro was the life of the party. A guy that loved the spotlight and knew how to party. Page 131

Nitro always threw parties back in the day. When he used to live on the East Side on East Orange Street. He would throw parties every weekend. It went from house parties to private parties at clubs and bars. Nitro knew all about the entertainment side of things. And would be a perfect partner for Chill. After thinking about it. Chill called Nitro and told him to meet him Downtown at HOP. To talk to Nitro about potentially being one of his partners in this club idea. Once they both arrived. Chill wasted no time telling Nitro why he wanted him to meet him down there.

"You know I've been in on this real estate thing with you and Kwame. But I'm also interested in building a nightclub. I know you know a lot about the party scene. So you can definitely help me out with that part of it. I just need a team of investors. We'll all be part

owners you dig. Wanted to see if you were interested"? Chill asked Nitro.

"Yeah. I'm down. I mean why not? There's a market in the city for another club. Downtown is popping more than it's ever been. But there's still enough money for us to do what we hope to do. So I'm in for sure. We can give all those Downtown bars competition like no other" Nitro replied.

"Word. That's what I'm talking about bro. Stretch this money out and put the crew stamp all over the city" Chill said.

"That's what it's all about at the end of the day man. We're from the 7th Ward playboy. All these muthafuckas from the outside. These county muthafuckas. They aren't giving us a chance in hell to succeed. But that's what makes this shit so much sweeter. When we prove all our doubters wrong. We'll start being in places where they THINK we don't belong. Give this city hope and give people from OUR neighborhoods hope. That they can do something greater than the normal stereotypical shit they believe we can do. Us owning our own club would be huge bro. Real big. I know we didn't get a lot of this money legally. But we're maintaining it legally. And we aren't hurting anyone in the process. It's been the other way around actually. We've given back to our hoods given back to the city. And that's all that matters" Nitro replied.

"That's a good way of looking at it. Most people around here that don't know us. The few. They think we're drug dealers. Yeah some of us got our hustle on in these streets. Shit some still do on the side. But that's not our primary source of income. We don't need to do that shit to survive. I just want us to build this club right. And take over the nightlife in the city. I was thinking that vacant building across from the stadium on Prince" Chill said.

The Clip was the stadium that was home to the city's Minor League baseball team.

"The big warehouse looking building? Yeah. No one has done shit with that building in a long time. And what's even better about that spot. Even though it's still considered Downtown being on Prince Street. It's a ways away from the rest of the bars Downtown. And that's a damn near perfect location too. Right across the street from the stadium. We have to get the money up for a liquor license. Getting that location from the city will be challenging though. I can't front, we're going to be in for a battle fam. But it'll all be worth it in the end" Nitro replied.   Page 132

"We're about to take over nightlife Downtown playboy" Chill said raising his glass. As the two men toasted and drank to that.

Meanwhile. Kwame had took a drive to Perry County. To just see the bank he and part of the crew were planning to rob. He drove his black Benz up and just sat in it. Watching the bank. Kwame had on black everything, including some shades. He parked a little ways away from the bank out of plain view sight. He went by himself too. He figured since he planned it, he should do that work. He sat and watched for almost an hour and then headed back to Lanc City.

The Summer was over and made way for Autumn and Fall. Kwame wanted to do this last heist while the weather was still somewhat warm. Wheels was learning more and more from Mr. Cee from a business standpoint. As opposed to being a customer. Mr. Cee went over a lot of things with Wheels over the last month. Getting him ready so he could soon take over. Wheels was still somewhat in awe over the fact he was going to be the new owner. Of a store he went to often as a child, teenager, young man. And now as an adult.

Out in Lancaster County. Rage was gearing up for a housewarming party. A few members of the crew were planning to attend. Him and his family were settled in their new surroundings. But like most people from Lanc City that move out of the city. They somehow and some way make their way back to the city. For him. He had to come back to the city to go to POS. To get some of their chicken that he loved. Plenty of nights, Rage would walk from his Beaver Street neighborhood to POS for their fried chicken. Coming back to the city just felt good to him. Before even going to POS. He went by his old hood on Beaver Street.

At first people from the block didn't recognize his truck. He had bought himself a brand new Yukon Denali Truck. When he first pulled up, no one knew who it was. That is until he got out of the truck. After he got out and people realized who it was. The whole block came and showed love. Rage felt like he should've felt. At home back in his hood. He stayed parked on Beaver Street chopping it up with people from the neighborhood. For about forty five minutes before he left and headed back to his new home. It was good seeing everybody from the old neighborhood. He hadn't been back since he moved over a month ago. Before he headed home. He decided to call Wheels and told him to meet him Down Bottom for a drink or two. Rage got there and was there for ten minutes before Wheels showed up.

"What's good bro? How's the County treating you"? Wheels asked Rage.

"What's good fam? Shit is good. Family has adjusted to life in Lancaster County. The quietness has been an adjustment for me. Nigga I'm used to Beaver Street. I heard you're about to take over the store. Good shit fam" Rage replied.

"Yeah man. Mr. Cee has been teaching me a lot of things about the business. I'm excited about taking over. And I'm ready to serve my community like he's done for so many years. It's truly an honor man. I'm just glad he gave me the opportunity" Wheels said.

"Indeed a blessing. Mr. Cee is a good man, always has been. And always ran an honest business. Congrats again homie. Proud of you.

I heard Kwame got some of the crew together for one last heist. I guess when we said no. He got the youngins to do it" Rage replied.

"Yeah. I definitely told him I was done. I got nothing else to prove to nobody man. I got the store now and I'm trying to keep it. I have enough money stashed to take care of myself with the store. The last thing I need is the law on my ass. You feel me"? Wheels said.

"Word. I hear that. I just bought my family a beautiful home and I'm not trying to have that shit either. Bought myself a new truck and I'm just enjoying life. You and I both earned our stripes in these streets. Now its on to bigger and better things. We don't have shit to prove. So why not just enjoy your life with your family like a real OG. I miss the block somewhat. Rode through and hollered at my peoples. Still doing the same shit is always. But they are my peoples. Had to stop through POS. You open my truck door now, nigga it smell like chicken" Rage replied as they both laughed.

The next day was Erotic's grand opening of her hair salon Erotic Styles. On Chestnut and Prince Streets. And from day one, her business took off. She hired some local talent to help her. Including a barber. Erotic was happy to have the talented men and women she had on her staff. She selected a diverse range of talented people. Who had different skill sets that made her business more rounded. Women who could do different types of hair and braid. Three hairstylists and one barber is what started with her day one. Angel and Tisha also helped out at the grand opening. A few of the fellas from the crew dropped by also. Like Travis and Desmond.

This was also the day before the heist. And after dropping by Erotic's salon showing support for her business venture. Desmond was back on the block on Green Street. He was home working on a new drawing. And just thinking about the next day. And the crew's last go round for hopefully their biggest take. At the same time he was somewhat torn about going through with the heist. After all. Travis is the one who came to him about it. And him being his right hand, he couldn't leave his guy out to dry. He knew he couldn't turn back now. Something about this whole situation didn't seem right to him. But there was no way he would cop out of it at this point. His crew members would never be able to trust him again. He had to do what he agreed on.

Desmond knew the crew had got away with robbing banks all across South Central Pennsylvania. And he wanted to keep it that way. But this was a different type of challenge. Not having as many people involved. And not having that back up getaway driver like all the other heists they did. Desmond was still confident they could do it. But just a little torn and skeptical. Either way. He wasn't letting his crew members down. They were counting on him and he was game.

The Day Of The Heist Act Five

Kwame woke up early that morning to a car parked outside banging music. It was Fall. As the wind blew a little. And the leaves blew off the trees as they scattered across front lawns on Ann Street. The wide street had beautiful homes up and down the block. Along with some rough looking ones in between. Ann was a block that could fool you. Being that it had so many nice homes on the block. The block was notoriously known for being one of the wildest blocks in the city. Kwame got up and went to his bathroom. Washed his face and brushed his teeth.

Kwame was real anxious about this heist. He just wanted to get it done and over with. And reach the crew's goal for this heist. A million dollars in cash. Kwame was confident but also a little uneasy.

He wouldn't have his main getaway driver Wheels with him this go round. Instead Kwame got Chino to do the driving on this heist. Chino had been waiting his turn to be apart of what the crew was doing. Now was his chance, and he was thrilled about the opportunity. But on the front lines would be the young guns Travis and Desmond. And Kwame alongside them. Travis and Desmond had never failed the crew and executed the plan perfectly. Kwame trusted them.

Chino came and got in the car Kwame got for the heist. Then they headed to Green Street to pick up Desmond. After that to Hill Rise to get Travis. And they were off to their final heist. As usual the car was quiet. A dead silence. Travis, Desmond, and Kwame were all stone face and not saying a word as Chino drove. Kwame just looking out the passenger window. Thinking about how far the crew had came since the beginning. How he got a bunch of men and women together. And formed a collective of people from the streets to get money in a unique way. A bank heist crew that was able to get away with a few high profile bank heists. Got away with a lot of money. And could live to tell it. Although they all were sworn to secrecy.

Kwame knew driving to that bank in Perry County. This was it. After this it would really be over. There was no turning back now, and this would be their most dangerous heist yet. After the hour and seventeen minute drive to Perry County. They had arrived at the bank. Chino drove past the bank and parked down the street. After Chino parked. Kwame got out of the car and walked up the street to the bank. Travis and Desmond both in the backseat waited patiently for Kwame's text. Gloves on and guns in hand ready to go. After another five minutes. Desmond and Travis got the text and quickly stormed out of the car. And headed towards the bank. Once they got in the bank. They drew their guns as soon as they entered.

"Get the fuck down!! Don't move and don't say shit!! Face down now!!! Stay calm and all of you will get out of here alive" Desmond said as he pointed his gun at the people in the bank.

Travis quickly led a teller back to the bank vault. Things seemed to be going as planned. As Kwame was emptying all the drawers in the front of the bank. Filling his bag full of money. Eleven minutes went by as Travis came sprinting from the back of the bank to the front.

Page 135

He had a bag full of money with him. That was Kwame's cue to get the hell out of there. And that's exactly what he did. He was right behind Travis. Desmond was still holding down the front of the bank. That's when Travis stopped and told Desmond to run ahead of him. And exit the bank. Desmond did and Travis was the last one out of the bank. As they raced down the street to the car where Chino was waiting. That's when the armed guard who was face down on the ground got up and grabbed his gun.

He quickly sprinted towards the doors that Desmond, Kwame, and Travis had just went through. By that time the crew had got to the car. But before they could speed off, the armed guard fired some shots at them. Desmond had hopped in the car and Kwame was already sitting in the passenger seat. As Travis attempted to get in, those shots narrowly missed him. That's when he attempted to return fire and was hit with two more shots the guard had fired. Travis staggered a bit and then fired two shots himself. At that moment Desmond had pulled Travis into the car as it sped off.

"Go Chino"!!! Kwame yelled as the car increased speed and was out.

As they were driving off, it was total mayhem in the car. As the crew realized Travis was hit twice. Once in the chest and once in the abdomen. And was bleeding heavily in the car.

"Fuck!! That guard got his gun and fired on us. fucking hit Travis. Shit!!! Hang on bro, hang on!!! Desmond yelled as he was trying to keep Travis up and conscious in the backseat.

Travis was just looking up at Desmond. Even smiled a little as blood gushed out of his mouth. He was bleeding so much internally that it was starting to ooze out of him. Blood was all over Desmond and it was bad. Real bad. But Desmond didn't want Travis to know it. He just kept talking to him and trying to keep him up.

"We have to get this kid somewhere man. He's bleeding a lot man. Fuck!!! We just have to drop him off at a hospital bro. We can't stay. Step on that shit Chino"!!! Kwame said. Sounding concerned.

They knew they had to get Travis to a hospital fast. There was no way they could drive all the way back to Lanc City. He was in a very critical state. They used GPS to route them to the nearest hospital. And immediately went there. They all knew, as hard as it was. Travis was dying. He had lost a lot of blood. But they had to at least take him somewhere where he could fight for what life he had left. And somewhere where his family could be notified. The worst thing Kwame could've ever thought would happen. Was happening right in front of his eyes. The crew had been successful in all of their heists. And never imagined anything like this would happen. But the reality was. It was always a chance it could happen in their line of work.

After both Kwame and Desmond carried Travis into the hospital. They laid him down and he was barely holding on and about to take his last breath as they walked away. Desmond was froze. Just staring at his best friend dying right in front of his eyes. Kwame grabbed Desmond's arm and reminded him they had to go. Page 136

Desmond was devastated. The car was in complete silence the whole ride back to Lanc City. Kwame being the mastermind behind the heist. Had every thought you could imagine running through his mind. From guilt to anger to shock to sorrow. When Desmond pulled Travis in the car. Travis dropped his 45 caliber handgun on the ground outside the car. They obviously left the gun behind. Perry County local law enforcement was sure to find it. Finding that gun meant a lot of things. Especially when it came to Travis. He was a shooter.

The crew finally made it back to Lanc City. And they headed straight to the warehouse in the Sixth Ward like always. After getting there they all just stood in silence once they entered. No one knew what to say. Until Kwame got the courage to speak. After all. This was his idea.

"Look. I'm sorry this happened. I really am. I know him and I bumped heads a few times. But at the end of the day. He was apart of this crew. And I handpicked him from day one. So it's only right that I pay for his funeral expenses. His family don't have to worry about shit because I got them" Kwame said.

Desmond was still quiet pacing back and forth. Chino was just standing there staring at Kwame. For his first ride with the crew. He had seen the worst he could have ever seen of them. They did get away with a nice amount of money. Bags of money but it didn't matter at the moment. All the men were thinking about was the reality of losing Travis.

"I'm getting the fuck out of here. I can't count no money right now. I'll holla at yall later" Desmond replied. As he walked out of the warehouse.

Chino and Kwame just stayed at the warehouse trying to make sense of it all. The heist went well up until the end. The crew had dealt with a crew member being shot before. Desmond was shot by an armed guard before. But not to this magnitude. The crew had lost one of it's members. And not just any old member. Travis was a wildcard, unpredictable wild and young. And a man accused of two murders himself. Was now dead. Killed in what was to be the crew's last bank heist.

"Just thinking. I should've just left the game when most of the crew did man. And being the OG I call myself. I should've kept the youngins out of this shit. I seen a great opportunity for us Chino. I did bro. That was a young dude man. A young dude with his life ahead of him, and could've done something with his life. And now he's gone. This shit is going to fuck with me for a long time. I have to get in touch with his family and let them know I got everything. This is a hard pill to swallow" Kwame said.

"It is fam. But you know how this shit works. Travis was a casualty of war. Wouldn't have been any different than him getting done in on the streets. Not trying to sound insensitive or anything. This shit is sad bro. The little time I knew him, he was cool" Chino replied.

"I guess we better get started on counting this shit" Kwame said as he sat down at the table that had bags of money on it. Page 137

Desmond returned to his house angry and upset at the same time. His ace was gone. He tore his house up. All his new drawings he ripped down in a rage. He just couldn't believe someone he was so close with was gone. Someone he was just with a few hours ago was gone. Desmond grabbed a bottle of Hennessey and started to reminisce. He remembered the time Travis sped down Green Street on his motorcycle. And he didn't know who the hell it was. Until Travis took off his helmet. The time he had a party in Hill Rise for the whole projects. And boy would Hill Rise miss him. Ever since he threw that party and had a rep on the streets as a shooter. He had become in a sense a popular figure in those projects.

Travis would be a legend of some sorts in the streets because of the way he lived and died. Travis life was summed up to living life to *the maximum and living life on the edge. It was the way he lived life every day until the end. Even in his final moments. After getting hit with two bullets in his torso. He still managed to fire back to the armed guard before being pulled in the car by Desmond. As the car sped away. Travis and Desmond had become so close, that they had keys to each other's houses. And they both made a pact being in the line of business they were in. With giving each other keys to each other's homes. That if something was to happen to either of them. They other would make sure that person's family got their money. And all their prized possessions would be taken and given to their families.*

That next day. Desmond did just that. Going to Travis apartment in Hill Rise. As soon as he walked in. He started reminiscing about all the great times they had in that apartment. The strippers they had over for parties they threw for just the two of them. With a few of their friends. The nights of just drinking and burning L's. And them just bullshitting. They had a lot of great times together for the short time they became close. They trusted each other a hundred percent. Travis had a safe in his bedroom that he told Desmond about and the combination. After opening the safe. Desmond found fifty thousand dollars cash inside. And information on a secret account in another state. Travis was a lot more on point and in tune with his future than most people thought.

Desmond quickly put everything in a bag and closed the safe. He figured that Police would soon come to Travis apartment. Desmond had on gloves the whole time he was in Travis apartment. After getting everything he came for. Including Travis damn near brand motorcycle. But before he walked out of the apartment. He seen a picture of him and Travis on Travis table. It was when they were in Atlantic City. The two loved hanging out in A.C. and had been a few times together. Desmond grabbed that picture off Travis table and took it with him before he left.

The money he got out of his apartment. And the money in the secret account would go to his family. Just like the pact they made said. Travis had a cousin in Delaware he was somewhat close with. Desmond knew about him. And planned to give Travis motorcycle to his cousin. News had spread quickly about Travis getting killed in a bank heist. Surveillance cameras at the hospital. Caught images of Kwame and Desmond carrying Travis into the ER and leaving him there. But the images didn't have a clear description of who Desmond and Kwame were. Page 138

Travis was a loose cannon when it came to the streets. And had some enemies. But he also had people who loved him. Wheels was someone who cared about him. He was like his big brother in a sense. Wheels tried his best to be a mentor to Travis. He looked out for him and encouraged him to do the right thing. Well most times. Travis was only 24 years old when he was killed. Travis had a little family in the area, although most of them lived in Florida. He had been on his own since he was seventeen. He had lived in various spots around the city. Getting his first official place on King Street. Before eventually moving to Hill Rise on the Howard Avenue side.

The crew, his family, and the community. All took his death hard. The funeral would be the next day. But before that. Desmond and Wheels met Down Bottom to have a few drinks. Trying to make sense of it all. Wheels wanted answers.

"Desmond. What the fuck happened fam"? Wheels asked.

Desmond took a deep breath before responding.

"Everything was going according to plan. We hit the bank and was doing what we do. There wasn't much resistance at all. We definitely didn't have to pop anybody. So we get in there, get what we could get out. We're all running towards the car. We get to the car, and Kwame gets in the passenger seat. And Travis and I get in the backseat. Well attempt to. After I got in I heard a shot, then

another. That's when I realized Travis wasn't in the car yet. So without even thinking, I grabbed his arm and pulled him in the car. That's when Chino took off. Travis fired two shots back before I snatched him in the car. And he was hit twice. Once we took off, I seen how bad Travis had been bleeding. That's when it was like mayhem in the car trying to get him to the hospital. Everybody was yelling. Especially Kwame and I. Shit is bad man, real bad. I feel angry as fuck at himself for letting Kwame and Travis talk me into this shit. When I should've talked Travis out of it. I can't regret shit now because what's done is done. But I can't front, I'm thinking about it now" Desmond replied.

"It's not about you and it's not on you Desmond. Aint shit you could've done to stop Travis from being Travis. And if anybody knows that, we know that. Because we knew him more than anybody. That kid loved money. He was going to get it any way he could. All we can do now is celebrate his life and remember the good times. And we had plenty of them with him. What we did was epic. Now we have to live our best lives Desmond. I started my journey by buying Mr. Cee's store. You can start yours by pursuing your love of art" Wheels said.

What Wheels said made Desmond think. So much so that he didn't even respond to Wheels. He just sat there deep in thought. Knowing he had lost focus on pushing his artwork. Desmond had a lot on his mind leading up to Travis funeral. Guilt, sorrow, anger, and shock. He kept having visions of him and Kwame carrying Travis into the hospital. And hearing his best friend take his last breath as he walked away from him. He needed to get back to his passion of drawing. And creating things he saw through his eyes. He remembered Travis encouraging him to follow his passion. He at least owed him that and owed himself that.   Page 139

The crew was more than what they did. That's why it was so important for them to give back to the community. They wanted *more out of life, anyway they could get it. And they knew the community did too. They all had families like everyone else. And no matter how they got it, they made good on it once they invested in it. They were hated, envied, and celebrated amongst their own community. But it never stopped them from giving back. The crew got a lot of love from their community also. Most people appreciated what they were doing.*

The day of the funeral had arrived. And as promised. Kwame paid for Travis funeral and Desmond gave the family his money in cash and his secret bank account. The funeral was held a local funeral home. And it was jam packed with people. All of Hill Rise came out to bid their farewells to the young, wild, crazy, two time accused killer. And project legend. The whole crew was there to pay their respects and homage to their fallen brother. Angel and Erotic who were good friends with Travis. Were overcome with emotion at the service. And had to be taken out for a moment. Kwame, Wheels, Chill, Nitro, Desmond, and Rage were all pallbearers. After a moving service, Travis was laid to rest at a local cemetery.

After everything. The crew decided to meet Down Bottom to get some drinks. The whole crew was there, along with some people from the funeral. There were conversations going on all over the bar. And then……

"Shoutout to all the OG's before us. The crews of this city that did their thing. CC, Reckless, HBO. Chester Street Crew. The posses and crews of the 90's. LSP, GSP, BSP, HPB, Colors, etc. But what we did was epic. And we kept shit popping in our community. Helping good people because we're good people. Today we celebrate the life of our brother Travis. May his soul rest in peace. We love you homie. Forever and ever" Wheels said. As everyone toasted to his memory.

While the crew was celebrating Travis life. Local law enforcement in Perry County had recovered Travis 45 caliber handgun at the scene. The armed guard that fired the fatal shots that killed Travis.

Had also been questioned at the scene. Local authorities were trying to piece together what happened in the bank. The crew like always wore masks during the bank heist. So there wasn't much of a description of suspects until Travis came up dead. His clothes that day matched the surveillance camera footage from the heist. That's another reason they knew Travis was apart of the bank heist crew.

Once the crew got back in Lanc City from the heist that day. They got rid of the car. It had a lot of blood from Travis in the car. So they quickly made the car disappear. The day of the funeral Kwame seemed in a daze. Kwame was a little broken and felt so much guilt about what happened. He knew in their line of business it was dangerous. And death could come at any time. But he never thought it would happen to anyone in his crew.

At Travis funeral there were at least five cop cars present. That was something that Kwame expected, but it still made him feel uneasy. He was a man dealing with a lot of anxiety. He was paranoid. Kwame didn't know if they were going to round the crew up or not. Either way he was ready for whatever. He had called his lawyer and told him to be ready when he would need him. He didn't know what was going to happen. But he wanted to be prepared. He had set some money aside for a situation if it went down. That was just Kwame, always prepared. His lady and kids also knew what was up and what to do. If he ever got bagged and had to go away. Kwame understood what he was apart of. And more importantly. He knew how to prepare and take care of his family in the event of his demise.

There was no shame in anything Kwame did or the crew as a collective. They made sure what they did, they did outside of the city. they kept the local beef to a minimum. Most of the crew members that were in the crew being together. That itself dropped the crime rate considerably within in the city. The crew took some of the money they made from the heists and gave back to their community. And was planning to continue to give back. With the upcoming turkey giveaway for the holidays. And there was so much more to come with Wheels taking over Mr. Cee's store. A neighborhood staple on the corner of Lime and Dauphin. Erotic had her new hair salon Erotic Styles. On Chestnut in Downtown Lanc City which was prime real estate.

Desmond would hopefully pursue his art dreams. Rage was enjoying his new surroundings in suburban Lancaster County. Nitro and Chill were still working on real estate deals. With Kwame also getting involved. Chill and Nitro were also hoping to open a nightclub in the city. In a spot that they believed would thrive. The next day after not sleeping much the previous night. Kwame awoke to some dogs barking. And they weren't his dogs because he knew his dogs. Kwame had two pit bulls. Kane and Abel. They protected his Ann Street home. He heard the dogs barking near the front of his house. Within minutes his two dogs got worked up once the other dog started going. He told his dogs to chill and got them calm down as we walked down his steps and towards the front door. He opened his door to find a young teenager in front of his house talking to another teenager.

After seeing Kwame. The teenager quickly kept walking up the street. Kwame didn't have to say a word. That's the respect he got on the block. Ever since Travis funeral, Kwame has had all kinds of thoughts running through his mind. He even contemplated going on the run. Before local law enforcement would be onto them. But his lady had convinced him not to. At least not just yet. As Kwame was laying in bed, wide awake. He got a call from Nitro.

"What's good OG? I'm downstairs. Come down let's take a ride bro" Nitro said. As Kwame looked out his bedroom window and seen Nitro's truck parked outside.

"Ok. Give me a minute. I'll be out" Kwame replied. Getting up and throwing something on.

He got himself dressed. Equipped with his 9mm handgun. Which he put in his waistband. Him and Nitro was cool. But at this point he was a little paranoid and didn't know what to think. Or how everyone was taking Travis death.   Page 141

Kwame didn't know if Nitro was blaming him for Travis death. So he packed his heat on him just in case. He was ready for whatever.

"So what's good homie? Haven't seen you since the funeral. I mean in a way I know why you've been laying low. I read they found Travis 45 at the scene. And you know like I know nigga. They're going to tie that shit to that double murder. They say the murder weapon in that double murder was a 45 caliber handgun. This nigga Travis loved that gun man. So much so the nigga was too stupid to get rid of that muthafucka. After he did that. or just didn't give a fuck. No need to talk the man down anymore. He's gone. I'll give him that respect of not talking him down. But that's the reality of it" Nitro said.

"Shit is what it is. When I put this together. I wanted us all to make it out safe and rich. We damn near did that. I know the heat is coming on us for this shit. I've thought about it a thousand times. We can't change shit now and we can't look back now. Hopefully this shit blows over. And we can move on with our lives" Kwame replied.

"You think your boy Chino going to be able to hold that? That was his first time in action. Hope he keeps his mouth shut if they grab his ass. Owning the warehouse has him out front dawg" Nitro said.

"You don't have to worry about Chino saying shit. He's a thoro nigga man. He's been in the joint before and he's been under pressure before. He won't break. He has too much to lose" Kwame replied.

"If you say so. I hope you're right" Nitro said. As he continued driving through Lanc City streets.

"So you have anything to tell me about this real estate shit"? Kwame asked.

"We're straight as of now. Might need another ten grand from each of us to get the ball rolling a little faster. You good man? You look tired and a little paranoid nigga" Nitro said.

"I'm good. Just haven't been getting much sleep lately. Things will get better, I'm just being patient. Like I said. Once we get past this, we can move on with our lives" Kwame replied.

Nitro nodded his head in approval as they continued driving until they got back to Kwame's Ann Street home. Nitro dropped Kwame off and went about his business. It was safe to say that Nitro was checking the temperature. Meanwhile Angel was preparing for college. Now that the crew was officially done and out the game of robbing banks. Angel felt like there was no better time than now to prepare for her future. She was planning to attend Temple University in nearby Philadelphia. She was going to study Business. But before she left, she made a few stops to say goodbye to her people for a little while. Even though Philly was only an hour and twenty minutes away. Maybe a little more in Philly traffic.

She planned to stay down there. She was renting an apartment in Philly. And would come back to Lanc City when she felt like it. She knew she didn't really feel like commuting. And she wanted to get away from the distraction that would come if she stayed in her own city.   Page 142

She stopped by her cousin Tisha's apartment in Garden Court. Angel gave Tisha ten grand for holding her money for her. And just for being the loyal person she's been for all of their lives. Angel and Tisha knew this really wasn't a goodbye. Angel would be back and forth between Philly and Lanc City throughout the year. But they wouldn't see each other for at least a month now. Angel wanted to get in her apartment and get settled. She wanted to get comfortable in her surroundings before coming back home.

"Cousin we had a lot of great times this summer. For real. We traveled. We went to Miami South Beach. That shit was lit. We had all the parties in the city. Splash Party in County Park was lit. Chill's cookout down Franklin Terrace. Nitro's birthday party at the CC. It was a fun summer, I loved every minute of it" Tisha said.

"Yes it was. And we're going to do it again sometime in the near future. Maybe Spring Break we can go to Miami again. Or somewhere else hot. Cousin just use that money wisely, I know how you like to shop. But I gave you that money to help you with anything you NEED" Angel replied. As they both laughed.

Although Tisha was the big cousin, she knew her little cousin was right. Tisha was notoriously known for shopping a lot. And she wasn't shy about it either. But she also earned her own money, so she had a right to.

"Girl you know damn well I'm going to buy me a few bags and outfits. Like clockwork" Tisha said. As they continued laughing.

Angel just shook her head. It was all in fun. They both knew each other so well.

"Cousin you take care. And I will keep in touch I'll be home in a month. And we'll go out and get our groove on. Go Down Bottom and get a few like we always do. Love you cousin" Angel said. As they gave each other a hug before Angel left.

"Love you more cousin. Call me when you get there. Safe travels"
Tisha replied.

Angel had also bought her a car before she left. A brand new Audi.
Her dream car. She was smart and saved a lot of her money. Mostly
for school, her apartment, and car. Only splurging she did was going
on the trip to Miami. And treating herself and Tisha to some
shopping. Tisha never asked Angel where she got all that money
again. Till this very day. And if she did, Angel wouldn't tell her
anyway. As long as Angel was safe and cool. And the Police wasn't
knocking on either of their doors. There were no more questions.
After leaving her cousin Tisha's place. Angel went Downtown to
Erotic's hair salon Erotic Styles. She entered Erotic Styles on
Chestnut Street Downtown.

*"Hey girl. What's cracking E? I see things are moving along in here.
Very nice. I see you E"* Angel said as she came in. Giving Erotic a hug
as they embraced.

*"Hey Angel. Yeah we're doing pretty good for a salon that just
opened. One day at a time. So this is it huh? Time to hit those books
sis. Good luck. Girl you got this. Just don't forget us little people on
your rise to the top"* Erotic replied.

*"I thought I'd stop by on my way out. And thank you. Girl you
crazy, I'm not forgetting about anybody"* Angel said.

*"I appreciate you and your cousin Tisha helping me out. Thanks
again. And when you come back home. Anything you want done
here, is on me. On the house"* Erotic replied.

*"Anytime girl. Anytime. It's a shame Travis didn't live through all
this. I feel like they shouldn't have done that last heist and Travis
would've still been here. I think Kwame was being a little greedy"*
Angel said.

"I don't think we could've stopped the inevitable. Travis was my boy, and I loved him like a brother. But Travis was going to do what Travis wanted to do. That's a fact. No one was going to stop what he wanted to do. Good or bad. It's like I'm waiting for him to come through those front doors like. "What's good E? It's still hard to believe he's gone" Erotic replied. Smiling with tears in her eyes.

"I know E. I miss him too. It's still hard to imagine that he's no longer here with us" Angel said.

Desmond, Angel, Erotic, and Wheels took Travis death the hardest. They were the closest to him. They were all still having a difficult time dealing with his death. The next morning. Cops were on Ann Street two cars deep. To arrest Kwame. They had information from a jailhouse informant that heard about an armed guard that got shot in a heist. And the guy that did it was from the Lancaster area. After reviewing surveillance camera footage after footage from all the recent heists. State authorities got a glimpse of license plate numbers of a few getaway cars. All registered back to Lancaster.

Why arrest Kwame? Because also caught on camera. Was an image that looked a lot like Kwame not too far from the Perry County bank. They had enough probable cause to believe that Kwame was at the bank that day. And might know he may have robbed it. Kwame wasn't shocked about being arrested. As soon as Travis was shot and killed during the heist. Kwame knew that the whole situation was going to get worse before it got better. That's why ever since it's happened, he hasn't got a full night sleep. He figured at some point the Police would come looking for him. And he had his lawyer ready.

Police took him Downtown for questioning. And his lawyer would meet him down there. Kwame's lady made the call before the police car had even pulled off. Kwame was a little confused as to how the authorities knew about him shooting an armed guard. Only crew members knew about that, because it was crew business. And each *person in the crew knew not to EVER speak on crew business. That was in case for a situation like this. It also was against the rules. Why would an individual want to incriminate themselves? That's why in their line of work. You keep your mouth shut. Page 144*

It didn't take long for law enforcement to let Kwame know how they found out. Someone had overheard Travis talking to someone about it. That someone ended up being the now turned jailhouse informant. He was still on the street when he heard it of course. Travis 45 caliber handgun that he dropped after being pulled in the car by Desmond. The day he was killed. Came back being the murder weapon from the double murder. It was official. Travis was the shooter in the double homicide. Kwame was still trying to come to terms with Travis saying anything about crew business. And the irony in that was. Kwame really didn't believe Travis had said it to incriminate him. He knew the type of dude Travis was.

He was disappointed a little. But it didn't take away from the respect Kwame had for Travis. They all knew the shit they were getting themselves into. Kwame was supposed to be chopping it up with Wheels and Chill. Instead he was in the back of a squad car. While Kwame was in Police custody. Wheels and Chill checked in on his family. Going by his Ann Street home to see how his lady and kids were. Kwame would be locked up until his hearing. And word was spreading fast amongst the city about his arrest. Wheels and Chill vowed to hold his family down while he was in Police custody. Plus Kwame had a stash that his lady knew about for situations like this. So his family was good. And they would be good for a while if need be. Rage would also look out for Kwame's family. It was a strange time for the crew. After losing Travis and now Kwame being locked up. Shit was tense. And other crew members didn't know if they were going to be locked up next or not.

Meanwhile Desmond was starting to get in a better space mentally. He was very depressed after Travis death. He wasn't working on his craft like he should. He had enough material to present to the Art Galleries. Some of the Downtown Art Galleries were interested in his work. Desmond was trying to decide what drawing he was going to use for his Art Gallery display. He was strongly considering the drawing that Travis really liked. The one he drew of his hood Green Street. That drawing was always special Desmond. Because it represented where he came from. Wasn't much thought. Desmond would use that very drawing for his display. In memory of Travis and to represent his hood.

Desmond walked Downtown on that windy Fall day. As soon as he walked in one of the Art Galleries the man remembered him right away. They talked for a little while and then shook hands. The man had agreed to display Desmond's drawing. It was great news on a great day. And something that made Desmond smile, he hadn't smiled in a while. The news was great for   Desmond's healing process after dealing with Travis death. He had something he was happy about that he did for himself. Something that kept his mind off what he was going through.

Drawing was therapeutic for Desmond. Like shooting baskets would be for a true baller that had immense passion for the game. It was his outlet. And now that it would be on display. His focus would be on growing his catalog and brand. Desmond defeated the odds in a sense. And brought a spotlight on the perception of Lanc City people to other areas around the County. A young man from one of the most notorious blocks in the city. Got his drawing of that same block in a Downtown Art Gallery to be on display. For the local art community.   Page 145

Later that day. Desmond got together with Wheels to have a conversation about everything that's happened recently.

"I still can't believe I'm finally getting my work on display for the whole city and county to see. Maybe even people from around the state. When they come through Downtown from out of town. Tourists are always Downtown. And that's where my work will be" Desmond said.

"Believe it homie. You put the work in and got good at your craft. Keep building. You deserve all the praise and accolades you get bro. I know it's your passion. You waited for this, and now it's here. Enjoy that fam" Wheels replied.

"Oh trust and believe I am. I know a lot of niggas didn't believe in me. They knew I had skills because they seen my work. But you know how some of these Lanc City niggas are. With that crabs in a barrel bullshit ass mentality. And I changed a perception of some outside of the city. And what they think of city people. I'm from Green Street and I'm a hell of an artist. And nobody can change that or take that away from me. You feel me. I heard Kwame got picked up. And no bail? I guess him shooting that guard got them on him hard. And to think. The nigga probably saved my life that day. That's why when I heard I felt bad. I knew he was taking that charge for saving my life. Anything his family needs I'm here for them. I know them muthafuckas were asking Kwame all types of questions" Desmond said.

"Kwame went over all this shit with us. And I know the man personally. More than you and Travis did. And I know Kwame's a real nigga. He's not ratting nobody out for shit. And believe it or not. The nigga might beat this charge of shooting the guard. He's got a good lawyer. He put me onto him for a few of my cases in the past. They can't give him a lot of time, if any. Because like I said. They have to prove Kwame was the shooter. And you know when we were in those banks. We always wore masks. So how much did they REALLY see on those surveillance cameras. That jailhouse snitch *might turn out to be a lying muthafucka just trying to save his ass from doing hard time"* Wheels replied.

"I believe you. But it's still some shit to think about big homie. I'm just getting this drawing shit off the ground. The last thing I need is anything fucking that up. Let's go get something to eat from HOP. My treat bro" Desmond said.

"Say no more. Let's do it" Wheels said. As they got in his car and went Downtown to the legendary establishment.

Chill was waiting on Nitro to pick him up. They were going to look at some homes for their real estate venture. Heading outside of the city. They had an interesting conversation.

"With Kwame down. I'm sure there will be eyes on us locally. That fucking Detective Boyd is probably following our ass right now. He's been on us since my cookout. He was an asshole when he was investigating my cousin's murder in Harrisburg. A few years back" Chill said.

"We're getting money the legit way now. They can't trace shit to those heists and us. They got Travis gun. And we now know what we already knew. Travis capped both them niggas on Duke and Church. And he was apart of the heists. But the thing is. A lot of us didn't hang together. We just did business together. Like we're doing now. We invested our money wisely. So as far as I'm concerned, they don't got shit on us" Nitro replied.

"Let's hope you're right. You've been in this real estate shit longer than me and your money is deep in it. I'm just trying to get my foot in the door. And hopefully in the near future. Get this club I was telling you about ready and lit. All this shit is still new to me bro" Chill said.

"And that's why I'm about to school you on how it works. Make you some easy money. Real money" Nitro replied. As he continued driving.

"We shall see" Chill said. As they both laughed a little.

"Dawg we're here. Let's get this money" Nitro replied. As they had arrived at the property.

Being around Nitro showed Chill another avenue how to make money. Because at the time Chill was somewhat unsure what he was going to invest some of his money on. Nitro got him hooked up with some people Downtown. People that could get him building permits. Because Nitro saw the bigger picture. And him and Chill's plans of eventually owning their own club. They needed to rub shoulders with a few people Downtown. Movers and shakers that could get them the club that they wanted. Chill now had a way of investing some of his money. That vacant building on Prince Street across from the stadium.

Chino was still on the streets. But he was nervous and paranoid as ever. With Kwame locked up, he didn't know what was going to happen next. He drove Ann Street after Kwame was locked up to see how the block was. Kwame kept his part of Ann real stable and business like. The youngins respected him as an OG. And never questioned his authority. And even while he was locked up. It was business as usual on the block. The youngins were instructed on what to do before Kwame was taken into custody by Police.

The plan from the very beginning was to make their money and invested it into something legit. And let their money grow. All the while giving back to the community. And the crew accomplished all of that. Took some loses along the way but they did what they set out to do. Chino knew that Kwame would never rat anyone out. So that was the last thing on his mind. But he was still paranoid about Police taking him into custody. Like Kwame. He had some sleepless nights. Chino's moment was coming sooner than he thought. The next day local law enforcement had him Downtown for questioning. Law enforcement wanted to look into Chino's warehouse in the Sixth Ward on the city's North Side. Which was something Chino really didn't want. He had been able to keep his warehouse real lowkey all this time. And he wanted to keep it that way.

As soon as Chino sat down at Police headquarters. Detective Boyd walked in the room. The same Detective Boyd that was at Chill's cookout in Franklin Terrace.   Page 147

"We meet again huh? I had a feeling we were going to see each other again. Today we have you down here because we have some suspicion about your warehouse on North Plum Street. We've had surveillance cameras on your warehouse over the last few months. And I'm sure you know there's been a lot that's happened over that time. There was the death of one Travis Clark. Did you know Travis Clark"? Detective Boyd asked.

"Yeah I knew him" Chino replied.

"How did you know Mr. Clark? Because the gun that Perry County law enforcement recovered from a bank heist there. Had Travis prints on it. That gun was the murder weapon in a Lancaster City double homicide. The murder took place on South Duke Street and Church Streets. Murder victims Antonio "Stacks" Smith and Charlie "Bags" Harmon. Do you know anything about those murders? Any information you give us, can only help you moving forward. Towards maybe reducing your charges or possible prison time" Detective Boyd said.

"I don't know anything about any murders. I just knew Travis. And I didn't even know him that well" Chino replied.

"You sure about that sir? Because we have pictures of you and Mr. Clark talking outside your warehouse on several occasions. So do you say you know Travis enough now? And what would you two be talking about"? Detective Boyd asked.

"Like I said. I know him but we aren't close like that. I was just talking to him about renting a space in my warehouse. He was thinking about storing his motorcycle there. But we weren't friends, it was just business" Chino replied.

The detective was trying his best to get Chino to flip on the crew. But Chino knew better. There was no way that he was giving up anyone in the crew. For two reasons. If he did rat on anyone, his life and his family's lives would be in danger. And secondly. He wouldn't be able to return to the same Lanc City streets he knew and loved if he was a snitch. Plus that wasn't Chino, he just wasn't that type of individual. If Chino had to do any time, he was prepared to do so. Especially with him being involved in the crew's last heist. They could only tie him to one of the heist and anything that happened at the warehouse. Which was the crew's headquarters for organizing and counting money.

Since being robbed by Stacks and Bags over a year ago. Chino had tightened up his security at the warehouse. Like Kwame had advised him to do after getting robbed. It was in the crew's best interest that the warehouse was secure. And it was in Chino's best interest to do so. Because he was getting paid by the crew for using his warehouse. What the crew didn't know was that law enforcement was watching the warehouse over the last few months.

But at the same time. Law enforcement didn't have cameras INSIDE the warehouse. There was no evidence of anything but them all just meeting at the warehouse. At the crime scene of the heist in

Perry County. There was a gun that was left on the ground. That gun was Travis gun. And local law enforcement had recovered it. Tests on that gun led to the owner and shooter in a double homicide. That person was Travis Clark. And since Travis was seen on camera with Chino and various others. That was why Chino was picked up. Law enforcement led by Detective Boyd were trying to piece together the trail to a bank heist crew. And they had strong suspicion that they may have found them. There was very little physical evidence tying the crew to those heists. Only Travis gun. Which placed him at the scene of the heist.

The robbing spree that dominated South Central Pennsylvania over the last year or so. Was still unsolved. Two armed guards were shot. One of them ended up being paralyzed from his injuries. The other one was still recovering from his. The crew took a lot of money and there was no trace of the money from any of the crew members. They had smartly invested their money or had their money in accounts they only knew about. No one was flashy with their money. Maybe more than any of them. Travis splurged a little. But Travis was dead. And couldn't tell law enforcement anything. Wheels had a BMW and Kwame had a Benz. But they weren't brand new vehicles. Nice cars but they weren't the most expensive. The other members bought cars that could be attainable for normal everyday working people. That weren't considered to be rich. The crew kept their money lowkey.

The crew were able to treat themselves and their families. As well as the community. And bring about positive programs like the turkey giveaway on Thanksgiving and the gift giveaway on Christmas. The crew was ingrained in the city and that's what made them legends in the city. A lot of legendary crews from the past had money at the height of their success. And then either got locked up and lost everything. Or fell off and disappeared. The crew was trying their best to avoid that fate. And for the most part they had done just that. The crew did a great job of hiding their identities and being as elusive as they were. It's what's kept most of them still on the street.

Their loyalty for one another was on another level and they kept their business between themselves. No jealousy or envy amongst each other. Because they all ate off the same plate and all got their equal share. There was no internal beef amongst the crew. A few members may have not got along like others. But they kept it together for the best interest of the business. The crew was untouchable in a sense.

There was a problem with the state's case against Kwame. They didn't have a weapon or any real physical evidence. They were basing their case on a jailhouse informant and Kwame's association with Travis. It was starting to look like Kwame would be home before he knew it. While in the County Jail. Wheels went to visit Kwame.

"What's good bro? How you holding up"? Wheels asked Kwame.

"I'm good man. I mean this is the County right? You know most niggas in the County anyway. I'm hoping to be home soon though. Page 149

I don't think they have much of a case against me. They don't have no weapon or no prints. They don't got shit on me. I'm thinking my lawyer will have me out soon. How's shit on the outside"? Kwame replied.

"It's cool. The store is doing well. I'm heading into my second week now. Have some good people working for me. People I can trust. As for the rest of the crew. I suppose they're doing well. The last one I talked to was Desmond" Wheels said.

"Have you seen or talked to Chino lately"? Kwame asked.

"No. I haven't seen Chino in a while. Why? Do I need to talk to him"? Wheels replied.

"I was just asking. I wanted to know if that detective was pressing him. Especially with me being in here. I believe they were watching the warehouse. We had thought that before, but we never really switched up. But then again. They didn't see shit we did in there" Kwame said.

"At this point. We can't do shit about it. So we move forward with our lives. Now that you know they have no case against you. I'm sure you'll be home soon. And we don't need that warehouse no more. Let them have that shit. Well I hope Chino don't lose his shit. But we don't need that spot anymore. We're done and out of the game" Wheels replied.

Kwame just nodded his head in agreement. The two men talked for a little while longer before visiting hours were over. Wheels needed to chop it up with his homie to get a sense of where his head was at. He knew Kwame was dealing with a lot of shit. Through it all Kwame remained head strong. And stayed sharp mentally. And that was good news for the crew. If they couldn't get Kwame, they weren't getting any of the other crew. This was one of the biggest cases in Detective Boyd's career. And he was eager to solve the case. Nothing else has mattered but the case. He wanted to solve the case more than anything. The double homicide was solved when Travis gun was recovered. The gun was his and it was the murder weapon. So it was pretty clear that Travis had killed Stacks and Bags. Travis being dead himself now, took the excitement out of solving that case for Detective Boyd.

But that's why solving this case meant so much to him. Witnesses in different bank heists and different locations. Said they saw as many as three people enter these banks. Doing the inside work in the bank. Along with a getaway driver. Law enforcement were looking for four people's identities. Of course they had two down. With Kwame and Travis. Chino wasn't talking. So at the moment law enforcement was stuck.

Meanwhile on the other side of the city. Downtown on Prince Street. Nitro and Chill were standing outside Nitro's truck. Just staring at the abandoned building warehouse across the street on Prince and West Clay Streets. Right across the street from the city's baseball stadium The Clip. Was the location that Chill desired to build his club at. It was somewhat prime real estate being Downtown. Even though it was a little ways away from Center City Downtown Lancaster.

"I see this shit blowing up and being big fam. I really do. It's away from the main strip Downtown. But still in the midst of everything. And it's right across the street from the stadium. Prime real estate. We have to get this spot Nitro. I'm sure we'll have plenty of opposition of us getting this location. Even though this shit has been sitting here vacant for decades. We've overcame a lot of shit over the last few weeks. And we're continuing to defy the odds. Why can't we do this"? Chill said. As he continued staring at the vacant building.

"Hell yeah. We can. I'm with you bro. We can make it happen. Somehow some way, we always do" Nitro replied.

"You go see Kwame yet"? Chill asked.

"No. I haven't been to see him yet. Not even sure I'm going to at this point. I want to stay as far away from that shit as possible. These detectives are trying to piece shit together. Basically trying to say guilty by association. I may have been apart of that heist shit. But that double homicide has nothing to do with either of us. I don't need that messy shit in my life right now. Crew or not. You feel me? Nothing against Kwame personally, but all this shit stems from that last heist. The shit got Travis killed. And I have too much money tied up in my businesses to fuck that shit up" Nitro replied.

Chill just agreed with him and understood. He himself was trying to build his business portfolio. And Nitro was helping him do just that. By teaching him what he knew. Chill knew Nitro was a loyal dude. But he also knew Nitro valued what he worked for and built. And there was no way he was losing anything he had worked for and owned. For anybody. Including crew members. He made that known from day one.

Kwame was still sitting in the County. But he was relieved to know that law enforcement had little evidence tying him to the crimes he was accused of. So although he was ready to come home. He felt good about his chances of that becoming a reality soon. Just being in the County the short time he had been in there. Kwame's mind changed a little. He had been to prison before, but this time was different for him. He was older. And had a different mindset. If he got out, he was thinking of leaving the area for good. That's how serious his mind was changing. It was all he thought about when he was in there. Taking the money he had and paying his lawyer. Taking his family and leaving town for good. And never looking back.

Kwame gave Nitro twenty grand before he got locked up on a real estate deal. Something he, Nitro, and Chill were working on. The last heist netted over $400,000. $600,000 short of their goal. But good money none the less. With that money. Each person involved in the heist was entitled to their half. That was Kwame, Desmond, Travis, and Chino. Of course Travis was deceased, so the crew would give his share to his family. After everything that happened the money didn't seem like it really meant anything. But it would come in handy for Kwame's legal fees. And his plans to relocate. He needed that money.

Chino with the help of Nitro. Got the money to an undisclosed place to count it. Things were a little out of control at the moment *for some members of the crew. Specifically the ones involved in the last heist. The money meant more to Chino than anyone else. This was his largest amount of money made in his life at one time. And his first actual action with the crew as the get away driver. He was beyond excited about the money. But still paranoid about law enforcement watching him. After being questioned by local law enforcement about the double murder and the bank heist crew. Amongst other things. So he let a few days go past after he was questioned. Before he called Nitro and told him to meet him down at Clairemont Homes. Down by the water. They both got out of their cars and talked. With the water being the backdrop.*

"What's good Nitro"? Chino said. Before being interrupted by Nitro.

"Yo"!! Nitro replied. Looking at Chino and then patting him down looking for a wire or anything else suspicious.

"Dawg I don't got no fucking wire on me nigga. Fuck off me"!! Chino said. Obviously annoyed of thought.

"You can never be sure. When the law is on a nigga's ass and he's under pressure. Even your closest friends will turn on you. You know the game nigga. So what's good"? Nitro replied.

"Fucking Detective questioned me Downtown and shit. Asking about bank heists. I guess because they can't pin shit on Kwame. They're trying to get other people in the crew. And now they're coming for me? I had nothing for them. But they've been watching my warehouse over the last few months. And they probably have footage of us coming from the heist that day. Fuck"!! Chino said. Angry beyond words.

"Shit is indeed fucked up. And you my friend better be careful of your moves in the future. Now that you know this shit. If the cameras would've been there all along. All our asses would be facing major time. I'm glad I'm out of that shit for good. I met you

only because you're somewhat apart of the crew. We used your warehouse. So I owed you this. But I'm sure this will be our first and last meeting. Kwame should be home soon, and I'm sure that nigga will need that money from that heist" Nitro said.

"Nigga. I'm trying to stay my ass out of jail too. This heist was huge for me. My first major payday. I needed this shit too. This is my life we're talking about" Chino said.

"I guess we shall see. You know I hope the best for all of you. You deserve that heist money for all the shit you been through to get it. But the shit was sloppy from the beginning. You went in with a skeleton team and one getaway driver. Which resulted in Travis getting killed, Kwame in jail. And your ass paranoid than a muthafucka. See what I'm getting at"? Nitro replied.

"Fuck you Nitro. I'm out" Chino said. As he walked away and got in his car and left.

"Yeah whatever nigga" Nitro replied smirking as he got back in his truck and drove off.

Kwame was very confident that he would beat any type of case the state had against him. He continued to stay strong and be in good spirits. And he was confident he was coming home soon. The crew or what was left of it. Were still doing their thing on the low. Mostly in all separate entities. Rage had his family life. And he was dedicated to that. Desmond had started taking his drawing seriously and had his work displayed at a Downtown Art Gallery. Chill, Nitro, and Kwame were all involved in real estate ventures. Angel was off to college at Temple. And Erotic had her hair salon Downtown. Four members were about to get a payday from the last heist. Actually only three. Travis share would go to his family. That next week. Kwame was released from prison like he had thought he would be all along. The state didn't have enough evidence to charge Kwame with shooting the armed guard in that bank heist. So they had to release him.

Law enforcement were very angry they had to release Kwame Richards. They thought for sure they had the man that was responsible for the bank heists. That were going on in and around South Central Pennsylvania. Kwame came home to his house on South Ann Street to his family. His family welcomed him home to an early Winter cookout. Knowing he was coming home with money coming to him. Felt even better. Kwame saved most of his money from the bank heists. Only splurging on his Mercedes Benz. And some work done on his house. He stashed most of it. But he did have legal fees that he had to pay. So the money would come in handy.

Wheels and Chill were amongst the people who helped welcome him home at the cookout. Later on Desmond would also join them.

"Thanks to all you guys for coming through man. Means a lot. I knew they didn't have shit on me all along. I knew they didn't have my identity or the gun. So I knew I was good. I'm glad everybody is good and continue to be good. I'm thinking about leaving here for good fam" Kwame said.

"Yeah man. You know we were going to hold shit down and be here when you got out. Good to see you home. Me running this store now has been the best thing for me bro. Keeps me grounded and on point with my shit. Productive and disciplined. The bonus is. It also makes me money. I can't complain. Nitro and this nigga Chill been doing their thing on that real estate shit. They're talking about building a nightclub on Prince Street. Tell him Chill" Wheels replied.

"Hell yeah. That's the plan. Hoping to get that spot on Prince and West Clay Street. Right now it's just a dream. But Nitro and I have been doing what we can to make it happen. Trying to secure that site, which won't be easy. But we can do it. Then get that liquor license and we're in" Chill replied.

"So yall doing it big like that? Huh? Ok. My homies doing their thing. I love it"!! Kwame said. Sounding excited for Chill and Nitro.

"That was also the plan right? We're just doing what we've set out to do" Chill replied.

"I wish yall the best in everything you do bro. For real. It's always good to see my people doing good for themselves. I know as far as me. I'm an Ann Street nigga. Ann Street niggas get money" Kwame said smiling.

"I know why this nigga came home in good spirits. He got that money from the heist waiting on him" Wheels said as him and Chill laughed.

"No homie. I'm just happy to be home. Because I knew damn well they didn't have shit on me. But coming home to this amount of cash does make it a little sweeter. You feel me"? Kwame said. As they all started laughing.

"I bet all those legal fees were a bitch. I been there. Exactly why I'm trying to keep my ass out of jail and out of the system. I like my money and I'm trying to keep my money. And spend it on me and mines, not no damn lawyers. Better get on some clean shit real fast Kwame. You know now that you beat this shit. They're going to be on your ass bro. Waiting for you to fuck up again, just waiting" Wheels replied.

"Man. You know I know. Chill. You and Nitro got some of my money on the real estate venture we're doing. And after I pay my lawyer the rest of the money I owe him. I'm thinking about taking my family and moving. Getting away from all this shit for good. I've been on Ann Street damn near all my life fam. Lanc City is always going to be home. It's just time for something else now" Kwame said.

"Where ever you go. I'm sure you'll do your thing like you always do. And if you do move nigga. Don't forget about us. And stop coming back to the city to visit. We'll do our best to visit. But you have to visit too. Happy to have you home bro. For real" Chill said. Before he left.

It was just Kwame and Wheels sitting there after Chill and Desmond left. Desmond had stayed only a few minutes. He had somewhere he had to go. It was a perfect time for Kwame and Wheels to have a conversation. A conversation that Wheels had wanted to have since it happened. But waited until now.

"I never got the chance to ask you what went wrong that day Travis got killed? Or what you thought went wrong that day"? Wheels asked Kwame.

"I don't think it was about what went wrong. That guard just surprised us that day. We never had that happen before. Once we got out of the bank, we were pretty much in the clear. I got in the passenger seat. And I assumed Desmond and Travis got in. That's when I heard two shots, and right after two more shots. Which we know now were the two shots Travis fired at the guard after he was hit twice. And right before Desmond snatched him in the car and we sped off. We really didn't realize how bad it was until Desmond pulled Travis in the car. He was bleeding like crazy. He was losing a lot of blood. I knew it wasn't good. But we tried our best to get him to a hospital as fast as we could. I was telling Chino we have to get this kid to a hospital.   Page 154

We dropped him off at the nearest hospital. Desmond and I carried him in. And then we were out. That day still haunts me. I'm actually surprised I could talk about it. Haven't said much about it since that day. I knew how close you and Travis were. That's why I'm only talking to YOU about this. Anybody else. I wouldn't discuss it with" Kwame replied.

"Yeah man. That was my young boy. His death still stings till this day. Travis was a wild youngin. And I miss him a lot. He had a lot of potential. He was smart man. And he was always on his shit. It's just fucked up he didn't reach his full potential. I'm sure he would've made something of himself. And I'm glad you're home. And now that you are. Let's keep our black asses out of jail and enjoy this money" Wheels said. As they both embraced and laughed a little.

Kwame knew how close Travis and Wheels were. And he felt he owed Wheels an explanation of what went down that day. Because Wheels genuinely cared. Despite Kwame and Travis having their differences. He still respected Wheels and Travis relationship after Travis was killed. Kwame and Travis had a business relationship. And not much of a friendship. After Kwame got out and was released from his short but annoying prison stint. He vowed to stay lowkey and out of the way. Just focus on his family and his business. That was the plan. And he was also hoping to eventually move away from the state of Pennsylvania period.

Kwame and Wheels knew each other since they were in Junior High School. And became closer over the years. And were still good friends till this day. Lanc City was always tricky when it came to the people. Just because you knew someone didn't mean you were cool with them, or that you could trust them. Trust wasn't a thing that existed on these streets. It's a small city where everyone is trying to get theirs. Much easier to step on one's toes when the space is limited. That's why the crew got their money outside the city. And outside the County also. Their faces were too familiar within the area. They didn't want anything to do with local beef unless it was something they had to handle. Especially when they were in the prime of their bank heist reign. Unnecessary bullshit brought local attention from local law enforcement. Which wasn't something the crew DIDN'T want.

It was the main reason Kwame always stressed to everyone to stay out of the bullshit and move accordingly. Plus the crew knew the city and it's people, and knew that. It was an unspoken rule really. Kwame just stressed it because he didn't want anything in the way of the money. Wasn't no money in local beef and bullshit. That's why they stayed clear of it. Well almost. Travis being Travis and doing what he does. Some things didn't change. But the crew was now out of the game and living normal lives and were blessed to still be alive and free to live their lives. A lot of men and women who lived similar lives as they did. Didn't have a chance to live and tell it. Or be able to say they pretty much got away with the money they took. What they did was epic on a lot of levels.

Chapter Seven "Evolution"

Angel was getting used to her new home on the Temple University campus. Over the past few weeks. She had put all her focus on her education. A great start to hopefully a successful college career. She had finally put the life of being apart of a legendary bank heist crew behind her now. And left her hometown of Lanc City behind and everything with it. Not to say she forgot where she came from, because she didn't. She loved her city. But she also knew that there was life outside her city and outside that life. She moved to Philly to sort of spread her wings. And as hard as it was. Concentrate on her studies and live a new life on campus. She had money and could've stayed in Lanc City. And flaunted her local celebrity status of being apart of "LANCREW". She wanted more. And something different in her life because she was still young.

After over a year off. Angel got herself back into college mode and hit the books studying Business. And after being down in Philly for the last month or so. She had gotten a little homesick and was thinking if she was home. She would be with her big cousin Tisha. So she decided to do the next best thing. She called her cousin Tisha.

"Hey cousin. What's good? What you been up to"? Angel asked.

"Hello Angel. Sitting here braiding my hair. How's school going"? Tisha replied asking.

"It's going pretty well. Getting used to everything and all. Have you seen Erotic lately? Or been to the shop"? Angel asked.

"No. I haven't been down there since you left. I'm sure she's been busy. A lot of people locally love the shop. I've just been chilling cousin" Tisha replied.

"That's good cousin. I should be home in another week or so. I will call you as soon as I get into town. Take care and I'll talk to you later" Angel said.

Talking to Tisha was just what Angel needed after feeling a little homesick. Even though she was happy to get away from her city. And start her new life. She still needed a taste of home from time to time. Home would always be home. No matter where she was. To her. There was no place like Lanc City. You had to be from the city to know what that meant.

Meanwhile Chill was seriously thinking about putting all his money into this dream of owning his own nightclub. The location was perfect, but they didn't secure the site yet. Once they got the approval on the property, they could start to rebuild. Chill was hoping and praying that it would happen. At the same time, remaining as patient as he could be.

It wasn't only Chill's dream. It was the vision of his and Nitro. Nitro partied more than anyone in the crew by far. The same man that threw himself a huge party Downtown at The Convention Center. This was definitely his lane. He knew that although Downtown had its bars and clubs. Most of Downtown catered to their County crowd. People that lived in the suburbs and outside the city. There wasn't a lot of bars or clubs that catered to the city people. The people that made the city what it is. Of course Down Bottom had catered to city people for decades. It was legendary in the city. But Chill's club would be on the other side of the city on the North Side. The location he wanted was right across the street from the baseball stadium. Perfect spot for a different type of entertainment in that area.

Having a nightclub in that area and playing the music that Chill and his partners planned to play would be huge for the city. Chill would not only be giving the people what they wanted, but also make money in the process. Living in the city as long as he has, Chill knew what the city needed. And now just recently released from prison. Kwame Richards would also be an investor and be involved with the club. So it was now more money invested in the night club. And even closer to reality as the days past.

Kwame finally decided to call Nitro. He hadn't spoken to him since he was released from prison. When he called Nitro was on Pershing Avenue just chilling on the block talking to a few of the youngins.

"What's good bro? I been home for almost a week now. Haven't heard from you, we need to link up" Kwame said.

"What's good man. I've been busy getting money out here. You know me. And handling OUR business. The real estate venture and now with us trying to get this club built. I know you just got out and all. But we have to stay on top of this shit bro. I'm on Pershing now, chopping it up with the youngins. You should come through. I'm sure you haven't been out of the house much since you've been home. Come through, we're out here" Nitro replied.

"You're right nigga. I haven't been out of the house much. And don't plan to. I'm trying to stay out of the mix. You feel me? But I might come through. Until then, I'll holla" Kwame said before hanging up.

About fifteen minutes later. And much to Nitro's surprise. Kwame's black Mercedes Benz pulled onto Pershing Avenue and parked. He got out and immediately went over to Nitro and his people. Handshakes and hugs as they all greeted each other. Not long after Kwame got out there, he pulled Nitro to the side. The stood in front of Kwame's Benz and chopped it up.

"What's been going on with our real estate venture"? Kwame asked Nitro.

"We're looking to expand our properties into a few other spots. On the West Side, the 8th Ward. Some even outside the city. There's a lot of money to be made Kwame. One thing we don't want to do is be like the rest of these muthafuckas. Who plan to gentrify our neighborhoods. The same neighborhoods we grew up in" Nitro replied.   Page 157

"Word. We've seen that happen in big cities and now they're doing that shit right in our backyards. Like anything you don't really feel it until it hits home. There's no place more home than the 7th Ward fam. Maybe we should start buying up the old homes in the 7th Ward and renovate them. Same shit they're trying to do. Only difference is. We could sell the homes back to the people who came up in the 7th Ward. And current residents of the 7th Ward. We can't let what happened in those big cities happen here. Depending on how our current real estate ventures go. We'll have the money to do so. It all sounds good. Let's hope and pray it works out. We shall see" Kwame said.

"That's a great idea. And I'm down if these other ventures go according to plan. For sure I'm in. But trust and believe that we can do this bro. It's not going to be easy, like I told Chill about getting the club. But if we stay in it, we could get this shit done" Nitro replied.

"Well it seems like you got shit under control. I just wanted to know what was going on. I just came home. And I hadn't heard from my nigga. So I had to reach out. But look I'm about to be out. I'm going to stop by Erotic's shop. I haven't seen her since I came home. So I'm going to head over there. I'll get up with you later. Stay up bro" Kwame said. Before he got in his Benz and left to Erotic's shop on Chestnut Street.

Meanwhile on Green Street. Desmond was putting the finishing touches on a piece he was hoping to show as his main display. At a few of the Downtown Art Galleries. It was a picture of a child of color with all kinds people and things going on around him. But the child stood out amongst them all. The child was larger than anything else in the picture. The message of the drawing was saying that the children are the center of the future. While other things are going on and the people around them were living their lives. The world and everything in it. A lot of Desmond's drawings had messages behind them.

And now even the mainstream audience could appreciate what he called "Urban Art". He was happy to share his gift with the world. Desmond was also thinking about moving off the block. He had money and could pretty much afford any place he wanted for the most part. He wasn't a millionaire by any stretch of the imagination. But he could afford a nice place. And he had just got some more money from the last heist. Desmond was good financially. He had no worries about money. There were some new Downtown condos on Chestnut. High rises. And Desmond had his eye on them. He would still be in the city, and it was walking distance to the 7th

Ward. It made sense. Every time Desmond would drive down Chestnut Street. He would look at them as they were being built. And he knew he wanted to live in them.

One day he decided to walk Downtown and look at one. When the man showed him one of the condos. He was a little surprised at first. Desmond always carried himself well. But like anything, sometimes people assume. The man that showed Desmond the condo wasn't expecting to see Desmond. It didn't stop Desmond from looking at the condo slowly and carefully. Being somewhat of a smart ass because of the way the man was acting. Desmond could feel the vibe as soon as he saw him. Page 158

Desmond could care less about people's opinion of him who didn't know him. He was business as usual when it came to things that required it. He was a city boy from one of the notorious blocks in the city. With a God given talent that no one could take from him. And a young man with money, who could really afford to live in those condos. Desmond knew how to interact with people from different backgrounds. That would prove vital if he wanted to be successful at his craft. No matter where he moved to or how successful he became. He would never forget Green Street and what it meant to him. The block kept him grounded.

As he was walking back home. He thought to himself. Just a few years prior he would walk past Downtown's Art Galleries hoping and dreaming. One day his art would be displayed there. And he was about to actually live that dream. Which was amazing in itself. It was something positive he could look forward to in his life. He had plenty of negativity in his life. Especially over the last few months. Losing one of his best friends Travis.

Chill had his share of the money to put towards the club. He was willing to spend whatever he had to make this club thing work. Chill was sure the club would be an instant hit in the city from day one.

And would maintain its popularity for a long time. Chill had other investments. Like his real estate venture with Kwame and Nitro. One thing was sure about the crew. They were smart. They were definitely street smart. But were getting sharper on the other side of things.

Wheels had been running his store for well over a few months now. And things were going well. Early on people were coming to the store on Lime and Dauphin. Expecting to see Mr. Cee standing behind the counter like always. But it was Wheels or one of his two employees he had working for him. Either way. The store was pretty much the same. Mr. Cee had built a great legacy with his business in the neighborhood. And Wheels wanted to continue that legacy with the same excellent service. Wheels talked Mr. Cee into giving him a picture of himself. So he could hang it in the store to honor him for his service to the community. After some talking to, Mr. Cee finally gave him and gave Wheels a picture. And Wheels did exactly what he said he was going to do.

Wheels appreciated everything that Mr. Cee did for him growing up on Lime Street. One day Wheels was in the store and Rage walked in. Much to his surprise.

"What's good bro? What are you doing on this side of town"? Wheels asked.

"I was doing some running around in the city and decided to stop by. Just because I moved to the burbs don't mean I can't come back to my city. I'm still a city boy, always will be" Rage replied.

"I know OG. You know I had to fuck with you. It's been a while since I've seen you. I'm glad you stopped by though. You can see me in my new element. This is my new life as a store owner, serving the community. I haven't made any drastic changes, because I believe the community loves the place how it is. I'll slowly put my stamp on things and come up with a few different things to implement. I'm *thankful Mr. Cee sold it to me. Keeps my ass focused and out of the bullshit. You feel me? All the while serving the community. I love it bro. I really do" Wheels said.*

"Can't agree more about that bro. It's good to do something positive and productive. You know Lanc City is the type of city. If you aren't doing something productive and positive. You could get into some shit real quick. That's why I'm glad everybody was smart with their money and invested. We lost Travis. I don't want to lose anymore of yall. I hope everybody remains smart and stays out of these streets. We're all too old for that shit now anyway. Well most of us are. Moving outside the city has helped me a lot. I don't have to worry about my peoples on Beaver coming to get me to handle some shit like in the past. All I hear now is birds chirping and shit. Moving outside the city and just visiting when I can. Has helped me a lot. And kept me out of a lot of shit. knowing me if I was still on the block I'd be tempted to get right back in" Rage replied.

"Whatever works for you and the family. And as long as you all are happy, that's all that matters. For me still living on Lime and having the store here is convenient. But I'm not going to front. I've thought about moving out of the city in the past. Maybe one day. But for now, it's business as usual" Wheels said. As he went over and waited on a customer.

"I'm going to get out of here bro. I like what you're doing with the store. Proud of you fam. We'll link up this weekend sometime" Rage replied. As he left.

They shook hands and Rage walked out of the store. After Rage left. It was a rare moment that Wheels was by himself in the store. Just reflecting on the last year or so of his life. All the shit the crew had been through. Of course the bank heists. And no doubt his little bro Travis. Travis death hit Wheels hard. And he wished Travis was still here. It was early in the afternoon right before the kids got home from school. After school was a busy time for the store, like it was back in the day. Kids getting off school and coming in the store for snacks before they went home. Corner stores were huge in Lanc City. And were in damn near every neighborhood in the city. It was a lucrative business.

A lot of residents in the city loved corner stores. They were very convenient to people who didn't drive. And people who didn't feel the need to go to the grocery store for a certain item. That's where corner stores made their money. Kids also came to the store in the mornings on their way to school. Business was steady during the day. Wheels was in a happy time in his life. He was carrying on the legacy of a great man in the community. And he was running a clean business, making money and just staying out of trouble. Wheels was content with his new life. He had been in the streets and did bids. And lived that life. Now he was happy to lay his head down at night. Without worrying about the Police kicking down his door in the middle of the night.

Those brutal Northeast Winters was also a time corner stores thrived. Wheels had two other corner stores up and down the block from him. One on Lime and Green Streets. And Ann and Juniata. The competition was there. So Wheels always made sure the store was his main priority. The store on Lime and Dauphin was special because of Mr. Cee and what he meant to the neighborhood and city. That alone made it special. And Wheels would take it into the future and uphold the legacy Mr. Cee had laid down for him.

On Ann Street. Kwame was sitting on his porch. Something he hadn't done in a while. He just sat outside and listened to the sounds of the block. He needed that. Still appreciating the fact he was home and thinking about his future. And realizing that things could be worse for him and he could still be sitting in prison. Kwame had not only got away with a lot of money from bank heists. He also got away with shooting an armed guard. Law enforcement couldn't prove that Kwame was the triggerman. That would've meant an even larger prison sentence. But as of now. Kwame was a free man and free of the charges they were TRYING to stick him with.

Chino on the other hand, wasn't so lucky. Local law enforcement had gotten a search warrant to search his warehouse. And they found illegal guns. And this wasn't Chino's first charge. He would more than likely get a long prison sentence for this. Law enforcement were pressuring him to take a deal to rat the crew out. If he did, he could possibly walk away a free man. Despite his charges. Chino was in a tough situation. But he couldn't be a rat. So he decided to take the years. Chino ended up being sentenced to 5 to 7 years in State Prison.

Nobody was able to talk to Chino just before he was taken into custody. The last person he spoke to in the crew was Nitro. And that didn't go too well. So the crew had no idea where his head was at. But they knew he wouldn't flip on them. Like anyone else in the crew that put in work. And eventually got locked up. The crew would make sure Chino's family was good while he was down.

Angel was on her way back home to Lanc City from Philly. She had gotten used to her surroundings on campus at Temple. And she liked living on campus and having a nice apartment that she had been in for a little while now. She was happy to be coming home. She hadn't been home in a little over a month. As soon as she got to her home on Chester Street. She took a power nap and then got up. Her cousin Tisha was walking over to her house from Garden Court. She was organizing some papers when she heard a knock on the door. It was her cousin Tisha of course.

"Hey cousin!! Welcome home girl!! How's Temple? You like it down there"? Tisha asked as she walked in.

"It's cool. Different. But yes. I like it down there. I have a nice apartment and I'm getting used to things down there. Specifically the school and campus. You know I've been to Philly plenty of times. How's things been around the city lately"? Angel replied asking.

"Same shit different day cousin. Not much going on at all. It's about to get cold. Niggas aint coming outside to be fucking around in these streets. Not many at least. I'm sure some fools are still out there. I seen Kwame the other day drive down Marshall Street in his black Benz. Not too many people around here have a black Benz like that. So I knew it was him. I was coming out of the corner store on East End and Marshall. I don't think he seen me either. But anyway. I seen him" Tisha said.

"Oh ok. Well we should go to dinner later. And catch up some more. My treat. I have this paper I have to finish and then I'll get a shower and get dressed. WE can go to dinner and then go Down Bottom for some drinks and music" Angel replied.   Page 161

"Sounds good to me cousin. But this time I got you. I'm buying dinner and I'm buying us drinks all night. You're home and I want to make you feel at home. So don't even think about disagreeing with your big cousin. I got us tonight" Tisha said.

The two cousins talked a little while longer before hanging up. Angel worked on her paper from school. Tisha went back to her apartment in Garden Court. And the two women did what they had to do before they would meet up later.

Kwame decided to go see Chino. He felt it was the least he could do. And he wanted to reassure Chino that the crew would look after his family while he did his time. He himself was fortunate to escape a potential long prison sentence recently. Kwame wanted to let him know he wasn't forgotten about and he appreciated everything he did for the crew. Before Chino was to go upstate to serve his 5 to 7 year prison sentence. Kwame went to see him in the County Prison.

"What's good man? I hope all is well with you. I just wanted to come and show my support and appreciation for all you've done for the crew. And we're going to look out for your family. While you're down bro" Kwame said.

Chino just stared at Kwame for a minute before responding.

"I would hope you all would. Remember. I was cool before you asked me to rent my warehouse. I'm taking the fall for the crew's shit. That means you all need to kick in. Including some of Travis cut too. He may be dead, but his money is still here. His death is the reason I'm here. We were free of this shit until he got hit" Chino replied.

"You hear what the fuck you're saying right now dawg? You want to take from a dead man's family? Remember when you got robbed at YOUR warehouse nigga? You know who made that right? And put them niggas in a graveyard? Travis. That's who. And now you want to take his money? The money he put his life on the line and died for? I told you, we got your family" Kwame said.

"I would expect that from you Kwame. We've known each other way too long for the bullshit. And you know I'm not saying shit. I'll take the time because I'm a stand up nigga. I never folded under the pressure of these muthafuckas. And I never will. You came and seen me. Which I was expecting you to do. Because if you didn't show your face, I might've had different thoughts about you. So I give you that" Chino replied.

"I'm always a man of my word. You know that Chino. So we're done here? Because I have to get going. And I'll make that trip to see you upstate when I can. Stay up homie and stay strong. I gave my number to your family if they need anything to call me" Kwame said. Before he got up and left.

Chino just nodded his head in agreement. And didn't say another word. As Kwame got up and left. Chino sat there for another minute before getting up and being escorted back to his cell.

After talking to a few people Downtown. Nitro was looking to meet up with Chill and Kwame about coming up with money to secure the liquor license for the club. That was half the battle, but they had to get started somewhere. They hadn't gotten word on if they had secured the location yet. But Nitro felt optimistic about it. Even though the site had been vacant for a long time. The city still considered it prime real estate. Being Downtown and across from the baseball stadium. Chill and Nitro wanted that spot badly, and they weren't giving up on it until they heard no from the city. Nitro needed to meet with Chill and Kwame. So he decided to meet them at one of the Downtown bars rooftop lounges. As they sat at a table overlooking the city's skyline, they discussed the plan.

"We get the liquor license. We got the hundred grand for that. We just need to put together a professional presentation for these big wigs Downtown. So they can believe in our plans. So we can secure that location for the build. Without that property, there's no club and the dream dies with it" Nitro said.

"If that's what we have to do, so be it. We have to come up with the best presentation we can come up with. I'm putting everything into this. This shit has to work, I want this club" Chill replied.

"I'm just going to sit back and let you two handle the hands on shit. I've invested my money. And I trust you two to make good with it. So whatever you two decide, count me in. I went and seen Chino the other day. He's a little bitter about him being the one doing the time. And we being the real ones in action" Kwame said.

"Bitter? Why? Because he fucked up? First this nigga gets robbed and then cries to us like we had some shit to do with it. Then he gets called Downtown about the double murder. And now he just got bagged for having illegal guns in that same fucking warehouse!! Nigga should be bitter at himself for being so sloppy. When you were in the County. I met him down by the water near The Clairemont Houses. He was bugging out. I thought he was going to flip on us then. But he didn't. So I give him that. He stood tall. But he shouldn't be bitter at us because we escaped the shit. I'm sure his fam will be straight with that money yall made from that last heist" Nitro replied.

"That's basically what I told him. His family will be taken care of. But you're listening to a man that just got sentenced five to seven years. A lot of shit can change in that time. Plus the man has already been locked up before. I understand his anger, it's just misdirected. He'll get over all that shit and do his time. I told him I'll come visit him upstate" Kwame said.

"Enough about that Chino bullshit. I got this chick Downtown that could help us. With the presentation. I just thought of her when we were talking. She's been dying to work with me. And this could be her chance. The main thing with this presentation is. We have to assure them the place will be professional and safe from any drama and bullshit. Especially with the stadium being right across the street. This is going to be our club. Playing the music we like and the community we come from likes. We set the trends like always" Nitro replied.

Page 163

"And be different and unique than any other club in the fucking city. Take over this nightlife shit in the city for real" Chill said sounding determined.

"We have the idea and drive no doubt. We just have to get to work and make it happen" Kwame added on.

Meanwhile Desmond decided to take a ride out to the cemetery. But before he did. He drove by Lime and Dauphin to see what Wheels was up to. As he drove through the block. Wheels was about to get in his BMW. Which was parked across the street from the store.

"What's good bro? I'm about to go out to the cemetery and see Travis. You down to ride"? Desmond asked.

"Hey bro. I just came from checking on the store and bringing my employee change. But yeah, fuck it. I'll ride out there. Haven't been out there in a while anyway" Wheels replied.

Wheels got in Desmond's car and they were out. They made their way out to the cemetery and to Travis gravesite. His family had bought him a nice tombstone. Wheels and Desmond stood there together staring at his tombstone. Neither of them had been out there since the day they buried him. They both missed him dearly. Especially Desmond. Desmond and Travis became close over that last year. Both young men with their whole lives ahead of them. Until Travis life was cut short. After standing out there for a little while longer. They both got in the car and left. On the ride home they had a conversation.

"Still crazy to believe that nigga is gone man. And not here to enjoy the money he made with us. As much shit as he did when he was alive. And how he really wanted to do the right things in life. It still seemed like he got robbed of it all in the end" Desmond said as he drove.

"I think about him often. He was like my little brother. And he did take some of my advice. Even though we both know Travis had a mind of his own. I would always try to steer him in the right direction. Well for the most part. Because I was doing my car shit. And I blame myself somewhat. Because when Kwame brought this bank heist shit to me. The first person I thought to bring in on it was

Travis. That was before you two became close. So in essence. I was the person who got him into some shit that eventually got him killed" Wheels replied.

"Can't none of us blame ourselves for what happened that day. And you weren't even there. I blamed myself for a while when it happened. Even long after the funeral. I just came to grips with the fact that I can't blame myself anymore. Whatever was going to happen that day did happen, and I have to accept it. We all do" Desmond said.

"I actually have made peace with it Desmond. Like you. At first I blamed myself because I wasn't there. And then I realized it wasn't my fault. And no matter how hard it was to accept that fact. I had to accept it. Just like you said. He'll live through us and our contributions in life moving forward. We were the two closest people to him in the crew. So WE have to be the ones to carry on his memory through ourselves" Wheels replied.   Page 164

"I just didn't want him to die for nothing. And as long as I'm breathing he didn't die for nothing. For him I'm going to be the best artist I can be. Because he wanted me to be just that. He always encouraged me to chase my dreams. Even though we were in the streets, he knew I had that talent. And he wanted me to maximize my potential. And I'm going to do it. And you're right, he'll live through us" Desmond said.

Desmond and Wheels had a nice moment reminiscing about their fallen homie. Someone they clearly missed. Travis might've been wild and crazy at times. But he was loyal to the crew, and his loyalty was unmatched.

Erotic Styles Hair Salon was doing great for a new business. The buzz about the shop was going through the city. And the shop being Downtown was attracting new customers. Erotic couldn't be more happier with her business. Kwame had to be driving through Downtown on Chestnut when he stopped by the shop.

"Hey. I see you doing big things E. How are you doing beautiful"? Kwame asked. As he came in the shop and gave Erotic a hug. And then sat down at one of the empty barber chairs.

"Thanks Kwame. I'm doing pretty good and business is going well. What brings you Downtown"? Erotic replied asking.

"I had to drop some papers off for my lawyer. And I was in the neighborhood so I stopped by. And I know I was here last week too. Just making sure my little sister is good is all" Kwame said.

"I'm good Kwame. I'm happy and very blessed. We all are. Since I've had this shop. I have no need to get myself in any kind of dumb shit. things that I used to do and wouldn't think a second about. That I knew wasn't the right thing to do. Doesn't cross my mind anymore. The old me would still be in the bullshit. Since having my shop I know I don't have to look over my shoulder anymore. I have a legit business now. I can sleep good at night and it feels good. And people know me now for doing hair and not boosting" Erotic replied.

"You evolved E. We all did. We're older now and thinking about our futures. That's why I told everybody to save and invest their money. And look at you now. Got your own business. Wheels got his store. Nitro, Chill, and I working on this real estate thing. Desmond has his art and Angel is down at Temple. We all did dirt and managed to clean our shit up when we needed to. Like you said. We've been blessed" Kwame said.

"Kwame I can see how you got all our crazy asses together too. Nigga you can talk your ass off. And talk people into believing in you and what you're selling. Thanks for always being the big brother you've always been to me. Love you bro" Erotic replied. As she gave Kwame a hug before he left.

Detective Boyd was back in Lanc City. After being in Harrisburg handling some other cases. But still following the investigations in the bank heists. He already knew who was responsible for the double murder.

Page 165

After it was proven that the murder weapon was Travis 45 caliber handgun. Which was recovered at the scene of the crew's last bank heist. Detective Boyd didn't have any more evidence than he had when he left Lanc City before. But he was still holding out hope that he could get more. He promised himself he wouldn't stay no more than a few days to get the evidence he needed. If couldn't get it in that time. He would focus on his other cases.

After Desmond had looked at the new high rise condos on Duke and Chestnut. He went and looked at one. He decided he would take it. And planned to move in a few days. Desmond had lived on Green Street all his life. All Desmond knew was Green Street. It was where his parents raised him until they were killed in a car accident when he was between eighteen and nineteen years old. He lost both his parents at the same time. Which would be devastating for any kid of any age to lose their parents so suddenly. Desmond had uncles and aunts that lived locally. But after his parents were killed. Desmond vowed to keep the family home, and he did. All through the years up until this point. Between hustling in the streets, the B&E game. Working jobs here and there and then quitting. Then finally getting up with the crew and doing bank heists is how he's survived all these years.

Desmond planned to rent his family home out on Green Street. The house had been paid for now for over three years. The future for Desmond was now. And he was making the necessary changes in life to evolve himself as a person. After he got himself together and established in the Art world. He planned to come back to the 7th Ward and offer classes for inner city kids who aspire to be artist. Kids from the city didn't just have to be sports figures and entertainers. Some could be artists, doctors, lawyers, judges, etc. Desmond was a success story in himself. Coming from where he came from and going through what he went through. Desmond had already spent some of his time volunteering at community centers art programs.

After having some of his pieces displayed at the Downtown Art Galleries. Desmond's face started to look familiar on Prince and Chestnut Streets. He became a fixture in the art scene in the city. From his new residence on Duke and Chestnut Streets. It would be a short walk to the Downtown Art Galleries.

Nitro and Chill had drew up the plans for their proposed nightclub. They hired a team of the best speakers and presenters they could find in the city. They wanted to be as professional as they could be. They knew what they were up against. There were rumors going around about local officials believing that the crew was behind all this. But it was just that......rumors. The day of the official proposal all three men were in attendance. Nitro, Chill, and Kwame were all there. And they were all dressed in suits and carried themselves like businessmen. They were all serious about this club they wanted to build. And you could see it in their swagger. They were determined to secure that location so they could start to build.

Angel had been home for a few days now. And after going out to dinner with her cousin Tisha. Angel stopped by Erotic's shop.

"Hey girl, how are you? Business seems to be going well. I just came home from school for a little. I hope you can do something with this hair too, before I head back to Philly" Angel said.

"Hey Angel. And don't worry girl I got you. How's school going"? Erotic replied asking.

"It's going well. And I'm glad business is going well for you. You know I had to come through and see my girl. I tell some of the women who come up this way to go to the outlets. To check you out when they come up this way. Come to the city and check you out" Angel said.

"Thanks for the plug girl. I appreciate it. New business is always good and welcomed. How long are you going to be home"? Erotic replied asking.

"I'm probably going to leave tomorrow sometime. Maybe we can hang out tonight. Go Down Bottom or something. It's been a while" Angel said. Before she left and let Erotic get back to her customers.

"Ok. Give me a call later. I'll be around. Need to get out anyway. It's been a while for me too" Erotic replied.

Rage continued living and enjoying suburbia. His family loved their new quieter lifestyle in Lancaster County. His children were involved in sports and activities at school. Soccer, basketball, football, drama club, chorus, etc. Rage and his wife were busy with that. Instead of being on the block, he was taking his kids to school. And to practices for the various sports they were in. It was a different life but a life Rage welcomed with open arms. Rage had a deck out back of his house that he enjoyed. Plenty of times after picking the kids up from school. He would grab one of his Cuban Cigars and a drink. Go out and sit on his back deck and relax. Rage was really enjoying his new life.

That next day Chino was sent upstate to serve his five to seven year prison sentence. Bittersweet day for him as well as the crew. It was like after this day today. It would officially end the crew's reign over being one of the best and most successful bank heist crews in American History. They could've tried to keep going. But it was clear the crew as a whole, were onto bigger and better things. Chino's warehouse in the Sixth Ward was the crew's headquarters during their reign. And played a major part in the whole process. It was where they counted the money. The first place they went to after doing their heists. Millions of dollars in cash money had been through that warehouse.

Chino was still angry about being the only one doing time. And also being the one that did the least amount of shit. But he also had to blame himself for having illegal guns in his warehouse. Something he had planned to do temporarily. But the local authorities ended up raiding his warehouse before he could move them. So he couldn't blame all of it on the crew. He had to stand tall and do his time like a man. And that's exactly what he planned to do. The crew stuck to their promise of taking care of his family. And getting Chino anything he needed while he was in there. No matter what. It would be hard for Chino being away from his family for at least the next five years. Page 167

The only one that visited Chino was Kwame. Which was to be expected. Because him and Kwame were close. And Kwame is the one who brought him in. Chino didn't have much of a relationship with the rest of the crew. It was just business with them. Getting on that bus and looking out that window as Lanc City streets got further and further away. Reality set in even more. He wouldn't see these streets again for a while. A lot of emotions ran through him. His family, his warehouse. That would now be seized by the city and state. Just the city itself would be long gone and behind him at this point. It was the harsh reality Chino was facing.

Later that night. Angel, Erotic, and Tisha all went Down Bottom for some drinks. And to dance. The ladies were all dressed and looking beautiful. As they listened to one of the local DJ's on the ones and twos. Wheels, Nitro, Desmond, and Chill joined the ladies at the bar. The crew was deep on this night. And having a good time taking pictures all around the bar. As people were coming in, they quickly recognized the crew. As did the local DJ. When he grabbed the mic and shouted the crew out. Everyone had a great time. And everyone was feeling the drinks like always Down Bottom. It was the first time most of the crew had been around each other since the early days.

"You see how live it is in this bitch? It's going to be even more live when we get that club. I'm going to be keep coming down here regardless. Because I love the hood. But that area where we want to build the club at. We have to take over this area and Downtown" Chill said taking a sip of his drink.

Thanksgiving was approaching and the crew was gearing up for their first annual turkey give away. And they weren't just giving away turkeys. They were serving full dinners. To anybody that wanted to eat. They served food all over the city in every community. At the community centers near each neighborhood. In essence they fed the city and were glad to do it. Angel was home from school and also helped serving food. There was also a huge set-up in front of where The Boys & Girls Club once was. For people who wanted to take turkeys home. Along with all the sides. A nice amount of people showed up and were grateful for everything the crew did.

It was part of what LANCREW was all about. All the hell they went through to get the money they got. Risking their lives and risking going to prison for a long time. it was all worth it, seeing the smiles on people's faces. Giving back to the community that raised them. And watched them all grow into men and women.

"Man look at this. This is truly amazing seeing all these happy people. I'm honored to be here. This city deserves this. There's a lot of homeless people in the city despite how small it is. Doing this is big, I'm glad we could do this. We didn't just talk about this shit, we did it" Kwame said.

It's definitely nice to see it. Seeing people that need it eat well for a change. Makes it all worth it fam. It really does. This is something we used to talk about when we first started this. It was a dream of ours. And seeing it become a reality is special" Wheels replied.

After serving the community for the holidays. Each crew member went to their respective homes and ate dinner with their families. The holiday, giveaway, and the serving of food all went well. Across the city in each location around the city. The serving of food went well and everyone was fed. The day was a success and the crew felt great about serving the community. It was a great turn out for the first year.

It was also around that time that Detective Boyd realized he needed to swallow his pride. And let the case he was pursuing go. It was the hard reality for Detective Boyd. And he couldn't stand the fact that he couldn't get the bank heist crew. All the work he put in, the long hours. And the only one convicted of a crime was Chino. Who wasn't necessarily an actual member of the crew. As Detective Boyd was cleaning out his makeshift desk on his way out of the door. He left Downtown Lanc City. After saying his goodbyes to some local law enforcement that worked with while in the city. He walked out of the Downtown Police Station into the Fall Lanc City sun to Downtown traffic.

Once he got in his car. He couldn't help but to drive through the 7th Ward one last time. Wondering where he went wrong as a detective. Even driving past the double murder scene. Detective Boyd was that deep in it. That case remained unsolved until a few days after Travis was killed himself. And his gun was recovered at the scene of his own shooting that resulted in his death. Travis never served a day in prison for killing Stacks and Bags. Because he met his own demise before he could. Detective Boyd wished he could bring Travis back to serve his time. And Stacks and Bags family could get the justice they deserved. But that would never happen now. And that's what disappointed Detective Boyd the most besides the fact he could never get the bank heist crew.

Detective Boyd really thought he was going to solve the bank heists that hit South Central Pennsylvania and surrounding areas. But in the end. He didn't have enough evidence to reach his ultimate goal of solving the case. He left Lanc City for good that day. And he left disappointed and angry. And didn't know what was next for him. The bank heist cases had him mentally drained. He swallowed his pride as hard as it was. And returned to his state office in Harrisburg.

Meanwhile Wheels was on Lime Street coming out of his house. And by now Fall had turned to Winter. And it was cold outside. Wheels had on a nice leather jacket with fur around the hoodie. And a skully on his head. He got in his BMW and was off. Riding through city blocks waving at those he knew. Banging some of the best music he could bang. Just enjoying the ride. Wheels would at times burn through city blocks. Meaning he would ride through for those that don't know the term "burn blocks". Or "burning blocks". He said it helped him clear his mind at times.

As he drove he began to reminisce about him, Travis, and Desmond. Being together on either Lime or Green Street. Or in Hill Rise. They all knew each other for years. But Travis and Desmond didn't get along too well at first. Two strong personalities clashed, but eventually became the best of friends. Wheels was of course older. But both Travis and Desmond knew and knew of Wheels from Lime Street. Once they banned together to be apart of the crew. Page 169

Their bond grew even stronger. It was an added plus that they were making money together. They bought cars and any other shit they wanted. Went on trips to A.C. and Vegas. They lived the life of having money in the fast lane. By this time Wheels was riding through the 8th Ward and heading back to the 7th Ward. To have a drink Down Bottom before he returned home. The drive did wonders for him. As he reminisced about all the good times they had. He experienced every emotion from smiling and laughing. To shedding some tears.

Sitting down at the bar and having himself a drink was just what Wheels needed. Things were going really well at the store. He had two dependable and responsible employees that he could count on. Working for him. He was in a great space in his life. He could now ease back a little from store's day to day operations. But that would be hard for Wheels. Because he lived right down the street on the same block. He was bound to visit his store daily to check on things.

On the other side of the city. Specifically on the North Side. North Prince and West Clay Streets. Looking at the abandoned building and still dreaming. And waiting to hear back from the city about their proposal to build the club on that property. As they stood there. Nitro's phone rang. As he was talking on the phone, and five minutes into the conversation. He tapped Chill on the shoulder, with excitement on his face. After finishing the conversation and hanging up. Nitro broke the news.

"Bro we got the property. You heard me? We did it fam!!! We fucking did it fam!!! We did that shit!! Yo"!!! Nitro said with pure excitement in his voice.

"Oh shit!! This is crazy bro!!! I can't believe this shit fam. We're celebrating tonight my G. For real" Chill replied.

They were both a little surprised they got the property. They were confident in their presentation and the people they hired to do it. Some of the best in the city. But they still thought they weren't going to be awarded the property in the end. To their surprise they were. And they both couldn't be any more happy than they were at the moment. The news was cause for a huge celebration and they planned to do just that. After securing the land. The men had to start working and brainstorming exactly how they wanted things. Most of that was done but they still had work to do. The men were serious about making this a success.

But before they could dive into the building process, the celebration was to take place. It would just be the crew, no outsiders on this night. Angel had stayed an extra night to celebrate with her brothers. She had class the next day. And since Philly was only an hour and twenty minutes away on a good day. She decided to stay longer. Chill and Nitro did it a little differently this time. They had a formal dinner party instead of a traditional party. At one of the trendy restaurants Downtown. Everyone would dress formal. Chill and Nitro were both in tailor made suits. Erotic and Angel both looked beautiful as ever in their beautiful dresses. That particular night at that spot. Only the crew was in attendance. The spot was rented out by the crew for the whole night. They were moving in on Downtown and making their presence felt right away. The crew was definitely in the building and throwing their weight around Downtown.   Page 170

"Look I know I'm a silent partner in this whole thing. I want to personally thank my brothers for getting it done. They did all the work. And I want to say you two brothers deserve the credit for this. Thank yall both and I love yall. Toast to my brothers for handling their shit like they said they was. Salute"!! Kwame said toasting to Chill and Nitro.

"Yes. Salute my bros. Kwame my other brother is drunk as shit right now but I got him. Salute my homies Nitro and Chill. And I want V.I.P. seats every time I come through too. Don't forget about me fellas" Wheels said. As everybody laughed.

Angel and Erotic gave the guys a hug and congratulated them on getting the location to build their club. Yet another member of the crew would be owning a business in the city. Chill and Nitro would be joining Wheels and Erotic. As people within the crew who had businesses. It was a great accomplishment for them all. They were once criminals that eventually became owners of businesses and leaders in the community. It was the first time the crew had been all together since Travis funeral. It was a great night and the crew was hoping for many more great nights in the future.

Rage and Desmond were standing off to the side of everybody else. Sipping on their drinks and talking.

"How's your drawing going? I heard you got some work of yours displayed in the Downtown Art Galleries" Rage said as he stood next to Desmond.

"It's going pretty well actually. And I've had a few of my pieces displayed too. Might have some buyers soon. I moved into those new high rise condos on Duke and Chestnut Streets" Desmond replied.

"Oh ok. That's what's up bro. Congrats homie. I'm happy for you fam" Rage said.

"Being close to Downtown has been better for me. I'm close to the Art Galleries. I lived on Green Street all my life, it was time for a change" Desmond replied.

"Word. It's all about evolving as a person bro. Growing into one's better self. Seeing shit differently than we did as young men. I couldn't be on the block doing the shit I used to do now. And I have a family. And kids looking up to me. You're still young and have your whole life ahead of you. You don't have any kids, you can do you. Live your life to the fullest and travel world man. I would if I was you. Let your art take you to the places you're meant to go" Rage said.

After leaving a Downtown restaurant the crew ended up at a rooftop lounge Downtown a few blocks away. Still celebrating Chill and Nitro getting the approval to build their club. The abandoned building for so many years. At North Prince and West Clay Streets. Would finally be brought to life. The crew ended the night on the rooftop. But before they did. They all took pictures with the city's two largest buildings as the backdrop. It was a fun night and a night that was memorable for so many reasons.

The crew wasn't known to frequent Downtown. But on this night, they took over the streets of Downtown Lanc City. And partied to the early morning hours of the next day. It was Christmas and the crew had one more obligation to fulfill. Their gift giveaway to the community. It was another way of giving back to the community they were apart of. They held the gift giveaway at the community building on Howard Avenue. Any less fortunate family, especially any that had children. Would get a cart full of gifts. There were plenty of gifts for everyone. As the crew shipped in truckloads of products to help local families and children. Having it on Howard Avenue was special for a few reasons. Howard Avenue was one of the oldest blocks in the city. And was also home to their fallen crew member Travis. Who was the same man that threw a party for all of Hill Rise. The whole projects. After he came into the money from the bank heists.

It was just a great day that day. A whole lot of love was shown. And a whole lot of families with and without children. Were happy after leaving the community center. The whole crew volunteered to help hand out gifts. Seeing the families faces meant everything to the crew. Regardless of what each individual did on the streets. And the shit they all did together with the bank heists. They all had good hearts and their hearts were always in the right place for the people that came from the same place they did. Without a doubt they had enemies that came to their cookouts and the Splash Party in County Park. Enemies that took full advantage of the good deeds they did for good people. Lanc City was very much a cutthroat city. You couldn't trust no one.

If you had a few people you did trust. You'd be best to remain with them and keep them within your circle. Because that was rare around these parts. Some of the crew didn't real hang together like that or considered themselves friends. But the ones that did, maintained a solid relationship. And nothing was going to come between that. No money or women or anything. Because they were used to it all. A snowstorm was coming. But the crew was able to pull off their gift giveaway without any problems. And they were thankful for that.

The next day. Kwame got a call from Chino. Asking him to come see him. He didn't really know what Chino wanted. But of course he had to be a man of his word, and visit Chino like he had promised him. He owed him that at least. So Kwame headed to Northwest Pennsylvania to visit Chino. Chino was in Camp Hill, Pa. As usual. Kwame went in and sat down and waited for a few minutes before Chino came out.

"What's good Chino? How are you holding up in here? Something wrong"? Kwame asked.

"I'm maintaining Kwame. But I'm going to keep it short and sweet. I need you to take fifteen grand of my money and take it to Duke Manor. And another fifteen grand across the street to Susquehanna Court. The rest to my family. They'll know what to do with it. They told me you guys have been coming through with the cash consistently. I appreciate that. That's the least yall could do anyway. I'm taking this one for the team" Chino replied.

Kwame just looked at Chino and smiled.

"Chino you're a funny dude fam. You had me thinking it was some real serious shit I had to handle. Don't worry I got you bro. Man we just did our gift giveaway yesterday. Down at the community center on Howard Avenue. He was a great turn-out and we made a lot of people smile yesterday. Wish you would've been there fam. We're doing our part like we promised ourselves we would. In the beginning. Sticking to our word. Like we've been to you and your family. Chino you know you're dealing with some real people. Not none of that fake bullshit. I told you that when I first put this shit together. I would never let a fake muthafucka be apart of this thing we call ours playboy. Don't ever forget that. When we say we got you, we got you" Kwame said.

Chino just stared at Kwame for a minute and then nodded his head in approval. He knew Kwame was right. They had stood by their word and took care of Chino's family while he was locked up. And also provided him with whatever he needed while he was in prison. Kwame would drop Chino's money off at the locations he desired. And give the rest to his family like he asked. Duke Manor and Susquehanna Court were two housing projects adjacent to each other.

A year later that Spring. Chill and Nitro's dream had come true. On the corner of North Prince and West Clay streets. A new nightclub was born name "Club Lanc City". And just like Chill had predicted. The club was an instant smash. You couldn't get in the club the nights it was open. Thirsty Thursdays, Fire Fridays, Sexy Saturdays, and Soothing Sundays. And all four nights the club was jam packed. The music playlist was diverse. From Neo Soul to Hip Hop to R&B to Reggaeton to Old-School. The club appealed to a broad audience who enjoyed Urban Music. The first week was truly amazing. And Chill and Nitro was overjoyed. The club also had two floors with two different DJ's rocking on each floor. V.I.P. areas on both floors. The buzz wasn't just in Lanc City about the new club. But all across Pennsylvania.

As Chill and Nitro stood in the V.I.P. section. Just looking and admiring what they built. Two kids from the 7th Ward that came from nothing. Had now got a hold of prime real estate Downtown to build a nightclub that took the city by storm. From day one. It was almost too good to be true. They worked hard to get where they were today. They had a dream and a plan. And saw it through. Neither men were angels by any stretch of the imagination. But they left the negativity behind them for more positive things. They were businessmen now. And they didn't work this hard and waited over a year to see their dream come true. For nothing. They had a legal business, and they planned to keep it.

"Man. Just seeing this shit up close and personal is crazy. It was just a dream last year. And we're here now actually living this shit. This is some true boss shit fam" Chill said pacing and fourth with his drink in hand.

"Hard work pays off homie. Hard work pays off. We put in the work.....THE MONEY. And we deserve all this shit my G. Enjoy it all Chill. Love you bro" Nitro replied. Clearly feeling it off a few bottles.

Kwame and a few other crew members had been to the club. A lot of them were there opening night celebrating with Chill and Nitro. Kwame was also part owner of the club.   Page 173

He was a silent partner. But he was part owner, after investing some of his money to build the club. But Kwame wasn't much of a club dude. And hadn't been since opening night. He let Chill and Nitro handle the day to day at the club. He was more interested in their other real estate ventures.

Desmond's art was getting more and more praise from the local art community. And it was starting to make waves throughout the state. And was quickly moving towards national recognition. He had re-dedicated himself to his craft. He was totally focused on his art. Something he promised himself he would do since Travis death.

Travis always encouraged him to follow his dreams in art. Desmond's re-dedication was dedicated to him. He would soon tour the United States and it's Art Galleries. Displaying his work and going to places he had never been. No matter how many places he toured or where he went. He would always remind everyone. That he was just a kid from Lancaster, Pennsylvania. Green Street to be exact. He was always proud of where he was from. And he felt even prouder now.

Touring meant a lot of time away from the city. The only place he knew for the most part of his life. But he was loving every minute of it. He was currently in Cleveland, Ohio. At an Art Exhibit. He was displaying some of his pieces. Afterwards going back to his hotel suite and relaxed as he watched TV. He decided to give Wheels a call.

"What's good OG? How's things going back home"? Desmond asked.

"Desmond!! Good to hear from you bro. You know Lanc City is always going to be Lanc City. The same shit, you aren't missing anything bro. Me and Kwame went to Club Lanc City last night. Hung out with Chill shooting the shit. We had a nice time too. So how's things going on the road touring? And where are you at now anyway"? Wheels replied asking.

"I'm in Cleveland now fam. And touring is great bro. And yeah. The club is nice. I'm proud of Nitro and Chill, they're doing big things. When I get back home we're all going to go out. Chop it up with my brothers, I miss yall man" Desmond said.

"You got any groupies out there on the road bro? I mean you're an artist now. And I know once women see your shit. They're going to be after you hard. I'm just saying. Enjoy that while you can, you're still young bro" Wheels replied.

"Man. There isn't no groupies out here for no artist who actually draw and paint. At least I haven't ran into any of them yet. Never know though. If I do eventually see one or come in contact with one. And she's bad? You know what it is OG" Desmond said.

"Listen. If you're successful and they know you're successful. They're out there bro. Trust me. I have a cousin that lives in Atlanta. This nigga is younger than me. My little cousin. Got his own practice. He's a doctor and those women know he's successful. And they love his ass. He's still single talking about his trying to figure things out. I'm like nigga. You're taking full advantage of your status. And that's cool. Because he's single like yo ass. And he earned it. Just like you're doing. All I'm saying is.

Be careful of course. But live your life and enjoy this moment bro. Some people that are from where we're from. Never leave. Never get the chance to tour the country like you're doing. Don't take this for granted. And I know you won't" Wheels replied.

"I hear you OG. Still the same Wheels. But this tour is really nice bro. Meeting a lot of interesting people through my art. People I didn't think I would ever meet. But it's been fun. And it's all about expanding the brand right? This is what the man above put me on this Earth to do. A God given gift. I'm blessed. Took some time for me to realize it. Being on this tour has brought so many things in perspective for me. Realizing what I have in front of me. And being away from Lanc City for the time I have. I've been able to think a lot more about things. But I can't front though. I miss home. There's no place like Lanc City" Desmond said.

"That's great bro. I'm glad to see you're maturing as a man. And looking at shit differently. That's what happens when you start maturing from life experiences. It's a natural progression for most people, but definitely not all. I'm glad you got it. Some niggas would still be out here doing the same shit. It's all about evolving as a person. None of us are perfect, we learn everyday. But you're well on your way youngin. I put some new flowers at Travis gravesite the other day" Wheels replied.

"There isn't a day that goes by that I don't think about my brother. And that day still plays in my mind till this day in real time. Shit plays in head a thousand times when I think of him. Not just that though. Of course the good times after I shed a few tears. He would be happy about everybody doing their thing now. How's the store going"? Desmond asked.

"Everything is cool. The store is doing well. I still have my two employees. And I work in the store myself sometimes. We make it work. I believe me, Kwame, and Chill are going to be the last niggas to move out of the 7th Ward. Out of the crew I mean. But then again maybe me, because my store is on the block I live on. Plus Kwame was already talking about moving. I thought about moving outside of the city. But I'm just so used to living on Lime Street. And my store being there, its more convenient. But I might change my mind. I could afford a nicer home" Wheels replied.

"Of course you could. I love my condo bro. And miss the hell out of it. But I have to get this money so I could keep affording to live there. You feel me? I can't complain about where I'm at. I'm Downtown where all the trendy shit is. All walking distance. I love it. Get you a condo bro" Desmond said.

"I might look into that. But I will let you get back to your relaxation. I have to head out anyway. Stay up bro. Crew" Wheels replied.

"Ok fam. Crew" Desmond said before hanging up.

Talking to his homie Wheels was refreshing to Desmond being on the road and missing home. They talked for a while that night. And remained good friends over the years. After Cleveland, Desmond would be off to Chicago. He had a fifteen city tour across the

country. Not bad for a kid from the 7th Ward.
Page 175

After getting off the phone with Desmond. Wheels decided to do a mid day pickup of cash from the store. Something he would do from time to time. It was also something that Mr. Cee told him he would do from time to time. To keep the cash at a minimum in the store. In case of a robbery or anything else. In which the store was never robbed. But times were changing and a new generation were a lot of the customers. And people respected Mr. Cee around the neighborhood enough to never do that. But Mr. Cee was no longer there. And Wheels had to be cautious at first. Wheels had a lot of the same respect around the neighborhood. But the younger generation. Some weren't really big on respect. Especially to their elders. The youngins that used to listen to the OG's like Desmond and Travis. Didn't exist as much.

After getting the cash. Wheels got in his black BMW and sped up Lime Street until you could no longer see him. Kwame eventually moved off Ann Street and relocated to Lancaster Township. That is for two years. That was his plan. And then he planned to move his family out West to Las Vegas. It was something about that city that intrigued him. Plus he always wanted to move out West. Until then. You could find him in the V.I.P. section at Club Lanc City from time to time. Other than that. He lived a private life with his family. Real lowkey and not wanting any attention drawn to himself. He was the mastermind of putting together one of the best bank heist crews in American history. A crew that got away with millions and lived to tell it. That life was far behind him now.

Desmond continued to have his Downtown condo. And enjoyed it when he wasn't travelling or touring with his art. Touring helped sell his work. The more he toured, the more money he made. He also had a lot of money he made from the bank heists still stashed. So he was stacking and enjoying his life as a young bachelor. Nitro was still doing his thing with the real state. And also co-owning the club with Chill. Chill was more of the physical presence at the club. Nitro would be there maybe 50% of the time. For the first three months Nitro was the face of the club. Being he was a people person that loved to party. He had to be the face of the club. People in the entertainment industry knew him. And that worked well for a while until Nitro got bored with it and went to do something else. Nitro wasn't one to stay stuck in one certain area. He was all over the place.

Chill enjoyed being the front man. After all this was his idea from day one. Chill was truly living a dream. Rage continued living in Lancaster County and enjoyed the normal righteous life he wanted with his family. Every once in a while coming into the city and stopping through his old stomping grounds on Beaver Street. He eventually went on a cruise with his family the next summer. Having the time of his life.

Erotic was still doing her thing. And her business was a household name not only Downtown, but within the city. It became one of the best hair salons in the city. You could see her work on many women walking the streets of Lanc City. Far from her Rockland Street days when she was boosting. Erotic had moved her and her grandmother into a new home outside the city. Things had truly come full circle for her. She didn't have to hustle looking over her shoulder anymore. She had a new clean hustle so she could sleep comfortably at night.   Page 176

Angel eventually graduated from Temple with a degree in Business. And was working for a company in New Jersey. She would still come home from time to time to her home on Chester Street. Angel's cousin Tisha had moved her parents down South and she moved to New Jersey. Not too far away from Angel. As the years went by. The crew watched as a new young generation was heavy in the streets. And they were totally different than when they came up.

With a different set of rules. There was no respect and no code. Just every man for himself. No loyalty and no honor amongst men. It was even more dangerous. There was little fighting and a lot more gunplay.

The crew by now. Were all just living normal lives. And they all didn't need for anything, them or their families. Because of their investments. They were all living comfortable lives. Had businesses or made investments that continued to make them money over the years. Desmond was home on a rare occasion for a few days. He had just got a brand new Cadillac Escalade and drove outside the city to the cemetery. He went to see Travis. He hadn't been since him and Wheels was out there. And he really wanted to come alone, so he did. He got out of his truck with a bottle. He poured a little bit of liquor on the ground. Before he spoke.

"What's good Travis. I miss you like crazy bro. I really do. I always remember that time you rode that damn motorcycle down Green Street. I was like. Who the hell was that? You had that helmet on that covered everything but the eyes. You came back up near my house. I'm like. Oh shit. it's Travis crazy ass. That motorcycle was fast. And you used to burn out on that shit every chance you could. I gave the bike to your little brother. I remember you telling me, he likes bikes too. He was happy I gave it to him too. I know you loved the hell out of that bike and your car. I'm not sure who has your car now. Your family is good though bro. I talked to your mom the other day and she said everybody is good.

I'm touring the country with this art thing man. Yeah. The art you told me to pursue. I'm following my dreams like you encouraged me to do bro. I've seen places I've never seen before. That's how far this art thing has taken me. I'm living the dream fam. And I wish you were here with me enjoying it with me. Well I know you're watching over me. Well I'm about to head out. But you know I'll be back. Love you bro. Crew" Desmond said before leaving.

He got in his truck and drove off. As Desmond drove back towards the city. 90's Hip Hop and R&B was banging on the radio. They lived a wild and interesting life during their reign. Survived some tragic and tense times. The ones that remained were successful and lived to tell it. They were legends. And when they were seen around the city. They were acknowledged with respect and honor. They weren't just legends for what they did in the streets. But they were legends for what they did for their community. The city appreciated them. They weren't only a legendary crew, but they started a movement and blueprint for future crews to follow. LANCREW.

Page 177

A year later. Wheels had bought a brand new tailor made suit. As he was driving Downtown to The Convention Center. The same Convention Center where Nitro had his birthday party some years back. But this time. He was here for something more dear to his heart. The city was honoring Mr. Cee for serving the city and community for so many years. It was well deserved from one of city's great men. An elder statesman that had a lot of wisdom that he shared with the youth growing up near his store on Lime Street. Wheels was honored to be invited and to speak on behalf of Mr. Cee. Who had become somewhat of a mentor to him over the years.

The event for Mr. Cee was jam packed with people. In one of the Convention Center's ballrooms. Mr. Cee sat quietly with his wife as each person got up and spoke about the man. It felt great to be appreciated. And Mr. Cee felt the love that night. Him and his family sat and listened to community leaders and citizens of the city. And they spoke fondly about the husband, father, Christian, store owner, and man in the community. Wheels sat and waited for his turn to speak. And then the time had come. It was Wheels turn to speak. As he got up out of his seat and walked up on stage. He grabbed the mic and began.

"Thank you to Mr. Cee and his family for having me here tonight. I can't begin to tell you all the impact Mr. Cee. Had on my life. As well as a lot of young men and women that grew up on Lime Street. And who were from Lancaster City. We all enjoyed Mr. Cee's corner store. And I personally loved the place so much I took over for him. And it's been an honor to carry on the legacy that this great man has paved along the way. He's been a father figure to me and a mentor. I just want to say. I love you and appreciate you Mr. Cee. Congratulations on your retirement" Wheels said. As the people clapped. And Mr. Cee nodded his head in approval from his seat.

It would now be the man of the hour. Mr. Cee would speak to the many that came out to honor him. It was indeed a special moment for Mr. Cee and his family. That included his wife and many children. Who were in attendance on this night.

"To God be the glory. I want to thank the city of Lancaster. The Southeast section of Lancaster City that I served and lived. For so many years. The people of Lancaster City that supported my business all these years. I'd like to thank my family. My wife and children who've been such a big part of why my business has survived for so many years. Without them, it wouldn't be no Mr. Cee. And last but not least. I'd like to thank the young man that's taken the store. And continued serving the community the way it should be served. Dondrake Wells has done a great job. And I want this community to continue to support him. And continue to support one another. Thank you. God bless" Mr. Cee said. Before returning to his seat to a standing ovation.

It was the end to a great night. Honoring a great man. After the speeches, it was time to eat. As dinner was served to the many guests. And soft Jazz played through the speakers around the ballroom. Mingling with some of the people he knew from the city that was among the guests. Wheels was then pulled to the side by Mr. Cee as he was walking back towards his table.

"Those were some kind words up there. I thank you. And my family thanks you for your kind words and your great work with the store. I knew when I chose you to have it. It would be in good hands. You make me proud son. Keep up the good work and keep growing in your life as a man" Mr. Cee said. Extending his hand to shake Wheels hand.

"No. Thank you Mr. Cee. It's been an honor running the store. It was an honor being here tonight. You've known me and my family since I was a kid. I grew up going to the store as a kid. And when you said you was thinking about retiring. I didn't want no one to have this store but someone from the neighborhood. Fortunately. I was in a position where I could do it. So I did it. And it's been the best thing I bought in my life. I'm going to carry on the legacy that you started Mr. Cee. And hopefully I'll keep making you proud. Thanks again for everything. Enjoy this night you deserve it" Wheels replied. Shaking Mr. Cee's hand and giving him a hug.

Kwame was finally about to make that move. He lived in Lancaster Township outside the city for over a year now. And he was financially secure enough to make the move. Club Lanc City was still thriving in the city. One of the hottest clubs in the state, and Kwame was part owner. Along with Nitro and Chill. Nitro and Chill were both still local. Chill was still the face of the club and Nitro was still heavy into real estate. And they all still had real estate ventures together. Being smart with their money with investments. Kept the money coming in.

Angel was moving up in management. And was now a Regional Manager getting paid a six figure salary. And enjoying her life. She eventually met a man that she was in a relationship with for about a year. And things were moving towards getting serious. They both were in the business world and were successful college graduates. Angel didn't come home as much anymore like she once did. And her house on Chester Street that her parents left her. She sold to her cousin Tisha. Who needed more room and moved from her Garden Court apartment to Chester Street. They were both still close and talked on the phone every other day. Angel's schedule just kept her busy and traveling.

Erotic Styles was still doing well Downtown. And Erotic started to travel with her team to hair shows and conventions. She was becoming more and more of a powerful business owner. Her business had already won awards in the hair industry. Desmond had traveled and toured nationally. And just like he had once promised to do. He returned home to Lanc City and formed a foundation for inner city kids and The Arts. Kids that had dreams of drawing and painting and wanted to pursue it further. He partnered with some local Community Centers to have Art classes and activities. Free to the public and any kid that was serious about pursuing Art. Desmond name the foundation The D&T Foundation For The Arts. The D&T stood for Desmond and Travis.

He dedicated his foundation to a good friend that always encouraged him to keep drawing and pursuing his dreams. Desmond felt it was only right. And the city received it very well. It was another way for Desmond to give back to his community in a positive way. And he loved that he could do it. His foundation meant a lot to him.

Nitro and Chill were sitting at the bar at their club. No one was there but one of the bartenders. Who happen to make Nitro and Chill all the drinks they wanted while they sat and chopped it up.

"Remember when this was just a dream of ours? And we were nervous as shit and didn't think the city would give us the location. No matter how nervous we were. We never gave up and believed we could get it done. And we got it done. Every time I come in this *place, shit bugs me out it's really ours. But we worked hard. And proud of us. Proud of you stepping to the forefront and handling shit at the club. While I'm on our real estate shit. That's how we have to continue to do it. This nigga Kwame calling right now. Let me put him on speaker" Nitro said.*

"What's good homie? How you"? Kwame asked.

"Just chilling at the club. Me and Chill sitting here. We got you on speaker. We're good over here. How's that Vegas life"? Nitro replied asking.

"Oh it's lovely fam. I love it out here bro. You and Chill need to come out and visit. We can hit the strip" Kwame said.

"Trust me playboy I plan to. I was just waiting for you to say the word" Chill replied as they all laughed.

"So I assume the club is still popping by these checks I'm getting sent out here to Vegas. That's what's up. I'm glad the city is still supporting us and the movement. That's why I always used to talk about giving back. They know all the money we made during our reign. We shared some of that money with the city. Had free events and fed the hood. They know that's important to us. And I plan to keep giving back in the name of the crew. And I don't even live in the city anymore. But that's home and I'll always give back" Kwame said.

"Nigga I know you love them checks. Business is great right now. Get used to it fam. And yeah. You know I love Vegas, so we'll be out there sometime soon" Nitro replied.

"Ok. I'm going to let you brothers get back to what you're doing. Me and the fam are about to go shopping and probably have a cookout later. Stay up. Crew" Kwame said before hanging up.

Nitro and Chill said crew back and the conversation was over. That's the way it was for most of the crew these days. They were all older and all doing their own things trying to maintain their finances. That's what it was about now. Maintaining stability. They were able to do what a lot of crews couldn't do. Avoid serious jailtime and never truly were convicted of the crimes they were accused of. AND got away with all the money they stole. Only a story like this could be fiction right? Or could it actually be real? Crew!!

This book is dedicated to all the Lancaster City residents we've lost over the years. And the city itself. My birthplace and the place that taught me how to be ME!! Page 180

Made in United States
North Haven, CT
25 August 2023

40724650R00182